She smelled as good as he remembered.

Sierra raised her arms, hesitated, then slid them around his neck, returning his hug.

Yes, nice. Really nice.

Wait, no. Clay reminded himself this was a friendly hug between two people whose only concern was the well-being of their son.

His body had other ideas, as did his hands, which skimmed her back over the material of her too bulky, too thick sweater.

He couldn't stop himself. Her curves were too perfect, her scent too intoxicating, her skin like satin.

Her skin?

When had his hand moved to caress her cheek?

"Tell me no." He bent his head, his lips seeking hers.

She didn't. She couldn't, not with him kissing her.

Dear Reader,

I'm often asked where I get ideas for my books. I have
to admit, many of them come from real life. Not my
own—I'm actually kind of boring. But other people's
lives, particularly people in the news. A few years ago I
read a story about a woman who adopted a child and
then later returned him to the adoption agency. I was
fascinated and couldn't help wondering how the birth
mother felt, if she even learned about her son being
returned.

When I first developed my Mustang Valley series, I knew
immediately that I wanted to use this real-life story idea
for my third book, *Baby's First Homecoming.* Sierra Powell
is a woman who made a terrible mistake when she gave
up her infant son for adoption, and now has the chance
to rectify it. She isn't counting on the baby's father, Clay
Duvall, being anywhere around when she brings her
toddler son home to meet her family.

Of course, he is there, and she must confess she not only
had their baby in secret, she gave him up for adoption.
It isn't an easy road for Sierra and Clay. Along the way,
they learn not only how to co-parent their son; they also
realize they were meant to be together always. I hope
you enjoy their journey and that it touches a place in
your heart.

Warmest wishes,

Cathy McDavid

P.S. I always enjoy hearing from readers. You can contact
me at www.cathymcdavid.com.

Baby's First Homecoming

CATHY McDAVID

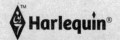

TORONTO NEW YORK LONDON
AMSTERDAM PARIS SYDNEY HAMBURG
STOCKHOLM ATHENS TOKYO MILAN MADRID
PRAGUE WARSAW BUDAPEST AUCKLAND

Recycling programs
for this product may
not exist in your area.

ISBN-13: 978-0-373-75401-4

BABY'S FIRST HOMECOMING

ABOUT THE AUTHOR

Cathy makes her home in Scottsdale, Arizona, near the breathtaking McDowell Mountains, where hawks fly overhead, javelina traipse across her front yard and mountain lions occasionally come calling. She embraced the country life at an early age, acquiring her first horse in eighth grade. Dozens of horses followed through the years, along with mules, an obscenely fat donkey, chickens, ducks, goats and a potbellied pig who had her own swimming pool. Nowadays, two spoiled dogs and two spoiled-er cats round out the McDavid pets. Cathy loves contemporary and historical ranch stories and often incorporates her own experiences into her books.

When not writing, Cathy and her family and friends spend as much time as they can at her cabin in the small town of Young. Of course, she takes her laptop with her on the chance inspiration strikes.

Books by Cathy McDavid

HARLEQUIN AMERICAN ROMANCE

1168—HIS ONLY WIFE
1197—THE FAMILY PLAN
1221—COWBOY DAD
1264—WAITING FOR BABY
1294—TAKING ON TWINS
1307—THE ACCIDENTAL SHERIFF
1318—DUSTY: WILD COWBOY
1345—THE COMEBACK COWBOY
1365—LAST CHANCE COWBOY *
1384—HER COWBOY'S CHRISTMAS WISH *

*Mustang Valley

To my son, Clay. You were without a doubt the cutest, most charming little boy there ever was. One day, I looked away for just a minute, and you grew up into a fine, talented, handsome young man. I am so very proud of you and all your accomplishments.
Love you always, Mom.

Chapter One

The Powell family home, more than a century old, had been transformed. Sierra Powell stood beside the open door of her Toyota SUV, assessing every change, comparing them to how she'd last seen the house, in shocking disrepair after ten years of chronic neglect.

Trees were trimmed, the yard's abundant desert flora and fauna manicured to tidy perfection. A fresh coat of dune-colored paint on the house's exterior gleamed to eye-squinting intensity in the midafternoon sun. Terra-cotta bricks lined the walkways to the front courtyard and back patio, resembling spectators at a parade.

The refurbishings pleased Sierra. It had taken a long time for her family to rebound from the emotional and financial ruin left in the wake of her mother's illness and death. These improvements to the house, she knew, mirrored the ones in her father and two brothers.

She envied them. The Powell men were healed and happy and well on the way to creating wonderful, exciting new lives for themselves while she had never been so terrified of the future or felt so alone.

What if her family rejected her? They certainly had good cause—she'd practically shunned them for almost two years. Now she'd returned, not just for her brothers' double wedding but to ask for her family's help, their love, their support, and, if they could see fit to give it, their forgiveness.

It wouldn't be easy. Sierra had made a lot of mistakes.

She stared at the back patio, working up the courage to head inside where her family and future sisters-in-law waited. Everyone was expecting her, possibly intending to confront her. There would be questions, especially when they saw the unexpected "guest" Sierra had brought with her and heard her request to—temporarily, she assured herself—move home.

By some miracle she'd been able to stand outside this long without being noticed. Maybe no one was home. She immediately dismissed that idea. Someone would be here to greet her. Her father at least, who'd insisted she come home for her brothers' double wedding.

Her brothers, Gavin and Ethan, could be elsewhere on the ranch—leading trail rides, teaching riding classes or otherwise making themselves scarce so she and her father could have a few minutes alone. She had hurt him the worst and owed him the biggest apology. It was he who had the power to grant or deny her request to stay.

Sierra might have been lost in thought indefinitely if not for a noise coming from inside her car. She opened the rear driver's-side door and stuck her head inside.

"Hey, handsome. You awake? How was your nap?"

Her son waved his pudgy fists and broke into a delighted grin that displayed six new teeth. His hazel eyes, the image of his father's, beamed at her as he babbled incoherently.

Her heart promptly broke open and spilled a torrent of love as it did every time he smiled or gurgled or nuzzled into her neck and sighed with baby contentment.

"Thank God I have you back," she murmured for the thousandth time, a catch in her voice, the wound within her still raw.

She didn't know what she'd done to deserve this reprieve.

This gift. This chance to right past wrongs. But she was bound and determined to turn her life around and make the best one possible for her and her son. If she needed to get on her hands and knees and beg her family, she would. He was that important to her.

"Let's clean you up a bit before we meet the folks." Using a cotton cloth, she wiped the smudges of dirt from his face and hands. "There. All better."

He kicked his feet, which were clad in white socks and brand-new red sneakers she'd recently purchased. In fact, she'd recently purchased all his clothes, the car seat, a portable crib and every necessity a child his age needed.

She reached onto the seat beside him and retrieved his favorite toy from where it had fallen. He grabbed the plastic pony and waved it in the air as if to say, *Where have you been? I was looking for you,* and stuffed the pony's entire head in his mouth.

With trembling fingers, Sierra unbuckled the car-seat straps. The distraction of caring for her son had worn off. She was once again dreading the prospect of facing her family.

They love you, she told herself. *They will love Jamie, too.*

But was it enough to make up for the last two years of shameful avoidance?

Drawing a deep breath, she hefted Jamie into her arms. When he was securely balanced on her hip and the diaper bag was slung over her shoulder, she picked her way slowly up the brick-lined walk to the back patio.

The kitchen door loomed ahead, the outline wavering as if she were seeing it though a very long tunnel. Her flats made scuffing sounds on the dirt and then clip-clopped across the Saltillo tiles, each beat matching her pounding heart.

Thank goodness she didn't have to worry about Jamie's father being anywhere near Mustang Valley. The last she'd heard, which was soon after their too-brief affair ended, he was married and living in Austin, Texas. Sierra had taken a risk returning to Arizona, but a small one so long as he stayed far, far away.

And she needed that distance, for her sake more than their son's. His betrayal—she couldn't think of it any other way—had shattered her. Granted, she'd been naive. That in no way made it acceptable for him to take advantage of her.

She reached the kitchen door and found it slightly ajar. Odd.

Knocking, she called, "Hello! Dad?" When there was no answer, she knocked again.

The door drifted open a few more inches. Sierra nudged it the rest of the way and stepped tentatively inside.

"Hello. Anybody home?"

The only answer she received was the soft humming of the refrigerator and the whirr of the slowly twirling ceiling fan over the kitchen table.

She frowned. This was more than strange. Her family knew she was coming. Heck, she'd called her father not an hour ago letting him know her anticipated arrival time.

She ventured farther in. It was then she noticed a large sheet cake in the center of the counter. Inching closer, she read the message scrawled with blue icing.

Welcome Home, Sissy. Her family's pet name for her.

Was it possible they weren't angry with her after all?

A dam broke, and the relief washing over her was so intense it stole every ounce of strength from her knees. She reached for the counter to steady herself before the combined weight of Jamie and the diaper bag dragged her to the floor.

"Surprise!" The resounding chorus of voices erupted from nowhere, echoing loudly off the walls. People, so many of them, converged on her from around corners and down the hall.

No, no!

Sierra's entire body jerked in response, out of alarm and fear. This wasn't how it was supposed to happen.

"You're here, honey!"

"Hey, Sissy."

"We've missed you!"

Jamie screwed up his mouth and started to wail. Holding on to her, he hid his beet-red face in her sweater. His beloved toy pony dropped to the floor, along with the diaper bag.

The room went instantly silent, like a TV when the mute button was pressed. Even Jamie stopped crying and turned teary eyes to the gathering of people gawking at him.

A young girl of about six or seven whom Sierra didn't recognize broke the silence with an excited, "You have a baby! Can I hold him?" She scrambled over to Sierra, her angelic face alight. "I'm Isa, your niece. Or I'm going to be your niece when my mama marries your brother."

"Hello, Isa." Sierra had trouble speaking and cleared her throat. "I've heard a lot about you."

Actually, Sierra had heard only a smattering about her future stepniece. She might have heard more if she'd answered her family's phone calls or read their emails.

Glancing around the kitchen, she took in the puzzled and shocked expressions on everyone's faces. Except for Isa, they kept their distance, as if waiting for someone else to break the ice.

What had she expected? She'd brought a fourteen-month-old child home with her, and had given them no warning.

Her oldest brother, Gavin, studied her with his usual seriousness. As a girl, she had been intimidated by that look. Living on her own since she was seventeen apparently made no difference.

Ethan, younger than Gavin by two years, nodded encouragingly at her. He'd always been there for her—except for when their mother had died almost a decade ago, and he'd run off to join the marines.

Everyone else was a blur. Some she recognized, like Ethan's fiancée, Caitlin. Others, she didn't.

"I like babies." Isa reached up to tickle Jamie under his chin.

He flailed and turned his head away from her. Isa pouted.

"He's a little shy," Sierra explained.

"Well, well." Her father finally came forward, breaking the trance that had fallen over everyone. The reserved smile he presented reassured Sierra not in the least. "Why don't you introduce us to this young man."

"Dad," Sierra said shakily, "this is Jamie. My...my son." Her hand instinctively cradled the side of the baby's head as if to shield him.

Her father's reserved smile dissolved into one that warmed her through and through. "I have a grandson. Oh, Sierra." He opened his arms.

She went to him, let him hug her and Jamie and, temporarily, set right a world that had been completely out of control for almost two years.

"I'm so sorry," she murmured into his shirtfront.

"Don't be. Everything's going to be fine. You'll see."

She wanted to believe him, and dared to let herself.

Jamie squirmed and started to cry.

Sierra drew back, reluctant to leave the comfort of her father's embrace. "He's hungry. I'd better fix him something to eat."

"Can I hold him while you do?" her father asked.

"He doesn't like—" She'd started to say *strangers*. Not wanting to hurt her father's feelings, she changed it to "New people."

He held open his arms. Jamie stared at them, a dubious frown knitting his otherwise perfectly smooth brow. When his grandfather clapped his hands and held them open again, Jamie twisted and reached for Sierra.

Her father's smile fell.

"He'll get used to you in a day or two," she reassured him, though, in truth, she didn't know what to expect. She and Jamie were still getting to know each other.

Her brothers came over next. Ethan's hug was enthusiastic. Gavin's less so. He loved her, but he was also angry at her for the pain she'd caused them and slower to let go of hard feelings.

"I'm so happy for you both," she said. "I can't wait for the wedding."

That seemed to ease the tension. More introductions were made. Sierra greeted Caitlin warmly, having known Ethan's fiancée since grade school. Sage, Gavin's fiancée, impressed Sierra with her genuineness.

"Your son is beautiful." Sage patted Jamie's leg.

He jerked his leg out of her reach.

Sierra smiled apologetically. "He's hungry and a little cranky."

While she warmed a jar of baby vegetable stew in the microwave, Jamie, still sitting on her hip, polished off a bottle of apple juice. Everyone began talking again, thank goodness.

After a while, Gavin's daughter, Cassie, came over. "I'm a good babysitter if you ever need one."

"Thanks." Sierra patted the girl's shoulder. "I'll keep that in mind."

She hadn't met Cassie before. The twelve-year-old had only come to live at the ranch last summer. Sierra noticed the affectionate glances Gavin sent his daughter from across the room. Maybe one day she'd have the same loving relationship with Jamie.

"It's so nice to have another baby in the family," Caitlin said, joining Sierra at the table where she fed Jamie.

"Another baby?"

"Sage is four months along, and I'm two."

"You're both pregnant!"

Sage dropped into the remaining empty chair. "Yes, so I guess it's a good thing the wedding's soon! I wouldn't fit into my dress otherwise."

"Congratulations." Sierra observed the joy in their faces and felt a pang of regret. Her face had been a mask of sorrow all during her pregnancy.

"Is Jamie's father in San Francisco?" Caitlin asked.

Sierra tensed. She'd prepared herself for this question on the long drive. "He's not part of mine or Jamie's lives. I'm raising him alone."

She couldn't tell her family the truth. If they ever found out Jamie's father was the son of the man who'd stolen their land and sold it to an investor, they'd disown Sierra and toss her and Jamie out on their rear ends.

Near the end of the meal, Sierra excused herself and went to the hall bathroom to clean up Jamie and change him.

On her way back, she was stopped outside the kitchen by a chorus of hearty welcomes and the sound of a voice that instantly ignited wave after wave of panic.

Clay Duvall.

Impossible! This couldn't be happening.

He was in Texas. And even if he wasn't, her family hated him. He wouldn't be allowed on the property, much less to set foot in the house.

"Sissy, come see who's here," her brother Ethan called to her.

She trembled so violently, she nearly dropped Jamie. He made it worse by wriggling.

"Hey." Ethan came around the corner. "Is something wrong?"

"What's he doing here?" she hissed.

"Clay? He came to see you."

"Why?"

"He's a friend."

"No, he isn't. His dad cheated us. You hate him. We all do."

"Not anymore."

"Since when?" she squeaked.

"Since we captured the wild mustang last fall. It's a long story, I'll tell you after the party." Ethan hooked her by the elbow and gave a tug.

She refused to budge.

"Come on. You haven't seen Clay since before Mom died."

Not true.

Ethan all but dragged her and Jamie into the kitchen where she stumbled into her chair, praying for invisibility. Her family and Clay were friends again? How could that be? In every scenario she'd devised, he'd been a thousand miles away.

He strode farther into the kitchen.

Please, please, don't come over here, she silently prayed.

Of course, he did, and she steeled herself.

"Hi, Sierra." His smile was friendly, his voice deep and honeyed like she remembered.

She looked up at him—how could she not?—and stared into the face of her baby's father. Her heart, open with love for her son and the recent reconciliation with her family, promptly closed tight.

SHE HAD A BABY.

Clay's stomach clenched as if someone had sucker-punched him with the business end of a baseball bat.

From the moment he'd learned Sierra was returning to Mustang Valley, he'd imagined them picking up where they'd left off. She'd generously overlook his incredible lack of judgment and brief, disastrous marriage, and they'd fall into each other's arms.

Only her arms were full of a bouncing baby boy. There went the happy-you're-home kiss he'd been counting on.

Instead, he squeezed her upper arm. "Good to see you again."

She muttered something about how nice it was to see him, too.

The boy's head tipped back, and his inquisitive gaze fixed on Clay's face. There was something about his eyes that struck a familiar chord, though Clay couldn't quite identify why.

Maybe he was wrong, and the kid wasn't hers. She could be a nanny or something.

"Who's this?" he asked.

"My, um, my…" She glanced down at the baby, held him closer. "My son."

Clay swallowed. So much for his nanny theory.

Which meant she'd been with a man. A man besides him. Jealousy sliced through him. Not that he had any claim on her. He'd forfeited it the second he'd stupidly left Sierra in order to reunite with Jessica, his then ex-fiancée and later wife.

In hindsight, hurting Sierra had been inevitable.

If Gavin and Ethan knew what he'd done to their little sister, he'd lose a lot more than their friendship. An arm. The use of his legs. And that was just for starters.

"What's his name?" Clay asked.

The baby babbled as if answering. He really was an appealing tyke. Clay felt an unfamiliar, but not unpleasant, tug inside his chest. He'd always liked kids despite having little experience with them and would be a father today if things had gone differently.

His loss still pained him.

Probably the reason he felt drawn to Sierra's boy.

She said nothing, acting as though she hadn't heard him. Loading a spoon with some vile-looking mush out of a jar, she tried to feed it to the baby. Wisely, the kid shook his head and grimaced. The stuff did look awful.

"No name, buddy?"

"It's Jamie," Isa piped up. She and Cassie had been standing behind Sierra and trying to distract the baby with funny faces. "Isn't that a cool name?"

"Yeah," Clay agreed, receiving yet another invisible punch to the stomach. "Cool."

His grandfather's name had been Jamie, short for Jamieson. Did Sierra know?

Yes, he'd told her all about his summers spent in Montana and about returning for his grandfather's funeral.

Coincidence?

It had to be.

"Nice to meet you, Jamie," Clay said and leaned down, extending his index finger.

The baby broke into a wide, rather comical grin and grabbed Clay's finger, holding it as he were shaking hands.

"He likes you," Cassie blurted.

"The feeling's mutual." The tug inside Clay's chest grew stronger, and he grinned back at the baby. Turning his head, he discovered Sierra's face mere inches from him. "Cute baby."

She stared back at him, her brown eyes wide with terror.

His grin dissolved, and he involuntarily straightened. The moment he did, she practically leapt out of her chair.

"I'd better clean this up." Grabbing the jar of baby food and empty bottle with her free hand, she cut past Isa and made a hasty beeline for the sink, Jamie riding on her hip.

What exactly had happened?

He would have understood anger. He'd treated her badly after all. But fear? No. Something else was definitely amiss.

Clay's glance cut to Sage and Caitlin still sitting at the table. Their expressions reflected a confusion similar to the one he was experiencing.

The celebration continued with cake and punch. Wayne Powell, Sierra's father, acted as host. The group of men, which included a few family friends and two of the Powells' longtime ranch hands, wandered to the living room. The women, girls and Wayne remained in the kitchen, hovering around Sierra and Jamie.

Clay stayed, too, using a conversation with Wayne as his excuse. While the older man talked, Clay kept one ear tuned to the discussion going on between the women.

Sierra had set Jamie on the floor, and he was toddling about by her feet. Isa knelt in front of him, making a toy pony that looked as if it had been mauled gallop in the air.

"How old is he?" Caitlin asked Sierra.

Sierra hesitated, thinned her lips and twirled a strand of glossy brunette hair around her finger. "About a year."

Clay knew that look and habit, having seen it a hundred times before. He'd spent almost as much time at Powell Ranch as he had his own family's while growing up. Sierra was the pesky, always-in-the-way little sister. While she didn't lie, exactly, she'd occasionally exaggerated, and the hair-twirling was a dead giveaway.

So, what was she exaggerating about this time?

"He's walking well for a year," Sage commented.

"Did he have his birthday already?" Cassie asked. "Maybe we can have a party for him."

Sierra thinned her lips again and twirled her hair even faster. "He already had a party."

Wayne said something to Sierra about her and Jamie staying in Ethan's old room, that her room had been given over to the girls.

Clay listened and watched.

Jamie fascinated him. He picked at the laces of Isa's sneakers with amazing determination and quickly had them untied. Clay admired that quality, having plenty of it himself. He'd inherited it from his father and grandfather Jamie.

Suddenly, the air was too thick to breathe and the room stifling hot.

Clay mentally calculated how long since he and Caitlin had last seen each other. Last slept together. Not quite two years. She had mentioned Jamie was about a year. But if he was older, say thirteen or fourteen months…

She'd lied, and not just about Jamie's age.

"Sierra." The volume of Clay's voice surprised not only himself but everyone else in the room. He didn't care. "We need to talk."

The fear he'd seen in her face earlier returned tenfold, only now he knew the cause.

When she didn't move, he started toward her. "Right this minute."

"I—I—" She bent and picked up Jamie, who was not happy about being separated from Isa and started to wail. "I really should unload the car."

"I'll help you."

"What's going on?" Wayne moved to stand in front of Clay.

"This is between me and Sierra."

Wayne might be pushing sixty but he presented a formidable obstacle when protecting his daughter. "Whatever you have to say to her, you can say to me."

"Is that what you want?" Clay's gaze locked with Sierra's.

"No." Her answer was hardly more than a whisper.

He went to the kitchen door, opened it and waited for her to join him.

"Sierra, you don't have to go with him." Wayne laid a protective hand on her arm.

She squared her shoulders. "It's okay, Dad."

She was brave, he'd give her that much.

"No, it's not," Wayne said. "I don't like him ordering you around." The glare Wayne shot Clay reminded him it hadn't been *that* long since he'd reconciled with the Powells.

He didn't care. He'd lost one child already, he wasn't about to lose a second.

"You harm one hair on her head—"

Clay cut off Wayne before he could finish. "I won't. I swear."

Wayne reluctantly backed off, his narrowed gaze informing Clay they weren't done by a long shot.

When Sierra reached the door, he held out his arms to Jamie. "Let me take him."

"No!" She curled her body away from Clay. "He doesn't like strangers."

Jamie made a liar of his mother by extending his arms to Clay. She held fast but lost her grip when Jamie squirmed and wriggled sideways.

Clay caught the boy easily and balanced him on his hip as he'd seen Sierra do.

"Give him back," she demanded.

"I will, after you and I talk."

Sierra went outside with Clay. Whatever she felt, she did a good job of keeping it to herself.

Clay was ready to explode.

They'd no sooner stepped off the back patio when he stopped and reeled on her.

"How dare you keep my son from me!"

Chapter Two

"Let me explain," Sierra insisted, jogging to match Clay's long strides.

"You lied to me."

He was right. She'd done everything in her power to hide Jamie's existence from him. Worse, if there was any way she could go back in time to an hour ago, she'd drive past her family's ranch and keep driving until she found someplace safe.

"Give Jamie to me, I can—"

"He's fine."

And he was fine, if his silly grin and happy babbling was any indication. Damn Clay.

She wanted to cry out, tackle Clay and wrestle Jamie away from him. It would be fruitless, of course. Clay was easily six-two and strong as a linebacker. What if he took off with Jamie? Made a mad dash to his truck? She might never get her son back.

"Please, Clay." She strived to maintain a reasonable tone. "If we could just talk."

"We'll talk, all right. But not here. I don't want your family interfering."

Her family! Oh, God, what must they be thinking? They'd barely begun to accept she had a child and now this. Surely her father was putting two and two together. They might have made their peace with Clay, but he'd still been their hated enemy when he and Sierra had their affair.

Clay crossed the open area and headed toward the stables, her son still clutched in his arms.

Her son.

Yes, his son, too. That, however, was a technicality. Clay hadn't wanted her when given the chance, had chosen to marry his off-again, on-again fiancée instead. As far as Sierra was concerned, he'd forfeited any and all say regarding Jamie.

It was an opinion Clay didn't seem to share.

"Wait!" Sierra hurried to catch up. "I'll carry Jamie. He doesn't like strangers."

"I'm no stranger." Clay didn't take his eyes off the ground in front of him. "I'm his father."

Anger bloomed inside her. "Clay, I said wait!"

He slowed, then, to her relief, came to a halt. She drew up beside him, weak-kneed from exertion as much as emotional overload.

Jamie hung on to Clay's neck and giggled.

Maybe he really did like other people, and she was the one with the phobia.

It was possible.

No one other than the pediatrician during their visit to his office last Monday had been allowed to hold Jamie besides Sierra. She didn't count the months between his birth and three weeks ago when he'd been returned to her. The Stevensons, the ones who'd cared for him, didn't matter. Didn't exist. Not after rejecting her child.

"Where are you taking us?" She captured Jamie's flailing foot in her hand and cupped the ankle, desperately needing the contact. He had been no more than an arm's length away from her since the minute she'd got him back.

"Ethan's apartment."

Sierra remembered now. Her brother had converted the old bunkhouse into an apartment after Sage and Isa moved into the main house.

"We can be alone there and lock the door."

"Lock the door?" She shook her head. "Aren't you being a little extreme?"

"No, considering the cavalry's almost here."

Sierra looked behind her. Her dad and brothers were indeed coming after them. The three sweetest, most important and ridiculously overprotective men in the world were going to rescue her. She had half a mind to let them. Then, she remembered Clay's hardheadedness. He wouldn't give up Jamie without a fight.

"Let me talk to them."

"I'll meet you in the apartment."

Inside? Out of her sight?

"No!" The mere thought of being away from her baby paralyzed her.

The muscles in Clay's jaw were clenching with anger or impatience or frustration, she didn't know which. "I won't take off with him."

She exhaled slowly. How to explain her crippling separation anxiety? She barely understood it herself.

"I'll go with you to Ethan's apartment. Anywhere you want. Just stay where I can see Jamie until I'm done talking to the family. Please."

"Fine, I'll wait for you on the porch."

Sierra mentally measured the distance. Thirty yards, give or take. It felt more like ten miles.

"You have about three seconds to decide."

Or what? He would go back on his word and run off with Jamie? Her temples throbbed. This day, her entire life, was unraveling at lightning speed.

"Okay."

As soon as Clay walked away, Sierra regretted her decision. He would be alone with her son. Never once had she imagined Clay would walk into her family's house and steal Jamie from her like an eagle snatching prey.

With one eye trained on Clay and Jamie, she braced herself for the confrontation with her father and brothers.

"Are you all right?" Wayne Powell demanded the instant he reached her. "What's going on?"

Gavin zoomed past without so much as a glance in her direction.

"Come back!" she called. When he ignored her, she hollered, "Gavin, don't make this worse than it already is."

That did the trick. Fists clenched at his sides, he returned, each step an obvious effort.

Sierra closed her eyes and sighed. Where to begin?

"Is he Jamie's father?"

She nodded.

"Son of a bitch," Gavin grumbled. "I'll kill him."

"Don't overreact. He didn't—" Sierra squeezed her eyes shut. "It was mutual. I knew what I was doing."

"If you loved him, why didn't you tell us?" Ethan asked.

How had he guessed? "You despised Clay at the time. Can you imagine your reaction?"

"Damn straight I can," Gavin agreed.

"Is that why you stayed away so long?" her father asked.

"Dad, I didn't mean to hurt you. I was confused. I came home for the wedding because I thought Clay was in Texas."

"He moved back a year or so ago. After his divorce."

"He's divorced?" She swayed slightly. "I didn't know."

Not that it made any difference.

Or did it?

No difference at all, she assured herself. There was nothing between her and Clay, now or ever again.

Except for Jamie.

"If you thought he was in Texas, why didn't you come home sooner?" her father asked, his eyes filled with sadness.

Guilt burned a brand-new hole in Sierra, bigger than all the other ones combined.

"It's complicated. And I'll tell you as soon as I finish with Clay."

He'd begun pacing on the porch. From this distance, Sierra couldn't tell if it was because he'd become restless or Jamie had or perhaps a combination of both. Neither man nor child possessed much patience, and both were prone to impulsiveness. They were also both charming to distraction when it suited them.

"You going to be okay?" Ethan squeezed her upper arm.

"With Clay? Of course. He's mad right at the moment, but he won't do anything drastic."

"I wasn't referring to Clay."

"Thank you for caring." She smiled tenderly at all three men. "I can't tell you how much I regret the way I treated you the last two years."

"Don't worry, honey." Her father gathered her into a hug and patted her head, much as he'd done when she was a little girl. "Everything will work out."

She wished she shared his optimism.

"We'll be right here if you need us." Gavin stared menacingly at Clay.

"Watch him for me, will you?" Sierra asked Ethan. "I don't want him going all big-brother on me."

"Don't be so hard on Gavin," her father said. "It's going to take us a while to get used to all this."

To say the least.

The walk to the apartment took forever and yet was over in an instant. Sierra climbed the three porch steps with leaden feet and a racing heart.

Clay stood by the door with one hand on the knob, his expression guarded and grave.

Her son's, on the other hand, lit up at the sight of her, and he babbled excitedly, just as he had three weeks ago when he'd seen her for the first time since the day he was born.

Giving Jamie up for adoption was the hardest thing she'd ever done.

Facing Clay, telling him about it, was coming in a very close second.

"HE WANTS DOWN." Sierra sat on the couch, assuming, hoping that Clay would sit there, too, and Jamie would crawl across the cushions to her.

Only Clay had chosen the chair, a hand-me-down that used to reside in the living room long before she'd left for college.

Jamie squirmed and wriggled and whined, pushing ruthlessly at Clay's chest in a bid for freedom. The resemblance between them, same hazel eyes and blond hair, same disarming smile, was striking enough for Sierra realize she wouldn't have gotten away with lying about her child's father's identity for long.

"I won't take off with him," she repeated his earlier promise.

Clay released Jamie, reluctantly depositing him on the hardwood floor. He immediately scrambled over to Sierra, then abandoned her just as quickly to explore the cozy apartment. The two-person breakfast set fascinated him. He squeezed between a chair and the table legs, then plopped on the floor beneath the table, cooing with satisfaction.

Sierra hadn't visited the old bunkhouse in years. As with the main house, the transformation amazed her.

"Why didn't you tell me about Jamie?"

It was like Clay to ask the toughest question first.

She collected her thoughts before replying. "The simple

answer is I found out you and Jessica were back together and getting married. Showing up at the wedding and announcing I was carrying your child didn't feel like the right thing to do."

"That's not reason enough. You denied me my son."

"Yes, I did." And she would do it again, given half the chance.

"Why?"

She wasn't going to admit she'd fallen in love during their two-week affair and that the announcement of his marriage so soon after it ended had crushed her. Clay would sense her vulnerability, and she wasn't about to give him any advantage.

"I denied myself my son, too," she said.

"I don't see how." He glowered at her as if she were a criminal when what she'd really been was a victim—of his callousness and the Stevensons' heartlessness.

"I didn't learn I was pregnant until after Dad told me you and Jessica had set a date."

"I'm sorry I didn't tell you myself." Clay's glower momentarily abated. "I owed you that much."

He had. And admitting it almost two years too late didn't diminish her anguish.

"I was never very regular," she continued without acknowledging his apology. "It wasn't until the flu bug I thought I'd caught didn't go away that I finally considered the possibility I was pregnant. You have to understand what a shock it was. We'd used protection."

"I do understand. But that's still no reason to keep Jamie a secret."

"I didn't tell my family, either, not that it matters."

"It does, actually. I was going to give Ethan and Gavin hell for not telling me."

"Today was the first I'd heard you and my brothers were friends again."

"More than friends. Gavin and I are partners in a mustang stud and breeding business, and Ethan works for me at the rodeo arena, breaking and training broncs."

"Wow!" Friends and business partners *and* coworkers. It was a lot for Sierra to absorb all at once.

"You'd have known we'd reconciled if you'd ever talked to your family."

"I deserved that." She may have, but it still stung.

"I didn't say it to be mean."

Hadn't he?

The glower had returned, raising her hackles.

"Regardless, at the time I found out I was pregnant, you and my family hated each other and had for years. Which is the reason we snuck around those two weeks."

"I wanted to tell them about us, if you remember."

"Right. Like I was supposed to say, 'Hey, Dad, I'm dating Clay, the son of the man who sold the land that was in our family for four generations.' They'd have disowned me."

"That's not true."

"They wouldn't have been happy. Dad despised your father."

"For the record, I never agreed with what he did to your family. We've hardly spoken in years."

"That's too bad."

"No, it isn't." Clay ground out the words as if they tasted foul.

Whatever had transpired between him and his father must have been quite ugly.

"He's family." Sierra was just now rediscovering how important family was, even when the parent was a soulless man like Bud Duvall.

"So is Jamie," Clay said. "My family."

They both looked at their son.

He'd grown bored with his pretend cave beneath the table and had crawled out. Before he could interest himself in an electrical outlet or a lamp cord, Sierra rose from the couch, located a ring of keys on the counter and gave them to him. Thrilled, he sat on the floor between the kitchen and living room and proceeded to investigate his new toy with avid concentration.

"I'd have taken care of you and Jamie," Clay said.

"You would have." His sense of duty was nothing if not strong. Unlike his father's. "Jessica, I was pretty sure, might have objected to you having a child with another woman."

He didn't answer, letting her know she was right.

"I refused to be responsible for ending your marriage before it even began."

"That was my decision to make. Not yours."

"Blame the hormones. I was confused and—" she decided to be honest with him "—hurt. I wasn't thinking entirely clearly."

She'd also been depressed. Deeply depressed. Enough that her obstetrician had become concerned and prescribed private counseling along with a support group. Sierra's health insurance didn't cover counseling, and she wasn't earning enough money to pay for it out of pocket. She did attend a support group. Three meetings. Talking with other single mothers in similar situations had only made her feel worse, not better.

Chronically sick, hormonal and at an all-time emotional low, she'd been an easy target for someone with a personal agenda. Like the Stevensons.

"I didn't intend to hurt you, Sierra. Those two weeks we had together were wonderful."

"Not wonderful enough, I guess." The wound he'd left her with ached anew.

"You were going back to San Francisco. My job was here. If I led you to believe we had a future—"

"You didn't."

Sierra had been the one to hope for the impossible. Clay and Jessica had dated for years. Six, no, seven. They were constantly breaking up, only to reconcile days or weeks later. Sierra had been a fool to think he wouldn't run back to Jessica the second she snapped her fingers.

"What made you decide to come home?" He'd gotten around at last to asking the second-toughest question.

She took her time, watching Jamie push the keys across the floor instead of answering Clay. It required all her will-power not to dash into the kitchen and grab Jamie. She didn't want to be here, didn't want to be having this conversation with Clay. What had made her think returning to Arizona was the solution?

"Sierra?"

"My brothers' wedding, of course. And I realized I needed help. Raising a child alone isn't easy."

"Are you home for good?"

"I…" Here was another chance to fib, but she couldn't. "I think so. I haven't discussed it with Dad yet."

"You weren't planning on telling me, were you? Not ever."

"I thought it best to get settled in first. Give my family time to adjust."

"Bullshit!"

"I told you, I thought you were in Texas."

"You could have found out easily enough if you'd bothered asking."

She shot to her feet. "You have no right to lecture me!"

"And you have no right to hide my son." He stood, too. "What was it? Revenge? Because I hurt you?"

"God, no!"

He snorted. "Right."

Jamie began to wail. One glance informed Sierra he was responding to her and Clay's escalating argument.

She went to him. Clay didn't object when she lifted Jamie into her arms. Patting his back, she murmured soothing phrases until he quieted. Before too long, he wanted down again.

When she released him, he toddled over to the cabinet under the sink where there was probably bleach, dish soap and a multitude of potentially dangerous cleaning products. Sierra opened an overhead cupboard and found some plastic cups and mugs. Sitting on the rug in front of the sink, Jamie proceeded to bang cups against mugs in a noisy symphony.

"You're good with him," Clay observed when she sat back down.

"I'm learning. Every day is a new experience. A new lesson." Many of them hard.

"At least you've had the opportunity these last, what? Fourteen months. I've missed out on everything."

She swallowed. Now that the moment had come to reveal the whole, horrible truth, she was having second thoughts. Clay was already angry with her. He might try to obtain custody of Jamie by proving her to be an unfit mother. He might win for, in her mind anyway, she was indeed the worst mother on the planet.

Lying to Clay and everyone else was the only way she could protect herself. Protect Jamie.

Her mind in a whirl, she opened her mouth, ready to blurt some concocted story. Clay's eyes stopped her cold. They were no longer ablaze with anger but filled with sadness and grief.

He truly regretted those missing fourteen months with Jamie.

Sierra's own heart shattered. Could she have been any

crueler? She'd done to Clay exactly what the Stevensons had done to her—stolen a child from his parent.

"I've missed out on everything, too." Tears pricked her eyes, and she brushed them away. "Except for the last three weeks."

"What are you talking about?"

There was no easy way to say it, no way to soften the crushing blow she was about to deliver. "I gave Jamie up for adoption when he was born. Last month, on January twenty-third—" she'd remember that day always "—he was returned to me."

His expression darkened. "I don't understand."

"I gave him up for adoption. His...caretakers—" she refused to use the word *parents,* even with *adoptive* in front of it "—changed their mind and returned him to me."

"You gave him up?" Clay recoiled in disbelief.

To Sierra, it felt like a slap.

"Why? How could you?"

Good question, and one she'd asked herself a thousand times.

"I was ill all during my pregnancy. Really ill. Day and night."

"That's no reason."

"I was also an emotional wreck. I took the news of your marriage hard." Boy, that was an understatement. "Maybe because I was pregnant, things overwhelmed me. I was alone. I didn't think I could confide in my family. My job didn't pay that well, had minimal benefits, and I was required to travel ten days a month. I wanted Jamie, truly I did. I just didn't know how I was going to manage everything."

"So, you decided not keeping your baby was easier."

The disgust in his voice cut her to the bone and echoed her own feelings about herself. This was why she hadn't come home before or confided in her family.

"It didn't happen like that. I was vulnerable, physically and emotionally weak. Confused and scared. I don't remember when my boss Ken first approached me about adopting Jamie. He was subtle, dropping tiny hints here and there, letting me get used to the idea slowly. The next thing I knew, I was in my last trimester and meeting with him and his wife and their attorney in order to finalize the adoption."

"You had to understand what was going on."

"I did understand." Sierra shoved her fingers through her hair. She'd gone over this again and again in her head, tried to justify what she'd done. So far, she hadn't. How could she expect Clay to understand? "They were very persuasive and nice. Or so I thought. Ken and Gail had been married twelve years and spent most of them trying to have a child. I was sure they'd be good parents, give Jamie a better life than I ever could. They helped me, supported me, paid my medical bills. I believed they wanted what was best for my baby. I didn't realize they were manipulating me."

"You wouldn't have had to go through that if you'd told me you were pregnant."

His sanctimonious attitude irritated her. "That's easy for you to say now that you're divorced."

"You're right," he admitted grudgingly.

"Believe me, I regretted my decision the moment I handed Jamie over to the Stevensons in the hospital."

"Why didn't you tell them you'd changed your mind?"

"I signed an agreement. And I was still convinced they'd be better parents than me."

"What happened?"

"Instead of getting my old life back or my new life together, I fell apart. Guilt, regret, remorse, you name it. Every aspect of my life suffered. I hit rock bottom and was about to lose my job, my apartment, friends, probably my family. I thought of hiring my own attorney, something I should have done in the first place, and seeing if I could get Jamie. Not long after that, Ken and Gail contacted me out of the blue. They didn't want Jamie anymore."

"What?"

"Gail had finally gotten pregnant. With twins. She was almost eight months along. Guess they were like those childless couples you hear about. They adopt, and suddenly the woman conceives."

"That's no reason to give back your child." Clay sounded as appalled and disgusted as Sierra had been. "He's not a shirt you decide you don't like once you get it home from the store."

"Gail said they never really bonded with him. And now that they were having their own biological children, they thought they'd give me first shot before their attorney arranged another adoption. She said they were also concerned about the baby's father."

"Me?"

"You didn't sign off on the adoption, which is usually required. Ken and Gail's attorney had advised them not to go ahead without your signature, but they were desperate and willing to take the chance you wouldn't appear one day. That changed when she got pregnant."

"And you decided to come home."

"I quit my job, gave up my apartment, cashed in my 401K and headed here. Now that I have Jamie, nothing or no one is going to take him from me again."

"I see," Clay said in a tone that made Sierra think he didn't see at all.

"I've been given a second chance, Clay. An opportunity to correct all the mistakes I made." The hell with her pride. She'd plead with him if that was what it took.

"Do those mistakes include not telling me?"

"I'm here now, and I've explained everything."

"Have you?"

Everything except the part where I fell in love with you. "Yes."

Jamie promptly abandoned the mugs and cups and waddled over to Sierra. She gathered him to her and kissed the top of his downy blond head.

Clay watched them. "We're going to have to come to an agreement about him."

"All right."

She'd let him visit Jamie at the ranch. A few times a week if he wanted. Then later, say next year, when she'd conquered her separation anxiety, Clay could take Jamie for the afternoon or maybe the whole day. Assuming she was still in Mustang Valley. She'd need a new job and these days a decent one was hard to find. Chances were she'd have to look outside the Scottsdale area, possibly outside the state.

"I'm glad you agree." Clay stood, went over to Jamie and patted his head, his smile tender and, this was a surprise to Sierra, almost fatherly. "I'll have my attorney contact you this week regarding the custody agreement."

"Custody agreement? Don't you mean visitation?" Sierra also stood, Jamie holding on to her leg.

Clay reached for Jamie, hefted him into his arms. "I want joint custody of our son."

"No! Forget it."

"We're going to raise him together, whether you like it or not."

She didn't like it. She didn't like it one bit.

Chapter Three

Clay rang his mother's doorbell. She always told him to use his key and just come in, but he didn't feel right about that. Perhaps because the spacious townhouse in the upscale Scottsdale neighborhood had never struck him as home.

His *mother's* home, he reminded himself.

The door swung open. "Clay, sweetheart! Come in." Blythe Duvall kissed his cheek. "I'm so glad you called. What a perfect way to spend a Saturday afternoon."

He gave her a fond squeeze before releasing her. "How are you, Mom?"

"Great. I shot an eighty-seven this morning. My best game in months."

All this time, and it still surprised him to see her in golfing attire. Or in the business suits and heels she wore to the title company where she worked as an escrow officer. She should be in jeans and boots and the floppy straw hat she'd refused to give up till it literally fell apart on her head.

Except she hadn't lived on a ranch in more than eight years and probably wouldn't ever again.

"Good for you." Clay followed her into the kitchen where a newspaper lay spread open on the breakfast bar.

"Can I get you something? A cold drink? Coffee?"

"Just ice water."

"You sounded so serious on the phone." She busied herself pouring their water. "Something the matter?"

"Not exactly."

He sat on a stool at the breakfast bar and let his gaze travel the stylish, ultra-contemporary kitchen, with its high-tech appliances and built-in flat-panel TV. Like his mother's clothes, the kitchen felt wrong. He remembered her cooking hearty meals at their huge gas range and a refrigerator covered with photos, reminder notes and school papers.

His parents had divorced about the time his father exercised a small-print clause in his contract with the Powells and sold off their land, effectively putting them out of the cattle business. Clay honestly didn't know if the sale of the land was the final straw in a marriage circling the drain or a last-ditch effort to save it.

The story changed depending on which parent was telling it.

Because his mother sided with Clay against his father regarding the Powells' land, they had remained close. Neither of them kept much of a connection with Bud Duvall.

"I have some news," Clay said. "Rather incredible news."

"Uh-oh." The twinkle in her eyes dimmed, replaced by worry. "The last incredible news you had was when you told me you and Jessica were getting married and moving to Texas."

They both knew how badly that had turned out. No two people had been more ill-suited for each other or more blind until it was too late.

"No, I'm not getting married again."

"What is it then?" She placed two glasses of ice water on the breakfast bar and slipped into the stool beside him.

He hesitated, honestly not sure how his mother would react. She wanted grandchildren. She also wanted Clay happily married and settled first.

"I told you Sierra Powell was coming home for the wedding."

"You did."

Clay's mother and Sierra's mother had been good friends before tragedy had struck, cutting Louise Powell's life short.

"She brought her young son with her."

"Really! I wasn't aware she had any children."

"No one was, including her family."

His mother's hands flew to her cheeks. "That must have come as a shock. Though I'm sure Wayne is overjoyed. He dotes on his granddaughter, Sage's daughter, too."

"He is overjoyed." Clay inhaled deeply. "There's something else you need to know. It's good news, I assure you. But unexpected."

"Now you've got me scared."

"Sierra's son… Well, I'm the father."

His mother stared at him blankly for several seconds. "How in the world did that happen?"

"The usual way."

"You haven't seen her since her mother died."

"I have. Two years ago when she came home for a visit. We didn't tell anyone. We thought it wise, considering how her family felt about me, us, at the time."

"You cheated on Jessica with Sierra?"

"No. Jessica and I were on the outs. I ran into Sierra at the Corner Diner. We got to talking, hit it off, and one thing led to another."

He summarized his brief affair with Sierra and what she'd told him about her pregnancy, Jamie's birth, adoption and getting him back.

"I can't believe it." His mother's happy smile warmed Clay. "I'm a grandmother. Wait till I tell—" She stopped, covered her mouth. "What am I saying? Poor Sierra. Such a terrible ordeal for her to go through."

Her? What about him? "She kept my son from me!"

"You dumped her."

"It wasn't like that."

"It was entirely like that. No wonder she was hurt and confused."

"She had no right to pawn Jamie off on strangers."

"We're all guilty of making bad decisions we later regret."

True. Clay was a walking, talking example. "I told her I want joint custody of Jamie."

"Is she agreeable?"

Clay thought back to how he and Sierra had parted yesterday at Ethan's apartment and her vehement protests. "She'd prefer I start with supervised visitation. I told I have no intention of being an every-other-weekend father."

His mother reached over and covered his hand with hers. "Please don't take this the wrong way, sweetheart, but why not?"

"I've always wanted kids. That was one of the reasons Jessica and I divorced."

"I remember how devastated you were when she miscarried."

"She didn't want children, Mom. She couldn't have been more relieved." Clay was the one who'd grieved over the loss. When he'd discovered not long after that Jessica was secretly taking birth control pills, their shaky marriage had rapidly deteriorated. "This is a second chance for me."

"I worry that you're so busy. You work seven days a week at the rodeo arena. You're at Powell Ranch at least two days a week helping Gavin with the stud and breeding business. And then there's the wild-mustang sanctuary. How are you going to fit raising a child, a *young* child at that, into your life?"

"I'll hire more help if necessary."

"I suppose you could."

"What happened to the happy grandmother?"

"I'm thrilled, of course. And I've always liked Sierra. It's just such a huge responsibility and an enormous adjustment. I think the two of you should proceed slowly. Whatever decisions you make must be best for everyone, especially little Jamie. Let him get used to Sierra before you start taking him."

His mother made sense, but Clay wasn't convinced. He had a lot of catching up to do with Jamie.

"Would you like to see him?"

She brightened. "I can't wait."

"Let's go over there now."

"This second?"

"Sure."

"Shouldn't you call Sierra first?"

"She's already expecting me. I told her yesterday I'd be by."

"But not that you'd be bringing me."

"You're Jamie's grandmother."

"Have you told your father yet?"

He shook his head.

"Don't you think you should?"

"I will. Later this week." Clay may be at odds with Bud, but he wouldn't deny the man his grandson. Not like Sierra had denied him.

"Tell you what." Blythe hopped off her stool. "You call Sierra while I change into slacks."

Two minutes later, Clay was shutting the Arcadia door behind him as he went onto his mother's back patio to make the call. He didn't want her hearing the conversation in case Sierra gave him more grief.

She answered the house phone on the second ring.

"It's Clay."

"Oh, hi."

He ignore her lack of enthusiasm. "I should be there in about a half-hour, forty-five minutes tops."

"It's not a good time. Jamie's napping."

"He'll wake up eventually. Won't he?"

"Yes—"

"We can wait."

"We?"

"My mother's coming with me."

Silence followed.

"We won't stay too long, I promise."

"All right. But in the future, I need more than a moment's notice you're bringing someone with you."

"She's my mother."

"Even so."

"Until we hammer out the custody agreement, I'm going to see Jamie every day. I'm more than willing to work out a schedule that's convenient for both of us."

"You don't get to dictate all the rules, Clay." There was an unaccustomed edge to her tone.

"Neither do you. Not anymore."

He heard her sharp intake of breath.

"Fine, I'll see you shortly." She hung up without saying goodbye.

Clay refused to get angry. This was only the beginning of a potentially long battle, since Sierra was intent on resisting him at every turn.

Unless…

The idea that had suddenly sprang to his mind quickly grew into a full-fledged plan.

And Clay liked having plans.

"YOU OKAY, SIERRA?"

She glanced up to see her future sister-in-law Sage enter the kitchen wearing her khaki uniform. She was a field agent for the Arizona Game and Fish Department and often worked on the weekends. Later, as her pregnancy advanced, she'd be assigned to a desk job.

"I'm fine." Sierra moved away from the wall phone. "Clay and his mother are coming over."

"From the look on your face, I'd say that's bad."

"I was hoping for more time alone with Jamie before pulling him in a dozen different directions."

"Kids are resilient and do better with change than we think they will. Especially at his age."

"You're probably right." She *was* right, Sierra thought. It was her and not Jamie who needed more time.

Sage reached into the refrigerator and came away with a piece of leftover pizza, which she then placed on a paper plate and put in the microwave.

"Miss lunch?"

"No." She smiled embarrassedly. "I'm just always hungry."

"Lucky you. I spent most of my pregnancy throwing up or feeling like I wanted to."

"You're also lucky."

"I am, but what are you referring to?"

The previous evening, after Clay had left, Sierra had finally unloaded the entire story about Jamie to her family. They were supportive, sad she'd gone through so much misery alone and ecstatic she and Jamie were reunited. They also didn't quite understand her reasons for not telling them about her pregnancy from the start and, at least in Gavin's case, were a little mad at her.

"You're lucky Jamie's father wants to be part of his life," Sage said.

Sierra leaned her back against the counter and watched Sage devour her warmed-up pizza. "I'm okay with Clay being part of his life. It's his need to control that bothers me."

"Wanting to see their sons every day is natural for most

dads. I wish my ex wanted to see Isa. Not for my sake, mind you. For hers. Gavin is wonderful and a hundred times the father my ex will ever be, but Isa still asks about her daddy and can't help feeling rejected. Jamie won't ever experience that."

The advice was good, and Sierra appreciated it. When she'd first got Jamie back, Sierra hadn't thought ahead to when he might ask about his father. Certainly not about what she'd say to him or how it would affect him.

Now it was irrelevant. Jamie would know his father. Very well, if Clay had anything to do with it.

"I just wish he'd calm down a little. Quit trying to run the show."

"That's Clay for you."

"Is it?" Sierra really didn't know him, not the adult Clay. The youth and teenager she'd grown up with had been a lot like her older brothers. Competitive, confident, a talented athlete and enormously popular with the girls. The Clay she'd spent time with two years ago had been vulnerable and wounded and unafraid to show his gentler side. That was the man she'd fallen in love with.

"He's a really good person, Sierra." Sage smiled fondly. "Hardworking, loyal, caring and sweet."

Sweet?

"He's not hard on the eyes, either," Sage added with an appreciative sigh. "You could do worse."

"We're not... There's nothing between us," Sierra protested.

"There was at one time."

Jamie's I'm-awake-where-are-you? cry carried through the house from the bedroom. "Oops." Sierra excused herself with a smile. "Someone's up from their nap."

"And demanding your attention. Isn't that just like a man? Big or little."

Jamie's crying stopped the moment Sierra stepped into the bedroom. He stood up in the portable crib, clinging to the side. One good growth spurt, and he'd be tall enough to crawl out on his own. She was going to have to buy a full-size crib soon, though she couldn't imagine where she'd put another piece of furniture in here.

She and Jamie needed their own place. Though she loved her family, she couldn't live *with* them and *off* them for long. Her pride wouldn't let her. In order to obtain her own place, however, she'd need a job. In order to get a job, she'd have to conquer her fear of being away from Jamie.

The solution was obvious. Find employment she could do from home.

That, she decided, would be the first order of business on Monday morning. She'd update her résumé and start sending it out. In the meantime, she'd offer to help around the ranch. Run errands. Answer the phone. Paperwork. Clean stalls if necessary, so long as she could have Jamie with her.

"Hungry, handsome?"

She hummed to Jamie as she combed his rumpled hair. He patted her face and made kissing sounds; at least, Sierra chose to believe they were kissing sounds.

For a moment, she lost herself in the miracle of her son and forgot all about his father coming over. It didn't last. No sooner did she walk back into the kitchen, Jamie toddling along beside her, then she remembered.

She'd just finished giving him a snack of juice and Cheerios, when a knock sounded.

"Sierra! It's wonderful to see you again." The hug Blythe Powell gave Sierra when she opened the door was warm and genuine and a good ten seconds long.

Her resistance melted. Here was someone from her past, an important someone. In a small way, hugging Blythe was like hugging her mother again.

Suddenly, Sierra wanted Jamie to meet his only living grandmother.

"Come in." Her pleasure was cut short when Clay sauntered into the kitchen.

He was carrying an old-fashioned wooden rocking horse, one that had been ridden hard and loved well, given the worn paint and frayed yarn mane. Once inside, he set it in the middle of the floor.

"I hope you don't mind I brought this along," Blythe explained. "It was Clay's when he was Jamie's age. His grandfather made it for him."

The grandfather she'd named Jamie after? Yes, she thought, observing Clay's features soften.

"Is this him?" Blythe approached Jamie, her hands clasped in front of her, her face an explosion of joy.

Jamie, excited over the commotion, started slapping the tray on his high chair.

"Hello there." Blythe bent so that her face was on Jamie's level. "Aren't you adorable?"

His eyes went huge, and his mouth started quivering.

"Goodness gracious, don't cry."

Sierra rushed over. "He's a little shy around new people."

Except when it came to Clay.

"It's okay," Blythe crooned, not appearing the least bit offended. "We'll get to know each other slowly."

Sierra removed Jamie from the high chair and bounced him in her arms, standing next to Blythe so he could get used to her. After a minute, he settled down. The next minute, he was reaching for Blythe's glasses.

She captured his hand, put it to her lips and blew a raspberry on his palm. Jamie snatched his hand back, stared at it in amazement, burst into giggles, then pushed it into her face.

"Ma, ma, ma."

Tears sprang to Blythe's eyes, and she laughed along with Jamie. "He looks just like Clay did as a baby."

Sierra didn't deny the resemblance, though she sometimes thought she saw some of her father in him, too.

After another two minutes and another dozen raspberries, Jamie was more than willing to go to his grandmother. She took him gratefully.

"Do you mind?" she asked, indicating the chair where Sierra had been sitting when they arrived.

"Sit, please." She caught Clay's glance and was struck still. The sweetness Sage had referred to earlier shone in his expression. "Thank you," he mouthed.

She shrugged, ignoring the mild thrum of her heartstrings. "Can I get you something?" she offered.

"I'm fine." Blythe and Jamie were engaged in a game of peek-a-boo.

"Me, too." Clay removed his cowboy hat and set it on the counter. At the table, he stroked Jamie's head. "The rest of the family out working?"

"Yes." Saturdays, as Sierra was learning, were the busiest days of the week for the Powell Riding Stables and Gavin's stud and breeding business. "Ethan's shoeing horses, and Gavin said something about new brood mares arriving. If you want to go talk to them, your mother and I—"

"I want to talk to you."

All the warm, cozy feelings Sierra had been having promptly vaporized. "Right this minute?"

"Mom can watch Jamie."

Blythe must have heard them, but she didn't look away from Jamie.

"I haven't hired an attorney yet," Sierra said softly.

"It's not that kind of conversation."

What kind was it, then? She'd much prefer stalling, except he would push and push and not relent until she did.

"We can sit in the living room."

"I was thinking of somewhere more private. Like the back patio."

"No. I can't see Jamie from outside." She couldn't see him from the living room, either, but he would be only one room away, and she could hear him. That would minimize her anxiety.

"Mom's not going to—"

"Of course she's not."

"Then why?"

"It's the living room or not at all."

Sierra couldn't explain her phobia to herself, much less other people. Losing Jamie had made her overprotective and unreasonably afraid. She would, she was convinced, improve in time. Everyone just needed to be patient with her.

"Okay." He led the way.

Sierra chose the chair closest to the hallway.

Rather than sit, Clay stood at the large picture window, studying the courtyard, beyond which lay Mustang Valley and the community of Mustang Village at its center.

He was, Sierra grudgingly admitted, a nice-looking man. Tall, broad-shouldered, lean-hipped and with a ruggedly handsome profile. His jeans were the same everyday brand her brothers wore. Not so his Western-cut shirt. She'd bet if she viewed the label inside the collar it would bear a designer name. His quality leather boots and belt were hand-tooled by expert craftsmen.

According to her brothers' account, Clay toiled laboriously running his various business ventures. He was apparently doing well.

A memory stirred of her nestled beside that tall frame, her fingertips stroking that rugged profile as early-morning light streamed in through the shutters. Even as she shoved the memory aside, a flush crept up her neck to her cheeks.

He abruptly turned, startling her, and she averted her head before he noted her flummoxed state.

When he sat, it was in the chair adjacent to hers, his knees separated from hers by mere inches.

"I don't want to make this difficult on you," he started, his voice low.

"I thought you said we weren't going to discuss Jamie's custody."

"We're not. Well, not the legal aspect of it."

"What then?"

He exhaled slowly. "Promise me you'll consider what I say before going ballistic."

"I don't go ballistic."

"You did a little yesterday and just now when I suggested we talk on the back patio."

"I told you, I get nervous when Jamie's out of my sight."

"Which is why I've been rethinking my paternity suit."

Thank goodness!

Her shoulders sagged with relief. "I swear to you, I'll be very generous with visitation."

"Oh, I still want custody of Jamie."

"What!" She sat up. "Not on your life."

"Not full custody."

Her patience snapped, and she pushed to her feet. "Quit playing games with me."

"Sit back down and listen."

She'd never heard him talk so sharply. Reluctantly, she lowered herself into the chair.

"Joint custody is more than shuffling a child between two residences. It's co-parenting. Both of us working as a team to raise our son. To do that successfully, we need to spend as much time together as possible. The three of us."

"Define *as much time as possible*."

"I'd rather define *together*."

"Go on."

"Twenty-four/seven."

"Forget it," Sierra bit out.

"Would you rather I take Jamie half the time? I will."

The thought of Clay taking Jamie for even an hour had her—how had he put it?—going ballistic.

"You can't stay here. There isn't enough room." If he thought he was sharing her bed, he was crazy.

"I agree." He leaned forward, pinning her in place with his unyielding gaze. "Which is why you and Jamie are going to live with me."

Chapter Four

Sierra would have liked to think she'd heard Clay incorrectly, except she hadn't.

"You say *going to live with you* like I don't have a choice."

"You do have a choice. Many of them, in fact. I just happen to think living with me is the best one under the circumstances."

He straightened in his chair, calm and cool and collected. Not one neatly trimmed hair sticking sideways or one droplet of perspiration dotting his brow. Her hair, on the other hand, was a mess, the result of constantly shoving her fingers through the thick strands. And the sweat-soaked collar of her shirt stuck to the back of her neck, intensifying her discomfort.

"Best for you," she snapped.

"For all of us. Jamie will have the benefit of both parents raising him, and you'll get to be with him most of the time."

As opposed to separated from him *half* the time, if Clay won his paternity suit.

Sierra already ached with loneliness. "I don't want to uproot him again. He's just getting used to me. To this place."

"You've been here...what? All of two days? I can't imagine he's become that attached."

"No." She shook her head. "I won't do it."

Clay continued talking as if he hadn't heard her. "The

rodeo arena isn't far from here, only a couple of miles. You can visit your family whenever you want or they can come over. Ethan's at the arena almost every day as it is, and Gavin once a week."

"You live at the rodeo arena?"

"Sometimes it feels like that, I'm there so much."

Not a place she saw herself either residing or bringing up her son. Too far from town. Too dangerous, what with horses and bulls and vehicles everywhere. It was probably also dusty and dirty. San Francisco was hardly perfect, but she'd resided there for the last seven years and grown accustomed to city life.

"The house is actually on the next parcel over," Clay continued. "I built it shortly after the arena was finished."

There were so many reasons to refuse his offer besides uprooting Jamie. She picked the first one.

"I've never shared a house or apartment with a man, and I won't unless he and I are in a committed relationship."

"I respect your principles, and I wouldn't ask you to compromise them."

Oh, okay. She hadn't expected him to give in so quickly. "Well, I guess there's no need—"

"I built a casita behind the house. It's not large, basically a bedroom, a sitting area and a bathroom. But you and Jamie could be comfortable there. You'd have to take some of your meals in the main house. With me," he added, his tone such that Sierra clearly understood shared meals were part of the deal.

"I can't live off you. It wouldn't be right."

"I'll be paying monthly child support for Jamie. Any rent, if you want, can be considered part of that support."

"It still feels like a handout."

"Fine. You can work for me."

"This is no joke."

"I'm not joking. I need the help."

She eyed him suspiciously. "With what? I was an assistant sales rep for a medical-supply company. I haven't been on a horse since…three years ago last Christmas."

Like the rest her family, Sierra had grown up on and around horses, but she had abandoned the cowboy lifestyle at seventeen when she'd left for college. What possible job could there be at a rodeo arena that didn't involve knowledge of livestock, expertise with a rope and excellent horsemanship skills?

"Office work mostly," Clay said. "Answering phones, correspondence, paying bills and depositing checks, livestock-rental contracts, maintaining liability waivers and promoting jackpot events."

That actually didn't sound too bad and like something Sierra might even enjoy, especially promotion. She was good with people and liked working with them. It was what had once made her the go-to assistant sales rep.

She could be that kind of worker again.

Wait a minute! Even if she could leave Jamie all day, she wasn't working for Clay. Not in this lifetime.

"You've thought of everything, haven't you?"

"I haven't. Which is why I need to run this by my attorney so he can draw up an employment contract."

She almost laughed. "You not only expect Jamie and I to live with you, you want me to sign a contract?"

"All my employees do."

She gaped at him. "How long are these contracts for?"

He didn't miss a beat. "One year."

"I can't put my life on hold that long."

"I'm not going to chain you to me." One corner of his wide mouth tipped up as if he were about to smile.

Did the idea appeal to him?

"What if I want to take a trip?"

"You can leave Jamie with me."

"Leave him?" Impossible. Clay *was* chaining her to him. "This is ridiculous."

"I disagree. It's a very fair arrangement."

"You're trying to manipulate me. And Jamie. Trying to force us to do what you want by threatening to take him away from me."

"Joint custody isn't taking him away from you."

It was. For seven out of fourteen days.

Hard to believe she'd once fallen in love with this…this… control freak?

"Talk it over with your family," he said, "and your attorney, when you retain one. Send me his or her name, and I'll have mine forward the documents."

"How long do I have to decide?" she asked snidely.

Clay ignored her tone. "A week."

"That's not enough time!"

"Ten days, then."

"Be reasonable."

His voice remained level, though his jaw muscles tightened. "I'm being far more reasonable with you than you were with me."

He was getting back at her. She didn't think he'd stoop so low.

Then again, she had done a terrible thing to him. He could sue for full custody, and he wasn't. She should be grateful for that, at least.

Sierra frowned. Come Monday morning, she wouldn't be sending out her résumé, she'd be finding an attorney to represent her.

Jamie suddenly let out a high-pitched squeal, and she shot out of her chair. How could she have forgotten about him for—what?—five minutes? No, seven. She dashed into the kitchen, Clay hot on her heels.

Jamie was sitting on the rocking horse, Blythe kneeling on the floor beside him.

Sierra came to a stop beside them, her breathing shallow. "What happened?"

"Jamie caught his shoe on the foot peg. When I stopped him from rocking in order to unwedge his shoe, he began squealing."

That was all? Sierra stroked Jamie's head to reassure herself.

His fingers gripping the hand pegs and feet properly positioned, he took off galloping again—which consisted of rocking the horse as fast as he could, his angelic face aglow.

Blythe watched him, her hand hovering protectively.

Sierra considered stepping in and lifting Jamie from the rocking horse. A part of her was angry enough at Clay to do it. But she'd never seen her son having so much fun.

Clay stepped around her, retrieved his hat from the counter and dropped it onto Jamie's head. Too large for him, it immediately fell forward over his eyes.

"Ride 'em, cowboy." Pride and affection shone in Clay's eyes. He tipped the hat back so Jamie could see.

Father, son and grandmother all laughed.

Sierra stood motionless, her emotions in a tangle.

This was the man she'd fallen in love with two years ago. The man who'd allowed her to dream of the impossible.

He was also the same man who'd broken her heart and left her miserable enough to make the biggest mistake of her life.

She would, she realized, have to guard her heart ruthlessly because it would be much too easy to fall in love with him again.

"I REALLY APPRECIATE you seeing me on such short notice." Sierra slipped into the visitor's chair, settled Jamie on her lap and looked across the desk at her attorney.

"No problem. I understand the urgency." Roberto Torres was Sage's cousin-in-law. He'd represented Sage during her custody dispute with her ex, and she'd highly recommended him to Sierra.

"Did Clay's attorney send over the papers?" She'd filled Roberto in on the situation during their phone call that morning.

"He did." Roberto picked up a stack of papers on his desk and passed several sheets to Sierra. "Here's a copy of the paternity suit and a proposed joint-custody agreement. I've only had time to skim both documents."

Sierra attempted to read the first page of the custody agreement but nothing made sense. It was the turmoil raging inside her and not the legalese that tripped her up. She'd been back in Mustang Valley a total of four days and, other than her family welcoming her home, nothing had gone as planned.

Blythe Duvall couldn't have been nicer or more considerate on Saturday, which Sierra appreciated. Things between her and Clay, however, had remained tense, continuing through yesterday evening when he'd stopped by the ranch while the family was having dessert. She expected more of the same when he visited today, especially as he knew she was meeting with her attorney.

"The terms of the custody agreement are pretty standard." Roberto laid down the papers. "You mentioned on the phone this isn't what you want."

"No, but I'm not sure I have a choice. I'm worried Clay will sue for full custody if I don't cooperate." Sierra held the papers out of Jamie's curious grasp. "Can he get it?"

"Probably not."

"But I gave Jamie up for adoption. Clay could use that against me. You said the attorney he hired is one of the best."

"You're not an unfit mother, Sierra, which is what he'd have to prove. Joint custody, however, is almost a given."

Sierra's hopes, small to begin with, plummeted. "What's this 5-2-2-5 parenting time schedule?"

"Basically, it's alternating weekends. A fourteen-day schedule that continually repeats."

"Sounds complicated." And awful.

"I'm told you get used to it, and that it's easier than a 7-7 schedule," he added kindly.

"What if I refuse?"

"The judge will likely order it."

And Clay wins again.

"I hate this feeling of helplessness," she said through clenched teeth.

"We can always try and negotiate the terms. Propose working up to the 5-2-2-5 schedule slowly."

"Clay won't do it."

"Let's ask. You'll feel less helpless if you have some say."

She flipped through the pages as best she could with Jamie in the way. "What else do you recommend?"

"A review of the schedule in three months to determine how well it's working and every six months thereafter. Also, what happens when Jamie's sick? Or you're sick? Or Clay? Grandparent visitations? Vacations—yours and his? Business trips? Babysitting? Day care? Preschool?"

Sierra wished Roberto would talk more slowly.

"I'm not sure about this employment contract," he said, pulling a sheet out.

"Employment contract?" She shuffled through the papers in her lap, dropping some. "I never agreed to work for him."

"No?"

"He mentioned it, but I didn't say yes."

"Well, I strongly advise you consider carefully before accepting. Living in his casita is one thing—"

"I'm not working for him," she stated flatly.

"All right then." He set several pages aside. "I won't review the employment contract."

Sierra fumed. Of all the nerve. She was ready to tell Clay he could shove the whole paternity suit where the sun didn't shine. Except that would gain her nothing and would quite possibly make matters worse.

Another thought occurred to her. "Will me not having a job hurt my chances?"

"I don't believe so. Are you currently looking?"

"I've just started. I'm hoping to find something I can do from home."

"We'll ask for day care costs. Keep in mind Clay will also need day care on his days with Jamie. You might want to use the same person or facility as him. Easier on Jamie that way."

"I'm not putting Jamie in day care. I can't."

Roberto gazed at her curiously, waiting for her to explain.

"I have trouble being separated from him. Even for short periods of time." *Like a few minutes.* "I thought I'd lost him forever. Since getting him back…" She hugged Jamie, her throat tight. "I'm scared to death of losing him again. I know it's completely unreasonable, but I can't help myself. That's why joint custody is, well, impossible for me. Can't we please start with visitation?"

"All we can do is ask."

Sierra bit back a sob.

"I've met Clay. He's not a bad guy. Have you talked to him about your apprehensions?"

"A little. That's why he suggested Jamie and I move into the casita."

Roberto reached into his desk drawer, withdrew a business card and handed it to her. "I'd like to make another suggestion. If I'm out of line, I apologize, but remember, I'm your advocate and only want what's best for you and Jamie."

She took the card and stiffened when she read the name of a psychologist on it.

"It's completely understandable for someone in your position, who's been through what you have, to suffer anxieties. Learning to cope with them will only improve things for you and Jamie." He waited while she flipped the card around in her fingers. "Dr. Brewster is someone we frequently refer our clients to, and she's very good."

"I can't afford counseling."

"Clay can. We'll include counseling in the agreement, both individual sessions for you and joint ones."

"He and I together?"

"You want to successfully co-parent Jamie. To do that, you and Clay have to get along."

"I'm not going to ask him to pay for counseling sessions. He might think I'm unbalanced and use it against me."

"The judge is going to order at least one counseling session, along with parenting classes. More sessions make sense and show you're trying your best to make the agreement work."

Sierra had her doubts. Could she trust Clay?

"Explore all your options," Robert said. "Visit his home and check out the casita. See if you and Jamie could be comfortable living there before we go any further."

"I assure you, I won't be comfortable."

"Maybe, maybe not. You don't know till you look."

Sierra and Roberto continued to discuss the paternity suit for another twenty minutes, until Jamie tired. They agreed on a follow-up meeting the next afternoon.

She couldn't wait to get out of the attorney's office. She kept hearing the phrase *make the agreement work* over and over in her head as she walked through the building's main lobby and out the double glass doors.

Granted, she didn't want a joint-custody agreement with

Clay. But this whole situation was starting to feel less like two people lovingly co-parenting their child and more like an impersonal business arrangement.

CLAY WATCHED FROM his front porch as Sierra pulled in beside his pickup truck and parked. Jogging down the steps, he headed for her car, intending to open her door. She was already at the rear hatch by the time he got there.

"You found the place."

"The signs along the road made it pretty easy." She removed a stroller and quickly set it up. For someone who'd been an active mother only one short month, she appeared to know what she was doing. "This is a busy place. I must have passed six horse trailers on my way in."

"There's a rodeo in Scottsdale next week. A lot of local cowboys are getting in as much practice as possible before then."

"That's what Ethan said."

She was being civil. On the verge of friendly. Not what he'd expected so soon following her appointment with her attorney. When she'd called him an hour ago and asked to see the casita, he'd stammered a surprised "How soon can you be here?"

He cautioned himself not to jump the gun. Her request didn't mean she'd changed her mind about living with him. But she was obviously entertaining the possibility, which was a huge step. Clay fully intended to obtain joint custody of his son. He'd rather accomplish it without battling Sierra.

"If you're interested, we can tour the rodeo facility and office when we're done here."

"Won't it be dark by then?" She pushed the empty stroller to the rear passenger door, then reached inside and lifted Jamie from his car seat.

"The floodlights will be on." Clay stood at her side, observing her every move. He had a lot to learn about caring for babies, too.

"Maybe." She set Jamie in the stroller. "I have an errand to run on the way home."

Jamie wiggled excitedly, and it took Sierra several attempts to get the safety straps buckled, his jacket zippered and his ball cap situated on his head.

Clay smiled and winked at his son and was rewarded with a silly giggle. Later, he would insist on holding Jamie. For now, Clay let Sierra be in charge.

"Do people always practice at night?" She handed Jamie his toy pony. For once, the boy disregarded it in favor of his surroundings.

"Depends," Clay said. "More often in the summer months when it's too hot during the day to ride. With the rodeo coming up, however, practice will last till midnight if I let it."

"Will you let it?" She tilted her head at an appealing angle.

Clay promptly forgot the question. "What? Oh, yeah. Practice. Probably not tonight. I don't have enough wranglers willing to stay late."

She took hold of the stroller's handle and released a foot brake. "Is Ethan here?"

"He is. We can watch him working the horses if you want."

"We'll see."

"That's right. You have an errand to run."

She didn't respond.

Clay wanted to ask her how her meeting with her attorney had gone but hesitated. Better to leave the joint-custody agreement to their respective representatives. He didn't want there to be any tension between him and Sierra while they were looking at the casita.

"You have a beautiful home." She took in the expansive grounds as they walked a shrub-lined footpath leading to the enclosed backyard.

"We can go inside when we're done with the casita. You'll like the kitchen. I designed it myself."

Would she like it? He realized after he'd made the comment he had no idea. He couldn't recall her spending much time in the kitchen as a teenager, and they'd either eaten out or grabbed a snack from the fridge during their brief affair.

Clearly she was wondering the same thing about him. Slanting him a curious look, she asked, "Do you cook?"

"When I have the time, which isn't often. I make the best country ribs and coleslaw you'll ever eat."

Funny, they could make a baby together and still not know the simplest things about each other.

"Hmm. I'm impressed." She carefully maneuvered the stroller over the uneven ground. "I haven't had ribs in years."

"Don't tell me. You're a vegan."

"No. I did try that once for a few months."

He could have sworn for just a second her mouth tipped up in a smile. His heart leapt. Maybe, possibly, the sense of humor that had charmed him two years ago hadn't entirely disappeared.

"This way." He gestured to their left to a small square building connected to the house by a wood-slat walkway. A small bridge rose at midpoint over the rocky bed of a natural wash.

Designed in the same Southwestern style as the main house right down to the red tile roof and carved oak door, the casita had its own private patio and a kiva fireplace with two wrought-iron chairs facing it. Leafy plants spilled over the sides of colorful ceramic pots placed on either side of the fireplace.

"The gate locks," Clay said, opening it so that they could enter the patio. "That way, Jamie can't get out. I'll also have extra dead bolt locks installed on both the casita's doors, high enough so he can't reach them. Right now, the heat's turned off, so it's a little cold inside."

Sierra didn't seem to notice that Clay was talking as though her moving in was a foregone conclusion.

She pushed the stroller through the front door and came to a sudden stop, her eyes wide. "It's bigger than it looks from the outside."

"Three hundred and sixty square feet altogether. I think the picture window and skylights give an illusion of spaciousness."

She continued past the recliner and queen-size bed to the tiny kitchen in the corner. There, she ran her fingers along the edges of the single-basin sink and three-burner stove. Last, she opened the mini refrigerator for a quick peek at the contents, which consisted of a can of tomato juice and a box of baking soda.

"No oven," Clay said, "so you can't prepare a huge meal. But between the stovetop and the microwave, you and Jamie won't starve."

"There's always the meals we share with you."

She *would* bring up that condition.

Leaving the stroller outside the bathroom, she went in to explore. Clay was glad he'd spent the extra money and had a whirlpool tub installed.

"This is great," she exclaimed.

He smiled to himself.

Was she remembering that night they'd spent at the Phoenix Inn and their room with the built-in Jacuzzi? They'd drunk champagne and eaten strawberries amid swirling water and shared a continental breakfast in bed the next morning. In between, they'd made love. For hours.

Then, a week after Sierra went home, Jessica had crooked her little finger and Clay went right back to her like a trained lapdog.

Would he have been so eager if he'd known Sierra was pregnant?

Definitely not.

He'd have done right by Jamie, been a better father than his own ever was—*would* be a better father than his own. Put his family first, not his insatiable greed.

And he'd have done right by Sierra, too. Married her if that was what she'd wanted. Taken care of her, certainly.

What if she'd told him about the baby *after* he and Jessica had renewed their engagement? Would he have still married Jessica?

Clay was honest enough with himself to admit he had his doubts. Oh, he'd have still taken care of Jamie and Sierra. But left Jessica? Hard to say. The spell that woman cast on him had been strong *and* blinding.

"Da, da, da!"

Clay swung around. Had Jamie just called him Dada? He went to the stroller and knelt in front of his son, who wore an enormous grin and waved his pony in the air.

"Da, da, da, ba, ba."

"Hey, pal." Clay tugged on the brim of Jamie's ball cap, emotion thickening his voice. "I'm here."

"Hard consonants are easier to pronounce than soft ones." Sierra had stepped out of the bathroom and was standing beside Clay and Jamie. "They aren't necessarily words."

Guess Jamie wasn't calling him Daddy yet. "Is that what the baby books say?"

She blushed guiltily. "I have been reading up."

Clay stood and waited. After a moment, she met his gaze. They were closer than he'd first thought. So close the fronts of their jackets brushed. With the wall on one side and the stroller on the other, there was little room to maneuver, unless Sierra twisted and ducked into the bathroom.

She didn't.

Her eyes, a vivid blue and by far her most striking feature, held him immobile. He had only to lower his mouth a few inches and he'd be able to taste her lush pink lips. Slide his tongue over them until they parted and she leaned into him…

"Da, da, ba, da."

Clay jerked. What the heck just happened?

He was angry at Sierra. Furious. Didn't trust her. And with good reason. He was not in any way whatsoever attracted to her.

His pulse and sudden rapid breathing were making a liar of him.

Maybe her living in such close proximity wasn't a good idea after all.

Chapter Five

"We'd better get a move on." Sierra slipped gracefully out from between Clay and the wall. "I have that errand to run."

Clay watched her lean down to fix Jamie's loose shoe. The curve of her shapely posterior didn't go unnoticed.

Dang. If she could have escaped all along, why hadn't she?

Perhaps this zing of attraction from out of nowhere wasn't entirely one-sided.

Naw. She didn't look like a person who'd just been emotionally knocked to her knees. Her movements were too steady, her demeanor too cool.

Clay, on the other hand, was only now recovering.

"Do you mind if I push Jamie?" Distractions. He needed distractions.

She hesitated.

"I admit, I don't have much experience but I think I can get him from here to the house without crashing."

"All right." She remained glued to his side, hovering with near obsessiveness as they left the casita.

"Any closer, and I'm going to run over you."

"Sorry."

Why had he opened his big mouth? Having her two feet away was infinitely less enjoyable than two inches.

The stroller wheels bumped over the wood slats as they

walked to the house. Jamie laughed with delight, and Clay could imagine him saying, *Again, Daddy, again.*

They entered the house through a pair of French doors opening to a spacious great room. Clay found himself looking at the decidedly masculine decor through Sierra's eyes. Did she find the leather furniture, floor-to-ceiling bookcases and pool table too much?

"You were right." She went straight to the kitchen with its antique buffet, plate racks and glass door cabinets. "It *is* fabulous." She turned in a half circle. "Look at that stove."

It was Clay's pride and joy. Six burners, a built-in grill, a conventional oven below and a convection oven above, the gas range had been designed to resemble one from the early 1900s.

She switched on a knob, and blue flames erupted from the front burner.

"You like to cook."

"When I get the chance. Same as you." The faint smile Clay had seen earlier in the casita reappeared and lasted two full seconds before fading.

Progress.

Jamie squawked and kicked his legs hard enough to shake the stroller.

"What's wrong?" Clay asked. If Jamie required changing, he'd do that, too, though he wasn't looking forward to it.

"I think he's tired of sitting."

That wasn't what had started Jamie fussing. He'd spied Oreo, who lumbered tiredly into the kitchen, his feathery tail wagging.

"Is that Oreo?" Sierra didn't wait for an answer. She reached down and scrunched the dog's ears in her hands. "He was old two years ago."

"Older now. Almost seventeen. He doesn't do much except move from one sleeping spot to the next."

And lick faces, present company included. Sierra laughed as she twisted her head out of Oreo's reach.

Jamie's kicking increased. "Da, da, da."

Great. His son was now calling his dog Daddy.

"His adoptive... The Stevensons had a dog," Sierra explained. "He's used to them."

"Go on, let them play. Oreo likes kids."

"Kids or babies? There's a difference."

"He's the gentlest dog in the world."

Oreo lived up to Clay's boasts. The moment Sierra set Jamie on the floor, he tumbled over to the old spaniel. Throwing his arms around Oreo's neck, he buried his face in the still-lustrous black-and-white coat and squealed excitedly.

Oreo's only reaction was to look up at Clay with a see-what-I-put-up-with-for-you expression on his face. Even when Jamie pulled on Oreo's fur, the dog's tail continued to wag.

"He *is* good with kids." Sierra smiled—*really* smiled.

The light radiating from it arrowed straight into Clay's chest. He wasn't sure he'd ever be the same.

He wasn't sure he wanted to be the same.

"I worry Jamie will get hurt." She nibbled her lip nervously. "He tried playing with Cassie's puppy Blue yesterday. It didn't go well. Jamie got too rambunctious."

"Did Blue snap at him?"

"No, no. Just yelped and scampered away. Which scared Jamie and he started crying."

"That won't happen with any dog of mine. Or horse."

"Just because Oreo's trustworthy doesn't mean you can put Jamie on a pony." She leveled a finger at Clay, her mouth set in a determined line. "Not happening, Clay Duvall. You hear me?"

How did she know he'd already contacted one of his livestock dealers about any ponies for sale?

"Not until he's older," she stated.

"How old?"

"Six, at least."

"I had my first pony at three."

"Three! Are you crazy?"

"If I don't buy him a pony, your dad or brothers will."

"No one is buying Jamie a pony."

Clay dropped the subject. For now. They'd compromise eventually. Clay was more concerned about Jamie living here with him.

And Sierra.

Taking both boy and dog with them, they toured the rest of the house. When they were done, they left for the arena. Oreo remained behind in the kitchen, to Jamie's acute disappointment. He wailed at being parted from his new best friend and didn't stop.

Clay hoisted Jamie into his arms, and the boy instantly quieted.

"That's better, pal."

Sierra pushed the empty stroller. "We can put him back now."

"He's fine."

She crinkled her brow. "You can't carry him all the way to the rodeo arena."

"Sure I can."

The horse operation was only about a hundred and fifty yards from the house. Close enough for Clay to keep watch on everything and far enough to afford him a modicum of privacy.

Sierra said nothing.

Jamie did. He would point to something that caught his attention, a horse and rider, a truck and trailer, one of the wranglers, and blurt a string of nonsense syllables as if he were commenting on what he saw.

Clay enjoyed every second and responded with "What do you think of that?" or "I know, it *is* big."

He observed the people they passed. Some openly stared. Clay waved or nodded, not minding the attention. He was proud to be a father. It was a feeling he treasured and, he glanced at Sierra, one he'd fight for if necessary.

"Most of the bulls, horses and calves are kept in pastures or paddocks over there." He indicated the acres and acres of open land behind the rodeo arena. "We transport them to the holding pens for practices and jackpot events. The maternity pastures are to the east."

"Maternity pastures?" Sierra asked showing the first hint of interest.

"Leasing livestock to rodeos is a large part of my business. Occasionally, I purchase livestock. Most often calves. For the larger stock, horses in particular, I've started breeding my own, which was one of the reasons I went into business with Gavin. I'm hoping Prince will produce quality bucking stock," he said, referring to the wild mustang he and Sierra's brothers had captured last fall. "I've bred him to three of my best mares."

"Hmm." Sierra's response was noncommittal but the spark remained in her eyes.

They watched the wranglers herd a new batch of bucking broncs to the holding pens. A few of the men were on foot, most on horseback, Ethan among them. When he was done and the bucking horses secured, he trotted over to Clay and Sierra and dismounted.

"Hey, buckeroo." Ethan poked Jamie on the nose. "Which of these bad boys are you going to ride tonight?"

Still in Clay's arms, Jamie grabbed for Ethan's horse. The big gelding was less enthused with the attention than Oreo had been and jerked back.

"He's not getting anywhere near a horse." Sierra planted herself between Clay and her brother, glaring at them both.

They exchanged glances and dutifully replied, "Yes, ma'am."

She harrumphed as if she didn't quite believe them.

While Clay and Ethan discussed the upcoming rodeo, Sierra kept watch on Jamie, ready to seize him from Clay if the horse got even one inch closer.

He decided to give her a break and handed Jamie over to her. Shoulders sagging with relief, she returned him to the stroller. Jamie objected loudly and pushed at the restraining bar.

"Cute kid," Ethan said to Clay. His manner had gone from lighthearted to serious.

"Yep, he is."

"Sissy told us about you wanting her and Jamie to move into the casita."

"I think it's a good compromise."

"You're my best friend, Clay. There isn't anyone else I want to stand up for me at my wedding next weekend."

Ethan's words warmed Clay. "I feel the same."

"The thing is, if you hurt my sister or her boy, it won't matter how good a friend you are."

Clay wasn't bothered by the thinly veiled threat. If he were in Ethan's shoes, he'd want to protect his sister and nephew, too.

"For the record, I don't plan on hurting either of them."

Ethan's grin, normally ear to ear, didn't reach his eyes. "Okay. Because I'd hate to have to hunt you down."

Sierra was too busy with Jamie to pay much attention to what Clay and her brother were saying. Something, however, must have changed for they were suddenly serious and, this was odd, posturing.

Really? Men!

She knelt down in front of Jamie so that their faces were on the same level.

"Hey there, handsome."

He ignored her, twisting his small body sideways to face Clay, his left arm extended.

"It's Mommy. Come on, look at me."

Jamie did, for a second. Then, his attention returned to Clay.

Not far away, a golden retriever stuck his head out of a parked truck window and barked.

"See the doggie, Jamie?"

He didn't care.

Sierra gave up and stood, not liking her son's fixation with Clay. She and Jamie were newly bonded, and she wanted to be the one he reached for. The one able to soothe him when he was distressed. The center of his small universe.

What would happen if—more likely, when—Clay was granted joint custody? Sure, he was an eager parent now. More than eager, almost obsessive. That could change. The Stevensons had been eager parents in the beginning, too.

Sierra would do whatever was necessary to protect her son from hurt and rejection. But how?

Live and work here, she supposed. That would enable her to stay close to Jamie, including the days Clay had him. She might even be able to convince him to postpone taking Jamie overnight until they were more settled, and she was on firmer emotional ground.

Jamie's excited chatter alerted her to Clay's presence behind her.

"Sorry about that," he said, his apology directed at Sierra but his disarming smile all for Jamie.

And it *was* disarming. She'd basked in it often two years

ago when, for a very short time, he'd forgotten all about Jessica.

Jamie's fidgeting returned Sierra to her senses. Thank goodness. She didn't need to be thinking about Clay's smile and how she'd basked in it.

Before she could dig Jamie's toy pony out of the diaper bag, Clay reached into his pocket and handed Jamie his set of keys.

He's learning, she thought. Clay might turn out to be a good father after all. Maybe even a better father than she was a mother.

Sierra bit down hard, determination overriding her insecurities. Jamie would love her so much he would never blame her for giving him up temporarily.

"Ready for the rest of the tour?" Clay asked.

She gripped the stroller handle and forced a smile. "Let's go."

He showed her the arena, bucking chutes, roping chutes and holding pens. Beside the bank of aluminum bleachers stood a two-story wooden structure with a staircase on the outside. Instead of windows, the second story was open on all four sides.

"Above is the announcer's stand." He opened a door on the ground floor and flipped on a light switch. "This is the first aid station."

She noted the room appeared well-equipped and neatly organized.

"It used to be my office, but I moved that to the barn after Caitlin started working for me."

Sierra had recently learned Ethan's fiancée, a licensed nurse, ran the first aid station for Clay during events. It was another reminder of how out of touch she'd become with her family.

She had to rectify that. She loved and needed her family. They would be all she had on the days Jamie spent with Clay.

"Can I see the office?" she asked, a heavy weight bearing down on her heart.

"Come on, I'll show you."

They started toward the barn. Other than being newer, it closely resembled the one at Powell Ranch.

Halfway there, Jamie started fussing again. Given that it was nearly six o'clock and two hours since he'd last eaten, he was probably hungry. She reached into the diaper bag. Too late, she remembered she was out of animal crackers.

"What's wrong with him?" Clay asked.

"He's hungry."

"Should we go back to the house and feed him?"

Prolonging her visit was the last thing she wanted. "He'll be okay if we don't take too long."

"He doesn't sound okay," Clay observed as Jamie's wailing gained conviction. "I have some instant oatmeal in the office."

"You eat breakfast in your office?"

"I like to tackle the paperwork before my day gets away from me."

Considering how late he'd worked the last two nights, he put in some mighty long hours.

They rounded the side of the barn. A flimsy plastic office sign was mounted beside a brown steel door.

Clay opened it.

Sierra made a face, recalling the barn office at her family's ranch with its perpetually grimy windows, scuffed floors and dust-blanketed desk. Not that she faulted her brothers. Who could keep an office clean in a barn?

Clay lifted the stroller's front wheels over the raised threshold. Jamie stopped whining—momentarily, Sierra was sure. If she'd learned anything about her son these last several weeks it was that he possessed a voracious appetite.

"Here we are."

Sierra prepared herself for the worst and stepped inside. She let out a small gasp. The office was not only spanking clean, it was attractive and housed state-of-the-art equipment. Framed photographs decorated the walls. A few featured Clay as a teenager, roping calves and riding bulls. Three photos were of the rodeo arena at various stages of construction. A large portrait of Prince hung over a cabinet.

As she had when she'd viewed his house, Sierra found herself stammering as she commented, "This is nice."

"I'm not the most organized person in the world."

She'd barely noticed the piles of papers and folders on the desk. "Who does your office work now?"

"Me, mostly. I also use a temp agency. They send someone out once or twice a week."

Despite her conviction not to be, Sierra was curious. "How many hours a day do you think would be enough?"

"Four, for sure. Maybe more the week before an event. We have a bull-and-bronc-riding jackpot next month."

As they talked, Clay went to a cupboard where he removed a bowl and package of instant oatmeal. Using water from a cooler, he prepared the oatmeal and heated it in the microwave.

Sierra lifted Jamie from the stroller and sat with him in the visitor chair. A minute later, Clay handed her the bowl of oatmeal and a spoon. Jamie ate as if he was starving.

Clay sat behind the desk, facing them. "I hope we're not spoiling his dinner."

"Are you kidding? This is just the appetizer. He'll have the main course at home."

"You're really good with him."

She couldn't look at Clay, afraid he'd see the blush warming her cheeks. Why in the world did his praise embarrass her?

"Thanks. I'm trying."

"I'd like to try, too. Feeding him, that is."

"Now?" She didn't want to give up Jamie. "He's almost done."

"So I see." Clay chuckled. "He definitely has my appetite."

Clay did eat a lot, Sierra remembered that about him. One would never know it to look at him, however. He didn't appear to have an ounce of fat on his lean, athletic frame.

Enough already with the personal thoughts about Clay, Sierra chided herself. Their relationship was already confusing enough.

While Jamie played with the spoon, Clay rambled on about the day-to-day office operations. Sierra listened, wishing she didn't like the sound of the job so much. If not for having to leave Jamie with a caretaker, and Clay being her boss, it would be a perfect job for her. Flexible hours, lots of customer contact and a variety of duties, some easy, some challenging.

"Then there's the mustang sanctuary," he said. "We're moving it from your family's ranch to here. I'm donating the pasture space, water and any feed and medical care above and beyond donations. Your brothers will still supervise the training. I'd like to organize a wild-horse auction to raise awareness and, hopefully, money. We're running low. I'd also like to investigate any potential government grants. You could be in charge of that."

"What about Sage?"

Sierra's future sister-in-law had founded the sanctuary shortly after Prince's capture in order to place formerly unadoptable feral horses in good homes. It was her hobby and her passion.

"Between the wedding, her full-time job and the baby due

this summer, she's had to step down. You'd make an excellent replacement."

Clay couldn't be holding a more tempting carrot in front of Sierra. Part of her former job had been planning client-appreciation luncheons, annual charity campaigns and employee retreats. She'd not only enjoyed the work, she'd shown a real knack for it.

"Babies are time-consuming," she agreed, thinking of those four-plus hours a day she'd be away from Jamie.

She didn't trust anyone to watch him, with the exception of her family, and they were far too busy with their own lives and livelihoods for her to ask such a huge favor.

Better she decline Clay's offer and find a job she could do from home. Then, once she'd saved enough money, she could locate her own place—and be miserably alone on the days Clay had Jamie.

Unless she moved into the casita.

Resentment, a frequent companion recently, built inside her. Clay had done nothing. Nothing *more,* anyway, than offer her a charming place to live and a great job. Yet she felt pressured again.

"Is there a sink where I can wash this?" She rose from the chair, Jamie in one arm, the empty oatmeal bowl in her free hand.

"I'll take care of it."

"You sure?"

"I can wash dishes." He flashed that disarming smile again. "In fact, I do it pretty regularly."

One good quality didn't cancel out all the bad ones.

"Clay…about the job. I appreciate the offer, but I have to say no."

"Why?"

She shifted Jamie to her other hip. "I need something I can do from home. So Jamie doesn't have to be left with a sitter or in day care. He's had so many disruptions these last few weeks, one more is just too much."

"Day care?" Clay stood up as well and came out from behind the desk. "I thought you understood."

"Understood what?"

"You can bring Jamie with you to work." He gestured to the corner. "Put a playpen over there. One of those bouncy-chair things. I don't care. This isn't exactly a professional office."

She stared blankly at him. "I can bring Jamie to work with me?"

"I told you that, didn't I?"

If he had, she hadn't heard him.

Clay moved closer, and Jamie reached for him. "I'd like it if you brought him. That way, I get to see him even more."

Another attempt to control her, or was he just being thoughtful and considerate?

Sierra wished she knew. Maybe then making a decision wouldn't be so hard.

Chapter Six

"He's forcing you," Gavin insisted, "and he has no right!"

Sierra loved that her brother was sticking up for her. She'd half expected him to support Clay, considering how traditional Gavin could be in his thinking and his past experience with Cassie's mother. Because of his ex, Gavin had missed out on most of Cassie's childhood and wouldn't wish the same on any father.

But he was also Sierra's big brother and for him blood was thicker than water.

"I don't know if he's forcing her as much as sweetening the pot." Ethan sat back, taking a sip of his coffee. While he was also concerned for her and Jamie's welfare, he happened to be best friends with Clay and would try hard to see both sides.

Gavin glared at Ethan. "You sound like you think she should do it."

"I think she should consider it. She said herself she freaks out if she has to be apart from Jamie. Even for a few minutes."

"He has a point," Sierra's father agreed. The four of them sat around the kitchen table, the dirty dinner dishes still in the sink waiting to be washed.

"She shouldn't have to be apart from him." Gavin pushed to his feet.

Ethan, the more easygoing of the two, stacked his hands behind his head and stretched out his long legs. "With joint custody, she'd get Jamie half the time. But if she lived with Clay, she'd get him *all* the time."

"I wouldn't be living with him," Sierra was quick to add. "The casita is entirely separate from the house."

"It's still on his property," Gavin grumbled.

"Technically, yes." She questioned how much of his annoyance at Clay was for her sake and how much was left over from when Bud Duvall sold their family's land out from under them. She'd thought Clay and Gavin had settled their differences when they became business partners.

Maybe not.

She was glad the rest of the family had driven into Scottsdale for some last-minute wedding preparations—which is what her brothers should be doing, too. The big day was Saturday, and there was precious little time left to handle the hundred and one details still needing attention.

Sierra glanced around the kitchen, her heart bursting with love. No way was she going to let her suit with Clay interfere with what should be the happiest day of her brothers' lives. She and Clay would have to get along, simple as that.

The debate between Gavin and Ethan continued with Jamie interjecting his two cents every now and then. He perched on his grandfather's lap, banging his toy pony on the table. Little by little he was warming up to his grandfather, uncles, aunts-to-be and cousins, which pleased Sierra immensely.

"Da, da, ba, be." Jamie pushed the toy pony into his grandfather's face.

"Hey, there." Wayne grimaced and averted his head. "Isn't it past your bedtime yet?"

"Bath first," Sierra said.

"Clay always thinks he's right." Gavin clearly wasn't letting the subject drop.

"And you don't?" Ethan slanted a good-natured grin at his brother.

"Sierra's place is with her family, and Jamie's place is with his mother."

"A father has a right to his child. You should know that better than anyone."

That shut Gavin up. There was nothing he wouldn't do, no lengths he wouldn't go to, to keep Cassie with him.

Was he any different from Clay?

Was she any different from Cassie's mother?

"I think you should move into Clay's casita." Her father's announcement brought a sudden halt to his brother's heated discussion.

"Are you serious?" Gavin demanded.

"Yes. For just the reason Ethan brought up. You went through hell those years you were separated from Cassie. We all did. It wasn't fair to you, to Cassie, and it wouldn't be fair to Clay."

"I'm not taking Jamie and moving across country," Sierra interjected. "Wherever I live, Clay will… He'll have Jamie half the time." Her mouth went dry at the prospect.

"The boy needs stability," her father persisted. "He's gone from home to home, parent to parent. You think shuffling him back and forth between you and Clay is going to provide him that stability?"

"No." Sierra reached over and patted Jamie's smooth cheek. "Which is why I'd rather have full custody and for Clay to have only visitation. For a while. Until Jamie adjusts."

"He can adjust perfectly fine at Clay's place."

Sierra wasn't sure she could, however.

"And you'd get to take him to work. How many employers will let you do that?"

"Day care wouldn't be an issue if I found a job I could do from home."

"Right. You look into that yet?"

"Some."

"Find anything that isn't telephone sales?"

"It's a tough job market. Something good will come along eventually." Hopefully her meager savings would hold out till then.

"Don't you want Sierra and Jamie here with us?" Gavin demanded of their father.

"'Course I do. But Clay's place is practically within walking distance. Riding distance, for sure. I can see my grandson every day if I want." Wayne lightened his tone. "Clay deserves the chance to raise his son. Just like you deserved the chance to raise Cassie."

"I like Clay, don't get me wrong."

"Then what is it?"

"Seems like the Duvalls are always taking from us."

Sierra thought her father might react more strongly to Gavin's statement, but he didn't. "Clay isn't his father. He's a good man."

"What about Sierra?"

"She'll be fine," her father said confidently. "Done pretty well on her own since college."

He was wrong on two counts. She hadn't done well on her own, especially during her pregnancy. And as far as being fine, the dispute was taking a terrible toll on her and that would continue even after it was settled.

She covered her father's hand with hers. "I'll always need you."

"And we'll always be here for you, sweetie pie."

Why hadn't she come home when she first found out she was pregnant instead of closing herself off?

Because her family had hated Clay until last fall when he and her brothers had reconciled after capturing Prince.

It still seemed strange to Sierra that he was treated the same as before Sierra's mother died—like a member of the family.

What would Louise Powell have wanted for her daughter and grandson if she were alive today?

Sierra didn't have to think twice. Her mother was as traditional as the rest of her family and believed a child's parents should be married. She'd insist Sierra move into Clay's casita on the chance the living arrangement would lead to a marriage proposal. And she'd have had Blythe's support. Sierra could just see the two women putting their matchmaking heads together.

Was her father also counting on Clay proposing? She wouldn't put it past him.

Jamie let out a whiny cry.

Sierra reached for him. "Sounds like one of us is getting tired."

"Can't he stay up a few more minutes?" Her father attempted to distract Jamie without success.

"I want to finish in the bathroom before Cassie and Isa get home." She was acutely aware of how big a disruption she and Jamie were to the girls' established routine. They'd been patient so far, but it was only bound to get worse.

"Whoa, there," Wayne said when a full-fledged cry erupted from Jamie's mouth.

"Sorry, Dad." Sierra stood and took Jamie, snuggling him close to her chest in an attempt to quiet him. "When he cries like this, he's reached the point of no return."

"I can give him a bath if you want," her father offered.

"What? And leave me with these two?" The look she sent her brothers said, *Talk about something other than Clay.*

They ignored her.

If she didn't dread more fallout, she'd tell them she'd mostly made up her mind hours ago. She'd just needed that last little push and to be reminded of what was most important. Jamie.

Tomorrow morning, first thing, she'd call Roberto and inform him of her decision. He could tell Clay; she didn't think she could handle it.

CLAY HESITATED JUST INSIDE the door. The noisy bar and grill was packed for a Thursday night. Then again, when wasn't it? He didn't frequent the Saddle Up Saloon for the very reason he'd come here tonight.

His father.

Bud Duvall could be found on his favorite bar stool most evenings from six to nine. Later on Fridays and Saturdays. He didn't have a drinking problem, none that Clay knew about anyway. Bud typically nursed two draft beers for as long as he stayed, always leaving a generous tip in exchange for "rent" on the bar stool. He often joked about the Saddle Up being his second home.

An unfortunately true situation that was no one's fault but his own.

Clay searched the large room, his gaze skimming a sea of cowboy hats and teased hairdos. He spotted his father in his usual place, center of the bar and, when the band wasn't playing, center of attention. Flanked by his regular cronies, Bud acknowledged everyone who passed by with a howdy or a firm handshake or, in the case of the fairer sex, a wide grin and appreciative once-over.

Some things never changed.

Clay crossed to his father, weaving right and left to skirt tables. Bud didn't see Clay until he was standing directly in the older man's line of vision.

"Lookie here, fellows," Bud boomed, his friendly voice a contrast to his wary eyes. "See what the cat drug in."

His father's friends greeted him warmly.

"Hey, Clay."

"Been a while, hasn't it?"

"Luke. Artie." Clay nodded, smiled. "How you doing?"

They exchanged small talk for several minutes before Luke and Artie offered flimsily concocted excuses and left. They probably figured if Clay had sought out his father after years of sporadic contact, it was probably an important and private matter.

"Buy you a drink?" Bud offered when the bartender made a pass.

"Club soda."

The bartender left to fill Clay's order.

"Since when you quit drinking beer?" His father studied him curiously.

"I haven't. Just not in the mood tonight." He didn't want any alcohol, even one beer's worth, dulling his senses. "Can we talk?"

"Sure."

"Some place less loud and less crowded?"

His father shrugged. He didn't relish abandoning his bar stool for any reason, including talking to his estranged son. "I'm free tomorrow."

Clay ignored the sarcasm. "This is important, Dad."

"Whatever you say." Bud drained the last of his beer and heaved himself off the stool. The same height as Clay, he carried an extra thirty pounds, most of it in the form of a spare tire hanging over his belt buckle.

Clay remembered when his father had been lean and muscled and strong enough to wrestle a full-grown steer to the ground one-handed. In those days, the Duvalls' cattle operation had been in full swing, and Clay and his father toiled twenty-four hours straight if necessary.

Bud sold the cattle operation when Clay was twenty-two. Clay had used his share of the proceeds, a share he felt he'd rightfully earned, to purchase the land on which he eventually constructed his rodeo arena. When his father sold the Powells' land two years later, Clay refused to take even one dime, though Bud had tried to convince him. They'd spoken rarely since then, Clay unable to get past what he considered his father's betrayal of a sacred trust.

In the span of a single day, the Duvalls had gone from being the Powells' dearest friends to being their hated enemies.

Was it any wonder Sierra had feared telling her family he was Jamie's father?

"There's an empty booth in the corner." Bud walked ahead of Clay.

Not exactly quiet, but the location was marginally more private. At least Clay wouldn't have to shout his personal business in order to be heard over the din. He and his father had already created quite a stir with the regulars.

They sat on opposite sides of the booth, the ancient cushioned seat beneath Clay giving in some places and lumpy in others.

"How's your mother?"

Bud's question didn't come out of the blue. He always asked after Blythe whenever he and Clay talked.

"She's good."

"Still liking her job at the title company?"

"Very much." Clay wasn't in the mood for pleasantries. "Dad, I have some news. Good news."

"You're not moving again?"

"No."

"Didn't think so." He scraped a knuckle along his neatly

trimmed salt-and-pepper beard. "Heard you're doing well with the rodeo arena."

Clay almost asked his father to repeat himself. The remark was the closest Bud had come to praising Clay since the day he'd brought home the state bronc-riding championship. Not long after that, Clay had cursed Bud and told him he didn't care if they ever crossed paths again.

He thought of Jamie. If someone had suggested to Clay ten days ago that he was the father of a toddler son, he'd have laughed in their face. Now, he was seeking custody and eager to turn his life upside down in order to have Jamie and Sierra included in it.

"I'm doing well enough. Being the only privately owned rodeo arena in Mustang Valley helps." Clay took a sip of his club soda, his throat inexplicably dry. Why was he suddenly nervous to tell his father about Jamie? "Sierra Powell is back in Mustang Valley."

"Been a while." Bud flinched ever so slightly. Someone who didn't know him might not have noticed.

Another time, he'd have tried to analyze that flinch. Tonight, he didn't care. "She brought her son with her. *Our* son."

Bud's brows rose until they disappeared beneath the unruly hank of silver hair covering his forehead. "You and her have a son? Why didn't you tell me?"

"I just found out myself. His name is Jamie. He's fifteen months old."

Bud chuckled. "I can't believe she let you within ten feet of her, much less into her bed."

Delivered with a humorous tone and coming from a friend, the comment could have been taken as a joke. From Bud, it smacked of an insult, and Clay's fingers involuntarily clenched.

"The Powells and I have made our peace," he said.

"Not then, you hadn't. When did you two hook up? Before or after Jessica?"

After? Did his father actually think Clay had violated his marriage vows? "Before. When Jessica and I were on the outs."

He didn't and wouldn't tell his father how devastated he'd been over Jessica dumping him—again—and how good Sierra had made him feel.

"What are you going to do?" Bud asked.

"Take care of Jamie. Sierra, too. I've filed a custody suit."

"What do you mean by 'take care of'?"

Be the best father I can, like you used to be, he almost said. "Provide financially and emotionally. Share the parenting with Sierra."

"Marry her?"

Clay thought carefully before answering. It wasn't as if the idea hadn't occurred to him. But having recently survived six months of a marriage made in hell, he wasn't ready or willing to take the plunge so soon.

"No, we're not getting married." Frankly, he doubted she'd accept even if he proposed.

"What's the matter with you?" Bud's voice rose loud enough to generate stares from nearby tables. "Didn't I raise you right?"

"You did," Clay answered evenly. "And I promise you my son will never go without."

"He deserves the Duvall name."

"He'll have it. My attorney is filing an amended birth certificate."

"That girl deserves your name, too."

"That girl?" Could his father not bring himself to say *Sierra?*

"Don't get smart with me."

A bar was hardly the place to engage his father in an argument, but Clay did it anyway. "How can you sit there and question whether you raised me right, when you stole six hundred acres out from under the Powells?"

"I did no such thing." Bud leaned forward, bringing his face closer to Clay's. "I gave them the money so Louise could have a heart transplant. A lot of money. It wasn't my fault she died. Or that Wayne lost interest in the ranch."

"You promised to give the Powells first chance to buy back the land."

"I did."

"That's a lie."

His father's face flushed a deep red. "I've done a lot of bad things that I'm not proud of, but lying isn't one of them."

"Wayne would have moved heaven and earth to keep his land."

"Maybe you don't know him as well as you think."

"What are you saying exactly?"

Some of the fight went out of his father, and he toyed absently with the happy-hour menu. "Wayne couldn't come up with the payment. Not even a partial payment. I extended the loan. Interest free. By then, he'd run their operation into the ground."

Clay reeled. He hadn't heard this version before. "Why are you only telling me now? Why hasn't Wayne said anything?"

"The man lost his wife. His business was hanging on by a thread. He wasn't about to admit he'd failed, and I wasn't about to publicly shame him."

"You should have gone to Gavin and Ethan. Given them the chance to repay the loan."

"Wayne asked me not to."

"Couldn't you have waited one more year?"

For the first time, Bud Duvall looked beaten and a decade older than his fifty-eight years. "Shoot, I'd have waited twenty years. A hundred years. Wayne was the best friend I ever had."

"So why ruin him?"

"You weren't even twenty when your mom and I split. There are just some things a kid shouldn't have to know about his parents."

"I'm not a kid anymore, Dad."

"You aren't, that's a fact." Bud tossed the happy-hour menu aside as if it irritated him. "One day your mother told me she was unhappy. The next day, she packed up, moved out and filed for divorce."

That was what Clay remembered, but he'd always assumed there was more to the story.

"Did you sell the Powells' land to try to get her back?"

"She tell you that?"

"No, I'm making a leap."

Bud chuckled mirthlessly. "Well, leap in another direction, pal. She forced me to sell the land because it was the only way I could raise enough revenue to meet her demands. She insisted on her half of our marital assets and refused to wait, even when I begged her."

Chapter Seven

Clay aimed his truck in the direction of Scottsdale and his mother's townhouse. Activating his Bluetooth, he pressed the speed dial. The call went right to voice mail, and he remembered her mentioning something about going to the theater with a friend. She held season tickets to ASU Gammage, had purchased them soon after she and his father divorced, the Director's Club, with preferred seating, backstage tours and VIP-lounge access.

Had she bought the tickets with money from the divorce? The Powells' money?

The possibility made Clay's stomach churn. For years he'd believed his father to be the bad guy. A traitor. A betrayer. According to his father, those descriptors belonged to his mother.

How screwed-up could one family be?

He drove to Powell Ranch instead of his mother's home. Ethan was probably in bed, or would be soon, which is where Clay should be. Like his friend, he had an early morning.

His mind, however, was racing too fast to let his body sleep. He needed to talk to someone, and Ethan, as his best friend, was that someone. He'd get Clay out of bed if circumstances were reversed.

Ethan's truck wasn't in sight when Clay rumbled slowly through the ranch and toward the converted apartment beside the stables. No lights came on in the main house, though the back-porch light shone for several seconds, then went off. Late-night visitors to the ranch weren't uncommon. People boarding their horses often came by at odd hours to administer medicine or change wound dressings, check on pregnant mares and, on really cold nights, ensure their horses were properly blanketed.

Parking in front of Ethan's apartment, Clay climbed the porch steps and knocked on the door. No one answered. He scanned the immediate area and noticed what he should have in the first place. Ethan's truck wasn't here. Clay was tempted to wait for Ethan. Naw, he was probably with Caitlin at her condo in Mustang Valley. That was where Clay would be staying if he was about to be married in a few days.

Married.

He could still hear his father asking him if he was going to do the right thing and give Sierra his name.

Clay tested the doorknob and found it locked. He couldn't even hide out till morning. About to turn around and go…he had no clue where…he heard the crunch of footsteps on hard ground.

"What are you doing here?"

He spun at the sound of Sierra's voice. She stood half in the shadows, half in the glow of a silver moon hanging high in the sky.

"Hey." Guilt ate at him—for what *both* his parents had done to her family. He swallowed before continuing. "I wanted to talk to Ethan."

"He's not here."

"So I see. What you are doing out so late?"

"One of us is having trouble sleeping." She stepped out of the shadows, and Clay saw that she was balancing Jamie on her hip. He had one fat fist shoved in his mouth and was making whiny, snuffling sounds.

"What's wrong?" Clay came off the porch, his worried glance taking in his son from ski-cap-bundled head to footed-pajama toe.

"He's teething. I was talking to an old friend from work earlier, and she suggested taking him outside. She said sometimes a change in scenery helps."

"With the pain?"

"It's more of a distraction tactic."

Clay could use one of those. Maybe he should stroll around the ranch, too. He liked that idea, but only if Sierra went with him.

"Hey, you okay?"

He caught her studying him. "Me? Yeah."

"You look upset."

He shoved his hands in his jacket pockets. "I am. A little. Had a talk with my dad tonight. Told him about Jamie."

"Is he mad?"

He heard the accusation in her voice. "Not at all."

Clay was the one who was mad. Even now, as he recalled the conversation at the Saddle Up, he realized his father hadn't asked one thing about his grandson or—this hurt the worst—if he could see Jamie.

Then again, Clay and his father had gotten off track. Way off track. And Clay had abruptly stormed out.

Damn it, none of this made any sense. His mother wouldn't have forced his father to sell off the Powells' land. She loved them.

Jamie whimpered.

"Can I hold him?" Clay asked.

"Um, sure."

He'd anticipated an argument.

Jamie went willingly into Clay's arms and quieted almost immediately. "Got a sore tooth, pal?" He tucked Jamie's head into the crook of his neck and closed his eyes. Not everything in life had come easy. Love for his son did. Very easy. "I know how painful that is. Had some bum teeth myself a few years back."

"Wisdom teeth?" Sierra asked.

"Impacted wisdom teeth. They pulled all four, which explains why I'm not very wise."

She smiled at his lame joke, the most relaxed he'd seen her since she'd arrived home. With moonlight turning her hair the color of quicksilver, she looked prettier than ever.

The pull of attraction he'd felt earlier when they were touring the casita didn't just return with a vengeance. It hit him like a sledgehammer to the gut.

"I'm sorry you argued with your dad."

"It wasn't an argument as much as a heated discussion."

"About Jamie?" Her tone became defensive again.

"My mom. Their divorce. The sale of your land." Without thinking about it, Clay had started swaying slowly, and Jamie's eyes drifted closed. "Can I ask you a question?"

"Sure." Sierra reached out and stroked Jamie's back.

Clay stared at her hand, recalling when she'd similarly stoked his back, offering comfort when he'd been heartsick over losing Jessica. It was the first time he'd noticed Sierra as someone other than his best friend's little sister.

His body stirred, reacting to the memory.

They'd made a baby together. But they'd also shared more than simple physical intimacy. He'd opened his heart to her, and she to him. If only he'd been smarter, seen that he and Jessica weren't cut out for each other.

He probably shouldn't have had those wisdom teeth removed, impacted or not.

"What did your dad tell you when mine sold off your land?"

The corners of her mouth turned down. "Why do you ask?"

"Did he mention my dad giving him an opportunity to buy back the land before he sold it?"

Her gaze clouded in confusion, then darkened. "I'm sure your father didn't give him any opportunity whatsoever."

Clay took that as a no.

If, as his father claimed, Wayne Powell had the chance to repay the loan and keep his land, why not tell his children?

Would Clay? Honestly, no. He'd have too much pride to admit to his children he couldn't come up with the money.

Had he really been wrong about his father all these years? His father had said he was protecting Wayne. But at the expense of his relationship with his son? It didn't make sense, not to Clay.

"Why are you asking?"

He considered telling Sierra the specifics of his conversation with his father, then decided against it. His dad could be lying. Clay needed to talk to his mother first. Even then, Wayne should be the person to tell his children the truth.

"My father mentioned something I hadn't heard before."

"What something?"

"It's probably nothing." He gazed down at his son who was soundly sleeping in his arms. When had that happened?

Longing squeezed his heart. This, a child of his own, was what he'd wanted, what he'd almost had and lost.

Only he'd always imagined having a wife along with his child. A wife he loved to distraction.

His gaze shifted to Sierra, slightly rumpled and yet incredibly appealing. She might have been his wife if things had worked out differently.

"Want me to take him?" she whispered.

"I'll carry him to the house if that's okay."

"Sure." She gazed adoringly at Jamie.

Clay almost felt like a heel insisting on taking Jamie half the time.

Not enough to alter his stand, however. Then again, he might be more inclined if Sierra ever looked at him the way she did their son.

They walked in silence to the house, entering through the kitchen door. Expecting Sierra to take Jamie from him, he was surprised when she said, "Do you want to put him to bed?"

They tiptoed down the hall and to the guest bedroom. The entire household appeared to be retired for the evening. In the room, Sierra switched on the nightlight. A ceramic teddy bear in pajamas sitting astride a calico pony provided enough illumination for Clay to see the portable crib on the floor beside the bed.

Together, he and Sierra gently removed Jamie's outerwear. Clay lowered Jamie into the crib, laying him on his back. His limp arms fell to his sides, and his mouth moved noiselessly.

"Is he talking in his sleep?"

Sierra smiled fondly. "Babies do that." She laid his jacket on the chair beside the dresser. "Once he's down for the night, he usually doesn't wake up till morning."

"Is it always so hard to get him to sleep?"

"Not usually."

"You tired?" Clay only now observed the shadows beneath her eyes and the lack of color in her cheeks.

"Some. You, too?"

"It's been a tough week."

"Yeah, it has."

They stood for a moment, Clay thinking what it would be like to hold her in his arms and have her rest her cheek on his jacket as Jamie had done.

Talk about making a complicated situation more complicated.

"I should get going."

"I'll walk you to the door."

He knew every inch of the Powells' home, having spent

endless hours there growing up. He could have found his way to the kitchen door with a triple blindfold.

Even so, he accepted Sierra's offer.

On the patio, he turned to bid her good-night.

She stood, nervously rubbing her palms on her pants.

"Something the matter?"

"I, um, was going to have my attorney contact you tomorrow."

"About the custody agreement?"

"Yes. And the living arrangements." She exhaled, clearly struggling with what to say.

She was turning him down.

Disappointment arrowed through him. Up until this moment, he hadn't realized how much he wanted her and Jamie to live with him. Granted, in the beginning, it had been a ploy to be close to his son. But that had changed.

"Take another day or two before you say no. It would be good for Jamie to have—"

"I'm accepting your offer."

His jaw went slack. "You are?"

"And the job, too."

"Wow."

"If you still want me to work for you."

"I do." He grinned. Stupidly, he was certain. "That's great."

"There are going to be some conditions."

"Naturally." His grin widened. "I figured as much."

"I'll move in and start work once we've ironed out the agreement."

He grabbed her by the waist and hugged her fiercely. Sierra and Jamie were coming to live with him! "Thank you."

She let out a startled gasp but didn't withdraw.

"I'm really glad you said yes." He breathed her in. She smelled as good as he remembered.

"Me, too." She raised her arms, hesitated, then slid them around his neck, returning his hug.

Yes, nice. Really nice.

Wait, no. He reminded himself this was a friendly hug between two people whose only concern was the well-being of their son.

His body had other ideas, as did his hands, which skimmed her back over the material of her too-bulky, too-thick sweater.

He couldn't stop himself. Her curves were too perfect, her scent too intoxicating, her skin like satin.

Her skin?

When had his hand moved to caress her cheek?

"Tell me no." He bent his head, his lips seeking hers.

She didn't. She couldn't, not with him kissing her.

BIG, BIG MISTAKE. Huge, like the size of an entire mountain range.

Exactly the kind of mistake that had gotten Sierra into trouble before.

She knew she should hightail it out of there as fast as her legs could carry her.

But she didn't move.

It wasn't Clay's arms circling her that prevented her escape. No, no. Or the sensation of his mouth, firm and warm and with just enough pressure to send a delicious thrill winding through her. A small part of her had wanted this kiss since she'd glimpsed him standing outside of her brother's apartment. Possibly since the first day she came home.

His lips moved her over hers, nibbling, teasing, coaxing a response from her. He got it, all right.

She sighed and leaned into him, anticipating the moment when he'd deepen the kiss. Soothe the needy ache inside her.

Just when things started to really heat up, he abruptly

withdrew. She almost lost her balance, and a startled sound escaped her.

A low groan escaped him. "I shouldn't have done that."

Yeah, and she shouldn't have turned into mush the instant their lips touched. What was wrong with her?

He studied her with a piercing stare that split her apart and, she was convinced, revealed every one of her secrets.

"Don't look at me like that. It was just a kiss."

"Right."

"Oh, please." She rolled her eyes. Clay wasn't going to learn how much the kiss had affected her.

His satisfied grin infuriated her. She was half inclined to tell him she'd changed her mind about everything, the casita, the job, the custody agreement, then she instantly reconsidered.

The better course of action would be not to lose her head again. She could do that. Keep their relationship strictly professional and avoid him as much as possible.

"See you tomorrow night." His voice was low and slightly husky and reminded her of other kisses shared beneath shimmering moonlight.

"What time are you coming by?" she asked with a not-that-I-care demeanor.

"I figured we'd meet up at the rehearsal dinner."

Shoot, she'd forgotten about the dinner. Well, it couldn't be helped. She'd agreed to attend even though she wasn't officially a part of the ceremony. Both Sage and Caitlin had offered to make her a bridesmaid, but Sierra had declined, preferring to watch Jamie and assist with the reception.

"See you there."

His gaze glided over her, slow and hungry. "You don't have to walk me to my truck."

"I wasn't going to." Of all the nerve.

He lowered his head.

For one wild second, she thought he was going to kiss her again. Her body ignored the directives her brain screamed at her and slowly drifted toward him.

"Jamie's crying."

She was so distracted by Clay's breath caressing her neck, what he said made no sense. "Excuse me?"

"Jamie. He's awake."

She listened and heard faint crying coming from inside the house. It galvanized her. "I'd better go."

With a final glance at Clay, she scurried inside and to the bedroom, hoping the noise hadn't woken up the rest of the house.

Jamie stood in the portable crib, clinging to the side, tears spilling from his eyes and red splotches on his cheeks.

"Sorry, baby." She lifted him into her arms and pressed him to her, alternately bouncing him in her arms and swaying back and forth. The wailing continued. Worsened.

How long had he been carrying on before Clay heard him? Sierra couldn't believe she'd been so wrapped up in their kiss she'd ignored her child's cries.

Then again…

She shivered at the memory of Clay's lips parting hers.

This absolutely had to stop! Jamie was her first and only concern.

"Definitely, positively, that is never going to happen again," she vowed aloud.

Aware of the sudden quiet, she peered down at Jamie. He'd stopped his fussing, and his hazel eyes stared fixedly at her as if he didn't buy a single word she said.

"Who was here?" Sierra's father stood in the bedroom doorway.

"Clay." At the mention of his name, a warm flush crept up her neck to her face. "Did Jamie wake you with his crying?"

Or, had her father been up already and seen her and Clay kissing?

Please, no!

"I was reading."

Whew!

Her father came into the room and smiled fondly at Jamie, who was fighting sleep tooth and nail. "Kind of late for a visit. What did Clay want?"

"He was looking for Ethan."

"Like I said, kind of late."

"He was upset. I guess he saw Bud and told him about Jamie. They got into some kind of argument."

"About Jamie? Of all the—"

"It had more to do with Bud selling our land and his parents' divorce."

"For the love of God! Why are they still rehashing that?"

Sierra thought her father's outburst a bit much but dismissed it. Between the wedding and her return, everyone's emotions were running a little high.

"Clay asked me if Bud ever gave you an opportunity to buy back the land before he sold it."

"What did you tell him?" There was no mistaking the apprehension in her father's voice.

"That Bud didn't give you *any* opportunities."

"Good. Because he didn't."

"Well, whatever Bud told Clay must have been pretty upsetting for him to drive out here at this time of night."

"He'll say anything to get out of taking responsibility for what he did to us. I hope Clay's smart enough not to be suckered in."

"I'm sure he is. Why else would the two of them have been at odds all these years?"

"If he wants to be part of this family, he'd better stay clear of Bud. I mean it."

Would her father really cut out his grandson's father from their lives?

"I think he's trying to mend broken bridges."

"No point in that."

"Really, Dad? Isn't that what *we're* doing?"

"It's different."

Sierra didn't agree. Bud Duvall had done a terrible thing to her family, but he'd also done one very kind and generous thing. He'd given them another fifteen months with her mother they wouldn't have had without the loan of his money for her heart-transplant surgery.

"I don't want Duvall coming to the wedding."

"He wouldn't dare. And Clay wouldn't dare invite him."

Her father grumbled to himself.

"Don't you think it's time to put the past to rest? For Jamie, and all your grandchildren."

Not that Sierra was ready to forgive Bud Duvall, but her own actions these last two years, her neglect of her family and their willingness to welcome her back with open arms, had given her a new perspective.

She might feel differently if her family was still on the brink of financial ruin instead of owning two thriving businesses, her brothers getting married and expanding their families.

"He took advantage of me at the lowest point in my life."

Sierra sighed softly. Continuing the discussion was useless. Her father harbored too much anger.

She lowered Jamie into the portable crib, and he went instantly to sleep. "This teething ordeal is awful."

"Ethan was the worst of you three."

"Seriously? He's always been so easygoing."

"Not when it came to teething or the terrible twos."

She followed her father to the door, glad to see him back

to his old self. "I have something to tell you. I've decided to move into Clay's casita."

"Makes sense."

His underwhelming reaction wasn't what she'd expected, considering how adamantly he'd supported the idea over dinner earlier.

"I'm moving as soon as the joint-custody agreement is finalized."

"Why the wait?"

"There are still some details we have to agree on first. And, besides, I don't want to be moving in the middle of the wedding."

"It probably sounds strange, a father encouraging his unmarried daughter to live with a man."

"Not *with* him, Dad. In the casita." The difference was important to her.

"In the casita," he repeated and smiled. "Much as I'm going to miss you, you're making the right decision."

Was she? If not, it was going to be one very long year.

"Good night." She stood on tiptoes and kissed her father's cheek.

"Sleep tight, honey." He started to leave, then stopped in midstep. "Promise me something."

"What's that?"

"If Clay does reconcile with Bud, and he starts hanging around Clay's place, don't talk to him."

"You know I wouldn't."

"Okay. See you in the morning."

She shut the door behind him, concern stealing over her.

Why had her father felt the need to extract a promise from her?

More worryingly, why had he refused to meet her gaze while doing it?

Chapter Eight

Sierra sat in the front row, Jamie perched on her lap, the fingers of one hand dangling a newly purchased plush toy in front of him. The fingers of her other hand were tightly crossed and had been for the last thirty minutes.

Please, please, don't cry.

All through the ceremony, Jamie had behaved beautifully. That could change in an instant. She'd hate for his wails to disrupt what had turned out to be a simple yet charmingly perfect country wedding.

The brides and grooms were exchanging their vows in the front courtyard of the Powell family home. Boughs from the paloverde and desert willow trees stretched out like reaching arms, providing a natural arch beneath which the wedding party stood. A golden afternoon sun glowed warmly, prompting several of the men to shed their suit jackets.

Two hundred white metal chairs had been rented and arranged to face a stunning view of Mustang Valley, at the heart of which lay Mustang Village. It was a fitting backdrop for the wedding ceremony. Mustang Valley had once belonged to the Powells, and even though civilization had encroached in recent years, the land would always belong to them in spirit.

More accurately, to her father and brothers. Sierra was still searching for where she truly belonged. She'd lived two-thirds of her life in Mustang Valley, and yet San Francisco felt more like home to her. She missed it. Her friends, too, and her job and even her tiny apartment.

On Monday, two days from now, she and her son would be moving into Clay's casita. She had yet to ship her personal belongings and furniture from San Francisco, preferring to "wait and see." In fact, she, her father and Gavin had gotten into a disagreement about it yesterday morning. They wanted her to have everything shipped now, make her return to Arizona permanent. Sierra had resisted, causing the argument to end in a stalemate.

On Tuesday, she'd start working for Clay at the rodeo arena. Mostly, she was terrified. She was also excited. About the job, not the move.

Living in close proximity to Clay worried her. She hadn't been able to fully suppress the fluttering in her middle that had started with their kiss the other night. How much worse would it get when she was sharing meals with him and passing him in the hall on the way to the laundry room?

Shifting Jamie to her other knee, she observed Clay from her place next to her father.

The two best men, Clay and Conner, another childhood friend of her brothers', wore black jeans, black Stetsons and bright turquoise Western shirts. Despite the casualness of his clothes, Clay looked handsome and mouthwateringly sexy. So much so, Sierra had to force herself to gaze at the brides and grooms.

Both women had chosen traditional white gowns, minus long trains. Sage's was high-waisted in order to draw attention away from her pregnancy. Gavin and Ethan, gorgeous in their black Western-style suits, couldn't take their eyes off their respective brides.

Isa stood by her mother and Cassie stood by her father. The girls wore matching turquoise dresses. Isa clutched the basket that had contained rose petals. She'd taken her job as flower girl very seriously and remained absolutely still, as she'd been instructed to do all last week. Cassie was the one fidgeting. When asked if she'd wanted to be a second bridesmaid for Sage, she had refused, opting instead to be the ring bearer. Her father had agreed but only if Cassie wore a dress. It was a compromise. She definitely preferred denim to taffeta.

Sierra's emotions, already riding close to the surface on this special day, overflowed, and she dabbed at her tears. She had always dreamed of a wedding like this. Not the country theme as much as having family and friends gathered in one place to witness the joining of two hearts, together forever.

She felt an invisible tug and lifted her head to find Clay staring at her, his expression unreadable. And then, suddenly, it wasn't. She saw longing and desire and a need that pierced her with its intensity.

No, she must be mistaken. He didn't want her like that.

She glanced quickly away, shaken by the raw power of his gaze. When she turned back a moment later, his attention was on the minister, giving her reason to suspect she'd allowed her imagination to run amuck.

"Gentlemen," the minister boomed, his crinkly smile taking over his entire face, "you may kiss your brides."

That was all the encouragement her brothers needed. While Gavin cradled Sage's cheeks tenderly between his hands and brushed his lips across hers, Ethan bent Caitlin backward over his arm and planted a toe-curling kiss on her mouth. The guests broke into cheers and applause.

Sierra leaned down and rubbed her temple against Jamie's. "Uncle Gavin and Uncle Ethan just got married."

"May I present Mr. and Mrs. Gavin Powell and Mr. and Mrs. Ethan Powell."

More applause accompanied the minister's pronouncement. Jamie joined in, squawking and clapping his hands. The wedding recession began, and the couples left the courtyard to the music of an acoustic guitar. The best men and maids of honor followed in the wake of the brides and grooms.

Connor had been matched up with Sage's cousin, Clay with Caitlin's roommate from nursing school. The woman was strikingly beautiful, with wavy brunette hair that cascaded down her back. Sierra tried not to think of what an attractive couple she and Clay made. How the woman's slim arm linked possessively with his. About the two of them chatting up a storm at last night's rehearsal dinner.

"You ready?" Her father pushed to his feet, his eyes misty. He'd mentioned several times today how much he wished Sierra's mother was there.

She stood, holding on to Jamie, and the three of them went down the aisle after the brides' families.

"I'm going to the kitchen to see if I can help with the food." A popular Mexican restaurant had been hired to provide the catering.

"You can't," her dad said, dragging her and Jamie through the house. "We have pictures to take."

Outside, the wedding party gathered in the open area between the house and the stables. With three families involved, there were a lot of people. Someone had laid out a large green indoor/outdoor carpet where the photos would be taken. Rental chairs were brought over for those who wanted to sit.

One of the Powells' wranglers led over Prince, the wild mustang her brothers and Clay had captured. The horse took one look at the brides in their billowing dresses and balked, snorting loudly.

"What are they doing with Prince?" Sierra asked her neighbor.

It was Clay who answered. He was, she noticed, minus Caitlin's maid of honor. "Your brothers decided they wanted him in some of the photos."

"I don't think Prince is on board with the idea."

"You could be right."

They watched and waited from a safe distance while Gavin and Ethan tried to calm the horse. It was a slow process. Sierra regretted not grabbing one of the empty chairs.

She was acutely aware of Clay. His height. His breadth. The rugged strength beneath his polished exterior. His undeniable sex appeal.

"I get that Prince played a part in bringing Gavin and Ethan together with their wives, but this might be going a touch overboard."

"What can I say? Your brothers are hopeless romantics."

"*My* brothers?" She gaped at Clay. "You have got to be kidding."

They both laughed. Sierra stopped abruptly when she caught Ethan staring at them, a knowing smile on his face.

Jamie chose that moment to start fussing.

"Hush now, baby." She wiggled the plush toy in front of him. He'd been so good. If not for the pictures, she'd put him down for a nap.

"You want me to take him for a bit?" Clay offered.

"Do you mind?"

"Are you kidding?"

Her arms were getting tired, and maybe a change would perk Jamie up. Prince was finally cooperating, and the photographer, a pretty young woman, was hurriedly snapping shots of him, Sierra's brothers and the brides.

Jamie, as always, delighted in going to his father. He immediately grabbed at Clay's hat.

"Later, buddy. When we're done with the pictures."

Finally, the wrangler led Prince away, or was it the other

way around? The photographer began calling out groupings. Clay, as best man, was in more shots than Sierra and Jamie. The minutes dragged on and on. Soon, Jamie started crying and nothing Sierra attempted quieted him.

Just when she thought they were done and she could leave, Clay put an arm around her shoulder.

"Can you take one of the three of us?" he asked the photographer.

"Certainly."

"Jamie's tired," Sierra protested. "And crying."

"This won't take long," Clay insisted.

"Can we do it later?"

"The photographer is leaving."

"I'd love a picture with Jamie, too," Blythe said. "Maybe one with Wayne and I and Jamie."

"Good idea!" Clay agreed.

Sierra fumed. This was the side of Clay she liked the least. The pushy one.

Unable to refuse without making a scene, she allowed the photographer to take several shots of them in different poses. Jamie cried in every one. When Clay suggested a shot with all "the men"—him, Jamie, Sierra's brothers and father—she reached her boiling point.

"Clay, it's time for Jamie's nap."

"One more."

Was this a preview of what it would be like when she and Clay shared custody of Jamie?

She allowed one more photo. When it was over, she wrenched Jamie from Clay much as he'd done to her before, and started for the house.

"Sierra—"

"He needs a nap, I need a rest and they're getting ready to serve the food."

Clay started after her only to stop when someone called

his name. Good. Hopefully, he got the message. He wasn't the only one in charge.

Was it too late to change her mind about the casita and the job?

Probably. She'd signed the custody agreement yesterday, along with the employment contract.

Escaping to her bedroom, she hastily changed Jamie and settled him in the portable crib, the plush toy beside him. Jamie protested loudly for about ninety seconds, then fell into an exhausted sleep.

Sierra sat on the edge of the bed, only to stand up again. She should be out there, mingling with guests, helping in the kitchen. Jamie would be fine without her. She really did hover excessively. Checking on him again, she stepped outside the room—and breathed. She was going to be okay. She couldn't leave the house without Jamie, but she could leave the room.

After visiting with a few old friends, she busied herself helping old Mrs. Ruesga serve up enchiladas and tamales while simultaneously protecting the three-tiered wedding cake from curious youngsters.

Cassie and Isa burst into the kitchen. "We're hungry," they said in unison.

The rest of the wedding party wasn't far behind. Clay came in last, Caitlin's maid of honor adhered to his side.

Hmm.

"Can I fix you a plate?" Sierra asked her brand-new sisters-in-law.

"I'm too excited to eat," Caitlin exclaimed.

"I'm not." Sage patted her stomach. "And don't be stingy."

After the initial rush of hungry guests slowed, Sierra and the other helpers began clearing tables.

"Cassie," she called. "Would you mind giving us a hand?"

"With what?" A hint of teenage attitude laced Cassie's voice.

"Take this empty garbage bag and go through the house, collecting trash."

Huffing impatiently, she grabbed the bag from Sierra.

"Did I say something to upset you?" She thought she got along well with her niece. She'd certainly made an effort since coming home.

"Nope." Cassie spun on her heels and left.

Sierra's first inclination was to do nothing. Cassie was probably in a mood brought on by all the excitement. Perhaps she was jealous of her new stepmother and all the attention Sage was getting.

On second thought, what kind of aunt would Sierra be if she didn't attempt to find out what was bothering the girl?

She went in search of Cassie and found her in the hall.

"Cassie, sweetie, what's wrong?"

She said nothing and dropped an empty plastic cup in the garbage bag.

"Come on. Talk to me."

To her surprise, Cassie whirled on her. "You're going to leave again."

"What gave you that idea?"

"I heard you yesterday morning with Grandpa and my dad. You won't have your junk shipped here because you're not sure you're staying."

"Sweetie, that's not the reason." Except it was. Somehow Cassie had figured out Sierra wasn't quite ready to put down roots.

"You hurt Grandpa. And my dad and Uncle Ethan, and you're going to do it again."

Cassie stormed off, leaving Sierra all alone to face the small gathering of stunned wedding guests.

"She doesn't mean it."

At the sound of Clay's voice behind her, Sierra cringed.

Of all the people to witness her scene with Cassie, Clay had to be the one. "You heard?"

"Most of it."

Damn.

"Come on," he said.

Not waiting for an answer, he took her by the hand. She accompanied him reluctantly through the living room and outside to the front courtyard. It was nearly empty. Most of the guests were congregating inside or on the back patio where tables had been set up. Clay and Sierra sat in chairs near the makeshift altar, far enough away so no one could hear their conversation.

"Cassie's a good kid," he began.

"I know that."

"She's very protective of Gavin. Of their relationship. She resents her mother for running off to Connecticut and not letting her visit Gavin until last summer."

Sierra stiffened. Clay was lecturing her, and she didn't like it. "You and Cassie have a lot of long talks?"

"Me and Gavin. He's the one Cassie has the long talks with."

Of course they did. Sierra was instantly contrite. "I'm not like her mother."

Clay, thankfully, didn't state the obvious—which was that Sierra was exactly like Cassie's mother.

No wonder the girl was angry at her and didn't trust her. There was a lot of that going around.

"If you give Cassie a chance," Clay continued, "you'll find a nice kid beneath that tomboy exterior."

"I like Cassie. And I'll talk to her. Tomorrow, when things aren't so hectic."

"Good. Now, about your furniture."

"Please, Clay. Not today."

"You're right. I guess I'm like Cassie, I don't want you to leave."

She gazed out at the valley below, remembering when she was Cassie's age and riding horses along the river with her brothers.

"I apologize for being prickly. Here and earlier during the photographs. I don't react too well to being pressured."

"Maybe that's something we can discuss during counseling."

She groaned. "Don't remind me."

They'd scheduled the first of their weekly sessions for this coming Wednesday.

"I admit, I can be a little pushy."

She wished his crooked smile wasn't so appealing. "A little?"

"What do you say we work with the counselor on our character defects?"

Against her will, she smiled. "There's still my dad and brothers. They're every bit as pushy as you."

"Afraid that's your problem to deal with."

She sighed. "Oh, joy."

"We're going to make this work, Sierra. You'll see."

He oozed confidence. She, on the other hand, wasn't sure about anything.

Meeting his gaze, she inhaled sharply. That same longing she'd seen on his face during the ceremony was back.

No man had ever looked at her like that before, unless she counted the night two years ago when she and Clay went from being friends to lovers in the span of a single heartbeat.

Suddenly nervous, she straightened. "I really should check on Jamie."

Clay didn't restrain her. Not physically. It was his eyes that cemented her in place, quickened her pulse, set her senses awhirl.

He raised his fingers to brush a strand of hair from her face.

Was he going to kiss her again?

Bad idea. They shouldn't.

She braced herself. Gave in. Gave up. What good would it do to fight the inevitable?

All at once, cool air struck her in the face. Clay had pulled back, was starting to rise.

Anger bloomed inside—at herself. What a fool she'd been. How often would he hurt her before she learned?

She stood so quickly her chair wobbled.

"Sierra, it's not—"

"Forget it."

"There you are!" Caitlin's maid of honor came up the aisle toward them, her sensual smile targeting Clay.

"Hey, Trista," Clay said.

Trista! That was the reason Clay hadn't kissed Sierra.

Relief filled her.

Relief that she'd been stopped in the nick of time from making another mistake. No other reason, she told herself.

"Sierra," Trista cooed. "I haven't had a chance to tell you how pretty you look. That dress really brings out the color in your cheeks."

Her dress? Hardly. Clay and their near-miss kiss was responsible.

"I came to tell you they're getting ready to pour the champagne and cut the cake. Clay, you have to make your toast."

"I'll join you shortly." Sierra exited the courtyard ahead of Clay and Trista, glad for an excuse to get away.

Smiling and saying hello to the guests she passed, she hastened to the bedroom. This was the longest she'd been away from Jamie, and she was proud of her progress.

Easing the door open, she stepped quietly inside the room and whispered, "Hey, handsome. You awake?"

She froze, staring at the empty portable crib. A strangled cry—her own—filled her ears.

Jamie was missing!

Oh, my God, oh, my God, oh, my God! Where was Jamie?

Terror assailed Sierra, shattering her composure, icing her blood. Grabbing at the sides of her head, she whirled, frantically scouring every corner of the room on the chance he'd managed to escape the crib and toddled off. Ripping the quilt aside, she fell to her knees and looked under the bed.

Nothing!

The closet was also empty.

Someone had taken him. *Stolen* him! Right out from his crib.

She tried to breathe but her lungs had collapsed. What was she thinking? She should never have left him alone for even a second.

Bolting from the room, she ran straight into Clay.

He grabbed her by the shoulders and steadied her. "Are you all right? I thought I heard something."

"Jamie's missing!"

"Missing?"

"He's not in his crib." She began to blubber. "I put him down for his nap, and now someone's taken him."

"Calm down, honey."

"I can't." She tried to shake free of his grasp. "I have to find him. Before something happens."

"You look inside, I'll look outside."

His calm demeanor outraged her. Did he always have to be in such freakin' control?

"No! I'll look outside." Sierra couldn't explain it, but she was convinced whoever had Jamie had fled the house and was already driving off.

Flinging aside Clay's hand, she tore through the house and out the kitchen door.

Clay called after her.

She ignored him. There were so many people. Hundreds, all of them talking and drinking and mingling on the patio. How easy it would be for someone to hide Jamie inside a coat or jacket and stroll nonchalantly away with him.

"Careful now, slow down," a man warned.

"Did you lose something?"

Yes, her son.

It occurred to her to stop and inform the guests of what was happening rather than plowing over them in her haste. Possibly enlist their aid. That would take too much time, however. The kidnapper was getting farther and farther away with each second.

Cars were everywhere. In the parking area behind the barn. Beside the stables. Next to the house. Her heart pounded inside her chest, hard enough to fracture her ribs. Where to start looking?

She heard an engine roar to life and ran in that direction. The heel of her shoe caught in a pothole, causing her to stumble. Regaining her balance, she surged ahead. Whoever had Jamie, they were not leaving this ranch. If necessary, she'd plant herself directly in their path and not move.

Then she saw it, a vehicle pulling out from behind the mare motel!

"Stop, stop," she hollered.

The vehicle came into view. Not a passenger car but a tractor with a feed wagon hooked to it. One of the ranch hands was getting ready to hay the horses.

She ground to a halt and blinked, her vision clouded from perspiration—or was it tears?

She was too late. Jamie was gone. Taken from her again.

The ground beneath her feet seemed to shift as if disrupted by tremors. A wave of dizziness left her faint and disoriented.

"Sierra!" Someone called to her from what sounded like a great distance away. "Sierra!"

She answered, except her voice came out a strangled sob. What should she do?

Call the police. Yes, right away. Before too much time passed. And obtain a list of the guests from her family.

"Sierra!" The voice drew closer.

Fighting another debilitating wave of dizziness, she tried to bring the figure sprinting toward her into focus. It was Clay, and he was wearing an enormous smile.

A smile! There was only one reason for it.

Her knees collapsed.

"We found him." He caught her as the last of her strength deserted her. "He's in the house."

"Thank God," she said and burst into tears.

He wrapped his arm around her waist, and she leaned heavily on him, appreciating his strength. They walked her back to the house. Sierra would have preferred to run but her bones had yet to solidify.

"Where was he?" she asked feebly.

"My mother has him."

"Your mother! Why?"

"I don't know. I didn't ask. I was just so glad to find him."

Well, Sierra was going to ask. And Blythe had better have a damn good reason for putting Sierra through hell.

She and Clay went directly to the living room. Blythe sat in a wingback chair, Jamie on her lap. Several people— strangers, all of them—surrounded her and bent over Jamie, speaking to him in baby talk. He fussed and writhed and made unhappy faces. While getting better, he was still leery of people he didn't know.

Sierra broke away from Clay. The second Jamie saw her, he opened his arms to her. "Ma, ma, ma."

Her throat closed. This was the first time he'd called her Mama. He must have been just as scared as she was.

"Hi." Blythe greeted her warmly. "I hope you don't mind—"

Sierra lifted Jamie off Blythe's lap and clutched him to her chest. She wouldn't let him out of her sight ever again, no matter what.

"How could you take him and not tell me?" she demanded, her voice cracking.

Blythe's jaw dropped. "I'm…sorry. I didn't think—"

"Obviously, you didn't." Sierra stroked Jamie's back, as much to reassure him as herself.

"Sierra," Clay said. "It's okay."

"No, it isn't. She had no right to take him."

Twin spots of color appeared on Blythe's cheeks. "I meant no harm," she said stiffly. "I just peeked in your room to show Lil and Beverly how cute he is, and he was awake, standing up in the crib. I brought him out here. I didn't think you'd mind."

"I do mind. Very much."

The half dozen pairs of eyes that had been fastened on Blythe switched to Sierra. She could feel the disapproval, the silent consensus that she was making a huge deal out of nothing.

She probably shouldn't have snapped at Blythe in front of her friends. But Blythe shouldn't have taken Jamie from his crib without telling Sierra.

"I apologize for losing my temper," she said. "I was upset to find Jamie gone."

"All you had to do, my dear, was look around."

Sierra bristled at Blythe's condescending tone. "I did look around. I didn't find him."

"Perhaps I should go give my respects to the brides and

grooms." Blythe rose from the chair, tall and slim and dignified.

In comparison, Sierra felt small, and not just in stature.

"Mom, wait." Clay reached for his mother, then said to Sierra, "This is just a misunderstanding. Let's not blow it out of proportion. Not today. Jamie's safe. No harm, no foul."

A misunderstanding? Sierra thought it was more than that.

Clay was right, however, about her brothers' wedding not being the time or place to discuss it. She would take the matter up later with him, and he could talk privately to his mother.

"Excuse me, please." Blythe slid past Clay, a thin smile on her face.

"It's all right," one of her friends soothed while casting Sierra an accusatory glance. "I'll come with you."

Fine, blame her. Sierra didn't care.

Okay, she did care. She didn't want her family's friends thinking badly of her.

"Mom," Clay said, his voice low but firm. "Sierra has a right to be upset. Don't be angry with her."

Blythe halted. "I'm not angry."

"Maybe *angry* isn't the word."

"She overreacted. I'm the boy's grandmother. Can't I pick up my own grandson from his crib when he's awake?"

"No one is saying you can't pick up Jamie." The look Clay gave Sierra was kind, not condoning. "She's been through a lot lately. More than you know. And if you did know, you wouldn't think she overreacted."

He was defending her. Taking her side. In front of his mother and her friends.

Gratitude vanquished the last of her anger, and she smiled at him.

He pinched Jamie's cheek. "Do you think this little guy's old enough for some wedding cake?"

"Plenty old enough."

She turned, intending to make amends with Blythe, only she and her friends were gone, and a heavy silence had descended over the room.

Terrific. Sierra had gone and spoiled her brothers' wedding.

Chapter Nine

Sierra answered the phone, a smile in her voice. "Good afternoon, Duvall Rodeo Arena. How may I help you?"

Clay sat in a visitor chair observing her at work, his open laptop computer balanced on his knees. Her first day on the job and already she sounded as if she'd been at it for months.

"Yes, I can get that for you. Hold on a second." She opened a three-ring binder containing the rodeo arena's rates and policies. "Are you interested in just bull-riding or also bronc-riding?"

Clay returned his attention to the monthly financial reports on the laptop screen, keeping one ear tuned to Sierra's conversation. They'd spent an hour when she first arrived at the office going over the types of calls she could expect and how to respond. Clearly, Sierra was a fast learner and not bragging when she'd referred to herself as the "go-to" assistant at her former job.

She'd spend the majority of yesterday moving into the casita and rearranging it to suit her tastes. He'd wanted to be more involved, his curiosity admittedly piqued. It was her father's help she'd enlisted, not Clay's, so he had yet to see the changes she'd made.

Frankly, he couldn't care less. He was just pleased that she and Jamie were here.

As if detecting his thoughts, his son banged his toy pony on the side of the playpen.

"Ba, da, da."

Clay put a finger to his lips. "Hush, son. Your mommy's on the phone," he said softly.

Jamie grinned, displaying yet another new tooth.

They'd set the recently purchased playpen up in the corner. Sierra had protested, not at the location but that Clay had refused to let her pay for it. He'd also purchased a full-size crib for the casita. In hindsight, he should have taken Sierra with him to the store. But then they probably wouldn't have agreed on which was the best brand. He and Sierra did have a tendency to take opposite sides of every issue.

Except for his mother removing Jamie from his crib during the wedding reception. His mother had been wrong, and he fully intended to discuss the subject with her when she came by in a little while to join him, Sierra and Jamie for dinner.

It had required almost no coercion on his part to convince both women to accept his invitation, and Clay was glad they seemed eager to make amends.

Before dinner, however, he needed to have a different discussion with his mother, this one about what his father had told him at the Saddle Up Saloon. Between kissing Sierra and the wedding, he'd gotten understandably sidetracked.

Jamie's banging escalated, and he emitted a loud shriek.

Sierra grimaced, though her tone remained pleasant. "Thank you for calling," she told the potential customer. "We'll see you tomorrow morning." Hanging up the phone, she sighed. "Baby, you have to be quiet."

Jamie grabbed the side of the playpen and rattled it.

"I think he's getting a little tired of being cooped up," Clay said.

"Yeah." She eyed Jamie worriedly, her thoughts clear. Their son was only going to get bigger and louder.

"Give him a chance," Clay said. "He'll settle down. Get used to the routine."

She didn't reply, merely got up from her chair and gave Jamie a toddler biscuit.

Clay hoped she'd eventually be agreeable to day care or a sitter, the sooner, the better. Her anxieties would be debilitating, for her and Jamie and Clay, too. He was counting on the counseling sessions to make a difference.

Sierra had been upset when she'd first learned she couldn't bring Jamie with them into the sessions and parenting classes and had almost backed out. Whatever argument her attorney had employed had had a positive effect. She'd consented to having Wayne accompany them to watch Jamie in the waiting area.

It was a step, and Clay was proud of her. When he'd told her so yesterday, she'd blushed. Very prettily, he might add.

He closed his laptop and got to his feet, purposefully distracting himself. This wasn't the first time he'd thought of Sierra as more than just the mother of his child. It wasn't even the first time today. He needed to get a grip on himself, and fast, before she sensed the change in him, panicked and moved out when she'd only just moved in.

That girl deserves your name, too.

Clay swallowed, his father's words ringing in his ears.

He wanted nothing more than to be the best dad in the world to Jamie. He *would* be the best dad. Did that require he marry Sierra? He found her attractive, desired her, thought there couldn't be a more caring and devoted mother for his son. But he wasn't ready to walk down the aisle with her. Not until he'd fully healed from the wounds Jessica had inflicted.

His gaze went to Jamie, his heart swelling with love. How could Jessica have been relieved to lose their baby?

How could Sierra have given theirs up?

"I'm heading outside," he told her, wanting to clear his

head. "Conner's delivering some of the mustangs from Sage's sanctuary, and then Mom will be here. Will you be okay flying solo?"

"As long as Jamie's quiet. He's usually napping by now. I think he finds the office too interesting."

"I like that he's taking an interest in the business."

Sierra laughed.

Clay didn't. If she decided to stay more than the three months they'd agreed to, this could truly be a family business.

He bent and kissed Jamie on the top of the head on his way out the door.

In the main arena, several pairs of team ropers were practicing, reminding Clay he should have Sierra confirm the herd of weanling calves scheduled to arrive this week. Also, check on the rental contract for the three bulls and seven bucking horses they would be sending to the Helzapoppin Rodeo in Buckeye next month. Batteries Included, his best bucking horse, had already earned enough money to support the rodeo arena through May. At this rate, the large gelding could easily qualify for the National Finals Rodeo in December.

He'd be Clay's first stock animal to qualify for a world championship event and could potentially bring in a slew of new contracts.

Not bad for being in business less than two years. If things kept on the way they were, Clay really would have something of value to leave to his children.

Children? As in plural?

He'd always envisioned himself with two or three. The head of a large, boisterous family. Being an only child, he'd missed having brothers and sisters. That was probably one of the reasons he'd been so close to Ethan and Gavin and had considered Powell Ranch his second home.

His son deserved siblings.

What if Sierra met someone and got married? What if she and her husband had children?

Clay didn't like that idea. He'd marry Sierra himself first, whether he was over Jessica or not.

He slowed his steps, slowed his racing thoughts.

Better to hold off, see how this co-parenting arrangement progressed. He'd married once in haste and entered into an affair in haste. Each time, someone had walked away hurt. He wouldn't make the same mistake a third time.

TEN MINUTES LATER, Clay rounded the corner of the main horse barn and spotted Conner's truck and trailer. His friend and fellow best man was at that moment unloading a pair of feral mustangs, one bay, one buckskin.

"Need some help?" Clay hollered, quickening his steps.

"Sure do. These two boys have yet to learn any manners." Conner opened the rear gate on the trailer. "Watch out!" he yelled a scant second before the buckskin kicked.

Clay ducked, the lightning-fast hoof missing him by inches. "I see what you mean."

Once out of the trailer, the horses behaved marginally better. They allowed Clay and Conner to lead them to a small pasture behind the main horse barn and well away from the other livestock.

Conner opened the gate. "Ethan sure has his work cut out for him when he and Caitlin return from that resort in Sedona."

Gavin and Sage were also on their honeymoon—at a five-star hotel in Palm Springs. Clay got a kick out of imagining his rough and rugged buddies in the lap of sophisticated luxury. Then again, they were newlyweds and were probably staying in their rooms till noon. Clay would if it were him.

He and Conner walked the young geldings along the pasture perimeter, acquainting them with the fenceline before removing their halters. Immediately, the horses galloped in circles, bucking and rearing playfully before investigating the feed and water troughs.

"They *are* a bit ornery," Clay agreed.

He and Ethan had decided before the wedding to bring these two horses to Clay's place as a first step in moving the mustang sanctuary from Powell Ranch. When Gavin and Ethan returned, they'd transport the rest of the horses and continue training.

"How 'bout you and me head to the Saddle Up for a beer and burgers?" Conner asked on the walk back to his truck. "My treat."

"Can't. Mom will be here any minute. She's having dinner with Sierra and I."

"Another one bites the dust," Conner grumbled.

"Why don't you come by this weekend? We'll grill some steaks and watch the basketball game."

"You sure Sierra will let you off your leash?"

"It's not like that," Clay insisted as his friend climbed in behind the wheel.

"Yeah, right." Conner started the engine. "See you Sunday." He slammed the door shut and, with a wave, drove off, the empty trailer making a clanging racket as it bumped over the rough ground.

Was it like that?

Things had definitely changed these last few weeks. Before Sierra came home with Jamie, Clay would have gone out with his friend in a heartbeat. Now, he had chicken and vegetables in the slow cooker and was trying to remember if he'd put out clean towels in the hall bathroom.

Wasn't all that different from being married.

Except he didn't get to wake up next to Sierra every morning.

A memory surfaced, one where he *had* woken up next to her at the Phoenix Inn. She'd been naked, save for a tangled sheet covering her shapely form. Her mussed hair had fallen appealingly over her sleepy eyes, and her tanned skin glowed from their long hours of lovemaking.

She'd never looked prettier or sexier.

He could think of worse things than waking up beside her every morning.

His cell phone rang. Nothing like the sight of his mother's number on his caller ID to banish all inappropriate thoughts of Sierra.

"Hey, Mom."

"I'm running a bit behind," she informed him.

"No problem. See you soon."

Clay conferred with his barn manager on the way to the house. He tried not to dwell on dinner. Just because Sierra and his mother had agreed to come didn't guarantee the evening would go smoothly. His mother pulled up just as he reached the driveway.

"Where's Sierra and Jamie?" she asked, kissing his cheek and handing him an apple pie to carry in.

"At the office."

"How's she doing?"

"Great. She's catching on really fast."

"No, I meant how's she doing after…the wedding?"

"She hasn't mentioned you once, if that's what you're wondering."

"It is." Blythe sighed wistfully. "I'm hoping she and I can put all that unpleasantness behind us."

"Me, too."

They made their way inside where Clay put the pie on the kitchen counter and checked on the chicken.

"How soon till she's finished work?"

He added water to the slow cooker. "About an hour."

"Do you have to rush back to the office or can we visit?"

"Actually, I was planning on you and I visiting." He attempted to keep his tone light.

His mother saw right through him. "What's wrong?"

Clay propped his back against the kitchen counter. "I spoke to Dad last week."

"Did you?" Blythe sat at the table. "You know I've always hated that you and he were estranged."

"No, Mom, I don't. I can't remember you ever telling me anything like that."

She hesitated, as if carefully considering her answer before responding. "That was a long time ago. I've moved on. I'm glad to see you're doing the same thing."

"My conversation with Dad was far from amiable."

"Oh, dear."

Clay crossed his arms. "He mentioned something. About you. Something that was news to me."

Her eyes grew wary. "What was that?"

"He said he sold the Powells' land because you forced him to. That you wanted your share of the marital assets and wouldn't wait. The only way he could come up with the money was to exercise the clause in his loan contract with Wayne."

She stared fixedly at her clasped hands. "He said that, huh?"

Clay's stomach dropped to his knees. It was true. He could read it in her expression. "How could you?"

"I didn't force him to sell the land. What assets he liquidated was his choice."

"What other assets were there to liquidate? He'd already sold the cattle operation." And given Clay half the proceeds, which he'd gladly accepted.

If only he'd realized his parents would be divorcing a few months later he'd have refused the proceeds in order to save the Powells' land. By then, however, he'd already purchased the property for the rodeo arena.

"I had no clue what other assets," Blythe said testily. "Your father handled all our finances. He told me only what he thought I needed to know."

She was right about that.

"But you did insist on your share in the divorce settlement."

"I honestly thought your father still had his share of the money from selling the cattle operation."

"What happened to it?"

She shrugged. "Between the time we drafted the property settlement and the divorce was finalized, he invested the money in stocks. The bottom fell out of the market, and he lost a considerable sum. He didn't tell me about it. Too ashamed, I guess."

Like Wayne had been too ashamed to tell his kids about his financial mishandlings.

"I'm sure your dad thought Wayne would make his payments. I assumed he was doing so all along. Certainly no one anticipated he'd sink into such a deep and lingering depression after Louise died."

Wayne's children had obviously thought the same thing as his mother had, and Wayne didn't correct them.

Clay rubbed the back of his neck. What a mess. And the ones who'd suffered the most were Sierra and her brothers.

"I was sick when I learned about the land sale. I loved Louise like a sister."

"Only sick? Weren't you the least bit guilty?"

"I barely slept for weeks. If I'd had any indication Wayne had defaulted on the loan and your father was selling the land, I'd have told him not to."

"You let me blame Dad all these years for something that wasn't entirely his fault."

Blythe squeezed her eyes shut. "I did, and I regret that."

"Why?"

"Divorce is complicated. I was furious with him. It skewed my thinking."

"Tell me about it. Been there, done that." Clay ground his teeth together. "I agree Dad can be a jerk sometimes. Tough. Strict. Uncompromising." He might have disagreed with his dad while he was growing up and rebelled more than once, but he'd always respected his dad until he'd sold the Powells' land. "But it's not like he gambled or lied to you or cheated on you."

"He didn't." His mother sighed. "He also wasn't entirely responsible for our marriage ending. It's taken me a while, but I see where I contributed. Greatly," she added, in a wobbly voice.

Clay wanted to vent more but he could see she was truly broken up.

"What are you going to do?" she asked.

"I'm not sure yet. Talk to Dad."

Tomorrow. After he'd had time to sort through everything.

This conversation would be considerably less heated and involve considerably more forgiveness.

"I CAN'T TELL YOU how sorry I am," Clay's mother said. "I was thoughtless and selfish. I should have sent someone to find you and let you know I had Jamie. Better yet, I should have found you and asked you myself if it was okay. Next time, I will. I promise."

"Thank you." Sierra smiled. "And I'm so sorry I snapped at you."

Clay watched his mother and Sierra make their sincere and heartfelt apologies to each other.

"Are we good then?"

"Yes, we're good." Sierra reached over and took Blythe's hand.

The three of them sat at the kitchen table, having recently finished Clay's chicken dinner. Jamie occupied his high chair, strategically placed next to Sierra. He evidently loved cooked carrots—smashing them into a pulp as much as eating them.

Everyone, including Jamie, was amused, until he started flinging carrot pieces onto the floor. Then, only Oreo was amused. The old dog lapped up the carrots with the dexterity and speed of an anteater.

"Enough of that," Sierra said and replaced the carrots with a sippy cup of milk.

Jamie immediately shared his milk with Oreo by tipping the cup over and spilling several drops on the floor.

"No, baby." She righted the cup. "Don't give any milk to the dog."

Jamie banged the tray and babbled as if to say, *But he's hungry.*

Oreo concurred and gazed at Sierra with soulful eyes.

"Honestly." She huffed. "Between the two of you, I'm going to have to break out the industrial-strength cleaner."

"Don't worry about it," Clay assured her.

"Nonsense. You cooked dinner, I'll wash up."

"Why don't we both wash up?"

"And why don't I watch Jamie in the family room while you do?" Blythe offered.

Clay waited for Sierra to say no. After her scare at the wedding, he doubted she'd leave Jamie alone.

"That would be great. And maybe you can give him a bath, too."

Blythe's hand fluttered her heart. "I'd love nothing better."

Sierra turned to Clay. "Is it all right if we use your bathroom?"

He cleared his throat, which had tightened during the last several seconds. "Have at it."

Over thick slices of apple pie, Blythe regaled them with stories of when Clay was Jamie's age, how cute he'd been and some of his more adventurous baby pranks. Normally Clay would have put an end to the torture. Instead, he let her talk uninterrupted. Sierra—where she got the patience Clay had no clue—listened raptly.

Jamie tossed several apple chunks to Oreo.

Sierra administered stern looks to boy and dog. "What am I going to do with you?"

Clay chuckled, only to be silenced by a sobering thought. He was having dinner with his family. How long had he wished for this very thing? A sense of amazement and profound satisfaction enveloped him.

It faded the next instant.

If Sierra decided she hated living here, took a job elsewhere, they'd be back to square one in three months.

Regardless what she did, wherever she went, he would not lose Jamie. He might be a brand-new father, but he loved his son more than life itself.

While Clay carried dishes to the sink, his mother filled the tub in the hall bathroom, and Sierra made a quick trip to the casita. She returned with a armful of bath paraphernalia. A towel, toys, three bottles, one of them shampoo, a hairbrush, a toothbrush, pajamas and some kind of ring contraption with suction cups on the bottom.

"This bathing stuff is kind of involved," he said as she traipsed through the kitchen.

"You have no idea."

After five minutes, he began to suspect Sierra wasn't able to leave his mother alone with Jamie after all. Well, next time. It was enough that she and his mother had resolved their differences.

He began loading the dishwasher.

Partway through, Sierra joined him. "That was a disaster."

Clay hid his pleasure. "What happened?"

"Jamie decided he needed a prewash in the toilet."

He grimaced. "I'm not going to ask."

"You're smart not to."

"I'm curious, what's that ring contraption?"

"To stabilize Jamie so he doesn't slip on the porcelain. He sits inside it."

"I guess our moms lived on the edge."

She laughed, a sound Clay liked to hear. "I admit, some of the baby safety gadgets these days are a little extreme. But most of them are clever and really useful."

They made quick work of the remaining dishes. When they were done, Clay fed Oreo. Dog food, not carrots and milk and apple chunks.

"I'm going to check on Jamie," Sierra said breezily.

Clay was impressed she'd gone as long as she had without dashing to the bathroom.

"While you do that, I'm going to take Oreo outside. He likes to go on a stroll every evening around the back pasture. His one shot at exercise."

"Wait a minute, and I'll go with you."

What?

Hell, yes.

He would, he realized, wait a very long time if necessary.

Chapter Ten

Clay retrieved his jacket from the hall closet and Sierra's old sweater from the back of the kitchen chair where she'd left it.

"Thanks." She tugged the bulky garment over her head, then freed her hair from the neck hole. The long sleeves hung past her wrists and the hem nearly to her knees.

Clay thought she looked pixieish and rather cute.

Like the time she'd worn an old work shirt of his with nothing underneath but a teeny-tiny pair of pink panties.

They'd spent a lazy Saturday afternoon lounging on his couch, eating popcorn and watching movies. By the middle of the second movie, she wasn't wearing anything at all, and his hands were caressing her silky bare skin.

A rush of desire plowed through him with the force of an avalanche.

"All set?" His fingers fumbled with the zipper on his jacket.

She rolled up her sweater sleeves. "I noticed earlier it's cold outside tonight."

Good. Bring it on. Cold evening air was just what he needed right now.

Oreo ambled slowly along behind them as they walked from the house toward the pastures. The pair of feral mustangs delivered earlier that day whinnied and ran over to the fence, snorting lustily as Clay and Sierra approached.

"We don't have to go very far," he said. "Oreo's not as frisky as he once was."

"He looks like he's doing okay. And so am I. You don't have to fret."

"I'm not." He was too busy entertaining inappropriate thoughts about Sierra to fret, or do anything else for that matter.

She checked her watch. "I have about fifteen minutes. That seems to be my threshold before I start going ballistic."

Was she ever going to let him live that down?

"You'll get better."

"I want to get better. I hate being this afraid. It's not healthy for either me or Jamie."

"The counselor will teach you how to cope."

"Among other things, I hope."

"Like what?"

"How to effectively communicate and negotiate." She slanted him an amused smile. "How to stand up to pushy people. How to conquer my insecurities."

What about them and their relationship? Clay was starting to think his goals were evolving from co-parenting Jamie with Sierra to co-habiting with her to—

Best stop there. He wasn't ready for what came next.

"You made my mother very happy tonight. You didn't have to let her bathe Jamie."

"I like your mother."

"She likes you, too." Where was a snake or bat when you needed one? Anything to spook Sierra and cause her to jump into his arms. "I'm going to invite my dad over this week to meet Jamie."

Sierra went abruptly quiet.

It killed his ardor better than the cold air.

He probably should have waited to tell her but he didn't dare risk her finding his dad at the house.

"He's Jamie's grandfather," Clay explained. "I want them to meet."

"I thought you and he didn't get along."

"We haven't been. I'd like that to change."

"Why now?"

He couldn't tell her his mother had allowed him to unfairly blame his father for years, not without dragging Sierra's father into the discussion.

"What if I said no?"

"I would try and convince you otherwise."

"And if I still said no?"

"Grandparent visitations are covered in the custody agreement. Monthly supervised visits."

"So, we're going by the agreement verbatim?"

"It's why we drew it up," he said reasonably. "So we wouldn't have these arguments."

"We're not arguing, Clay."

Not yet, but the mood had certainly shifted—downward. "Have you asked your dad about mine lately?"

He sensed more than saw her withdrawal.

"The other night, when you came by."

The night they'd kissed.

"I told him you'd seen your dad earlier at the Saddle Up."

"How did he react?"

"Is it important?"

"I'm just curious to know if he's any less angry."

She chuckled mirthlessly. "He's not. In fact, he warned me to stay away from your dad."

Clay would give anything to know the reason why. Was Wayne afraid Clay's dad would give away his biggest secret? Or were his parents distorting the truth in order to make themselves appear better?

"We should get back." Sierra stopped and peered anxiously over her shoulder. She'd apparently reached her threshold.

Clay reversed direction. "Oreo's getting tired anyway."

"Can I ask you a personal question?"

"Fire away." He'd asked one of her. She deserved the same.

"Why did you and Jessica divorce?"

That came out of the blue.

Then again, maybe not. Sierra was living with him, more or less. She was naturally curious about his ex-wife, as he was curious about the men in her past.

"I think the better question is why we married in the first place."

"You were in love."

"Not the healthy, happy kind of love. Not the kind that sustains two people for a lifetime."

"Lust?"

"There was that, I won't lie." He paused, waited for Oreo to catch up with them. "Jessica infatuated me from the moment I met her. And she knew just how to work that infatuation to her advantage. She always held back a little, enough to keep me on the hook. She'd break up with me then take me back with no rhyme or reason other than her own unpredictable whims."

"It was a game to her."

"Not entirely. That was just how she operated. I'm not sure she was even conscious of it."

"Didn't you get fed up with her manipulations?"

"I did. And when that happened, she'd pile on the charm. Next thing, I'd be suckered in all over again."

"What prompted the divorce?"

"She didn't want children. Not right away and possibly not ever."

"Isn't that something you decided on before you got married?"

"I talked about having kids all the time and failed to notice her lack of enthusiasm. My mistake was assuming the absence of a no meant yes. Shortly after we married, she got pregnant."

"She did?" Sierra let out a soft gasp.

Clay had told only his mother and a few close friends about the baby. It was too hard on him, too many sad memories.

Not, he noticed, with Sierra. The pressure in his chest wasn't there, and he could breathe without experiencing a sharp, stabbing pain.

It had been the same two years ago when he'd poured out his heart to her after his and Jessica's latest breakup.

"I was thrilled. Jessica wasn't. I figured she was simply scared about being a first-time mother."

"What happened?" Sierra asked, her voice low and strained.

She must have realized that she and Jessica were pregnant at the same time, Sierra further along by a few months.

"She miscarried. At fifteen weeks."

"Oh, Clay. How tragic." Sierra touched his arm, let her fingers remain.

"It was rough. I was disappointed."

Disappointed and devastated and guilty. He could still hear the doctor gently advising them it wasn't their fault the fetus hadn't thrived.

How could the baby not thrive when he'd already loved him or her so much?

"Jessica, on the other hand, was relieved. She went right out and changed her birth-control method to something more reliable. Didn't bother telling me. I had to accidentally discover her stash of pills."

"Nothing is worse than losing a child." Sierra stared at the ground in front of them.

"For some of us." He covered the hand she'd rested on his arm. "If I overreacted when I first learned Jamie was mine, I apologize. I had a knee-jerk reaction."

"I'm glad you told me. It explains a lot."

"I did tell you because I want you to know how serious I am about being a good father and making this arrangement of ours succeed."

"I am, too."

She met his gaze boldly, and, for the first time, Clay believed her.

"SOMEBODY'S TIRED." Clay's mother cuddled with Jamie on the family-room sofa. All the lights were dimmed and soft music played from the sound system's built-in speakers.

Clay tarried behind while Sierra went over and peered down at grandmother and grandson, her features radiant.

"It's almost his bedtime."

Jamie lay with his head in the crook of Clay's mother's arm, sucking his thumb, his eyelids drooping heavily. Oreo lumbered over to the rug at their feet and dropped onto it with an exhausted sigh.

"Looks like it's someone else's bedtime, too." Clay grinned. He himself was too wired to sleep after his conversation with Sierra.

Sierra held out her arms to Blythe. "I'll take him and put him to bed."

"So soon?" The corners of his mother's mouth fell. She brightened almost immediately. "Thank you again for this evening. It's been wonderful."

"Anytime."

Did she mean it? Clay hoped so.

His mother stood and carefully passed Jamie to Sierra. "I think he's getting used to me."

The baby immediately wrapped his arms around Sierra's neck and snuggled his face in her sweater. She kissed the top of his head.

Jamie might be getting used to Clay's mother but he loved Sierra more than anyone.

She turned to Clay. "I'll see you in the morning."

He wasn't ready for the evening to end. "Can I go with you?"

"What about your mother?"

"Don't let me keep you, I have to leave anyway." Clay's mother went to the long breakfast bar separating the kitchen from the family room and retrieved her purse. "I'm scheduled to be at the office early for a big real-estate closing."

Sierra could still say no to Clay's request, manufacture an excuse. Lucky for him, she didn't, though her hesitancy left something to be desired.

"Good night, my dear." His mother dispensed hugs to Clay and Sierra, then tenderly kissed Jamie's forehead.

"I'll walk you to your car, Mom."

"Don't bother. Go put your son to bed."

She showed herself out.

"Come on," Clay said to Sierra when they were alone. "There's all the bath stuff."

"Leave it till the morning." Better yet, leave it and let Clay give Jamie his bath tomorrow night.

"Wait a sec. I'll be right back."

Before Clay had a chance to react, Sierra pushed Jamie at him. He took the sleeping boy and held him as he'd seen Sierra do. "Hey there, buddy."

Jamie protested grumpily but quickly drifted off, resting his cheek on Clay's chest.

Protectiveness and possessiveness welled inside him. This was his son, and Clay would do anything, give everything he had, to safeguard him.

"I love you, Jamie." He nuzzled the boy's downy hair. Hearing a noise, he looked up to see Sierra, her arms loaded with bath items. She stared openly at him.

"Is everything okay?"

"Yeah. Fine."

She appeared more rattled than fine.

Clay grabbed an afghan from the couch and draped it over Jamie to ward off the night chill. His son slept through the entire walk to the casita. Inside, Clay noted the changes. An old quilt on the bed. Clothes hanging in the closet. A floor lamp where there had been none.

The crib he'd purchased was no longer barren. Sierra had added colorful bedding, a mobile with shooting stars and quarter moons and an entire zoo's worth of stuffed toys.

"Is there room in there for him?" Clay asked.

She shoved some of the toys aside. "Now there is."

"Should we change him first?" Clay wasn't sure how often a baby needed changing, but it seemed like a lot.

"I think he's okay for now."

"Still sleeping though the night?"

"He didn't last night. I'm sure he will again as soon we get settled per—" She cut herself off.

What was she going to say? Permanently?

Clay liked her near slip.

He laid Jamie in the crib, stroked his back. "Sleep tight, buddy."

Feeling Sierra's gaze on him, he turned his head and met her bottomless blue eyes.

"I'm sorry," she said in a broken whisper.

"For what?"

"Not telling you about Jamie. I was wrong."

She'd admitted as much before but not with such genuine emotion. "Can you forgive me?"

"I already have. Jamie, the two of us raising him, is what's really important."

Every cell in Clay's body urged him to kiss her. She was close enough, all he had to do was tilt his head, lean in.

Every cell in his brain warned him not to give in to his impulses. He and Sierra were making progress. She'd moved into the casita. Started working for him. Agreed to counseling sessions. Let his mother watch Jamie for a full fifteen minutes. Voluntarily handed Jamie over to Clay. He'd be a fool ten times over to screw it up by making an unwanted advance.

He took a step back from the crib. Before he could take a second step, Sierra reached for the collar of his jacket and pulled him toward her as she stood on her tiptoes.

"Sierra?" Her name came out a breath against her lush lips. Instantly, he plummeted, falling into her softness.

God help him, he never wanted to leave.

Her tongue touched his, and it was all over. Clay gave up resisting and kissed her with the voracity of a starved man. She responded, moaning low, setting every nerve in his body on fire. The control he thought he had snapped, and he threaded his fingers through the strands of her silky hair.

She came to her senses first and broke off the kiss.

"What was that for?" He had yet to release her, might never release her.

"I'm not sure," she said shyly. "It just felt right."

He couldn't agree more.

In fact, everything about her was feeling right as rain.

Even the idea of marrying her didn't scare the pants off him anymore.

Ten forty-seven a.m.

"How is the living arrangement working? Are you comfortable in Clay's casita?"

"It's very nice." Sierra smiled tightly.

Dr. Brewster, the counselor her attorney had recommended, waited patiently for Sierra to elaborate.

So did Clay. He sat beside her on the couch, tapping his foot.

"Nice as in the quarters are attractive?" Dr. Brewster had one of those open, pleasant faces that inspired confidence. "Nice as in you like being close to Clay and sharing parenting duties?"

Ten forty-eight.

Sierra wrung her hands. How was Jamie doing? Was he giving her father any trouble? She'd been to the reception area twice to check briefly on them.

They were fine. Managing well enough, other than the magazine Jamie had torn to shreds.

Still, she couldn't shake the intense agitation that gripped her with vice-like tenacity.

She started to rise. "I'll be right back."

"Can you possibly wait?" Dr. Brewster asked. "We only have a few more minutes before the session's over."

Sierra didn't want to wait. She really didn't want to be here at all. But a deal was a deal.

Who knew it would be so difficult?

"Okay. I'll wait." She perched on the edge of the couch cushion and checked her watch again.

Still ten forty-eight?

She shook her wrist. Maybe her batteries were dead.

"About the living arrangement…" Dr. Brewster prompted.

"The casita is charming. Quite comfortable."

"And what about residing so close to Clay? How does that make you feel?" Dr. Brewster had asked the same question six times regarding six different topics.

Sierra had yet to meet anyone so concerned with how she felt.

"It's a little early to tell. This is only our third day." Sierra strained to hear through the closed door.

Silence. No crying, no screaming. No shattering of glass or the crash of bookcases toppling.

Had her father left with Jamie? Taken him on a stroll around the building? He wouldn't do that, would he? He'd promised to stay in the reception area until Sierra and Clay were done.

Ten forty-nine.

This session was never going to end.

"Well, *so far,* how's it going?" Dr. Brewster's question disrupted Sierra's thoughts.

"Okay."

"Just okay?"

Clay hadn't had any trouble when it was his turn to talk. He'd spent the first half of their session rambling on and on about how much he enjoyed being a father, how great it was having Jamie in his life, his plans for the future, blah, blah, blah.

Not that Sierra didn't think all that was wonderful. She just couldn't open up to a complete stranger as he could.

"Are you two growing closer?"

Sierra's knee jerked.

Clay raised his brows as if to say, *Tell her.*

She was not mentioning their kiss. Kisses, plural. Dr. Brewster would probably ask Sierra how she felt about them.

How did she feel?

Like she'd been lost forever and finally come home.

Wouldn't Dr. Brewster have a field day with that?

Sierra shouldn't have kissed Clay. The first one was kind of, sort of, understandable. He'd been excited that she'd agreed to move into the casita and accepted his job offer.

The second one? No excuses.

His story about Jessica's miscarriage and his tender confession of love for Jamie had moved her. As a result, she'd let down her guard. Boy, had she let it down.

What if he hurt her again?

He wasn't the same man she'd had an affair with two years

ago, but he wasn't that different, either. She couldn't take a second devastating loss. And there would be no hiding from her family this time.

Ten-fifty.

"We're getting along better," Sierra hedged, "if that's what you're asking."

"Tell me more."

Dr. Brewster's second-favorite phrase.

"We were able to discuss Clay letting his father meet Jamie without screaming and shouting at each other."

"Very good. I'm impressed."

And not long after that, I kissed him.

She was growing closer to Clay, all right, in every sense of the word. The power of their connection, the depth of their attraction, scared her. She didn't like feeling vulnerable.

There, Dr. Brewster. What do you think of that?

"It's interesting you say you didn't scream and shout because I sense tension between you two."

"There's bound to be some tension," Clay said. "Just like any couple."

They were a couple now?

He covered Sierra's hands with his.

It was the first time he'd touched her since their kiss, other than to take her elbow as they were crossing the parking lot into the building. That touch had sent a tingle soaring through her. This one sent a wave of pleasure.

She had to force herself not to curl her own fingers around his.

Dr. Brewster glanced at their joined hands and jotted a note on her pad.

Great.

Ten fifty-one.

Sierra began rocking nervously.

"I'd like to make a suggestion," Dr. Brewster said. "Some homework for you to do between now and your next session."

"What kind of homework?" Clay leaned forward.

Sierra sat back, a sinking sensation in her middle.

"I know you mentioned that the two of you are having dinner together every night. And that you've done some activities with Jamie, like taking him on walks and putting him to bed."

And standing beside his crib, kissing.

Clay sent her a not so discreet glance. Was he thinking the same thing?

"What I'd also like is for you to practice some trust-building exercises."

Could trust be built with exercises? Sierra thought it had to be earned.

"For starters," Dr. Brewster said, "when you go on those walks with Jamie, I want you to tell the other person a quality or trait about them you appreciate and admire. Stick to those that relate to raising your son. Maybe, Clay, you admire Sierra's devotion to Jamie and maybe, Sierra, you admire Clay's protectiveness. Don't bring up anything negative and steer clear of your personal relationship."

That didn't sound entirely awful.

"Next, I want you to practice eye contact. It will help you be more comfortable with each other, more relaxed. Once a day, perhaps after your dinner together, you sit and stare into each other's eyes for a full sixty seconds."

Was she joking? If Sierra stared into Clay's eyes for sixty seconds, she'd wind up locking lips with him.

"No glasses or sunglasses and no squinting." Dr. Brewster smiled expectantly.

"Sounds okay to me."

Clay *would* agree.

"Do I have a choice?" Sierra asked.

"Of course," Dr. Brewster answered. "No one is going to force you to do anything you don't want to. I'd like you to consider the exercises, however. You might be surprised at the results."

Ten fifty-three.

Two more minutes and Sierra could leave.

The sound of a muffled chime sounded from the other side of the door.

Sierra stiffened. "What was that?"

"My eleven o'clock appointment arriving, I imagine."

Another patient. Of course.

Dr. Brewster took out her calendar. "Next Wednesday at the same time?" She looked to Clay and Sierra for confirmation.

"Sure," Clay answered for them both, already entering the appointment into his smart phone.

Hurray! It was over. Sierra sprang to her feet.

"And what about you, Sierra? What day works best for your individual session?"

Ah, yes. The individual sessions. Another agreement she'd made. More torture for her while Jamie and her father waited in the reception area.

"Mornings are best," she said. "I work in the afternoons."

"Friday at nine?"

She nodded.

"See you then."

Sierra raced to the door. Flinging it open, she burst into the reception area.

Her father stood at the window, Jamie beside him, busily leaving fingerprints all over the sparkling-clean glass.

"How was he?" Her heart didn't stop hammering until she'd lifted Jamie into her arms, inhaled his baby scent.

"Pretty good. He might have mutinied without those animal crackers you left me."

No one said much on the drive back to Mustang Valley. Clay dropped Sierra's dad off at the ranch, then drove home. She planned to feed Jamie lunch before heading to the office. Work would be a welcome distraction after the counseling session.

"See you at one?" she asked when Clay pulled into the driveway. He was going to show her the accounting software this afternoon.

"More like one-thirty. I have an appointment with the photographer from the wedding."

"Okay." Sierra thought that was strange but didn't ask. When it came to work, she was determined to maintain a strictly professional relationship with Clay.

"I'll bring her by the office when we're done touring the arena and barn since you'll be the one coordinating with her."

"I will?" Now she was really curious.

"She volunteered to take pictures of the feral mustangs for the sanctuary's newsletter and website. We're hoping professionally taken shots showing the horses at their best will generate interest and promote adoptions."

"What a great idea."

Clay lifted Jamie out of the car seat. "I think so, too. She and I talked about it at the wedding."

When was that? In between his conversations with Caitlin's maid of honor?

Sierra forgot about the photographer once she and Jamie returned to the casita. Feeding him lunch, freshening her makeup for the office and trying not to think about trust exercises occupied most of her thoughts.

In the office, she settled Jamie in his playpen. The morning's trip must have tuckered him out for, after only a few minutes of quiet play, he fell asleep.

Sierra checked the voice mail and email messages, responding to those she could and saving the others for Clay to handle. She was opening and sorting the daily mail when he brought the photographer into the office.

Sierra had forgotten how pretty the young woman was. Today, her highlighted hair was caught up in a high ponytail, and her brown eyes sparkled, especially when they lighted on Clay.

"Sierra, this is Dallas Sorrenson."

"Nice to meet you again." Sierra shook her hand.

"Same here. I'm really excited about this project and can't wait to get started. Animal causes are kind of my passion. I've also done photographs for several no-kill animal shelters."

They talked in subdued voices so as not to disturb Jamie.

"Are you a horse person?" Sierra asked.

"I was. Until college. Then, unfortunately, I had to sell my mare. Not enough money for board bills and tuition." She showered Clay with a gorgeous smile. "Clay says he'll take me riding."

"He did?" For some reason, Sierra's voice had risen half an octave.

"And let me watch one of the bull-riding practices next week. I love anything to do with rodeos."

She was sweet. Very sweet.

Sierra watched through the office window as Clay escorted Dallas to her car.

What was wrong with her? She wasn't the jealous type. And yet, here she was, spying on Clay, fuming because Caitlin's maid of honor had fawned over him at the wedding and he'd shown the photographer around the arena.

Maybe she should ask Dr. Brewster about it in her individual session on Friday. No, that would be too humiliating.

Big whoop. Sierra and Clay had kissed. Twice. That didn't mean there was anything between them.

She was about to leave the window when Dallas and Clay

suddenly hugged. A second later, she slid into her car, and Clay shut her door.

What the—! Did he hug all his business associates?

When he came into the office, a smile splitting his handsome face, Sierra met him in front of her desk and did as Dr. Brewster suggested, staring into his eyes for a full sixty seconds.

Just what she thought. She didn't trust him any more after the exercise than she had before.

Chapter Eleven

Clay craned his neck in an effort to see over the block wall to the casita. Nothing. Sierra still hadn't emerged from inside.

Did she have a case of cold feet? Had she allowed her anger to win out?

Frankly, he'd been a little surprised that she'd agreed to let his father meet Jamie today. When he'd initially broached the subject a couple of weeks ago, she'd been resistant.

Perhaps the counseling sessions they'd been attending were responsible. The positive effects were evident in other areas. Sierra was now able to leave Jamie with either Wayne or Clay's mother for a full hour with only mild anxiety. She and Clay were mostly on the same page regarding Jamie's upbringing. And the trust exercises—Dr. Brewster had added two more—were beginning to eradicate the barriers between them, enabling them to develop a sincere respect for each other.

Clay wasn't so optimistic he didn't anticipate setbacks. Like today, for instance.

He paced back and forth beside his truck, repeatedly checking the time on his smart phone. If they didn't leave soon, they'd be late for the picnic.

A Sunday afternoon at the park had been chosen for Jamie's first get-together with his other grandfather. Neutral territory, kid-friendly activities and plenty of other people providing a buffer. Sierra would feel less pressured, or so Clay hoped.

Dr. Brewster supported the meeting and the location. She believed Sierra and Jamie would benefit greatly from the experience.

Had Sierra changed her mind?

Or maybe something was wrong with Jamie. Forget pressuring her or being too controlling—her major complaint about him to Dr. Brewster—he was going to the casita to find out what the hold-up was.

He didn't get far. The side gate opened, and Sierra emerged, Jamie in one arm, an overflowing diaper bag in the other.

Relieved, Clay rushed toward her. "Here, let me help."

"Sorry I took so long. Jamie wasn't cooperating."

They added her diaper bag to the assortment of picnic stuff crammed in the truck's back seat.

"Should I bring the stroller?" she asked once Jamie was situated in his car seat.

"Probably."

She hurried back to get it.

Clay watched her, noticing her jeans and sweatshirt were far more "countrified" than her usual attire. It was a style that looked good on her. Almost as good as the little black dress and heels she'd worn to dinner the night they'd spent at the Phoenix Inn.

He winked at Jamie. "Your mama sure is pretty."

"Ma, ma, ma."

"That's right."

Sierra reappeared and, after loading the stroller in the truck bed beside the three folding lawn chairs, they left for the park.

She alternated between yapping a mile a minute and long stretches of silence.

"Are you nervous?" he asked.

"Some."

"We don't have to stay long."

"Will you mind greatly if I don't join in too much?"

"Naw. I'm just pleased you're going."

Clay had considered and reconsidered telling Sierra about his conversations with his father and mother, that his father had given Wayne ample opportunity to repay the loan. Ultimately, he'd decided against it.

He didn't know everything that had happened between his parents and Wayne. As the old saying went, there was more than one side to every story. If Clay interfered, Sierra might wind up angry at him, too, not just at his dad. It was a risk he wasn't willing to take.

He'd casually suggested on several occasions that she speak to Wayne about what had happened. For Jamie's sake. She'd refused. Her last reply was "Why rehash a past we can't change?"

That sounded more like Wayne than Sierra.

The only way they'd ever discover the whole truth, once and for all, was to approach Wayne, and Clay wasn't about to do that. Not when Sierra had finally consented to Jamie meeting his father.

She was staring out the window, gnawing on her lower lip.

"Dallas came up with a good idea the other day."

"Dallas?" Her head snapped around. "She was at the arena?"

"No, she called." Was it his imagination or did Sierra's eyes narrow? "I mentioned we were brainstorming fundraisers for the wild-mustang adoption."

The event was scheduled for next month. Sierra had been toiling diligently, often long into the evenings after Jamie went to bed. Ethan and Gavin had planned a demonstration to show how well-trained the mustangs were and their suitableness as Western pleasure mounts. Cassie was riding one of the older, gentler geldings. Dallas had volunteered to take pictures.

"She suggested we sell photos with Prince, charge people a nominal fee."

"I'm not sure about that." Sierra scowled. "Remember the wedding? Prince spooks easily."

"Dallas suggested we practice with him."

"Huh."

"He's a local celebrity. It's a good idea. I'd like you to coordinate with her on it."

"Whatever you say, boss. You're in charge."

Clay let the remark slide, attributing her surliness to nerves.

The entrance to the park came into view. Sierra offered no more than a murmured comment or two while they unloaded Jamie and the picnic supplies, which took an absurdly long time.

Clay surveyed the enormous pile. "I could use a third arm about now." His attempt at levity was ignored. "Sierra, you okay?"

"Don't worry about me." Her weak smile barely lifted the corners of her mouth.

How could he not worry? This meeting was important to him. She was important, too.

"Why don't we come up with a safe word? If things get too much for you, just say, 'Jamie's tired,' and we'll cut the visit short."

"You'd do that?"

"After all you've done for me? You bet."

She stared at him, as she did when they were practicing their trust exercises but not exactly. It was as if she wanted to see *him,* the real person inside, wasn't merely going along with Dr. Brewster's homework assignment.

Clay had been waiting weeks for just this moment.

JAMIE SAT IN THE MIDDLE of the blanket, picking raisins off the lint-ridden material and popping them into his mouth.

Sierra clasped her hands behind her back rather than whisk him away. She kept assuring herself babies didn't get sick and die from eating raisins off old blankets.

Bud Duvall, who also sat on the blanket, inched closer to Jamie. "Are those tasty?"

The boy glanced up from his task but didn't smile back at his grandfather. The older man's exuberance faltered briefly before he shored it up.

"It takes him a while to warm up to people," she said, then almost bit her tongue.

They'd been at the park half an hour, during which they'd laid out the blanket, set up the chairs and unpacked the food. This was the first Sierra had spoken to Bud.

"Well, that's just fine," he said, "because I'm in no hurry to leave."

Sierra was, but she had to admit Bud was being cordial and considerate. Not the least bit annoying or overbearing, which was what she'd feared. He was, she almost hated to admit it, the man she remembered from her childhood. Her father's closest friend. The husband of her mother's best friend.

How could that be? How could a considerate man practically destroy her family's lives and livelihood?

"He's teething," Clay explained. Like Sierra, he occupied one of the lawn chairs. "Makes him a little fussy."

"I had a root canal a few weeks ago. Hurt like a son of b— Like a son of a buck." Bud hooked a finger on his lower lip and tugged, showing Jamie his bottom teeth. "Right there," he muttered.

Jamie gawked at him with hugely round eyes, then burst into giggles.

"You like that?" Bud pulled the other side of his lip down.

Jamie shoved his own fingers into his mouth.

Bud chuckled and pinched his chin.

If Sierra didn't dislike the man, she'd have been enamored by the charming exchange.

"Anyone want a sandwich?" Clay popped the lid on the ice chest. "I have ham and Swiss, and peanut butter and bananas."

Peanut butter and bananas? Her guilty-pleasure favorite.

He'd remembered.

She'd made them for him one day when they'd driven to Saguaro Lake to watch the sunset. They'd taken the sandwiches with them and strolled the lakeshore until they found a solitary spot. Such a simple date and a simple meal. Yet it had been the most romantic day of her life.

"I'll try one of the ham and Swiss." Bud pushed to his feet with a grunt and sat in the empty lawn chair.

Clay rambled on about the wild-mustang adoption while they ate.

"That's a worthy cause, son." Bud dusted crumbs off his lap. "It does my heart good to know there's mustangs in the valley again, even if they aren't running wild."

"Did you ever see wild mustangs here?" Sierra asked.

"I did," Bud said. "I was just a boy. Nine or ten. The mustangs had all but disappeared before I was born. The tales my dad would tell…" He smiled, more to himself. "A small herd of horses made their way into the valley one winter from the mountains. They were skin and bones, and sick to boot. Didn't put up much of a fight when we rounded them up. There was a yearling, his dam, another mare and a stallion. Never saw horses that abhorred captivity more. They refused to eat and almost died."

"My dad saved them," Clay said.

"I don't know if I saved them exactly. I'd mix up a bucket of warm mash and feed the yearling by hand. The poor critter was timid as a church mouse but, eventually, he friendlied up and started eating. After that, the other horses did, too. Turned into some of the best horses we ever owned."

"What happened to the yearling?" Sierra asked.

"I kept him. Rode him nearly every day for the next twenty-six years, then retired him. Damn horse survived to be almost thirty. I must have covered a million miles of mountains and valley on his back. Speaking of teeth, his were so bad at the end and he grew so frail, I was back to feeding him warm mash by hand. I buried him at the trailhead behind the back pasture."

Sierra sat, transfixed. By the recounting and by Bud. His love of the land and the animals sang in his voice. She could see him as a young boy and an adult, patiently tending his beloved horse.

How could he have sold off her family's land? It didn't make sense.

"I'm sorry, Sierra. You must hate me, and I deserve it."

She drew back. Were her thoughts that apparent?

"Dad, you don't have to—"

"I do. Not a day goes by I don't think how different things might be if I'd told that investor no."

"Why didn't you?"

Sierra's question hung between them.

"At the time, I didn't believe I had a choice."

It wasn't much of an answer, but it was evidently the only one Sierra was going to get.

Bud stood, gathered up their trash and disposed of it in a nearby barrel. "You think Jamie would like to play in the sandbox?"

"I don't know." Clay turned to Sierra. "Do you think he's tired?"

Their safe phrase. All she had to do was agree with him, and, they could leave.

She started to say yes, but the desperation in Bud's expression halted her, caused her to reconsider.

"No," she told Clay. "I think he's okay for now."

FOR THE SECOND TIME that day, Clay craned his neck, seeking a glimpse of Sierra. Tonight, he was in the great room, staring out the French doors at the casita. A light shone in the front window, an indication she hadn't gone to bed yet despite the lateness of the hour. After almost three weeks of living with him—*at his place,* he corrected himself—he'd learned her habits. Sierra was early to bed, early to rise.

Should he check on her? What if Jamie was teething or coming down with a bug? The next instant, he changed his mind. She wouldn't appreciate him knocking on her door at nearly eleven o'clock, even if his intentions were good.

Were they good?

Clay had wanted to talk to Sierra since they'd left the park. She'd been somber and distant on the ride home and unresponsive when he'd queried her.

They'd parted in the driveway, and he left her alone the rest of the day. It had been an emotionally draining afternoon for all of them. And, for Clay, deeply satisfying.

Yet, instead of sleeping, he was pacing the floor and borderline stalking Sierra.

Enough was enough. He had a full day tomorrow. Some of the bucking stock were returning from the Parada del Sol rodeo in Scottsdale, the feed bins had to be cleaned in preparation for Monday's grain delivery and he had a conference call from a rodeo promoter out of Salt Lake City.

Clay was about to head to his room when the door to the

casita opened. Sierra stepped outside, the exterior light bathing her in a hazy yellow glow. She wore scruffy slippers on her feet and a blanket wrapped around her like a cape. She went to the wrought-iron chairs in front of the kiva fireplace and plunked down.

Even at a distance, Clay could see her movements were slow and weighted, her shoulders slumped in exhaustion.

Clearly, Jamie wasn't teething or sick. Sierra wouldn't have left his side.

Perhaps she also had insomnia.

Stalker-like or not, he watched, unable to tear his gaze away from her. She opened the front of the blanket, revealing Jamie in her arms. A faint cry carried across the yard.

Clay didn't think twice before he fetched his jacket. At the door, he shoved his bare feet into the pair of athletic shoes he'd worn to the park. Only when he stepped outside and cool air blasted him did he remember he wore nothing other than cotton pajama bottoms beneath his jacket.

Sierra glanced up the moment his feet struck the wood-slat walkway, the clacking sound echoing in the still night. If she was surprised by his appearance, she gave no indication. Not even when he hopped over the low gate.

Jamie stopped crying upon spotting Clay but still fussed.

"You okay?"

It seemed as though he was always asking her that question. During their dinners together. After their counseling sessions. At the end of her work day. Before meeting his dad today.

"Jamie's been crying for the last two hours. I don't know what's wrong with him. The teething gel hasn't helped, if it's even that. He doesn't have a diaper rash. No fever. No stuffy nose. No throwing up." She jiggled him on her knees. "I wish you could talk, baby. Tell me what's wrong."

Jamie hiccupped and shuddered slightly as a muffled sob escaped.

"He probably had a rough day like the rest of us."

"And he's overtired. He didn't get much of a nap this afternoon." She lifted by his underarms and stood him on her thighs. "I came outside hoping the fresh air would relax him."

Clay considered offering to hold Jamie. Then, he had a better idea. "Why don't we take him inside the house?"

"Yours?"

"He can play with Oreo, and I'll make us cups of that herbal tea you like."

"I used my last teabag this morning."

"I have a box. Bought it at the store the other day."

"Really?"

He could tell the extra effort he'd taken on her behalf pleased her. "We could warm up a can of formula for Jamie."

"You have toddler formula, too?"

"I think that's what it is. There's a picture of a kid about Jamie's age on the label. Supposed to be more nutritious than plain milk."

"I suppose you have a bottle, too."

"As a matter of fact..." He'd been preparing for when Sierra was ready to leave Jamie with him for extended periods.

Or when she moved out into her own place and Jamie stayed with Clay on "his days." Just because things were progressing extraordinarily well was no guarantee they'd stay that way.

He and Sierra hadn't kissed since that night by Jamie's crib. Not that Clay didn't want to or didn't think about kissing her. Day in, day out. But Jamie was their priority and main focus.

"Come on, let's go." He inclined his head toward the house.

She wavered.

He stood, held out a hand to her. She allowed him to assist her to her feet.

Her fingers were small and soft and warm inside his.

Jamie's fussiness ceased the instant they entered the house. The fluorescent lights in the kitchen seemed to fascinate him. Tilting his head back, he gawked at the ceiling.

Sierra gawked at Clay, making him a tad self-conscious. He'd taken off his jacket and left his shoes by the door, forgetting that all he wore was his cotton pajama bottoms.

Well, she'd seen him in less before. A lot less.

He boiled water for the tea while Sierra set Jamie on the floor and prepared his bottle of toddler formula. He lost interest in the lights the moment Oreo meandered into the kitchen. The dog licked Jamie's face, then bowed down in a huge stretch and yawned expansively.

Clay patted Oreo's head. "I see one of us isn't having trouble sleeping."

When the tea was ready, he transferred the steaming mugs to the table. Sierra tried to pick up Jamie, but he scrambled away from her. Rather than fight, she gave him the bottle, which he drank while sitting on the floor next to Oreo.

"I've been thinking about what your dad said today." She plucked nervously at her oversize T-shirt and sweatpants.

Clay was going to bring up the wild-mustang auction. This was an unexpected, and better, subject. "You want to discuss it?"

She grimaced. "You sound like Dr. Brewster."

"Sorry." The counseling sessions had definitely influenced him. "Thanks again for letting my dad meet Jamie. Not that you care, but it meant a lot to him."

"I did it for Jamie."

"And me?"

She averted her gaze.

Sometimes saying nothing spoke volumes.

"I don't expect you to forgive him," Clay said.

"Have you?"

Clay spoke slowly, aware that if he leveled with Sierra he'd be treading on dangerous ground. "I'm trying. We've had some conversations lately. There's more to my parents' split than either of them told me."

"Isn't that common in divorce?"

True. He'd certainly kept facts about his own divorce private. Never at the expense of another person, however.

"My mom let me make assumptions about my dad and didn't correct them. Harmful assumptions."

"Why would she do that?"

"Their divorce was complicated. She was angry at him. When I confronted her with what my dad said, she admitted misleading me."

Sierra shook her head. "I can't see your mom lying."

"She didn't lie so much as omit."

"They divorced years ago. Why is this even important?"

"Closure, I suppose. It started when I told Dad about Jamie. Apparently my parents didn't want to drag me into the nasty details of their divorce or acknowledge the mistakes they'd made."

"Like your dad selling my family's land to an investor?"

Up till now, Clay had danced around the subject of Wayne. He decided the time had come for frankness. "There's more to the sale of your family's land than either of our parents told us. Ask your dad."

"What purpose would that serve?"

"Learning the truth."

She snorted indignantly. "The truth is your father breached the contract he had with mine. Just because he didn't think he had a choice doesn't make it acceptable or forgivable."

"Sierra—"

"My dad was depressed for years. He's finally his old self again. I'm not risking a relapse by hammering him with questions about the darkest days of his life."

"Okay. I didn't mean to push you." Clay had been struggling to temper that least-desirable trait of his.

"And I didn't mean to get defensive."

They sipped their tea wordlessly for several seconds.

Sierra broke the lull. "What do you want from our relationship, Clay?"

"To be great parents to Jamie."

"Is that all?"

Dr. Brewster had encouraged direct questions. Sierra was apparently taking the advice seriously.

"If we weren't already in an unconventional relationship, I'd pursue a conventional one."

"You'd ask me out?"

"Yes."

"But we *do* have an unconventional relationship."

He turned the tables on her. "What are you really asking?"

She sighed, propped her chin on her hand. "Things keep changing on me. The last two years have been a roller-coaster ride. I know I want stability and permanence, for me and for Jamie."

"You don't have that here?"

"Come on. There are two legal agreements binding us together and both of them expire at the end of three months. That's not exactly permanence."

"I won't kick you out of the casita or fire you."

"You say that now. What if you meet someone?"

"That isn't likely."

"You've said that before."

She had every reason to doubt him. He'd given Sierra a similar assurance right before reconciling with Jessica. "Can we take this one day at a time? Not worry about what hasn't happened and probably won't?"

"You're right." She sighed.

Could she be searching for more than permanence? A home rather than a place to live? A career with potential rather than a plain old job? A loving, committed relationship rather than a man with whom she shared parenting duties?

Clay's aversion to marriage had lessened considerably in recent weeks, but he still remained cautious. Sierra was astute and probably sensed his reservations.

"I'm attracted to you," he said, gauging her reaction. "I think that's obvious."

"A little." She smiled. A spark lit her eyes.

His pulse jumped. "Unconventional relationship or not, we could still go out."

"As in a date?"

Start with a date, he was thinking, but said, "Yeah. Take Jamie along."

Her smile turned mischievous. "Then it wouldn't be much of a date. What if I want to go to a grown-up restaurant, not a pizza place with games and ten million screaming kids?"

His pulse went from jumping to leaping. "You okay with someone watching him?"

"Your mom or my dad. For a couple of hours."

What would Dr. Brewster's reaction be to them going on a date? What about their attorneys?

"Ah!" Sierra's expression melted. "Would you look at that."

Clay followed her gaze to Jamie, sound asleep on the floor beside Oreo. The dog, snoring quietly, rested his head on Jamie's bottom.

"I should put him to bed."

"Wait. Not yet." Clay retrieved his smart phone from the counter and snapped several pictures.

"You're not going to email those to all your friends and family and post them on Facebook?"

"What kind of dad would I be if I didn't?"

"I want copies, too."

When he finished with the pictures, she bent and tugged Jamie out from under Oreo.

The dog grunted his displeasure at the loss of his pillow.

"Where'd I leave that blanket?" She glanced around, Jamie draped limply over her shoulder.

"Don't leave yet."

"It's almost midnight."

"You haven't finished your tea." Or their conversation. "The cold air might wake him up."

"Umm…"

"Put him in the playpen."

"You have a playpen? Where?"

"In the living room. I just bought it."

"Along with the toddler formula and bottles?"

"And some more baby junk."

"Just how much baby junk did you buy?"

Clay grinned like a boy on his first pony ride. "Put Jamie in the playpen and I'll show you."

Chapter Twelve

Sierra waited while Clay spread an old afghan in the bottom of the playpen. She laid Jamie on top of it and used a corner to cover him up.

Amazingly, he didn't stir once.

"Where are all these new purchases?" she whispered as they padded on bare feet to the hall.

"This way."

Clay took her to the den. There, on the couch, were bags and bags of baby things. On the floor beside the couch was a tricycle.

"You've really outdone yourself." Sierra went to the tricycle and lifted one of the brightly colored streamers hanging from the handlebars. "He's not quite old enough for this. Or this." She dug out a skateboard and rolled her eyes. "And here I thought a pony was bad."

"I bought a helmet and knee pads. They're in one of the bags."

"Clay Duvall, you're impossible." She laughed. Easily, naturally. Wasn't that a nice change from the glum mood she'd been in after the picnic at the park?

"Granted, I may have gotten carried away," he confessed.

"You think?" Still laughing, she came over and pressed a hand to his cheek. "You're a very a sweet man. Jamie's a fortunate boy to have you for his father. Not just because of what you can buy him—" She moved her hand from his cheek to his chest and laid it over his heart. "Because you love him."

"Thank you. For Jamie and for working so hard to make this relationship of ours work."

"It's not as bad as I thought it would be."

"No, it isn't."

Her gaze roved his face, settled on his eyes. This was no trust exercise. She looked at him for the sheer pleasure it gave her.

Drawn by an irresistible pull, she swayed toward him.

He circled her waist with his arms, narrowing the distance between them to nothing. "Sierra, I—"

"Don't say anything." She pressed a finger to his mouth. "Show me instead."

He groaned and brushed his lips across hers, slowly, purposefully. She leaned into him, fitted her body to his and pressed her breasts against him. The passion that had swept them up before instantly reignited.

Two years ago, Clay had desired her. Not because he loved her or even wanted her. He'd been needing a balm to soothe the ache left by Jessica. Sierra had been available and willing to provide that balm.

Tonight was different.

Jessica was buried deep in Clay's past where she belonged. It was Sierra's name Clay murmured as he trailed kisses along her jaw and down her throat. It was her eyes he lost himself in before claiming her mouth again. It was her desperate need he was eager to satisfy.

Emotions gathered inside her, then tumbled out in a shiver that left her simultaneously weak-kneed and exhilarated.

Clay ruthlessly broke off their kiss, gasping for air as if every molecule of oxygen had been sucked from the room.

He tried to talk and couldn't.

She enjoyed leaving him speechless.

"We'd better stop while I can," he managed in a choked voice.

"Do you want to stop?"

"What do you think?"

She thought he'd like to take her to bed.

Were they ready?

This was new territory they were navigating, despite having slept together before. Common sense dictated they proceed slowly.

Sierra had been listening to her common sense for two years and was tired of it.

"I could go, but I hate to wake up Jamie."

"If you stay, I don't want Jamie to be the reason."

If she stayed, there would be no going back. Ever.

His breathing steadied, and his muscles relaxed.

She liked him better when that infuriating control of his was about to snap.

"It would be a shame to wake him up." She smiled seductively.

"A crying shame." Clay hauled her off her feet for another kiss and carried her down the hall.

His bedroom was large and the decor masculine, like the rest of his house.

The bed was simply too far away and Sierra in too much of a hurry.

"Put me down."

Clay set her on her feet in the middle of the room. She didn't wait for him to undress her but tugged off her T-shirt.

"Wow." He filled his hands with her breasts. "You are gorgeous."

She felt gorgeous. And daring and, yes, timid. She was taking a chance, putting her heart out there again with no protection.

"I won't hurt you, I promise."

Her fears must have shown on her face.

She covered his hands with hers, let the silky sensations his touch evoked slide through her.

"Let's just concentrate on the here and now," she said. "Not worry about what hasn't happened."

Hadn't he told her the very same thing earlier?

He kissed her mouth, her shoulders, tickled the tops of her breasts with his five o'clock shadow. His restraint was maddening. When had he gained control and she lost hers?

"Clay, please." She arched her back, and he reached between her legs.

"What do you want? Tell me."

"You, naked, inside me."

They tumbled onto the bed, the rest of their clothes dissolving in a mad frenzy. When she would have straddled him, Clay took his time exploring every inch of her with intimate touches and sensual caresses. Not to mention kisses. Lots of them. All over.

Her hands weren't still, either. She traced the contour of his broad chest, his lean thighs, his tight buttocks. His body had always fascinated her, and she reveled in the rediscovery.

She bit his earlobe as her fingers found his erection. "I want you inside me."

"Not half as much as I want you."

Rolling onto his side, he opened the drawer of the nightstand and removed a condom. Swiftly covering his erection, he pushed her onto her back and entered her.

Sierra gasped in astonishment and delight, rising off the mattress as every one of her muscles contracted. The next instant, her limbs turned to liquid as he thrust in and out of her, his rhythm steadily increasing at the same rate as her excitement.

Heaven help her, she wanted more.

"Touch me."

At her bold demand, he drove into her harder, his hand stroking her where she craved it the most.

The connection was electrifying.

Within seconds, she reached a spectacular climax that triggered an onslaught of emotions. Tears sprang to her eyes. She blinked them away, hoping Clay wouldn't notice.

He did. "What's this?" He wiped her moist cheek.

She started to tell him it was nothing. Except that would be a terrible lie.

"Make love to me." That was as near as she could come to telling him what lay in her heart.

His breathing grew shallower, and his thrusts went deeper. She clung to him, told him how incredible he felt and how good they were together.

He shuddered, buried his face in her neck and let go.

She enjoyed his release almost as much as she had her own. Clay might be bigger and stronger than her, but she was capable of reducing him to a weakling simply by moving her hips a certain way.

"Stop that," he growled, "unless you mean business." He captured her wrist and brought her hand to his mouth.

She sifted her fingers through his short disheveled hair. "I'm glad Jamie was fussy tonight."

"You have no idea how often I've wanted to walk over to that casita." His smile was little-boy charming.

"I'm not sure the evening would have ended the same if you did."

"Me either, to be honest." He rolled off her onto his side.

Sierra missed him immediately and was glad when he scooped her into his arms. She reciprocated by curling her leg around his calf.

"This is nice," he said, his voice tinged with sleep.

Sierra was suddenly tired, too, and her own eyelids drifted shut.

The day had been filled with ups and down, highs and lows and unexpected turns. Being physically sated contributed to her sleepiness. So did being cocooned in Clay's arms.

She'd started to drift off when he kissed the back of her neck. "I have an idea."

"Mmm, what's that?"

"Let's get married."

Her eyes flew open, and she came instantly wide awake.

SIERRA SAT UP AND swung her legs over the side of the mattress, her back to Clay. "That was out of the blue."

"Was it?" He propped himself up on one elbow and stroked her arm, the sleepiness vanished from his voice. "Can you honestly tell me you haven't thought about marrying me?"

She had, a lot. Two years ago. She'd dreamed of nothing else after returning to San Francisco. Even when she heard he and Jessica had reconciled, a small part of her hoped they'd break up again. Then, she'd received two stunning blows. She was pregnant, and, a week later, she learned Clay and Jessica were engaged.

"It's too soon for us to think about marriage. This… We…" Sierra waved a hand at the bed. "Everything is happening really fast. We haven't gone on our first date yet."

"Jamie is our son. You and he are my family. I think it would be best for him if we were married. You said you wanted stability and permanence."

All right, people married for the sake of their child every day. Clay's proposal wasn't as out of the blue as she'd claimed. But Jamie wasn't enough of a reason for her to accept. Clay felt compelled to "do the right thing," which was why she hadn't told him about her pregnancy in the beginning.

"I do want stability and permanence," she said. "I also

want to marry for love. To be in a committed relationship with a man who adores me and can't bear to live without me."

"I adore you, Sierra. You're a beautiful, smart, talented woman. An incredible mother. Everything I want in a wife."

Do you love me?

He hadn't included that in his list of the perfect-wife qualities.

Do I love him?

She did. Despite all the doubts and uncertainties, she'd been steadily falling for Clay since her return home. If she didn't love him, she wouldn't be in his bed now.

"Hey, come on, look at me." He reached up and, taking her chin between his fingers, forced her to look at him.

His vulnerable expression turned her insides to mush.

"Won't you at least consider my proposal?" he asked.

"I'm not ready. We have too many unresolved issues."

There was sufficient moonlight streaming in though the shutters for her to discern the flare of disappointment in his eyes. Had she crushed his ego or did he truly care for her?

He must. No man made love with the kind of intense passion Clay did without caring for his partner.

She'd feel a whole lot better about them and their future if he'd say those three little words.

"I'm touched by your proposal." She cupped his cheek, attempting to restore their former mood.

"I can see where I might have jumped the gun."

"You do that sometimes." Though there was a big difference between buying a one-year-old a tricycle and proposing marriage.

"The control freak strikes again."

She smiled. "You said it, not me."

He returned her smile. "Why don't we just live together?"

"Live together," she repeated slowly.

"Yeah. We practically already are."

"No, we're not." She stiffened. "We have completely separate residences."

He sat up beside her, his thigh brushing hers. "What's wrong?"

"You're pressuring me."

"Take your time deciding. I'm in no rush."

"I'm not sure of your motives."

"For asking you to move in with me?"

"That and proposing."

"I told you, Jamie and you."

Right. To give her stability and permanence. Not for love.

Another legal agreement binding them together. This one a marriage license.

She should drop the subject before either of them said something they'd regret.

He tucked a lock of hair behind her ear. "If I'm pressuring you it's because you mean the world to me, and I don't want to lose you."

Funny, she was afraid of losing him.

"That still isn't a good reason to get married or move in together. Those are huge steps."

"You're right. It's just that tonight was amazing. Not only the sex. And make no mistake, that was mind-blowing. I'm talking about the emotional connection. I've never felt so close to anyone."

Almost a declaration of love.

Maybe he was one of those men who couldn't say it out loud.

"Oh, Clay." She bent and kissed his cheek.

"I'm sorry I botched this."

"You didn't. You've let me know we have enough between us to build a solid relationship. We love Jamie and want what's best for him. We also have some pretty powerful feelings for each other. Maybe, if we go slow, we can have something really special one day."

"I said you were smart." He kissed her mouth thoroughly. "Will you at least spend the night with me?"

She laughed and slid her foot along his thigh. "I'm not going anywhere, cowboy."

And she didn't, for another hour.

After a second round of love-making, Sierra tiptoed to the living room and checked on Jamie. He continued sleeping peacefully in the playpen, Oreo on the floor beside him.

She scratched the dog's ear. "Watch out for him, will you?"

Oreo's tail thumped.

Rather than immediately return to bed, Sierra stood over Jamie, considering the night's events yet again.

She had thought herself the insecure one, plagued by doubts and anxieties, and Clay the confident, self-assured one. Yet, he wasn't always confident and self-assured.

Which might explain why he had reconciled with Jessica rather than attempt a long-distance relationship with Sierra. And why he always strived to be in control. He was compensating for his fears.

The two of them were a study in contradictions.

She sighed. This new relationship of theirs would either be a stupendous success or an equally stupendous failure.

"I'M PRETTY SURE the three of us bought out the entire store!" Sage laughed as she climbed awkwardly into the front passenger seat of Sierra's SUV, her growing stomach hampering her movements.

"If you don't tell Ethan, I won't tell Gavin." Caitlin made funny faces at Jamie as she hopped in the back seat next to him.

Sierra buckled the harness on his car seat and shut the door. She and her sisters-in-law had spent the entire morning shopping at baby boutiques in nearby Scottsdale. Actually, Sage and Caitlin had done most of the shopping. After only a month at the rodeo arena, part-time at that, Sierra was still carefully managing her disposable income.

Clay would buy her anything she had a hankering for, and that was the problem. She didn't want to take advantage of him. Their *dating* relationship, while in the early stages, was going well. More than well, in fact, and she'd hate to mess it up by giving him reasons to think her feelings for him were based solely on what he could provide her.

"I'm not ready to go home yet," Sage announced. "Are you?" She looked to Sierra and Caitlin for confirmation.

"Me, either." Caitlin yawned and stretched. She'd only recently started showing, and most of her purchases today were maternity clothes.

"You sure? You look tired."

"Nothing a little pick-me-up won't cure. Anyone hungry?"

"Starving!" Sage rubbed her belly. "Junior, too. Why don't we stop for lunch at the Corner Diner?"

"What do you say, Sierra?" Caitlin smiled winningly. "My treat, in exchange for you driving us around all morning."

Sierra glanced over her shoulder at Jamie. He was as energized as his Aunt Sage and as content as his Aunt Caitlin. "Sure. Why not?"

Twenty-five minutes later they were being seated at the busy diner, Jamie in one of the restaurant-provided high chairs. Sierra automatically dug several of his toys out from the diaper bag. He was far more interested in the plastic-laminated dessert menu.

Once they placed their orders with the waitress, the conversation returned to where it had been most of the morning—babies.

"Did you know you were having a boy?" Caitlin asked. "Ethan wants to find out the baby's sex, but I don't."

"I refuse to find out," Sage chimed in. "We already have two girls. I'm worried Gavin will be disappointed if we have another one."

"Oh, Gavin won't care." Caitlin dismissed her sister-in-law with a shrug, and, thank goodness, forgot about Sierra.

She'd dreaded having to answer the question. It brought back too many sad memories. Once she'd agreed to the adoption, the Stevensons had insisted on learning if her baby was a boy or a girl, even accompanying Sierra to an ultrasound appointment.

Knowing she was carrying a boy had made those last few months of Sierra's pregnancy excruciatingly difficult. She was no longer carrying a baby, she was carrying her son.

A son she was abandoning.

"How're things going with you and Clay?" Sage asked, nibbling a cracker. She gave one to Jamie.

This question was easier to answer, yet Sierra hedged. What if talking about her and Clay jinxed their relationship?

"Fine."

"That's all?"

"Okay, really fine."

Clay had broken the news that he and Sierra were seeing each other to Sierra's brothers. Ethan had been happy for them. Gavin, as usual, expressed reservations.

"Have you moved in with him yet? What?" Caitlin objected when Sage sent her a warning glance. "Am I being too nosy?"

"I'm still in the casita and he's still in his house."

Technically, that was true. Sierra insisted on maintaining her residence in the casita in order to minimize disrupting Jamie's schedule. Clay hadn't insisted on taking Jamie during "his days," though he could if he chose to enforce the custody agreement.

"We eat breakfast together every morning and dinner together every evening. In his house," she added. "We also have Friday date nights and family Sundays."

And, almost always, Clay spent the night in the casita with her. That probably wouldn't last much longer. Jamie was getting too big to be sleeping in the same room with his parents.

The thought of him occupying his own room didn't distress Sierra anymore, thanks to her counseling.

Or maybe the reason was sharing her bed with Clay. She definitely felt calmer and slept better snuggled against him.

What she refused to tell her sisters-in-law was that the last family Sunday had been spent with Bud Duvall, this time at an indoor playground with an activity center designed for toddlers.

If Sage and Caitlin found out, they'd spill the beans to Sierra's brothers, and she wasn't ready to deal with the inevitable fallout. Ethan might understand but Gavin and her father would come unglued.

She couldn't keep it from them forever. Jamie was quickly coming to adore his other grandfather. Bud had won him over at the playground by climbing into the ball pit with him and chasing him through the tunnels.

For her part, Sierra continued having trouble reconciling the horrible man who'd destroyed her family with the kind, caring grandfather who doted on his grandson.

"How's the job going?" Caitlin asked.

"I love it." Sierra smiled broadly, glad for the distraction. "The work's really interesting, and there's a lot of it. I'm busy every minute."

"I'm jealous," Sage said. "You get to take Jamie with you to the office. I'll have to leave Junior here in day care or—" she sighed despairingly "—with Gavin."

"It's not always easy, believe me. Jamie can be very demanding. And loud. It's embarrassing when I'm on the phone and he starts wailing."

She should arrange day care. But every time she imagined leaving Jamie with someone else, she was reminded of the Stevensons and panicked.

"I'm thinking of hiring Cassie this summer to watch him while I work."

Sierra and Gavin's daughter had engaged in a long talk after the wedding. They'd both regretted the incident and wanted to make amends.

"That's a wonderful solution," Sage gushed.

Yeah, other than Cassie wouldn't be off school for three more months. Thank goodness Clay was patient.

"How's the wild-horse auction coming?" Sage asked. "I can't believe it's in two weeks. I'm so excited. I wish I could be more involved."

"We're on target. The horses are ready. We've hired the auctioneer. Arranged for Cassie's equestrian drill team to run the concession stand. My big concern is publicity. Ads are appearing in the newspapers this week and next, and I've contacted five local TV stations. So far, only one has committed. I worry I haven't done enough."

"Gavin tells me Prince is ready for his picture-taking," Sage said. "They've been practicing."

Sierra was less sure. About Prince, not Dallas. She and the photographer had gotten to know each other over the last couple weeks and had become friends. Sierra was mortified to think she once suspected Dallas of going after Clay.

Their food arrived, and Sage dove into her sandwich with gusto. "This is delicious."

"Hey, I've just had the best idea." Caitlin put down her fork and grabbed Sage's arm. "Let's throw Jamie a belated birthday party."

"Yes, we should!"

"No, no," Sierra protested. "He doesn't need any more presents. Clay's bought him too many already."

"But not the rest of his family," Caitlin insisted. "We want to dote on him, too."

Sierra wavered, remembering Gail Stevenson's baby shower. She'd tried to coerce Sierra into attending, but she simply couldn't bring herself to go. That evening, Gail had shown Sierra all the baby gifts her family and friends had given her, never noticing Sierra's anguish.

"You have enough on your plates already," Sierra insisted, "getting ready for your own babies."

"Are you kidding?" Sage exclaimed. "It'll be a blast. We'll have it next weekend. Before the horse auction."

"Is that enough time?"

"Plenty."

"I don't know."

"Please, Sierra." Caitlin touched her arm. "The party isn't just for Jamie. It's for all of us. We love him and you."

How could Sierra say no to that? "All right."

Sage and Caitlin chatted enthusiastically about the party, with Sierra insisting they limit the guest list to a reasonable number.

"My mom will want to come." Caitlin had taken out a pen and paper and was making notes.

Jamie, who'd been good as gold up till now, decided to drop his spoon and bowl of applesauce on the floor.

Sierra leaned over to retrieve it. She sat up and saw a hostess escorting two women to a booth. Her breath caught as she recognized the younger one.

Jessica Rovedatti. Or Jessica Duvall if she hadn't taken back her maiden name after her divorce from Clay.

An invisible wall of ice slammed into her, shaking her to her core.

Sierra set the bowl and spoon on the table, fumbling slightly.

"Honey, are you okay?" Caitlin asked.

"I'm… Um, yeah."

Caitlin turned her head and hissed, "Oh, my God! I don't believe it."

She'd recognized Clay's ex-wife, having grown up in the area and dated Ethan for years.

"What?" Sage shifted in her seat to see. "Who?"

"Please," Sierra implored in a hushed voice. "I don't want her looking over here."

Too late. Jessica acknowledged Sierra with a cool nod, no smile, and returned her attention to her lunch companion.

Sierra drew in a shaky breath.

"Who is she?" Sage demanded.

Caitlin pushed aside her empty plate. "Clay's ex-wife."

"Oh. *Ooohh.* I thought she lived in Texas."

So had Sierra.

"Wonder what she's doing here?" Caitlin peered across the dining room, trying to be discreet and not succeeding.

Sierra clasped Jamie's hand protectively in hers, the image of Jessica's cool nod replaying over and over inside her head.

The waitress couldn't come fast enough with their tab.

Chapter Thirteen

Sierra put Jamie down for his nap shortly after returning from the diner. Taking the nursery monitor with her, she crossed the backyard and went into the house.

"You home?" she hollered.

"Hey!" Clay's voice carried from the living room. "In here."

She found him on the floor, surrounded by an assortment of large plastic pieces and a sheet of instructions lying open beside him. He wore basketball shorts, a sweatshirt with the sleeves cut off and a backward baseball cap. A far cry from his typical cowboy shirt and jeans.

If she weren't upset over seeing Jessica at the diner, she'd joke with him about his attire.

"What are you doing?"

"Putting this together." He pointed to an empty cardboard box. On the side was a picture of a miniature slide and a child going down it, his arms lifted high over his head. "He had such a good time at the indoor playground, I thought he'd like this."

She wanted to admonish Clay for spoiling Jamie but held her tongue. "Where are you going to put it?"

"I thought on the back porch." He glanced at the nursery monitor in her hand. "Jamie asleep?"

"Yeah. He's wiped out after our shopping spree." She sat

on the sofa and watched Clay. He assembled the slide with the meticulous attention of a master craftsman.

"Have fun with the girls?"

"I did." For most of the morning. "We had lunch at the Corner Diner."

He must have discerned the tiny note of distress in her voice for he asked, "Everything all right?"

"Something did happen."

"What?"

"Jessica was there. At the diner."

He set the plastic pieces he'd been holding aside. "She was?"

"Having lunch with a woman I didn't recognize. I'm surprised she's back in Mustang Valley. I thought her family moved to Avondale."

Clay picked up the slide pieces he'd set down and attempted to fit them together. When he spoke, his tone was measured. "She's in town visiting her godmother."

"You knew?"

"I talked to her recently."

The revelation shocked Sierra almost as much as seeing Jessica. "When?"

"She called last week to tell me she was coming to Arizona for a couple weeks."

"I see." Every insecurity Sierra had thought she'd beaten, every fear she'd set to rest, returned in one violent, blinding wave.

Clay had been in contact with Jessica. Behind Sierra's back!

"It's not unusual for divorced people to stay in touch," he said.

"Are you in touch with her a lot?"

"Once in a while we email or talk on the phone."

"You couldn't tell me this?"

"I didn't want to upset you."

"Is there anything else you're hiding from me?"

He got to his feet and joined her on the couch. "I'm not hiding anything from you. I swear."

Why then did she feel betrayed?

"Does she know about Jamie?"

"Yes."

"You told her when she called you last week."

"Before then."

Once in a while was beginning to sound like every week.

"I told her about *us* when I saw her the other day."

"You *saw* her?" Anger seeped in, filling the cracks he was leaving in her heart.

She couldn't sit here another second and listen to him try to convince her that communicating with Jessica was perfectly normal.

"There was a form she needed to sign so I could remove her as beneficiary on my life insurance policy and add you and Jamie."

He'd added *her* and Jamie as his beneficiaries? That took some of the wind from her sails.

"I could have shipped the form to her," Clay went on to explain, "but when she said she was coming to town for a visit, I decided to handle it in person. Jessica's forgetful sometimes, and I wanted to make the change now."

Everything Clay said made sense. And yet…

"Didn't you take her off your insurance policy when you divorced?"

"Honestly, it didn't occur to me until I went to renew the policy."

"Do you still love her?"

He reached up and rubbed his knuckles along Sierra's cheek. "I haven't loved her for a long, long time. But I did once, and she was a big part of my life for many years. It isn't always easy to let go, even in the wake of hurt and resentment."

"You can't let go of Jessica?" How could he still cling to her after what she'd done to him?

How could he ever love Sierra?

"Believe me, I have. She's just a person from my past. You and Jamie are my future."

Suddenly, comprehension dawned. "She's the one unable to let go of you."

"I think being single again isn't as much fun as she anticipated."

"Poor Jessica."

Clay pressed a light kiss to Sierra's mouth. "You have nothing to worry about where she's concerned."

No? Jessica had always exuded a sort of power over Clay. He'd been crazy mad in love with her, and she'd expertly wrapped him around her little finger.

Sierra wanted her back in Texas in the worst way.

God, why had she agreed to joint custody? She should have fought tooth and nail for sole custody.

Then, she wouldn't be scared to death "the other woman" would be helping Clay raise Jamie on the days he had his son.

"Morning." Clay breezed into the kitchen, tucking his shirt into his jeans.

Sierra stood at the counter, fixing breakfast—for Jamie.

Not that Clay expected her to cook for him, they usually shared the chore. But since they'd taken their relationship to the next level, so to speak, whenever she scrambled eggs and toasted bread for Jamie, she made extra for Clay.

He could always have oatmeal in the office, he supposed.

"What's on your schedule for today?" he asked, kissing the top of Jamie's head. The boy sat in his high chair, Oreo beside him, waiting for any food that found its way to the floor.

Clay would have kissed Sierra, too, but she'd remained aloof since yesterday afternoon and the Jessica conversation. What were the odds his girlfriend and his ex-wife would be at the diner the same time?

In hindsight, he should have told Sierra about Jessica's visit and the beneficiary form. Live and learn.

"I need to run to the discount store today for diapers and baby food," she said. "Then hit the office."

Pouring himself a cup of coffee, Clay sat at the table and combed his fingers through his shower-dampened hair. "I assume you're still mad at me."

"I'm not mad." She set a plate in front of Jamie. He immediately fed a toast triangle to Oreo. "No, honey bun, those are for you. Oreo's already had breakfast." She handed Jamie a baby spoon for his eggs.

He preferred using his fingers.

"You sure you're not mad?" Clay presented his most appealing smile. "Because you're acting it. I know you didn't sleep well last night."

"You explained everything. I have nothing to worry about, right?"

"Right."

She started loading the dishwasher. "Okay then."

It wasn't as if anything had happened with Jessica. She and Clay had met at a coffee shop, she'd signed the form, he'd showed her pictures of Jamie, they'd talked for ten minutes, and then he'd left.

Wait a minute! On second thought, something did happen. A big something. When he'd left the coffee shop, he didn't glance back once or give her a moment's consideration until Sierra mentioned seeing her.

What a relief. He hadn't lied. He was finally and truly over Jessica.

Before he could tell Sierra, her cell phone rang. She retrieved it from the counter and glanced at the caller ID, her expression puzzled.

"Hello. Yes, good morning," she said brightly after a pause. "I'm still interested." Casting Clay a guilty look, she walked into the family room, the phone pressed to her ear.

She didn't want Clay to hear her conversation. Naturally, his curiosity skyrocketed. He went over and played with Jamie, stealing bites of his eggs and toast, much to Jamie's amusement. Clay heard only a word here and there of Sierra's phone call, not enough to decipher it.

"Thank you very much for considering me," she said. "I look forward to the call."

Clay clearly heard that last part and frowned.

She returned to the kitchen, murmuring, "Sorry about that," and resumed loading the dishwasher.

The hell with respecting her privacy. "Was that about a job?"

She pivoted to face him, her mouth set in a determined line. "Yes."

Holy cow, she was really mad at him.

"I didn't realize you were looking for a new one."

"I'm not. This is a company I applied to before I started working for you. They're hiring a new position and going through the résumés on file."

"Are you seriously considering it?" The few bites of Jamie's breakfast Clay had eaten sat like stones in his stomach. She was quitting him.

"It's pays well and the hours are flexible."

"I'll give you a raise."

She exhaled sharply. "It's just a phone interview. I'm one of a dozen."

"We have an agreement." He was ashamed at himself for sinking so low as to use their employment contract.

"This job doesn't start till May, after the contract expires."

"It automatically renews."

"If I don't opt out."

"Are you ready to put Jamie in day care?"

"I think I will be by then."

"You're doing this because of Jessica."

"She has *nothing* to do with me considering a potential job opportunity."

"Yes, she does. You're mad because I met her the other day and didn't tell you."

"I don't care who you—" She stopped, let her shoulders sag. "That's not true. I do care. Jessica is a sore spot with me. But I'm not mad at you, just hurt."

Clay rose from his chair and crossed the kitchen in three strides. Wrapping his arms around Sierra's waist, he pulled her to him.

"You have every right to be hurt. I was an insensitive dope. I thought I was avoiding an argument with you. Instead, I lost your trust."

"You haven't lost my trust. Maybe dented it."

"I promise, if I see or hear from Jessica again, not that I plan to, I'll tell you." He squeezed Sierra tight, needing her to squeeze him in return. She didn't. "Interview with the company. If they make you an offer, I only ask you give me a chance to beat it."

"We'll see."

He set her away from him and studied her face. "You won't?"

"No, I'll see about interviewing. I'm not that interested in the job."

He kissed her, drank her in, was reborn when she at last responded.

Given his choice, he'd carry her to his bedroom, make endless love to her until he wiped Jessica completely from her mind and heart. Unfortunately, they couldn't leave Jamie in his high chair and there were a half dozen phone calls waiting for him to place the second he set foot in the office.

"I'll see you later." He nuzzled her ear before reluctantly releasing her.

She usually giggled when he did that and told him not to tickle her.

"I'll be in after lunch. I have to type up those new contracts for your signature. And I'm hoping to hear back from the TV stations. Did I tell you I might have a lead on some grant money?"

She was all business. Normally, Clay liked talking shop with her. Today, it felt as if she'd erected a ten-foot wall to keep him at a distance and her heart safe.

Sierra perched on the wingback chair in her family's living room, a pile of unopened gifts on one side of her, a pile of opened gifts on the other. Jamie sat on the floor, shredding wrapping paper and unraveling bows. When Cassie and Isa weren't fussing over him, they picked through the gifts, deciding which one Sierra should open next.

The women guests huddled close to her, oohing and ahhing at the appropriate moments. The men occupied the farther corners of the room, conversing amongst themselves and participating as little as possible.

Sierra was reminded of the wedding last month when Caitlin and Sage had sat in this same room, opening their gifts. She couldn't believe all the trouble they'd gone through for her. In a week, they'd pulled together a baby shower that was better than anything she could have hoped for.

The Powell house and ranch, a sad and lonely place for so many years, was bursting with people and activity and, most importantly, love. Not to mention children. From none to five in barely over a year. That had to be some kind of record.

Seeing her brothers and father content warmed Sierra's heart. She'd been happy like them for a while, too. Then, she'd found out Jessica was back in Mustang Valley and Clay had had a meeting with her. Sierra really didn't think anything had transpired between them other than signing the form.

It was the what-might-happen that had her sleeping poorly, phone-interviewing for a job she had no interest in and watching Clay's every move, searching for telltale signs that he was sneaking away to be with Jessica.

"Open this one." Cassie set a large box in front of Sierra. "It's from Grandpa."

She pasted a happy smile on her face and attacked the wrapping paper. "Dad, this is huge and heavy." The plain cardboard box containing the gift revealed nothing about its contents.

"I hope Jamie likes it," he said.

Sierra cut through the tape, opened the top of the box and peered inside. "What! You didn't." She rolled her eyes. He was absolutely hopeless. "A saddle? You bought him a saddle?"

Jamie came over to investigate.

"Let me see that." Clay scooted forward from where he'd been sitting on the couch. He pulled a child-size saddle from the box, holding on to it by the horn for everyone to see. "Look, Jamie, now all we need is a pony."

"No pony!" Sierra protested.

The women agreed. The men acted like they didn't hear.

"Thanks, Wayne," Clay said, still admiring the saddle and showing it to Jamie.

"Yeah, thanks, Dad," Sierra muttered.

"I didn't know what toys to get him." Her father's pleased-with-himself grin stretched from ear to ear.

"I'm surprised no one here got Jamie boots," Blythe remarked.

Ethan's face instantly drooped.

Sierra glowered at him. "Don't tell me."

"A cowboy needs boots."

Sierra wanted to be mad, but it was impossible in the presence of such love and generosity. She was truly blessed.

"Open this one." Isa handed Sierra a shirt box wrapped in paper with cartoon horses galloping over plains. "It doesn't say who it's from."

A card lay atop a miniature cowboy outfit, complete with Western shirt, jeans and even chaps, all about three sizes too big for Jamie.

"How adorable," Caitlin crooned.

Isa held the card out to Sierra.

"You go ahead and read it, honey." She was busy admiring the chaps, which appeared custom-made.

"It says 'to Jamie from Grandpa.'"

"Dad! Another present?"

"Huh?" Wayne squinted at the card. "I didn't buy that."

A jolt went through Sierra, and the chaps fell into her lap. *Not now, not yet, not today.*

Her gaze flew to Clay. He knew, too.

Before either of them could react, Blythe dropped the bombshell. "It's from Jamie's other grandfather. He asked me to bring it."

"Other grandfather?" Isa examined the card as if it held the answer.

No one else spoke. Moved. Breathed.

"Yes, dear. Clay's father."

"Dammit to hell!" Gavin slapped his thighs and shot

from his chair. "What's that bastard doing sending Jamie a present?"

"Sweetheart, the girls." Sage's eyes cut to their daughters.

Blythe looked stricken. Her fingers covered her mouth, and her cheeks drained of color.

Sierra's father's cheeks flushed a vivid red.

As if by silent consensus, everyone not a Powell or Duvall or married to one left the room.

"Cassie, would you and Isa take Jamie to the den for me, please?" Sierra was amazed at the steadiness of her voice.

They did as she asked, grabbing some of the new toys.

"Why would Duvall send a gift?" Gavin repeated. He was up and pacing the floor.

"He's Jamie's grandfather," Clay said.

"I wish he wasn't."

"Gavin!" Sage gasped.

"That man is a snake."

"Watch what you say," Clay warned, rising from the sofa. "You may be my business partner and buddy but I won't tolerate you insulting my family."

"I thought you hated him, too."

"I don't. I was angry at him. But I've since learned he's not entirely responsible for what happened to you."

"You're screwed in the head if you think that."

"Enough," Ethan barked at Gavin. "Sit down, both of you, and shut up."

"You're siding with Clay?"

"I'm refereeing."

Clay sat. Gavin resumed pacing.

"I'm sorry," Blythe murmured miserably. "When he asked me to deliver the gift, I didn't think it would be a problem. Considering you've reconciled, and he's been seeing Jamie."

"You let him near Jamie?" Gavin raged at Sierra. "How could you?"

She straightened her spine defensively. "I know how you feel about Bud—"

"I assumed I felt the same as you."

"It's my fault," Clay interjected. "I insisted on Jamie meeting my dad. Sierra didn't want him to."

"But you still allowed it?" Gavin demanded of her.

He was Sierra's big brother, used to ordering her around. She was tired of it, of all the men in her life thinking they knew what was best for her, including her old boss. Who was Ken Stevenson to judge how fit she'd be as a mother?

"I did allow it, and I'm glad. Bud is a good grandfather to Jamie."

"He's a thief."

Sierra stood and glared at Gavin, hands on her hips. She refused to let him intimidate her. "He gave us fifteen more months with Mom we wouldn't have had without that heart transplant."

"Then he stole our land."

"He did no such thing." All eyes turned to Sierra's father, his earlier flush replaced by a mask of pain and devastation. "I lost our land."

"What are you talking about?" Some of the razor-sharp steel had left Gavin's voice.

Yes, Sierra thought, what *was* her father talking about?

"Never mind." He turned his head to stare out the window.

"Wayne." Clay's gentle tone was in stark contrast to all the yelling. "It's time. They have a right to know, and you have a duty to tell them."

Her father coughed, and Sierra saw he was biting back a sob.

"It's all right, Dad."

"No. Nothing's been right for years."

His listlessness reminded her too much of those desperate days during his depression. "You don't have to say anything."

"I couldn't make the payments. The loan was due, then overdue, then long overdue." He cleared his throat, sniffed, returned his attention to the room. "Bud gave me plenty of chances. I didn't take them. I'd lost your mother, lost myself to grief, then the business. I couldn't have scraped enough money together to buy back ten acres, much less all six hundred. I was sure if you kids found out, you'd leave me, too, like your mother did, and I'd be all alone."

"You *let* him sell our land?" Gavin's incredulousness mirrored Sierra's and everyone else's.

Her father was mistaken. Confused. He wouldn't have intentionally allowed an investor to buy their land and then tell everyone Bud stole it. That would be…a lie.

"Dad," she insisted, "don't feel the need to cover for Bud just because I let him see Jamie."

"I'm not covering for Bud." Her father's sad gaze pleaded for understanding. "He's covering for me."

"You're wrong, he stole our land. Who would allow people to think the worst of them all these years if they did nothing wrong?"

"Someone who's a better friend to me than I was to him."

Sierra covered her face with her hands.

Gavin sat on the couch, then sank defeated into the cushions.

"I'm the one responsible," Blythe said softly, her eyes misting. "I didn't realize Bud would have to sell your land to settle our divorce. I thought you were making the payments."

"Not your fault, either, Blythe. I should have leveled with my kids. Been honest from the start."

Conversation continued around Sierra, but she hardly heard a word.

Her father, not Bud, was responsible for them losing their land. Their cattle business. Their reputation. Their heritage. How could he? And how could he have committed such an appalling injustice to a friend? A man who'd given him money for his wife's heart transplant surgery.

"I apologize, Clay. And to you, Blythe."

They assured Sierra's father they held no grudge against him.

What about Sierra and her brothers? Didn't their father owe them an apology, too?

Their lives would have been entirely different if he'd told the truth. Her brothers and Clay would have remained friends rather than become enemies. She and Clay wouldn't have had to hide their affair. He and Bud wouldn't have been estranged for years. She could have come home when she got pregnant instead of giving Jamie up for adoption.

Oh, God, what had her father done?

She thought of Clay's betrayal when he'd reconciled with Jessica and married her. It was nothing compared to this. He hadn't wiped out two families.

Suddenly chilled to the bone, Sierra rubbed her upper arms.

"Dad felt awful about having to sell your land," Clay said. "He wanted to extend the loan again, but he lost money in the stock market."

Sierra's hands stilled. "You knew about this?"

"Dad told me last month."

"Another conversation you decided to keep from me?" She ignored the stares from her family members.

"I didn't keep it from you," Clay said, his voice annoyingly reasonable. "I told you more than once to ask your dad."

"You didn't say he was lying to me."

"It wasn't my place. And I'm not sure you'd have believed me if I had. If anything, you'd have packed up and moved out."

True enough, but that didn't temper her mounting anger and resentment.

Suddenly, the room tilted at an odd angle. Dizzy and nauseous, Sierra caught her head as it fell forward.

Clay appeared beside her. "Are you all right?"

"No, I'm not." The world as she knew it was forever changed.

He stroked her hair. "We're going to sort through this."

She almost laughed. Hysterically. He'd said *sort through this* as if they were evaluating a collection of old odds and ends in the garage. "I don't think it's as simple as that."

"Sierra, sweetie," her father implored, "I can see you're upset."

Upset hardly described her current emotional state. She stared at him. His features were the same as always, and, yet, in some ways, they were those of a total stranger's.

Her legs started to tremble. "I have to go."

Clay took her elbow and steadied her.

She pulled away and snapped, "I don't need your help. Some truthfulness, now *that* I could use."

He stepped back, her hurtful remark hitting the bull's-eye dead center. She stormed off.

Gavin called after her. Ethan, too. She didn't answer.

The other guests had assembled in the kitchen. Sierra hurried past them and out the door. Reaching the sanctuary of the patio, she burst into tears.

So much deception. All of them. Clay, her father, Bud, the Stevensons. And let's not forget herself. Was she any better than her father just because she'd come clean sooner?

Poor Jamie deserved better role models than the ones he had.

What would Dr. Brewster say when she heard about this?

Sierra did laugh then. Bitterly.

"Hey."

She jerked at hearing Clay. "What are you doing here?"

He approached slowly, concern etched on his features. "I hate seeing you distressed."

"Then get back in the house because I'm going to be distressed for a while."

"Come on. Let's take a walk."

"I don't want to walk."

"What about a glass of water?"

"I'm fine."

"What can I do?"

"Check on Jamie for me."

"Is that all?"

She faced him. "Clay, there are just some things you can't control. My entire life going to hell in a handbasket is one of them."

"I'll be waiting inside."

She'd wanted him gone, and she'd got it.

A moment later, she was alone, drifting in what felt like an alternative reality. She hadn't meant to bite Clay's head off. He was trying to be supportive in her time of need.

Why, then, couldn't she turn to him and accept that support?

Because he'd been secretly communicating with Jessica and had had a meeting with her.

And she'd borne Clay's son and gave him up for adoption without telling Clay.

How could the two of them have a secure and happy future with a foundation based on deception?

Leave. Now. The urge came on her again.

She did better on her own, when she could hear her own thoughts, organize her priorities, gain a different perspective.

But where to go?

Removing her cell phone from her pocket, she dialed her attorney Roberto's number, vaguely aware she'd done this before, with disastrous results.

It didn't stop her.

Roberto answered with a brisk "Hello, Sierra."

She didn't miss a beat. "I'm sorry to impose on you, but I don't have anyone else to call."

"What is it?"

"I need a place to stay for a few days. Possibly a week."

Chapter Fourteen

Clay could be patient when the situation called for it. Not today. He was on the verge of exploding.

Sierra had been in the casita for the last hour while he occupied himself in the house and yard with a dozen menial tasks. He'd given her the space she'd asked for, at her family's home and here. But he wasn't going to be shut out indefinitely.

After she'd abandoned the birthday party to sit alone on the back patio and, in his opinion, brood, he'd spoken to her father and brothers. Gavin stayed sore at Clay but did shake his hand eventually. Tensions had remained high, however, and he couldn't wait to leave.

Wayne had significant lost ground to make up, and Clay felt sorry for the man. His first concern, however, was Sierra.

She'd received a momentous blow. But she would recover, and they'd move on. Clay was practical that way.

Crossing the yard, he opened the gate to the casita's small courtyard, remembering the night they'd first made love and he'd jumped the gate in haste. The door was slightly ajar, an indicator that Jamie was napping. Sierra never left the door unlocked if he was awake in case he wandered outside.

Clay knocked and called softly, "Sierra."

She didn't answer. Was she napping, too? Probably. Emotional displays were exhausting. He stood there a moment, debated whether to knock again or return later.

"Come in."

Apparently, she was awake.

He entered quietly so as not to disturb Jamie and came face-to-face with her packing a suitcase.

"What are you doing?"

"I'm leaving for a while, taking Jamie with me. I need some time alone to think."

Leaving? Was she joking? "You can't think here? I won't bother you if that's what concerns you."

She set a pair of folded slacks on top of the already full suitcase and pressed down on the clothes to compress them. "I'd rather get away from everyone and everything. Clear my head. Gain some perspective. Being here reminds me of everything. Confuses me and clouds my judgment."

"And your judgment isn't clouded at your dad's?"

"I'm not staying there."

When she'd originally said she was leaving, Clay had been mad. Now, he was scared. "Where, then?"

She glanced at Jamie sleeping in the crib.

"Sierra. Tell me."

"My attorney's home."

"For how long?"

"Three or four days."

"This is bullshit," he spat out.

"Not so loud, you'll wake up Jamie."

Reining in his frustration, he continued in a lower voice, "You can't just leave."

Her chin jutted out. "You promised me when I moved in that I wasn't chained to you or this place."

"You're not. You can go anytime. But I'm asking you to stay. We can't work on our relationship when we're apart."

"This is about a lot more than our relationship."

"We're in the same boat, Sierra. My dad lied to me, too."

"There's a difference. Your dad's motives were good—to spare his friend embarrassment. My dad's motives were to save himself. I want to forgive him, and I will. I just need time alone and to talk to someone who doesn't have a personal stake in this."

"Good idea. We can see Dr. Brewster together."

She closed the suitcase lid. "Don't take this wrong, but you have a strong personality and strong opinions, and I'm too easily influenced. If I talk to Dr. Brewster, it will be by myself."

"Go easier on your dad. None of us is guiltless when it comes to lying."

"None of us perpetuated a lie for years and years."

She might have, if he hadn't been there for her surprise party the day she arrived home.

His face must have reflected his thoughts for she zippered the suitcase closed with an angry jerk of her hand.

"Are you punishing me for Jessica?"

"Don't be ridiculous." Her denial was weak at best.

How long until she forgave *him?*

"Okay, stay at your attorney's house for a few days. Just leave Jamie with me."

"What!"

"Jamie's head doesn't need any clearing, and his perspective is fine."

"Absolutely not."

"You've said yourself over and over that he's had too much disruption in his life. I don't think we should put him through any more, especially when it isn't necessary."

"I'm taking him with me."

"We have a joint-custody agreement. I want my five days starting now."

"You can't do that."

"I'm pretty sure I can. If need be, we'll let a judge decide."

Her chest rose and fell rapidly. "You haven't enforced the custody agreement before."

"That's because you were living here." *And we were sleeping together.* "Now, you're leaving."

"I'll be gone a week at the most."

"No problem. I can watch Jamie for a week."

"Don't do this, Clay."

"I'm asking you the same thing."

"I can't stay here," she said in a thready whisper.

"Why?"

"It's too confining. Too crowded."

No more confining or crowded than her attorney's home. "That's what you do, isn't it? When things get tough, you run for the hills."

"I do not!"

"Oh, come on. You turned down a full-ride scholarship and instead went to college in another state right after your mom died and the ranch started to fail. You cut off your family and me when you found out you were pregnant. You left your old job and your friends in California to come here because you couldn't handle your anxieties and being a single mother. And now you're slinking off to your attorney's house after a fight with your dad."

"It was more than a fight."

"Grow up, Sierra. Start facing your problems instead of avoiding them."

"How dare you criticize me!" Anger flashed in those wide eyes. "I may not cope well with my problems but at least I'm not a control freak."

"This isn't a matter of me trying to control you. It's you taking my son from me. *Again!* If clearing your head and getting perspective is really your goal, you can do that without Jamie."

"You know I can't be separated from him."

"You should have thought of that before deciding to leave."

"I'm not the bad person here. My dad is."

"Don't go, Sierra. When has leaving ever worked out for you?"

"When has pushing people into doing what you want ever worked out for you? Is that why Jessica left?"

Clay recoiled as if stabbed with an iron poker.

Was Sierra right? Had he pushed Jessica into having children when she wasn't ready? Put his own desire to start a family ahead of hers for a career?

"What about your job? You leaving that, too?"

"I'm sorry to put you in a spot."

"We have an employment contract."

"That allows for sick time."

"You're not sick."

"Whatever." She grabbed a tissue from the box on the nightstand and dabbed her nose. "Short my pay."

"The wild-horse auction is next weekend. Everyone is counting on you."

"All the files are in order, and I left detailed notes on the desk. A temp can handle the rest."

"Is there nothing you care about more than yourself?"

"Is there *anything* you care about *besides* yourself?" she shot back.

"You. My son. Our dads. Patching up this god-awful mess and putting our families back on track. I'm not sure how to accomplish that, but I damn well know the answer isn't running off to my attorney's."

She set the suitcase on the floor. "You pegged me earlier. I fold under pressure. And whether you intend it or not, you pressure me. I'm not the kind of person who stands up for herself well."

"You're standing up to me."

"Are you really going to fight me for Jamie?"

"If you walk out that door, I most certainly am."

"What if I don't go to my attorney's? What if I stay at my dad's instead?"

"I thought you said you couldn't go there, either."

"I'm thinking you're right. I should face my dad. Deal with his lie."

"Then by all means, go." He was through pleading with her. "But leave Jamie here."

"You can visit him every day at the ranch."

For someone so adamant about not seeing her dad a minute ago, she was making a pretty quick turnaround.

"Do you really need space or do you simply want to get away from me?"

She closed her eyes. "I don't know anymore."

Nothing she'd said until now hurt worse than that. "We have a custody agreement, and we're going to stick to it."

"It feels like you're the one punishing me." She pressed a hand to her chest, rubbed it as if her heart ached. "Why don't you just admit it? You don't trust me."

"Should I? You did hide my son from me."

"And you've hidden things from me, too. Pretty recently, in fact."

"I told you, I was trying to avoid an argument."

"Well, big surprise. We're arguing."

Clay lost his temper, aware he was exhibiting the very stereotypical control-freak trait she'd accused him of. "I've bent over backward for you. The casita. The job. Letting you take Jamie with you to the office. The counseling sessions. I've given a hundred and ten percent."

"I've given, too. I agreed to move in with you for Jamie's sake and our relationship. And I've been a damn good employee."

"Good employees don't quit with no notice."

"I'll be back."

"Permanently or to pick up Jamie?"

"That's not fair."

Clay expelled a harsh breath. "I can't live every day wondering if you'll disappear because my preference to eat dinner at six is too controlling."

"I'm not that extreme."

"I've been committed to you and Jamie since the day you returned. I wish you could say the same."

"A short breather to reevaluate and take stock of the situation isn't a lack of commitment."

Jamie woke up and started to cry. Incredibly, he'd slept through the entire argument.

Sierra and Clay started toward him and bottlenecked at the foot of the crib. They stared at each other in stormy silence for several seconds, neither giving an inch.

Finally, Clay let her pass. Apparently his dad did raise him to be a gentleman.

Sierra lifted Jamie into her arms. The second he saw Clay, he reached for him, his face puffy and mottled from sleep.

"Hey, there, pal."

"Da, da, da, da."

Sierra's features caved, her pain striking him square in the gut.

In one afternoon she'd had her entire belief system felled. That would send even the strongest individual retreating to lick their wounds. He was about to tell her to take Jamie with her when she abruptly handed him to Clay.

"All this fighting is getting us nowhere."

He went weak with relief. She'd changed her mind. They were going to solve their problems and everything would go back to the way it was.

"I agree," he said. "Let's not talk anymore tonight. We'll have some dinner, take Jamie on a walk."

"You can. I won't be here." She went to the bed and grabbed her suitcase. "We'll start with two days, then go to five. I'll see you Monday evening when I pick up Jamie. Or you can drop him off at Dad's, whichever's more convenient for you."

Clay held Jamie close, like a shield, words escaping him.

Of all the times for her to spontaneously overcome her separation anxieties.

"I love you, honey bun." She gave Jamie a desperate hug and kiss on the cheek. Then, looking straight ahead, marched out the door, the only sign of her distress a slight wobble in her gait.

She was either the bravest person Clay knew or the biggest coward.

What about him?

Right this moment, he was alone.

"Ma, ma, ma." Jamie poked Clay on the side of the head.

He could imagine his son saying, "Hey, idiot. You just let the woman we love leave."

And he'd be right.

THE WILD-HORSE AUCTION was starting in—Sierra glanced at her watch—two hours.

Unable to completely walk away from the job, she'd handled several last-minute tasks from home—her father's home—and spoken daily on the phone with the temp Clay had hired. It wasn't the same.

She could see the auction unfolding in her mind's eye.

The ranch hands grooming and exercising the mustangs under her brothers' careful supervision so they would look their best and behave well. The foreman and his crew grading the dirt and insuring the arena was in tip-top condition, the bleachers swept, the pens tidy and the grounds spotless.

Any minute, the auctioneer and his assistant would arrive

and set up in the announcer's booth. Dallas was probably arranging her photographer's table and inventorying her supplies. The media would arrive soon. One local TV station had agreed to send a reporter and camera operator and a small local paper had promised coverage.

The only individual not showing up was the head cashier. Her.

Sierra had recruited Sage to take over rather than simply assist, as was the original plan. Cashiering wasn't complicated, and there were the notes Sierra had left. Sage would have no trouble.

Sierra moped. She was a good employee, not the kind who abandoned ship in the middle of a big event.

Yet she'd done exactly that. Left her job, her son and Clay.

Talk about selfish.

She missed them. All of them. Clay, too.

Those last weeks together were the happiest she'd had since their affair. If only he'd given her those few days she needed to think, trusted her enough not to take off with Jamie, she'd be with him now.

No sooner had she shown up on her father's doorstep a week ago than the two of them had talked. Unresolved issues remained, but they were making headway. With Gavin and Ethan as well. Not that Ethan had been upset with her. Gavin—that was a different story. He was disappointed she wasn't working the auction. After several awkward meals, they'd cleared the air enough to eat companionably if not noisily and rowdily like before.

Sierra hadn't realized how similar she and her father were—they both tended to avoid their problems. Where they differed was that she ran while her father shut down completely.

Checking her watch again, she sighed. She should be at the auction.

After all the hurt she'd caused her family, all the assistance they'd given her, she owed them not to bail at the last hour. In this valley, mustangs were synonymous with the Powell name and the plight of wild horses was close to their hearts, a vital part of their personal history to pass down to their children and grandchildren. To Jamie.

It was also a cause important to Clay.

He had Jamie, would for another four days as per their parenting schedule.

She hadn't forgotten about her son. Heaven forbid. But she didn't obsess about him when he wasn't with her. Not anymore. The breakup with Clay—she'd stopped kidding herself and calling it "time away"—had had one positive impact on her. She'd mostly gotten over her separation anxiety. There were moments, but then she'd remind herself Clay was a good father and wouldn't let anything happen to Jamie.

She wished he'd taken the same tender care of her love for him.

Sierra didn't regret her decision. It really was for the best, as she kept telling herself. Clay must agree. He didn't act as though he wanted a reconciliation when they met to hand over Jamie.

God, that sounded awful. Their son wasn't a borrowed tool to be exchanged when the other person was done using it.

She wondered if Clay had Jamie with him at the auction or if he'd hired Cassie to babysit. No, her niece would be with her fellow equestrian drill team members selling refreshments at the concession stand.

Did the drill team need more ice? Sierra could buy some and take it over. She'd be welcomed.

What message would that send Clay? She'd been wrong? She was sorry? She wanted to try again? She wasn't a quitter and finished the jobs she started?

Apparently she was less dedicated to relationships than jobs.

She'd been so scared after seeing Jessica in the diner and discovering Clay had met with her, terrified when her father's duplicity was revealed. It was too much like looking at her own reflection.

Sierra had once viewed honesty as fluid, able to change shape depending on the individual's needs.

It was an excuse she'd used to justify her own actions.

The last few weeks had taught her much.

What to do with her new education?

She tackled the laundry in an attempt to stop dwelling on the auction and Clay. In her bedroom—the bedroom that would belong to Gavin and Sage's baby once he or she was born—she grabbed the laundry bag.

Finding a new place to live and a new job were a priority, but she'd been dragging her feet, even turning down a second, in-person, interview with the company that had called. When she'd mentioned her lack of motivation to Dr. Brewster, the counselor had turned the tables on Sierra by posing questions like "Why do you think you're procrastinating?" and "How do you feel about quitting your job?"

Miserable, all right? I feel miserable.

Sierra took her frustration out on the dirty clothes, ruthlessly stuffing them into the washing machine. As she was making a second trip to the laundry room with some of the girls' clothes, the doorbell rang.

She glimpsed through the peephole but didn't recognize the caller, whose face was averted as she dug through her purse. It must be one of the ranch customers with a problem. Sierra opened the door.

"Hello, can I—" Her vocal chords froze.

"Hi, Sierra. I'm glad you're here. I hope you don't mind me showing up without calling first."

Oh, yes, she minded.

"I wasn't sure you'd see me."

No fooling.

"Can I come in? I promise to take no more than a minute. I'm leaving for Texas tomorrow and wanted to talk to you."

Convinced she was making a giant mistake, Sierra stepped aside to let Jessica enter.

Chapter Fifteen

"Care to sit?" Sierra indicated the living room with a flimsy wave of her hand. Had she really just invited Clay's ex-wife into the house?

Jessica's gaze swept the interior as she followed Sierra. "I'd forgotten how charming and homey this place is."

"It's been a while, I suppose."

"Years."

Jessica had visited the Powells on occasion when she and Clay were dating.

"I'm sorry about your divorce." Good grief. Could Sierra have made a stupider remark? Her brain must have disconnected from her mouth.

"Thank you." Jessica sat on the sofa, brushed her stylishly messy bangs from her face and smoothed her wrinkle-free pants.

"What do you want to talk about?" Her initial surprise having passed, Sierra was curious, though she remained cautious.

"I came to apologize."

"What for?" Her stomach tightened. Something more had happened at Jessica's recent meeting with Clay.

Were his denials nothing but more lies?

"Stealing Clay away from you. Your life, his, and that of

your son, would be vastly different if I'd been less jealous and able to admit Clay wasn't the man for me."

"I'm confused. Are you referring to two years ago?"

Jessica nodded. "I'd heard you and he were seeing each other. Mustang Valley is a small community. I didn't want Clay for myself, but I didn't want anyone else to have him. Not so soon. Not before I'd found a new man." She smiled sadly. "I wasn't the best person in those days. Marriage, failing at it and surviving divorce changed me. Oh, gosh." She looked chagrined. "Did I just utter a cliché?"

Jessica had changed. Goodie for her. As far as Sierra was concerned, one I-came-to-apologize speech didn't make everything okay. Jessica's fickle whims had wreaked chaos on too many lives. "Isn't it a little late for this?"

"Possibly. Possibly not. I heard you had moved out of Clay's casita."

"He told you?" Sierra's twisted stomach turned inside out. He was still communicating with Jessica despite his promise.

"I haven't seen or spoken to Clay since we met at the coffee shop and I signed the insurance form."

"Then how—"

"I saw Caitlin at the clinic yesterday. My godmother's blood-sugar level dropped, and I rushed her in for a quick check. Caitlin mentioned you. Actually, I asked how you and Clay were, and she reluctantly told me."

"Oh." Sierra had jumped to conclusions.

"You know, Clay always wanted children, and he adores Jamie."

"Yes, he does."

"He loves you, too."

Sierra must have misheard. "I beg your pardon?"

"I think he fell in love with you two years ago, he just didn't realize it. He and I had dated a long, long time. Old habits are hard to break." She stood, smoothed her pants again. Caitlin now recognized the gesture as a nervous one. "Don't let him get away again."

The last person in the world Sierra thought she should take advice from was Jessica.

Except the advice was pretty darn good.

She left, and Sierra shut the door behind her, slumping against it. Clay loved her! At least according to Jessica he did.

Sierra had been a fool, and not for the first time. She'd permitted her fear of rejection to color her judgment, manufactured reasons to reject Clay before he rejected her.

How to tell him she loved and trusted him in a way he couldn't possibly misunderstand or misinterpret?

Easy. She'd go to the auction. Where she should have been all morning.

Changing her clothes, she dashed outside to her SUV. The minute she hit the end of the driveway, she pulled her cell phone from her purse. The first call she made was to her father, the second one to Blythe. They were both at the auction. Sierra's request, the same to each of them, was readily and excitedly granted.

Parking at Clay's house, she half walked, half jogged the short distance to the arena. The place was already packed, the bleachers full. She searched frantically for Clay and Jamie, responding with a distracted "Hi, have you seen Clay?" when people greeted her. She finally spotted him near the announcer's stand, being interviewed by the TV reporter. A moment later he noticed her and briefly lost his train of thought before continuing.

She stood to the side and waited until the interview was concluded. The reporter thanked Clay and left with the camera operator to film more footage. Sierra approached slowly.

"If you're looking for Jamie, he's with my mother."

"I know. I didn't come here to see Jamie." She longed to throw herself at him, but his wary expression held her at bay.

"Then why?"

"I've been stupid lately. About work and…other things."

"What other things?" His control cracked a tiny fraction.

She intended to split it wide open. "Give me my job back and I'll tell you."

"THAT MARE AND COLT are the best of the bunch," Ethan observed. "They should bring in decent money."

Clay stood at the far end of the arena fence, half listening to his friend, his attention all over the place. He couldn't take his mind off Sierra.

She'd come back for her job.

Not him.

She'd barely made her cryptic remark about "other things" when Clay was called away to resolve a problem. With a "We'll chat later," she'd hurried to meet with the auctioneer and his assistant. Clay had glimpsed her a short time later scurrying across the open area to the office in the barn.

He'd wanted to talk then, not later, but the auction had started and was quickly in full swing. As cashier, Sierra would be busy processing paperwork and accepting funds for an hour or two after the auction closed.

Could he wait?

"I'm glad the other horses were adopted, I just wish they'd brought higher prices," Ethan continued, unaware of Clay's turmoil. "Unless that grant money comes through, the sanctuary will go broke in a few months."

"We'll think of something," Clay muttered distractedly.

"Hey! What's up?" Ethan elbowed Clay in the ribs. "Sierra tying you in knots again?"

"I'm concentrating on the auction."

"It's like that, you know."

He glanced over his shoulder at the office in the distance. Sierra hadn't emerged since going inside. "What is?"

"When you're in love." Ethan shook his head as if accepting a dismal truth.

"I'm not in love."

"Yeah. Sure. And the sky is green."

Was he in love with Sierra? Clay gave his head a dismal shake mimicking Ethan's.

He was sunk. In love with a woman who didn't love him.

But she had come back. Asked for her old job. Mentioned being stupid about "other things."

"I need to find your sister."

"Wait." Ethan grabbed Clay's jacket sleeve and restrained him. "The bidding is starting on the mare and colt."

They watched as the last two horses up for auction were led into the arena. The auctioneer recounted their history to the audience, when, where and how they'd been rounded up and what training they'd been given. Then he talked up the duo's good qualities, emphasizing their potential as all-around Western pleasure mounts.

"Okee dokie, ladies and gents." His voice rang out from the speakers. "What do you say we open up the bidding at two hundred dollars for the pair."

At first, no one raised their hand. When the price dropped to twenty-five dollars, the bidding took off and didn't stop. The wranglers kept the mare and colt calm while the ring men stationed themselves in front of the bleachers and alerted the auctioneer with a loud whoop when a bid was made.

Before Clay realized it, the price was up to a thousand. Then, two thousand. Twenty-five hundred. Three thousand.

What the heck?

He scanned the audience, trying to determine who was bidding so furiously on the horses. He didn't recognize either of the men, one an old-timer and the other a businessman in a suit and tie.

"Twenty thousand dollars." The call came from the businessman.

The audience fell silent for several shocked seconds, then broke out into hoots and hollers.

"I have twenty thousand dollars," the auctioneer shouted, disbelief in his voice. "Do I have twenty-one thousand?"

"Dang!" The old-timer threw up his arms in defeat. "I'd have to rob a bank."

"Going once, going twice, sold to number…" He waited for the buyer to hold up his card. "Eighty-six."

"Hot damn." Ethan grabbed Clay's arm and jostled it, grinning ridiculously. "That's enough money to run the sanctuary for a year, maybe two."

"Who is that guy?"

"Let's find out. Looks like that TV reporter is about to interview him."

They made their way across the open area to the crowd that had formed around the businessman and the reporter. Sierra waited on the other side. He'd have gone to her but then noticed a man standing beside her. Before he could manage a closer look, someone stepped in front of him and blocked his view.

"Wow," the TV reporter gushed as the camera operator filmed and Dallas snapped pictures, "that was some purchase. Tell us about yourself and your plans for the horses?"

"I didn't buy them for myself. I'm a broker with MRB Trade and Commerce, acting on behalf of my client. He's the one who purchased the horses."

"Can you give us his name?"

"Certainly. He's here, in fact." The broker inclined his head. "Mr. Bud Duvall."

"Your dad?" Ethan exclaimed in a booming voice. "He bought the horses?"

Clay's thoughts exactly. "Excuse me." He wedged between two people in an attempt to get closer, Ethan behind him.

His dad stepped up to the reporter, taking the place of his banker. Sierra, holding Jamie, and Wayne were with him.

What in the world was going on?

Finally, when Clay's patience was about to snap, he and Ethan broke free of the crowd.

The rest of Ethan's family surrounded Clay's father. Gavin, Sage, Caitlin and the girls. Clay's mother was also there.

He went to her. "Mom?"

She took his hand and patted it, then told him, "Shh, your father's talking."

"People who've lived in these parts a long time know that the Duvalls and Powells were once close as kin." Clay's dad nervously wiped his sweaty brow with his handkerchief. "Unfortunately, we had a bit of a falling-out, I guess you'd say. Spent a lot of years being needlessly mad at each other. It took this little guy here to bring us to our senses." He ruffled Jamie's hair. "And this here gal." He squeezed Sierra's shoulder.

Clay watched, stunned.

"I'd like to present this check, twenty thousand for the purchase of the horses and an additional twenty thousand dollars for the Powell Wild Mustang Sanctuary."

A gasp erupted from the crowd.

"I make this donation in memory of Louise Powell." He handed the check to Sierra. "Late wife of my friend Wayne. It can't change what happened, but maybe it, and this boy, will give us a second chance."

Wayne extended his hand to Clay's father, visibly moved. "I can't thank you enough. For *everything*."

"Water under the bridge, pal. Water under the bridge."
Clay's dad pulled Wayne into a warm bear hug.

The rest of the families converged on them. There were
more hugs and tears. Everyone stood back a moment while
Gavin and Clay's dad exchanged words and shook hands.

Clay didn't join his family—his *two* families. He made
straight for Sierra and Jamie.

"You knew about the donation," he said.

"Not until right before the auction started. Your dad met
me in the office."

"He's always liked being the center of attention." Clay
chuckled. "In this case, I approve."

"I was thinking." She jiggled Jamie, who'd started to fuss.
"About *other things?*"

"Yes. If our dads are able to put the past behind them,
maybe we can—"

Clay cut her off with a kiss. Then another and another until
Jamie protested noisily at being squished between them.

"There's something I've been meaning to tell you," he said.
"Something I should have told you weeks ago."

"What?"

"I love you." He lost himself in her startling blue eyes.
"And I want to marry you. Not just because of Jamie, but
because I can't live without you one more day. I know I'm
being pushy."

"You're not." She looped an arm around his neck. "I love
you, too."

"Let's start over. Take it one day at a time. You can move
back into the casita, if you're comfortable with that, or stay
at your dad's."

"I'd rather live in the house with you."

"Okay. On two conditions."

"More legal agreements?" She smiled coyly.

"Not exactly. First, you accept my proposal."

She captured Jamie's chin and turned his face toward hers. "I'm not sure. What do you think, honey bun? Should I marry your daddy?"

Jamie squealed and babbled, "Da, da, da, be."

"I think that's a yes. What's the second condition?"

Clay struggled to get a grip on his soaring emotions. "We tear up that employment contact. I don't want you working for me."

"No?"

"I want you to be my partner in the rodeo arena."

"Seriously?" Her eyes glittered with excitement. "Because I'd be good at that, and I'd—"

He kissed her again, and it was the sweetest one yet.

"I called your mom and my dad on the way here," she admitted, reluctantly extracting herself from his embrace. "They've agreed to share babysitting duties. As much as I love having Jamie in the office with me, it's too hard to get my work done and take care of him, too."

"Are you ready for that?"

She gazed lovingly at him. "I'm ready for anything, cowboy."

Clay reached for her.

"Hey, you three," Ethan hollered, "break it up. We're in public."

"I'll kiss my fiancée in public or anywhere I want," Clay answered without looking away from Sierra.

"Fiancée!" Blythe charged them, the rest of the Powells hot on her heels. "I'm so happy for you. I've been hoping and praying you two would get married."

"Wait!" Dallas called, her camera in hand. "We have to take photos. Everyone, squeeze together." She snapped away. "Now, one of Clay, Sierra and Jamie."

"Can we get an extra copy?" Clay asked, already intending to display the picture with the others in his office.

"You bet!"

"How you holding up?" he asked Sierra when the commotion started to die down.

"I'm great. Happy." She kissed Jamie's cheek, then Clay's. "I can't believe it. Last January, I was alone. Cut off from my family, turning my back on my friends, losing my job and my apartment. And now…this. Jamie. You. Our families reunited. I have to be the luckiest person alive."

"We could get luckier." Clay arched a brow at her. "Have another kid or two. If that's not too controlling."

"Maybe a younger sister for Jamie." She smiled coyly, and Clay fell deeper in love. "But I have my own condition."

"Name it."

"We get married first."

"You free next weekend?" he joked.

She called his bluff and rocked his world by answering with a resounding "Yes!"

* * * * *

HEART & HOME

COMING NEXT MONTH
AVAILABLE MAY 8, 2012

#1401 A CALLAHAN WEDDING
Callahan Cowboys
Tina Leonard

#1402 LASSOING THE DEPUTY
Forever, Texas
Marie Ferrarella

#1403 THE COWBOY SHERIFF
The Teagues of Texas
Trish Milburn

#1404 THE MAVERICK RETURNS
Fatherhood
Roz Denny Fox

REQUEST YOUR FREE BOOKS!
2 FREE NOVELS PLUS 2 FREE GIFTS!

LOVE, HOME & HAPPINESS

YES! Please send me 2 FREE Harlequin® American Romance® novels and my 2 FREE gifts (gifts are worth about $10). After receiving them, if I don't wish to receive any more books, I can return the shipping statement marked "cancel." If I don't cancel, I will receive 4 brand-new novels every month and be billed just $4.49 per book in the U.S. or $5.24 per book in Canada. That's a saving of at least 14% off the cover price! It's quite a bargain! Shipping and handling is just 50¢ per book in the U.S. and 75¢ per book in Canada.* I understand that accepting the 2 free books and gifts places me under no obligation to buy anything. I can always return a shipment and cancel at any time. Even if I never buy another book, the two free books and gifts are mine to keep forever.

154/354 HDN FEP2

Name _____ (PLEASE PRINT)

Address _____ Apt. #

City _____ State/Prov. _____ Zip/Postal Code

Signature (if under 18, a parent or guardian must sign)

Mail to the Reader Service:
IN U.S.A.: P.O. Box 1867, Buffalo, NY 14240-1867
IN CANADA: P.O. Box 609, Fort Erie, Ontario L2A 5X3

Not valid for current subscribers to Harlequin American Romance books.

Want to try two free books from another line?
Call 1-800-873-8635 or visit www.ReaderService.com.

* Terms and prices subject to change without notice. Prices do not include applicable taxes. Sales tax applicable in N.Y. Canadian residents will be charged applicable taxes. Offer not valid in Quebec. This offer is limited to one order per household. All orders subject to credit approval. Credit or debit balances in a customer's account(s) may be offset by any other outstanding balance owed by or to the customer. Please allow 4 to 6 weeks for delivery. Offer available while quantities last.

Your Privacy—The Reader Service is committed to protecting your privacy. Our Privacy Policy is available online at www.ReaderService.com or upon request from the Reader Service.

We make a portion of our mailing list available to reputable third parties that offer products we believe may interest you. If you prefer that we not exchange your name with third parties, or if you wish to clarify or modify your communication preferences, please visit us at www.ReaderService.com/consumerschoice or write to us at Reader Service Preference Service, P.O. Box 9062, Buffalo, NY 14269. Include your complete name and address.

HARIIB

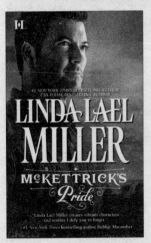

*After a bad decision—or two—Annie Mendes
is determined to succeed as a P.I. But her first assignment
could be her last, because one thing is clear: she's not cut
out to be a nanny. And Louisiana detective Nate Dufrene
seems to know there's more to her than meets the eye!*

*Read on for an exciting excerpt of the upcoming book
WATERS RUN DEEP by Liz Talley...*

THE SOUND OF A CAR behind her had Annie scooting off the
road and checking over her shoulder.

Nate Dufrene.

Her heart took on a galloping rhythm that had nothing to
do with exercise.

He slowed beside her. "Wanna ride?"

"I'm almost there. Besides, I wouldn't want to get your
seat sweaty."

His gaze traveled down her body before meeting her
eyes. Awareness ignited in her blood. "I don't mind."

Her mind screamed, *get your butt back to the house and
leave Nate alone.* Her libido, however, told her to take the
candy he offered and climb into his car like a naughty little
girl. Damn, it was hard to ignore candy like him.

"If you don't mind." She pulled open the door and
climbed inside.

The slight scent of citrus cologne, which suited him,
filled the car. She inhaled, sucking in cool air and Nate.
Both were good.

"You run often?" he asked.

"Three or four times a week."

"Oh, yeah? Maybe we can go for a run together."

Her body tightened unwillingly as thoughts of other
things they could do together flitted through her mind. She

shrugged as though his presence wasn't affecting her. Which it *so* was. Lord, what was wrong with her? *He* wasn't her assignment.

"Sure." No way—not if she wanted to keep her job. As he parked, she reached for the door handle, but his hand on her arm stopped her. His touch was warm, even on her heated flesh.

"What did you say you were before becoming a nanny?"

Alarm choked out the weird sexual energy that had been humming in her for the past few minutes. Maybe meeting him on the road wasn't as coincidental as it first seemed. "A real-estate agent."

Will Nate discover Annie's secret?
Find out in WATERS RUN DEEP by Liz Talley,
available May 2012 from Harlequin® Superromance®.

And be sure to look for the other two books
in Liz's THE BOYS OF BAYOU BRIDGE series,
available in July and September 2012.

HSREXP0412

"You do realize that we're going to need to stay here together."

...ooked around the room. "...'ll have to ...e the bed took up ...ace. "...ng" ...e the bed. Is

She shrugged, ... "Well, it won't be the end of the world. We're both adults. We can——"

Graham made a chopping sign with his hand. "Don't sound like an innocent child. How do you expect me to share ...d with you and keep my hands off you?"

She looked up at *him in* surprise. "You make me sound like some kind of irresistible siren, Graham."

"I'm not sure how to break the news to you, but I don't have an overabundant supply of willpower where you're concerned."

Dear Reader,

Welcome to the fourth great month of CELEBRATION 1000! We're winding up this special event with fireworks!— six more dazzling love st... es that will light up your summer nights. The festivities ... with *Impromptu Bride* by beloved author A... s and Broadrick ...ile running for their lives, Graham ...wedding ...Katie ...caid had to m... will their h...

Favorite aut... or Elizabeth Augu... ...lasting lov... with *The Forgotten Husband* ... knowing the real reaso... ...other memori... Jonah Tavish. But ... her searching for the truth.

This month our FABULOUS FATHER is *Daniel's Daddy*— a heartwarming story by Stella Bag...

Debut author Kate Thomas brings a tale of courtship— Texas-style in— *The Texas Touch*

There's love and laughter when a runaway heiress plays *Stand-in Mom* in Susan Meier's romantic romp. And don't miss Jodi O'Donnell's emotional story of a love all but forgotten in *A Man To Remember*.

We'd love to know if you have enjoyed CELEBRATION 1000! Please write to us at the address shown below.

Happy reading!

Anne Canadeo
Senior Editor

Please address questions and book requests to:
Silhouette Reader Service
U.S.: 3010 Walden Ave., P.O. Box 1325, Buffalo, NY 14269
Canadian: P.O. Box 609, Fort Erie, Ont. L2A 5X3

Annette Broadrick

IMPROMPTU BRIDE

Silhouette
ROMANCE™

Published by Silhouette Books

America's Publisher of Contemporary Romance

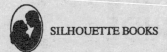

SILHOUETTE BOOKS

ISBN 0-373-19018-2

IMPROMPTU BRIDE

ANNETTE BROADRICK

believes in romance and the magic of life. Since 1984, when her first book was published, Annette has shared her view of life and love with readers all over the world. In addition to being nominated by *Romantic Times* as one of the Best New Authors of that year, she has also won the *Romantic Times* Reviewer's Choice Award for Best in its Series for *Heat of the Night, Mystery Lover* and *Irresistible;* the *Romantic Times* WISH award for her heroes in *Strange Enchantment* and *Marriage Texas Style!;* and the *Romantic Times* Lifetime Achievement Award for Series Romance and Series Romantic Fantasy.

Dear Reader,

I was delighted to be asked to write another story to help celebrate the Romance line for Silhouette. My first novel was a Romance, published ten years ago. What better way for me to celebrate those ten years?

There's something special about Romances. They seem to touch the heart, pluck at the heartstrings and at times bring a lump to the throat. Maybe that's because they reflect life.

Life isn't always sunshine and smiles. We don't always get exactly what we ask for. But have you ever noticed that many times we get something better, even if we didn't recognize it at the time?

I believe these stories offer us a great deal of promise and hope for tomorrow. For a little while they get our minds off some of our own problems. Once finished, they sometimes help us look at our life with a new perspective.

What a fun opportunity it is for me to be able to share my view of love and life with you.

Here's to our next ten years together!

Best regards,

Annette Broadrick

Chapter One

"Wake up, Katie! You've got to get out of here. Now."

Katie Kincaid awoke with a jolt, wildly looking around her. She was supposed to be alone in her hotel room. She stared up at the man leaning over her and groaned. She sincerely hoped she was only in the midst of an unpleasant dream and that Graham Douglas hadn't actually appeared in her life once again.

She realized she was not asleep when she forced herself into a sitting position. Once again she glanced around the dimly lit room before returning her gaze to the man who had now straightened and stood watching her, his expression enigmatic.

"Graham?" she mumbled, her tongue still asleep. "What are you doing here in Dalmatia?"

The small, mid-European country had sprung into world prominence the week before with the assassination of the ruling monarch, and the newsmagazine she worked for as a photojournalist and reporter had sent Katie to cover the story.

The country's capital had been ominously quiet since she'd arrived, although there had been no easing of the tension between the government and the rebel leaders who claimed responsibility for the death of the leader. Verbal volleys had flown between the opposing factions, which had kept her busy tracking down and confirming quotes as well as researching background material.

She squinted at her watch and saw that it was a little after three o'clock in the morning.

"We can catch up on our schedules some other time, Kincaid," he growled. "Now get your rear out of bed before we both get killed!"

As though on cue, a spattering of gunfire echoed outside, effectively punctuating his words.

"Oh my God," she breathed, throwing back the covers and darting toward the windows to see what was happening. "War has broken out!"

Graham grabbed her arm as she dashed by him and spun her around to face him. "Stay away from there or you're going to become one of the casualties in this mess. If a bullet doesn't get you, shattering glass will. C'mon! If we don't get out of here before the hotel is captured, there's a good chance we'll be held as hostages."

An explosion nearby shook the building. Plaster dust drifted from the ceiling while a wall hanging hit the floor with a thud.

Katie could feel the adrenaline pumping through her as she turned to do his bidding.

"What's happening, do you know?" she asked. "Who began the shooting?" She grabbed her camouflage fatigues and hurriedly pulled them on over her cotton pajamas, then crouched on the side of the bed and jerked on her socks and boots.

Another explosion shook the building, this one even closer. The light flickered, then went out, leaving them in darkness.

Katie didn't have to worry about locating Graham in the ensuing blackout. His highly profane, unprintable comments came from somewhere across the room, near the door. Katie felt around on the table for her camera, fumbled for the knapsack that carried her film and the few basic necessities she'd brought into the country with her, then headed toward the sound of his voice.

Graham's voice was the first thing she'd noticed about him the first time they'd met. She'd never been able to figure out why its deep timbre made her spine tingle every time he spoke. No one else had ever had that effect on her.

He could have made millions of dollars if he'd chosen a career in television news reporting. With his dark, lean good looks, the viewing public would have tuned in to watch him announce anything. Unfortunately for female viewers, Graham Douglas preferred a less visible life-style.

She thought of him as a phantom of the night, with his penchant for wearing black and his habit of appearing wherever political tensions exploded around the world. So why was she surprised to see him in Dalmatia?

The first time they met she'd attempted to interview him, since he'd explained his presence in the area was as an observer for the U.S. government. She'd quickly discovered his skill at making evasive responses to her most pointed questions.

In the years since then, she still knew next to nothing about him . . . except that he was the most irritating, aggravating, arrogant and elusive man she'd ever met. She considered herself a professional and took pride in the fact that few things could rattle her. Somehow, some way, Graham Douglas managed to do just that, seemingly without effort.

Now—once again—he'd turned up in her life, although this was the first time he'd ever come to her bedroom!

Another explosion rocked the room, this one so close that her ears rang. Muffled screams and the sound of falling debris came through the closed door. Shouts echoed in the streets, filtered through the windows that overlooked one of the city's main thoroughfares.

Katie felt her way across the room. When her outstretched hand brushed against Graham's arm, she experienced a sense of relief that she wasn't alone. How strange. She'd been on her own for several years. She was used to reporting from dangerous locations.

She was a strong, independent woman with a demanding job to perform.

So what was this ridiculous feeling of gratitude that Graham had come in search of her? Was she losing her edge? She found the thought revolting.

He jerked open the door into a hallway that looked like an artist's depiction of hell. A red glow from the emergency lighting system gave the passageway an eerie atmosphere. Plaster dust filled the air, causing many of the panic-stricken occupants of the hotel to gasp, cough and choke as soon as they dashed out of their rooms. Pandemonium reigned over the scene.

Graham grasped her hand in his and pushed his way into the crowded hallway, the fear and confusion surrounding them as claustrophic as the dust-filled air. Katie covered her mouth and nose with her free hand and stayed close behind him.

The door to the stairway was located halfway down the long hallway, next to the elevators. The crush of the crowd increased the closer they got as people fought to reach the stairwell. Graham paused for a moment and pulled Katie against his chest, wrapping his arms around her as the pushing, shoving people hurried to escape.

Keeping one arm firmly about her shoulders, Graham worked his way around the surging crowd, away from the stairs, until he and Katie reached the other side of the hallway.

People continued to come out of their rooms and head for the stairs. Ignoring them, he continued down the hallway to where it ended with a large window.

The glass had been shattered, leaving the frame open. Graham stepped through the frame to the fire escape, then turned and helped Katie through.

Katie looked around her. The fire escape was located on an alleyway, which seemed to be deserted. Taking a deep breath, she filled her lungs with fresh air, relieved to be out of the crush of people on their floor.

"Are you okay?" Graham asked, his hands still resting on her waist.

She nodded. "What's going to happen to the people staying in the hotel?"

"It depends on who gains the upper hand in this thing. Most of the guests are either tourists visiting the country when the assassination occurred, political observers who arrived shortly after, or—like you— reporters covering the news. If the rebels take control, it will be anyone's guess how they'll treat outsiders."

Katie shivered. Although she'd covered many hot spots in the world, this was the closest she'd come to becoming a part of the unfolding drama. Despite her edgy reaction to the man, she was glad that Graham had come after her.

"I didn't thank you for getting me out of there. I appreciate your taking the time to wake me. Are you staying here?"

"No."

She frowned with puzzlement. "How did you know I was here? How did you know where to find me?"

She couldn't see his face, but she heard the amusement in his voice. "Believe me, it wasn't easy." He pulled her toward the stairs. "C'mon. We aren't much safer up here than we were in the room." He started down the stairway. Katie stayed close behind him.

"Where are we going to go?"

"The fighting's just started. The rebels have troops surrounding the city. If we can figure a way out before they get a complete stranglehold on the area, we should be able to reach the mountains and slip across the border with relative ease."

He kept his voice low while he agilely moved down the metal steps. Katie hurried to keep up with him, the continuous gunfire and sporadic explosions adding urgency to their situation.

Being taken hostage was a scary thought. However, danger was always a consideration in her job. She tried to be wherever the news was breaking. The Gulf War, Somalia, Bosnia, Haiti—she'd covered them all. She lived with the knowledge that she placed herself at risk whenever she worked. Graham wasn't exaggerating the dangers. However...

Katie waited until they were on the ground, crouched in the concealing shadows of the alleyway before she said, "I appreciate what you've done for me, Graham, but I can't leave the country. As soon as we get out of the city, I need to find a place where I can contact my office and let them know what's happening."

"We'll discuss your commitment to your job some other time," he muttered. "In the meantime, our number one priority is to get out of here before we get killed. Stay close and follow me. I managed to get my hands on a car that will get us out of town. Let's just hope no one has found it.''

He grabbed her hand and headed to the end of the alley.

The street lamps of the main thoroughfare revealed an eerily empty view, although shouts and gunshots could still be heard. Somehow, the lack of movement around them seemed more ominous than the sight of an angry mob.

Graham stayed in the shadows close to the buildings. Katie pulled her hand free so that she could follow him in single file. Keeping his dark form in view, she hurried behind him.

He paused at one of the side streets, looked both ways before whispering, "Run!"

She didn't need a second prompting as they darted across the street to the shadowy safety of the other side.

The sound of gunfire and accompanying noises seemed to fade somewhat as they continued to sprint down the street. Katie had no idea where they were going, but at this rate they were going to get there in a hurry.

"I left the car over there," he said, pointing. She noted that he wasn't even breathing hard. "It should be just beyond that— Yes! It's there, all right."

He'd left the car in a small parking area behind a row of shops. As soon as they reached the car, he opened the passenger door and said, "Get in." By the time she closed the door behind her, he was already inside, starting the engine.

Although she prided herself on staying in good physical shape, Katie was winded. She glanced at Graham. In the dim light from the dash, she could see perspiration along his hairline, dotting his upper lip and under his eyes. She smiled to herself, amused by the reassurance that he was human, too, and not some inexhaustible robot programmed to perform upon command. There were times when she had wondered about his uncanny ability to know what to do in any given situation. Tonight, that ability had removed her from a potentially dangerous situation.

He cut his eyes in her direction before focusing on the street and surrounding neighborhood. "So far, so good," he muttered. "Now, if we don't run into some trigger-happy, gun-toting adventurers, we should be okay." He flexed his shoulders as though trying to relax the muscles there, then started to move the car out.

"You never cease to amaze me," she said, watching him more than the area through which they were passing.

Without looking at her, he said, "I don't know what you're talking about."

"How is it you always show up at the exact moment to help me out of trouble? This isn't the first time you've come to my rescue since I met you."

He didn't answer right away. When he did, he sounded very casual. "Has it ever occurred to you that you have a talent for getting yourself into trouble?"

She shrugged. "I don't do it on purpose, you know. It's my job."

"You obviously chose your vocation because you found it appealing. There aren't many women who choose to be foreign correspondents."

"How is it that whenever I ask you a question, we wind up discussing me?"

He grinned, but made no response.

She decided to share her fantasy with him. "I have this theory about you."

"Oh, yeah?"

"Uh-huh. You've never seemed quite real to me."

The low rumble in his chest could have been a chuckle. "Oh, I'm real enough."

"Maybe so, but you have to admit that the way you keep turning up in my life is unusual."

"In what way?"

"Take tonight, for example. You appeared to get me out of danger before I was even aware of the danger."

"You rarely admit to being in any danger at all," he responded wryly.

"What I'm saying is that you just suddenly appear in my life—like the first time I saw you. I'd flown to Baghdad to get the latest information on whether promises made to the U.S. were going to be honored. You walked up to me in the lobby of my hotel, introduced yourself, quickly flashed some credentials and strongly suggested I leave the country immediately."

"Which you refused to do, as I recall."

"Well, I did, eventually.... With your help, of course."

"So what is your point?"

She grinned. "Well, I've decided that you were only pretending to work for the government. That you are, in fact, a supernatural hero here to help save humanity from its own follies.''

He looked around at her in disbelief. "You *are* kidding, aren't you?''

She laughed. ''Well, maybe, but there seems to be a grain of truth in there, somewhere. I mean, in the years since I've known you, we continue to run into each other, invariably when I can use some help.''

''What are we talking about here? Do you see me as your guardian angel or as some superhero?''

''You're certainly not my idea of an angel!''

''Ah, then you see me as a superhero, out to rescue his ladylove.''

''Something like that,'' she replied, wishing she'd never brought up the subject, especially when he asked: ''Do you see yourself as my ladylove, by any chance?''

Katie could feel her cheeks glowing. Thank God for the concealing darkness. ''Of course not, it's just that I find it rather an unlikely coincidence that we should keep turning up in the same places, don't you?''

''Not at all. We're both on assignments that take us to some highly flammable situations.''

''But why did you decide to help me rather than some of the other reporters, that time in Baghdad?''

He was quiet for several minutes before he answered. ''Actually, I did give them my advice. Many of them took it, but not you, as I recall. That's when I began to pay attention to you.'' He smiled in memory. ''I remember the first thing I noticed about you was that unruly mop of russet curls and the determined tilt to your chin. I was intrigued. Finally, I asked one of the correspondents who you were, introduced myself and the rest you know.''

She looked at him in surprise. ''You mean, you deliberately picked me up?''

''Why do you call it that? Because we weren't formally introduced?''

''No! You weren't helping me because I was a reporter. You were helping me because I was a woman.''

''Woman or not, you looked like you could use some help. You appeared very grateful at the time, as I recall.''

''Well! Of course I was grateful, but that's not my point.''

''All right. The point is . . . ?''

''You were coming on to me!''

He shook his head, grinning. ''Ms. Kincaid, I hate to disagree with your arguably irrefutable logic, but if I'd been coming on to you back then, you wouldn't just now be aware of it, believe me.''

''Oh.''

''I can't tell if you're disappointed because I wasn't coming on to you or for some other reason.''

''I'm not disappointed at all. Your insistence on being so blasted mysterious just irritates me, that's all.'' She was quiet for a few moments. ''I seem to overreact whenever you're around me, which is annoying, since I take pride in keeping my composure regardless of the circumstances surrounding me.'' She absently pushed her fingers through the curls that had slipped out of her single braid.

"For the record, I can't afford to become interested in you personally. But there's nothing to stop my professional interest in you."

"Is that what it is, professional interest? Tell me, are we talking about your profession or mine?"

"Both. There are times when you've come close to jeopardizing intelligence operations by reporting too much too soon."

She thought about that for a while. "Do you mean you've deliberatedly removed me from potentially dangerous areas in order to stop me from getting the story I was after?"

"You've always reported your findings."

"True. But there have been times when I had to change my focus and sometimes even my subject because of you."

"You're a fine investigator and writer, Katie. You just take too many chances at times. If I can keep you from getting your pretty neck broken, I don't feel it's too far out of my job description to do so."

Katie lapsed into silence, realizing that Graham had revealed more of himself to her in this one conversation than he had in all the years she'd known him.

He still refused to tell her what he did for a living, his purpose for being in Dalmatia or any of the other countries where they had met. However, he'd admitted to being attracted to her by the very words he used to describe her.

What amazed her most was the fact that she was touched by his unconscious admission. Was that what all of her anger was about where he was concerned? Was she actually attracted to him, as well? Had she felt ignored and continuously in the wrong whenever they met?

The startling peek into her unconscious responses gave her pause.

Her career had been her number one priority for years. The only men in her life were co-workers and friends from college who made the effort to stay in touch with her. If anyone had asked, she would have said that she was too busy to concentrate on a relationship, but the truth was, she was uncomfortable whenever any man showed a personal interest in her. She'd grown up in a household of females, raised by a mother who had spent most of her life trying to care for three daughters.

She didn't remember her father. He'd left her mother by the time Katie was three years old. She'd learned a valuable lesson growing up that she'd never forgotten—when the chips were down, a man couldn't be relied on to stay and face his responsibilities.

Because she'd been such a tomboy as a child, she had acquired many male buddies and friends, but whenever they attempted to form a closer relationship with her, she ran.

Now that she thought about it, she and Graham had a great deal in common. Neither wanted a personal relationship. They both had chosen careers that had them traveling all over the world. They thrived on danger, if the exhilaration that had flowed through her earlier tonight was any indication.

Or was it because, deep in her heart, she was excited to see Graham Douglas once again?

Katie decided she didn't want to pursue that line of thinking. She had other things, more productive and less threatening things, to consider.

By now, they were out of the city and following a winding highway into the foothills.

"If you'll let me out at the next town, I'll find someplace to stay where I can call in my story."

"Katie, this isn't the time to be hanging around here. The entire country is going to blow up into a full-fledged civil war in the next few days."

"Which is exactly why I have to stay. I appreciate what you've done for me, Graham. Once again, you got me out of a bad situation. Thank you for your help. But it isn't possible for me to leave right now, can't you understand that?"

Through gritted teeth, he muttered, "Fine. Stay here and get yourself killed. You won't be the first news journalist to die trying to get a story."

"You don't understand! It's my job to—"

"To get yourself killed? Somehow I doubt that your employer expects quite that much devotion."

Lights on the curving road ahead caused him to slam on the brakes. Armed men milled around in the bright lights of a roadblock.

Graham muttered something obscene.

"Who are they?" Katie asked as Graham threw the car into reverse. "Can you tell?"

"At this point, it really doesn't matter," he said, turning the car around. "With the outbreak of fighting, no one is going to listen to us explain that we happened to be in the wrong place at the wrong time."

He spotted a side road and immediately whipped the car into a turn. The narrow lane headed deeper into the mountains.

Negotiating the road appeared to take all of Graham's concentration. The woods around them thickened as they climbed higher. Katie could see nothing around them but unrelieved darkness. She had no idea where they were going or what they might find along the way.

Recognizing that there was nothing she could do about their present situation, Katie deliberately returned her attention to Graham, knowing that the longer they were forced to be together, the greater were her chances of discovering more about him.

"You never told me what you're doing in Dalmatia," she said.

"At the moment? Trying to get out of here alive."

"I mean, what brings you here?" she persisted. "Are you here on official business?"

"What is this? An interview, or background material for your next article?"

"I've never used you as a source and you know it, Graham. Can I help it if we keep turning up in the same parts of the world at the same time?"

He glanced at her from the corner of his eye. "You're right. We're really going to have to stop meeting this way."

"You know, Graham, you've got all the instincts of a seasoned reporter. A real nose for where action is going to develop."

"It didn't take a giant mind to figure out that the assassination was going to throw the Dalmatian government into chaos."

"How did you find out that the rebels were going to attack tonight?"

"It's part of my job to know those things."

End of discussion. She could hear the implacable tone of his voice.

"How did you know I was here?" she asked.

"I knew you wouldn't waste any time getting here once news of the assassination went public. Your articles always reflect the latest-breaking stories."

She looked at him in surprise. "You read my stuff?"

"Is that so surprising?"

She smiled. "Well, I'm flattered."

"Why? Surely, you're aware you're a good reporter."

She sighed. "Sometimes, I wonder. It's tough trying to stay objective...particularly in places like Somalia, Sarajevo, Haiti."

"Why do you do it? Why take so many risks?"

"Because people need to be told what's happening to humanity. If they don't have the information, they can't make informed choices and decisions." She paused, realizing she was allowing her emotions to creep into the conversation. She decided to redirect the discussion. "Why do *you* do it? Why do you take so many risks in your line of work?"

He shrugged. "No particular reason. I've been trained to take carefully calculated risks...and I guess I'm good at saving my own neck."

"And mine," she added quietly. "Thank you for that. I still don't know how you knew what hotel I was in, what room and how to get inside."

He grinned, that same lopsided smile that seemed to stick in her memory long after he was gone. "I can't give away all my secrets, now, can I?" He shifted the car into a lower gear as they continued to climb.

"Do you have any idea where we are at the moment?" she asked, peering out the window.

"Vaguely."

"That's comforting," she replied dryly. "I've always admired a man with confidence."

One moment they were relaxed and teasing, the next moment the dark night seemed to explode all around them. They had come around a sharp turn and found themselves in the middle of an armed camp.

Graham flattened the accelerator, causing the car to shoot through the sudden onslaught of beams and gunfire. "Get down!" he shouted. "And hang on!"

She'd already dropped to the floor by the time he said anything, praying that none of the bullets would hit Graham. The glass in the back window shattered but the pace didn't slacken.

They were leaving the encampment behind, Katie decided, as the gunfire seemed to have abated somewhat. She took a deep breath to congratulate him once again on his quick thinking when a blinding white light and a concussive explosion somewhere close behind them caused the car to buck like a horse and go into a spinning skid, out of control.

Chapter Two

Graham fought the wheel of the car in an effort to regain control, but he was unable to do more than hang on. Katie scrambled back into the seat with some idea of trying to get out of the sliding, skidding car.

As though it had a mind of its own, the car charged at an alarming rate toward the side of the road and the nearby trees.

Graham threw his upper body over Katie, covering her as much as possible while the car went off the road and slid downward, coming to a metal-grinding, screeching halt against a tree.

The mind-numbing silence that followed was a startling contrast to the previous noise.

Dazed, Katie felt Graham's weight against her chest, his arm draped protectively over her head. She shifted slightly and felt a rush of relief when he, too, slowly raised his head and looked around.

The headlights shone into a wall of foliage. A tree limb had come through the windshield and had lodged in the seat where Graham had been. If he hadn't thrown himself over her, he would have been impaled.

She took a shaky breath. Then another one.

"Are you all right?" he asked.

"I think so."

Graham reached across her and opened the passenger door. She needed no more urging. Grabbing her knapsack, she scrambled out of the car and waited for him to join her.

"We've got to get away from here before they come to see what damage they caused," he said in a low voice. He reached into the back and grabbed a small bag before he took her hand and guided her down the sharp incline that led deeper into the woods and away from the road.

The reflected glow from the car's headlights helped them to pick their way through the dense underbrush. Graham took the lead and moved quietly, holding branches for her and guiding her through the woods. He halted when they heard voices along the road above them.

He pulled her against him and they stood there, listening.

Katie rested her head on his chest, her ear pressed to the comforting rhythm of his heart. Being this close to him unnerved her. His sheer maleness was overwhelming. His body bristled with energy, almost quivering with a suppressed need to act.

She had a hunch that if she hadn't been there, he might have waited at the car for the men, rather than slipping away into the underbrush. She knew that her heart was racing with fear, just as she knew that his was racing with excitement.

He was in his element fighting against the odds.

They stood that way for untold minutes, waiting to see if the men were going to search for them. When she raised her face toward his, he immediately clamped his hand over her mouth. She dropped her head to his chest and he removed his hand.

What felt like several years later, the men's voices grew fainter. They must be returning to the camp. But would they return later to search for the occupants of the car? she wondered.

Long after all the sounds were gone, Graham continued to hold her tightly against him without moving. Eventually, she lifted her head again. This time, instead of covering her mouth with his hand, he covered it with his lips.

Katie stiffened with shock. She placed her hands on his chest in order to push away from him, but the tautly muscled expanse distracted her from her intention. So did the firm pressure of his lips, coaxing her to respond.

Her already-racing pulse discovered a reason to increase its tempo—this time from pleasure, not fear. Instead of resisting, Katie found herself yielding to the temptation of his sensuous touch. With a tiny moan, she relaxed against him, going up on her toes to bring herself closer to him. New sensations raced through her, swamping her with emotion.

Graham wrapped his arms around her and pulled her even closer while he continued to kiss her senseless. When eventually he loosened his hold slightly, she pulled away to fill her lungs with much-needed air.

He nuzzled her forehead, placing kisses along her hairline and down her cheek. Katie couldn't seem to get enough air. She kept gasping, reminding herself that air was essential to her well-being but finding herself holding her breath every time his lips brushed against her face.

"Graham?" she finally whispered.

"Hmm?"

"What do you think you're doing?" she managed to say past the constriction in her throat.

He leaned his forehead against hers and sighed. "Rotten timing, huh?"

That made no sense whatsoever.

Finally getting her hands to cooperate, she pushed away from him. It was too dark to see his expression. "What's going on?"

He didn't answer right away. When he did, he only muttered, "Sorry. I didn't mean to take advantage of the situation." After another silence, he said, "We've got to make tracks before they start searching for us." He turned and continued moving away from the road.

Katie hurried to keep up with him. She didn't relish the idea of getting lost in the brush. As soon as she caught up with him, she paced herself, staying a few steps behind him, her mind still racing. She was having a problem reconciling the actions of the man she thought she knew with what had just happened between them.

One thing she had to say for him—Graham was no novice when it came to the art of sensual persuasion. For a few moments, she'd forgotten where they were and what had just happened to them. His kiss had wiped her memory clean of everything but him.

Graham turned and held out his hand. She took it and allowed him to guide her to a stop beside him. "I've found a path," he whispered. "I think we should follow it so that we can find help."

Katie nodded before she realized he couldn't see her. "Fine."

Night had faded into dawn before they reached a clearing where a small cottage sat amid tall dewy grass. Graham paused at the edge of the clearing.

"Stay here while I check the place out."

Without waiting to see if she had followed his instructions, Graham strode away from her. Nothing stirred. With daylight, Katie felt a little more safe. She watched Graham's lithe figure move silently toward the building. After disappearing around back, he eventually came into sight and beckoned her to join him.

As soon as he reached her side, he said, "The cottage is empty. I think we'll be safe enough if we stay here for a few hours." He started back to the cottage. She followed. "If the owner shows up, we'll explain that we were hiking and got lost in the mountains."

"That wouldn't be a lie," she said, catching up with him.

He glanced down at her boots and serviceable fatigues. "At least you're dressed for the part. There's no telling how far we'll have to go to reach a border."

This wasn't the time to argue with him about their destination. She certainly couldn't report anything that had happened since the shooting had started, so she might as well relax and follow Graham's lead.

"At least we managed to grab our bags," he said, nodding toward the knapsack she'd slung over her shoulder, then at the duffel bag slung over his shoulder.

"How far do you think we've come?"

"I'm not certain. Distances in the mountains are deceiving."

Dark stubble showed on his jaw and chin and his eyes looked tired. She glanced at the cottage. "Can we get inside?"

He nodded. "The door's around on the other side." He turned to retrace his steps. "Luckily, there's no lock, but the door was closed, which has kept animals out." He paused and pushed the partially opened door wider. "I've stayed in worse places."

The cottage was one large room with a small loft. Though simply furnished, it had the well cared for look of somebody's home.

Summer light filtered through the windows, giving the place a cheerful appearance.

"I wonder who owns this place?" she asked, standing in the middle of the room.

"Hopefully, an understanding person, if they show up while we're still here." He walked over to the kitchen area and peered into the cabinets. "I don't know about you, but I'm starving."

She reached into her bag and brought out some food bars and trail mix. "Here. Help yourself." She turned away and surveyed the small living area. A thick braid rug lay before the empty fireplace. She walked over and knelt down. "I'm asleep on my feet," she muttered. She stretched out on the rug, using her knapsack for a pillow. "Wake me up when it's time to leave."

Graham leaned against the wall, watching her sleep, and caught himself smiling. He didn't understand why this woman had the ability to get under his skin, but somehow she always managed the feat with little effort.

She was so exasperating, so stubborn, so blasted independent. He should have left her there in the hotel. By slipping into the capital to find her, he'd risked incurring the wrath of his boss. If he'd gotten caught, it would have been an embarrassing situation for the State Department.

What he'd learned since arriving in Dalmatia had convinced him that he had to do what he could. Angry citizens were even now working into a gigantic clash of political views.

He should have crossed the border last night. Every hour counted. He knew better than to take a chance on being captured.

After finishing off the food she'd so casually tossed at him, Graham pulled out a map of Dalmatia and intently studied it. He found the road and the approximate spot where they had been attacked. If his calculations were correct, they weren't too far from the village of Etrusca. He'd heard of it, but had never been there.

If they could reach the village, he'd see about finding them some transportation. Hopefully, the borders were still open.

Once again he glanced at the sleeping woman who had now curled up on her side. He needed some sleep, too. He couldn't remember the last time he'd gotten any rest. Things had been happening too fast and furious for him to do anything but keep going.

He climbed the steep stairs to the loft, found a couple of blankets and brought them downstairs. He arranged one over Katie, then stretched out beside her, willing himself to sleep.

Instead, his mind teased him with the memory of their shared kiss. He almost groaned out loud. How could he have been so stupid? Of course, there had been the danger of their getting caught. He hadn't wanted her to make a sound, but that was no excuse for kissing her.

The problem was that he'd wanted to kiss her for some time now. Having her in his arms had been too tempting to resist.

Katie Kincaid had an unforgettable grip on his imagination. She had never shown any personal interest in him, had never encouraged him to believe that she found him attractive, but that hadn't discouraged his fantasies about her.

In his line of work, permanent relationships were frowned upon. They became distractions that could be dangerous. Not that he was considering having a relationship with Katie, permanent or otherwise. Just because he found her intriguing and unforgettable meant nothing in the overall scheme of things.

Graham closed his eyes, allowing his body to relax. Katie stirred beside him, drawn to his warmth. Without conscious thought, he slipped his arm beneath her neck so that her head rested on his shoulder. Feeling curiously at peace, he fell asleep with Katie in his arms.

Katie stirred, disoriented. Her hotel bed had grown harder and her covers were— Her eyes flew open. She was lying on her side. The warmth of a large, warm body pressed against her back and down the length of her bent legs. When she attempted to move, the band at her waist tightened.

She glanced down and saw a dark-clad arm securely fastened around her. Only then did she remember Graham, their escape from the hotel room and the long hike ending at the small cottage.

"Graham?"

"Mmph?"

"How long have we been here?"

He moved away from her, freeing her to sit up and look around. The light coming through the windows was dim. Had they slept the whole day?

She stood and walked across to the closest window. Dark clouds scudded angrily across the sky. A rising wind whistled along the eaves, bending the branches of the nearby trees in a frenzy of movement.

"I think a storm is moving in," she said quietly, before turning to face the man who still lay on his back on the floor, one leg bent at the knee. Did he have to be so ruggedly attractive?

His hair was rumpled, his face unshaven, his eyes sleepy. Slowly, she retraced her steps to his side. "When's the last time you had any sleep?" She knelt beside him, studying him closely.

"I don't remember. It's been a while."

"I'm sorry I woke you. From the looks of the weather, we'd be foolish to move around in the mountains at the moment." A flash of light appeared at the windows, followed closely by thunder. "A mountain storm isn't anything to ignore," she added.

Graham sat up so that he was facing her. He rubbed the heels of his hands across his cheeks and eyes, then shoved his hair away from his face. "I didn't mean to sleep so long." He glanced at his watch in disbelief. "We've been asleep for almost eight hours."

Katie glanced around the room. "I wonder where the occupant of this cottage has gone? More to the point, when will he or she return?"

Graham massaged his back. "Nobody will be coming around for a few hours with this kind of weather."

"By then it will be dark."

They stared at each other in silence.

Katie had never spent so much time with Graham before. Each previous encounter had been under tense circumstances, which hadn't allowed for social niceties or polite conversations. Now, for all intents and purposes, she was marooned with him in the mountains for at least another night.

"I'm sorry that I wasn't able to get you to a village sooner," Graham said. "I know you needed to call your office."

"It can't be helped, although they must be worried about the reports coming out of this country. My silence could be interpreted to mean that I was hurt."

"Or worse."

"Yes."

Once again, they studied each other without speaking. Unable to hold the eye contact, Katie stirred. "I could see what's in the kitchen to eat. Surely our absent host wouldn't begrudge our eating something."

"I plan to leave a note and some money when we leave."

She scrambled to her feet, relieved to have something with which to occupy herself. A new tension had crept into the room since she'd awakened. Was it finding herself once again snuggled against Graham, being made aware of him as a very attractive male? She didn't have a clue to his feelings. He was excellent at masking what he was thinking.

She found some can goods that could be combined to make a savory soup. After lighting the old-fashioned stove and locating a large cooking pot, she asked, "Do you know how to speak the language here?"

"A little, but not much. One of my army buddies years ago was conversant with it. His parents had emigrated from here. I've always been fascinated by languages. It's been a hobby of mine to learn about them."

"Do you know enough to explain why we are here?"

"Even if I did, I don't think that would be a good idea."

His last words were directly behind her. She turned around and found him leaning against the small table by one of the walls, his legs crossed at the ankles. Although he was still unshaven, his eyes looked a little more rested. The lines around them weren't quite so pronounced. She ducked her head and forced herself to concentrate on what she was doing.

"Katie?" The low timbre of his voice zipped through her system like an electric shock.

She jerked her head around to look at him again. "Yes?"

"Are you afraid of me?"

She stiffened, feeling insulted that he should consider such a thing. "Of course not!"

"Something's bothering you. Is it the storm?"

Hard rain hit the side of the cottage, pinging against the glass like pebbles. The wind continued to build, causing the structure to shudder from time to time.

"Not really, although it does sound ferocious out there. I don't like the inactivity, sitting around waiting for something to happen."

"Are you feeling a bit trapped?"

"I suppose."

He straightened, moving closer. He stroked her cheek with the back of his hand. Her skin tingled where the warmth of his fingers grazed it.

"I would never take advantage of the situation, you know."

His words rang out in the quiet, calling her attention to the outside noises and the inside stillness. She swallowed, trying to think of something light and casual to say in reply. Nothing came. Her nerves were leaping inside her.

A sudden crash outside made her jump.

Graham spun away from her and sprinted for the door. He swung it open, quickly filling the room with gusty wind and spatterings of rain.

Darkness had fallen early, but there was still enough light to see that one of the trees across the meadow had lost a giant limb filled with thick branches. Drawn by the awesome majesty of the storm, Katie moved to the door.

"If that had been closer, it would have fallen through this place," she said.

"It's my guess that's the reason there are no trees nearby."

The long grass around the cottage was flattened by the wind and rain. They continued to stand there and watch the storm race overhead.

Finally, Graham shut the door, forcing their attention to the small room. It had grown even darker.

"I think I saw a lamp over here somewhere," he said, heading toward the fireplace. "It probably wouldn't be a bad idea to build a fire to keep the chill out tonight."

Katie returned to the kitchen, glad that the cookstove used bottled gas. She was also thankful that there was running water and a small bathroom off the rear of the cottage, obviously added after the original cottage had been built.

This was someone's home and had been built to be as comfortable as possible, given its remote location. Perhaps the person who lived here had gone to the closest village for supplies. After checking the provisions in the kitchen, she'd noted that many of the staples were low. It made sense that the storm had stopped the owner from returning today.

She found a couple of large bowls, ladled the soup into them and set them on the table. She filled glasses with water before she looked around to see what Graham was doing.

The fire was catching, she noted, while he patiently fed it twigs taken from a woodbox nearby. Seen in profile, Graham's noncommittal expression reminded her of how little she knew about him...how mysterious he truly was.

Was she afraid of him as he'd suggested? she asked herself, searching for an honest answer from deep inside. Or was she more uneasy about her own reactions to him? He had a definite effect on her, one she'd never had around anyone else. Her reaction unnerved her, to be sure.

What was it about Graham that made him so different from other men she knew?

A thought suddenly flashed into her mind. He was totally self-sufficient...a loner who needed no one.

With that thought came another realization, one that she'd not considered. She, too, was a loner, proud to be self-sufficient, needing no one.

They were two of a kind, thrown together by unusual circumstances. Instead of feeling threatened by

their similarities, Katie almost smiled, relaxing for the
first time in several hours.

She'd just come face-to-face with her alter ego, the
masculine mirror of her own personality.

She'd finally come into contact with the one person
who could see through all her defenses, understand her
reactions and motivations, pull down all her walls.

With her new knowledge, she realized she could do
the same with him.

Chapter Three

Dinner had been over for a while, the storm had moved through their vicinity, leaving the rain pattering on the roof, and Katie sat beside Graham on the small sofa in front of the flickering flames in the fireplace.

At first they had been silent, enjoying the hot meal, the warm fire and the coffee they were currently drinking. However, as they continued to sit side by side, they began to reminisce about their childhoods.

"I spent most of my free time as a teenager in Oregon, hiking in the mountains in and around Mount Hood," Graham was saying. "Weekends, we'd go over to Detroit Lake or the Three Sisters. Sitting around a campfire at night was the reward for all the aching muscles." He took a sip of his coffee. "What about you?"

"There weren't many mountains in east Texas," she said, "although I did go to summer camp several years in a row in the hill country of central Texas. We learned how to swim, canoe, hike, that kind of thing."

"I noticed that you didn't have much trouble keeping up with me during our long trek after we lost the car. I must admit that I was impressed that you weren't complaining."

She grinned. "Some of my muscles have been, believe me. I'm more out of shape than I want to acknowledge." She rubbed her calf and ankle ruefully.

"What attracted you to working as a photojournalist?" he asked.

"I got a camera for Christmas when I was eight years old, one of those point-and-shoot kind that are foolproof. From that time on, I spent most of my weekly allowance on film and processing fees. Eventually, I learned how to develop black-and-white film, and I discovered a whole new world."

"How about your writing skills?"

"I majored in journalism in college. I wanted to paint mind pictures with words. I hoped to show people my perspective of the world." She rested her head against the sofa, remembering the child she had been. "I had very decided opinions back then about everything. I was a real pain to some of my professors, who were always trying to get me to write more objectively, with less inflammatory adjectives."

She turned and looked at him. "How about you? How did you come to be whatever it is you are—an observer, I believe you once said."

"I was in ROTC in college, went directly into the army after graduation. Because of my love of languages and foreign locales, I was eventually moved into the intelligence section of the armed forces... translating, decoding, that kind of thing." He got up and added more wood to the dying flames. After rebuilding the fire, he continued speaking. "When it came time for my discharge, I was asked to either stay in the military or to take a civilian job doing basically the same type of work. I chose to become a civilian and moved to D.C."

"You enjoy it, don't you?"

He thought about that. "Yeah, I guess I do, although I haven't thought about it for a long time. I mean, it's just what I do. It fits my personality, and I like the life-style."

Katie refilled their cups. "Do your friends ever pester you about settling down and having a family?"

He grinned. "Whenever they can find me. I went to my college reunion a couple of years ago. Most everybody I knew back then are completely ensconced in their professions. Some are already into their second marriages, making child support and alimony payments. They thought *I* should envy *them,* but I think, secretly, they wished they had the freedom I have in my life."

"I get the same thing, particularly from my two older sisters. They're both married and have made me an aunt several times over. I keep pointing out to my mother that she has plenty of grandchildren without my contributing to the noisy family gatherings."

He shifted so he was able to see her more fully. "Don't you ever intend to marry?"

"No."

"Not ever?"

"No."

"You seem very certain."

"I learned a long time ago not to rely on anyone but myself."

"What painful lesson taught you that?"

"Not painful. Just necessary."

"If you say so."

"What about you?" she asked with more interest than she would have admitted to having. "When are you going to acquire all the trappings of a stable home life and raise the prescribed number of offspring?"

She expected him to reply with a facetious quip or to change the subject, or even to tell her that it was none of her business. He did none of those things. Instead, he surprised her by saying, "I've been asking myself the same question, lately. Two years ago, I would have said I had no interest in having a wife and family, especially after seeing what's happened to some of my former college classmates. Now, I'm not so sure. The idea seems to have more and more appeal to me." He stretched his legs out in front of him. "I keep thinking about how nice it would be to have someone waiting for me when I get home, instead of walking into an empty apartment.... To have someone who cares that I've been gone and is glad to see me back. I'll admit that I still enjoy my freedom, but I miss having someone with whom to share my life."

She wasn't sure why she found his words so alarming. They had absolutely nothing to do with her. She certainly didn't care if Graham Douglas decided to marry. What he did with his life was none of her business. So why did the vision of some beautiful blonde greeting him at his front door in a filmy, provocative negligee make her blood run cold?

Katie stood and gathered up their cups. "I'm about to fall asleep sitting here," she announced, the lie tripping off her lips with ease. "I'm going to shower and change out of these clothes." She still wore the camouflage fatigues over her cotton pajamas. Actually, the pajamas had helped to insulate her from the chilly mountain air last night. They were no doubt the reason she felt hot and bothered now.

"Why don't you sleep in the loft tonight?" Graham said, rising. "I'll stay down here and keep the fire going. I'll also be here if our host suddenly appears."

Distancing herself from Graham was the best idea she'd heard in hours. "Fine. I'll wash these cups, then get ready for bed."

He rubbed his stubbled jawline. "I think I'll shave while you do that. There's no reason to scare our kind host, if he should show up, by looking like a mountain bandit."

Katie turned her back to him, busying herself in the kitchen. She didn't care what he did. She just wanted this night to end so that they could get out of here. She didn't want to be seduced by their isolation, the cozy chat before the mesmerizing fire or the sight of Graham's rugged good looks.

Why had she thought getting to know him better would ease the tension between them? If anything, it had made it worse, as far as she was concerned.

She owed him her gratitude for getting her out of a dangerous situation. She would make certain that she expressed her thanks once they reached civilization. Then she would be on her own once again.

Katie didn't want to be reminded of his dark, hooded gaze, his flashing smile or his ridiculous yearning for a mate. It probably had something to do with hormones. Who said that men didn't have some kind of biological clock working in them, as well?

"It's all yours," he said cheerfully several minutes later. Katie turned to face him and almost groaned out loud. The man was driving her crazy.

He'd obviously decided that a shower sounded good. He'd taken his small bag into the bathroom and from its contents donned a pair of black jeans that had obviously seen better days. They clung to his hips and thighs, molding his masculinity and causing her to avert her eyes to his chest, which unfortunately for her peace of mind was exposed by his unbuttoned shirt. Black, of course.

"What is this need of yours to dress as Zorro?" she asked, hearing the waspish tone in her voice and unable to disguise it.

"Zorro?"

She waved her hand. "You know. He was supposed to have lived in early California, robbing the rich and helping the poor like a New-World Robin Hood."

"Don't tell me he pranced around in tights, too?"

"No. He just dressed in black all the time, like you do." She forced her gaze away from the broad expanse of muscled chest revealed.

He crossed the room in his bare feet and nonchalantly spread the blankets they had used earlier into a makeshift bed on the rug in front of the fire. "My only motive is ease of dressing. I don't have to worry about matching colors this way."

He sounded so blasted reasonable that she felt like a fool, wanting to find something to fight about. How could he be so relaxed in their present circumstances? They'd been alone together for hours now. Didn't that bother him at all? Did he just see her as one of the guys? Didn't she affect him in the least?

What was she thinking? Was she out of her mind? Did she want him to come on to her, for Pete's sake? Where was her professionalism? Where was her common sense?

At this precise moment, she felt as though it had taken a long vacation somewhere in the South Sea Islands, leaving her quivering with ridiculous ideas. . . .

She muttered something inane and grabbed her knapsack before disappearing into the bathroom.

The room still carried a hint of his after-shave. Not fair. Not fair at all. She checked the water pressure and found it weak. The water was no more than tepid, but she didn't care. The thought of getting clean appealed to her immensely.

By the time she finished her shower, dried off, wrapped her wet hair in a towel and rummaged in her bag for something fresh to sleep in, Katie felt much better. Graham had absolutely no power to upset her.

None at all. He was a common, ordinary man who—
Well. Maybe not common, exactly. Certainly not ordinary. All right. So, he was a very attractive, charis-
matic man who made her insides shiver every time he
gazed deeply into her eyes and spoke to her in that
deep voice of his.

She'd met other attractive men. Lots of them. They
hadn't even slightly affected her.

The same couldn't be said for Graham Douglas.

All right, she muttered, pulling out an extra-large,
long-sleeved sweatshirt from her bag and studying it
critically. So she reacted differently to him than she did
to other men. So what?

She shrugged into the sweatshirt and peered at herself in the mirror. The soft material felt good against
her skin and the shapelessness of the garment reassured her that Graham wouldn't mistakenly think she
was dressing to call attention to herself.

After devoting several minutes to getting the tangles out of her hair, Katie stuffed her clothes into her
bag and went back to the other room.

Graham looked up from his contemplative stare into
the fire when the click of the bathroom door announced that Katie would be rejoining him. What he
saw made his heart race.

She stood looking like a little girl in the doorway,
her wet hair forming a cape over her shoulders. The
sweatshirt completely dispelled any misconception that
the woman coming toward him was a little girl, softly
clinging to the womanly curves of her breasts and hips
and ending at midthigh, revealing legs a show girl
would envy.

He forgot to breathe.

"I hate to disturb you," she said, approaching him, "but I need to dry my hair a little more before I go to bed."

He was very glad that he'd had the presence of mind to drape the blanket over the bottom half of his body, particularly since he'd dispensed with the jeans as soon as she'd shut the bathroom door.

He felt like somebody's maiden aunt when he pulled the blanket up over his bare chest in a ridiculous parody of modesty. "No problem," he muttered, watching her kneel in front of the fire and flip her hair over her head.

The light from the fire made her skin glow, highlighting the lighter strands of hair into gold and burnishing the rest. He had a sudden longing to run his hands through the cascading waves, clenching them before allowing the silken mass to slide through his fingers like an exotic waterfall of color and texture and light.

He closed his eyes before he embarrassed himself by doing something unforgivably crude, like grabbing her and hauling her upstairs to that bed in the loft and spending the rest of the night making passionate love to her.

As he lay there with his eyes closed, hearing the soft sounds she made as she brushed her hair, Graham faced the sad truth for the first time. This was not the first time he'd fantasized about making love to this woman. It probably wouldn't be the last.

Why was it that one particular pair of calm gray eyes had such a powerful effect on him, when other eyes, filled with much more promise, could leave him feeling detached and unfulfilled?

How could the memory of a determined chin, the flip of a chestnut braid, a husky chuckle, more fully involve all his senses and responses than the actual presence of another woman eager for his advances?

Why, after meeting this particular woman, had he become more and more aware of his loneliness and started looking at his life with new eyes?

Graham had a strong hunch he knew the answers to those questions.

Fat lot of good the answers were to him.

Katie had made it clear that she was content with her life. She'd made it even clearer that she had no intention of becoming romantically involved with anyone.

What he had to do was pack up his fantasies and file them away. If he was seriously considering a more balanced life-style, then he'd make it a point to get out more in social situations whenever he had time. He'd start meeting—

"Graham?" she said softly.

He opened his eyes. Not a good move. Her hair was drier now, falling in luxurious, cascading waves over her shoulders and breasts. She had moved closer and now leaned over him.

"Yeah?" he muttered, praying his body wouldn't betray him.

"Why don't you sleep upstairs where it's more comfortable? I don't mind staying down here."

Since he was wearing only his briefs, he did not think moving around was a very good idea.

"I'm okay."

"The floor's awfully hard," she said.

He knew all about that particular condition and decided that no comment was by far the best way to go.

She touched his forehead lightly, brushing his hair away from his face. "I can see you as you must have been when you were a teenager, sleeping around the campfire. You look so young and innocent, lying there with the firelight highlighting the contours of your face."

Katie leaned down and brushed her lips against his cheek. "Pleasant dreams," she whispered.

Achieving sainthood had never been one of his goals. Not this lifetime. He'd resisted the temptation she'd unknowingly presented these past few hours. He'd done everything in his power to blot out the sight of her, but his resistance gave way completely when she touched him.

He reached for her, his hand sliding through the silky veil falling around them until he touched the nape of her neck. With a motion as natural as breathing, he came up on his elbow and found her mouth with his.

In some part of his mind, Graham realized that she was not resisting him. Instead, her lips parted slightly... shyly... beneath his.

He sat up and tugged her into his lap without releasing her mouth. She felt wonderful in his arms—better than he'd remembered from the adrenaline rush of the night before. She slipped her arm around his neck, clinging to him.

Graham forgot everything but the woman he held—the wonderfully responsive and obviously innocent woman who seemed to welcome his exploration.

He cupped her breast in his hand, causing her to stop breathing for a moment before giving a soft sigh of acquiescence.

She tasted of minty toothpaste and freshness, her scent a commingling of roses and sunshine. Graham knew in that moment that this woman had managed to wrap herself firmly around his heart.

By the time he raised his head so he could catch his breath, he was trembling badly.

She lay in his arms, her eyes closed, her chest moving rapidly. He could feel her heart racing beneath his palm. He brushed his lips against her ear and whispered, "I want to make love to you, Katie."

She sighed. "I know."

"Is that what you want?"

Her lashes seemed weighted as her eyes slowly opened. "Nobody has ever affected me like this before," she murmured.

"Same here."

She swallowed. "I mean, I've never been this intimate with anyone before."

He raised his head and glanced down at her in surprise. The hem of the sweatshirt had ridden up on her hip, showing him her white cotton panties.

What she'd just admitted shook him badly.

"Never?"

She shook her head.

No wonder her kisses had been so shyly innocent. Now what? he asked himself. He had a hunch she wouldn't stop him if he continued, at least not for a while. But then what? When would she draw the line? When would she point out that she had no intention of giving up her innocent state to him or to anyone else?

For a moment, a shaft of pure possessive jealousy shot through him. The idea of another man touching her infuriated him, which shocked him further.

"You'd better go on upstairs," he finally muttered, lifting her out of his lap in a pained determination to remove the delicious temptation she presented.

"I thought you wanted—"

"I'm not going to take advantage of this situation. You've made it clear that you have no intention of becoming involved with anyone."

She looked dazed and confused. "Yes. I mean, that's true. I guess I never realized how—" She paused, searching for words. "How...it would feel," she said haltingly. "I've never wanted to be kissed...or touched...before. But with you, it's...it's..." Her words trailed off.

"It certainly is," he finished grimly. "I've never taken advantage of a woman's innocence in my life, and I sure as hell don't intend to start now."

As though suddenly aware of herself, Katie straightened the hem of her sweatshirt and came up on her knees, facing him. "I guess you thought that's what I was asking for when I offered you the bed upstairs." She made a face. "I guess I wasn't really thinking about how it would sound...or look. I honestly—" She paused, looking startled. "Honestly," she repeated slowly. "If I'm really honest with both of us, I think I've been wanting you to kiss me again ever since last night." She looked bewildered, sitting back on her heels in surprise. To Graham, she looked absolutely adorable.

"That makes two of us," he admitted, unable to hide his grin.

"But I've never— That is, I don't usually. It's just that ... You must think I—"

"I think we both got a little carried away, that's all." He didn't believe anything of the sort, but she was already beginning to look horrified at what she'd done. He made a strong effort to sound casual. "The thing is, we've both been under a strain since last night. Danger has an annoying way of playing around with our emotions."

"I guess this sort of thing happens to you a lot," she offered quietly.

He couldn't tell what she was thinking. Her expression was calm, as was her voice. "No. I don't spend much time with women in my line of work."

Her expression lightened. "Oh?"

"What? Do you think I'm some kind of Casanova, chasing women while I'm supposed to be working?"

"I'd have no way of knowing, would I? I really don't know much about men."

"Well, they come in all shapes, sizes and attitudes, just like women do. So don't generalize. I'm not a lecher preying on unsuspecting women."

She chuckled and his heart lurched. There was that husky sound of amusement that he found so endearing. It was a good thing she had no idea how strong a hold she had on him.

"Look," he said. "We both need some sleep. Go on upstairs. There's no need to blow this thing out of proportion." He glanced around the room. "Let's face it, this is a perfect setup for a seduction scene. So we both succumbed a little. There's nothing wrong with that. Just shows we're human."

She stood, exposing those show-girl legs to him as she stepped away from his side. He fought to hang on to his composure. "Well, this has certainly been an enlightening evening," she said with an unsteady laugh. "I must seem like a relic from the dinosaur age. High school girls these days have more experience than I've had."

Since he couldn't get up, he pulled his knees up to effectively camouflage his rather painful condition. "In this day and age, you're being very wise."

She turned away, pausing at one of the windows. "I think the rain has stopped," she said, and he knew she was trying to put things back on a more even level. It was a nice try, but he knew that nothing in his life would ever be the same. Not after this particular trip.

"Good. We'll wait for daylight and look for a pathway to one of the villages. According to the map, we aren't too far from Etrusca."

She paused at the top of the steps and said softly, "Thank you for being so understanding, Graham. You've been very kind."

"Good night, Katie. Pleasant dreams."

He heard her move around in the loft, heard the ancient bedsprings groan as she crawled into bed, heard the rustling of the bedclothes while she settled into place.

He rested his head on his clasped hands. Katie was right. This had been an illuminating evening in several respects. He couldn't believe how he'd kidded himself about his interest in Katie's safety these past several months. He couldn't get over how deeply he'd been denying to himself his feelings for her.

Now that he knew, he didn't have a clue what to do about them.

Chapter Four

Neither one of them had much to say the next morning. Graham felt as though he'd been trampled by a herd of water buffalo in mating season. Or maybe he was the one who suddenly felt like declaring mating season.

He sat at the small table and watched as Katie heated up the remains of their soup from the night before, serving it to him along with freshly made coffee.

"It looks like a beautiful day for hiking," she offered when he didn't say anything.

"Yes."

She glanced down at her wrinkled clothes. "Believe it or not, these fatigues are clean, although they are my last pair. I hope we can find a Laundromat sometime soon or I'm going to be in big trouble." Her smile invited him to see the humor in their situation.

All he could see this morning was that she was glowing with new energy and vitality, obviously having slept the night through without any of the dreams that had haunted his fitful sleep. Now, after his bout of painful self-honesty, he found her exciting and appealing in her camouflage fatigues, wrinkled or not.

She had rebraided her hair so that it hung once again in a thick rope over her shoulder. Her face was freshly scrubbed and shining with good health.

She seemed to have put the events of the previous night behind her, where they belonged.

Good for her, he thought to himself savagely. He swallowed the hot coffee as though punishing himself for his lascivious thoughts.

"How long until you're ready to go?" he asked gruffly.

Her smile faded. "As soon as I clean our dishes."

He pushed away from the table. "I want to look around outside to see what kind of paths I come across." He placed some money and a note, written in English, on the table. "I can speak a little of the language, but don't know how to write it. The money is probably self-explanatory."

He grabbed his bag and slung the strap over his shoulder. "I'll be outside whenever you're ready."

Katie watched him until he disappeared from view. Mr. Graham Douglas had certainly lost his rather charming personality this morning, she decided. She'd hoped the coffee would help to put him in a better mood. That's what he got for insisting on sleeping on the floor last night.

She glanced over at the rug where he'd slept. By the time she'd come downstairs this morning, he'd dressed, cleaned out the fireplace, folded the blankets and had been pacing up and down the room, obviously impatient to leave.

Of course she wanted to get away, too. She had a job to do, a war to report, a career to maintain. However, was there any real need for him to be so abrupt and uncommunicative?

Men really were a breed apart. Maybe they *were* from another planet, as the title of a book she'd seen indicated. She just knew that she didn't understand them. Both of her sisters had found loving husbands who were caring fathers to their children. Her mother had never remarried, though, indicating to Katie that her heart had been irreparably broken when her father had left.

Katie had no desire to discover what a broken heart felt like. She had a hunch, however, that if she spent much time with Graham Douglas, she might be in real danger of finding out.

By midafternoon they saw the spires of a church nestled in one of the valleys and knew that their long trek would soon be over.

Katie was relieved that their forced togetherness would end shortly.

Not that Graham had been anything but polite. He'd been almost too polite, treating her like an aging aunt, carefully assisting her over the rough portions of the trail he'd found that morning, then keeping a respectable distance between them during the rest of their hike.

She would be glad to pull off her boots and rest her feet. They paused at the brink of the downward slope of the path in silent unison now that their destination was in sight. Katie sank to a nearby boulder and fanned her face with her hand.

"You okay?" he asked, showing no sign of being tired.

"Never been better," she said cheerfully. She refused to show him the vulnerable side of herself again. In another hour or so, they would be in the valley below them. She'd find some kind of transportation that would take her back to the capital, bid him goodbye and pray that any future encounters they might have would be fleeting.

"Hungry?"

"Not at all." She held up half a food bar she clutched in her hand.

He turned away and looked out at the view. It really was spectacular. After being raised in the flatness of east Texas, she would always notice and appreciate the grandeur of the mountains. She watched him study the map in his hand, tracing lines with his finger before returning it to his pocket.

She stood, rolling her shoulders and shifting her knapsack on her back. She'd been snapping pictures all day with the camera that hung from its strap around her neck, determined to enjoy every moment.

They'd come across a female deer with twin fawns hugging her side. All three had bounded away as soon as they spotted intruders, but not before Katie had gotten a picture.

Graham started down the path and wordlessly Katie fell in behind him. His continued aloofness reinforced her earlier opinion of him. Thank heavens she hadn't succumbed to his mesmerizing charm the night before. She would certainly have been kicking herself all the way down the mountainside today if she had.

Of course, technically speaking, she *had* succumbed. If he had continued to kiss and caress her— the mere thought of which filled her cheeks with heat—she would have ended up making love to him right there on the floor.

It was amazing what a few kisses could do to a woman's judgment. Absolutely amazing.

A sudden shout from the trees stopped them both in their tracks. Armed men came running toward them, at least five of them.

Graham immediately put his hands in the air to show them he was unarmed. She quickly did the same while she moved closer to Graham's back. The leader came nearer, calling something to them.

Katie had worked with an interpreter since she'd arrived in the country. Now she was at a loss to understand the man.

Graham gave a halting answer in return.

The armed leader said something to him in staccato speech, and Graham answered. Then the man motioned with his rifle and the other men surrounded them.

"What did you say?" she whispered.

"Not much."

The leader signaled for them to follow him. He stepped on the path in front of them and led the way.

"Where's he taking us?"

"I assume to the village."

"Did you tell him we're Americans?"

"I don't think he cares."

Graham had lowered his arms once he'd begun to speak to the man, so Katie had lowered hers, as well. Now she was itching to take some more photographs, but suspected that if she tried it, her camera would be confiscated. It wasn't worth the risk. She had to let Graham deal with the situation and hopefully get them some transportation out of there.

The trail eventually led them to a small village built around an old church. A cobbled courtyard with a fountain and formal garden was next to the church. The group of men surrounding Katie and Graham motioned for them to enter the garden, which they did, looking around them.

The village was quiet. Few people could be seen stirring. Katie wondered if fighting had broken out this far. Surely they would have heard it in the mountains. She'd heard nothing in the past thirty-six hours to cause her to believe the fighting had been anywhere in this area.

She looked at Graham who was looking past her shoulder. She turned and saw a priest coming toward them. The armed men stepped aside and allowed the holy man to come into their midst.

He nodded gravely to Graham and Katie, then said something to the leader. The armed man immediately responded, his tone sharp, his gestures angry. Graham and Katie watched the two men, the priest continuing to ask questions, then making comments before he finally turned to Graham.

He spoke in a quiet and sober tone. Graham responded in the same tongue, his words halting. The priest surprised her by saying, "Ah. You are Americans." He spoke with a strong accent but she had understood him. If anything, the priest looked even more serious then, which certainly wasn't a good sign.

Katie started to say something when Graham took her hand, giving it a squeeze, which she interpreted to mean that she was to let him do the talking.

Fair enough.

"Yes, Father. And you are—"

"Father Xabier." He turned to the men watching them so intently and spoke to them at length before the leader nodded slowly. They moved away but did not leave. "I am sorry about the men. We received word yesterday that there was fighting in the capital. We are naturally suspicious of any strangers at the moment. Particularly foreigners."

Graham nodded. "I understand." He looked around. "Is there somewhere private where I might speak with you?"

The priest nodded to the church. "My office, perhaps?"

"Thank you." He turned to Katie and in a low voice murmured, "I need to speak to Father Xabier for a few minutes. I've got to decide how much to tell him about why we are here. Will you wait here in the garden for me? I'll be back as soon as possible."

"But why—"

She started to ask why she couldn't go with them, when he shook his head. "You'll be safe enough. I want to offer an explanation for our presence here and I may not be able to tell him the truth. I don't want you looking surprised if I decide to make up something."

"Why do you need to make up anything? Why can't you just tell him the truth?"

"Because they may not let us leave here if they know why we're in the country. I want to feel my way with him and hopefully get some kind of an idea about where he stands. I'm prepared to lie if I have to, but it would be easier if you weren't standing there looking on."

She glanced at the priest, then at the men watching them so intently before returning her gaze to Graham. "I don't see why there's any need to lie. We aren't a threat to the village, but go ahead if you really believe we're in some kind of danger.... Oh, and see if there's a phone I can use, would you?"

"I need to make some calls, as well. I'll see what I can do." He gave her hand a reassuring squeeze before releasing it and joining the priest. The two men turned and walked toward the church.

Katie sat down on a bench near the fountain. The day had continued to be warm and sunny, but the cool breeze kept it from being uncomfortable. Now that they had found a village, she could take the time to enjoy the quaintness of the area and its people.

A young mother with two small children came toward her. They stopped about ten feet away and looked at her. The woman could have been about Katie's age. Katie smiled. The woman smiled back.

She walked over to them. "Hello. My name is Katie." The woman shrugged and shook her head.

Katie held up her camera. As she spoke, she gestured with her hand. "May I take a picture of you and your children?" She pointed to each of them and to the camera.

The woman smiled shyly and nodded, grasping the children's hands in each of hers and straightening to her full height.

Katie hid her smile and busied herself with her camera settings. After taking several pictures of the small family, she turned and took pictures of the church, the garden and of some of the nearby homes.

The woman spoke to her, gesturing to one of the houses. Katie smiled and shrugged. The woman laughed, shrugging, as well.

The armed men had moved away, still in a group, but they continued to watch her. No doubt Graham would not be pleased with her for taking photographs, but it was what she did, not only for a living, but whenever she was nervous or didn't know what to do with herself. It gave her hands something to do, and her mind something on which to concentrate.

After about fifteen minutes or so, she saw Graham and the priest reappear. Father Xabier was animated, looking cheerful as he pointed first to her, then to the woman standing nearby, before returning his attention to Graham.

"I wonder what that's all about?" she muttered, glancing at the woman as she responded to Father

Xabier's beckoning motion. The woman joined the two men and listened while the priest spoke on at length.

Finally, the woman nodded her head vigorously, smiled shyly at Graham before she turned away and retraced her steps.

Once again, she gave Katie a big smile, said something in a cheerful voice, then took her children's hands and hurried down the street.

Katie felt as if she were watching a foreign film with no subtitles, and found it frustrating not to have an interpreter at her elbow to explain. She watched the woman enter the home she'd pointed out earlier. Ah. At least that explained a little. She'd been pointing out where she lived.

Graham materialized beside her.

"Friendly people, aren't they?" she offered.

"Amazingly so," he responded, sounding somewhat hesitant.

"Did you explain to Father Xabier that we aren't here to make trouble for any of them?"

"I think I convinced him finally, yes." His voice still sounded a little strange.

"Did you find a phone we can use?"

"Yes. In fact, Father Xabier was kind enough to allow me to call one of my contacts in the capital to get the latest news. Of course, I didn't tell the priest who I was calling or why."

"And what did you find out?"

"The fighting hasn't slackened. The rebels have run into more opposition than they expected. The situation remains tense. The government is trying to reassure the people in the remote areas such as this village that they will come to no harm, but, obviously, the government has no control over the rebels. There's no predicting what's going to happen in these outlying areas in the weeks to come.''

"What about transportation? Did you ask Father Xabier if someone in the village can help us?"

"I, uh, didn't get to the subject, but I don't think there's going to be a problem." He surveyed the area before taking her arm and guiding her to the bench she had occupied earlier. Once they were seated, he said, "The priest is quite worried about his people. He told me that they don't want anything to do with the uprising going on in the capital. They're afraid that we're bringing unwanted trouble by showing up like this. ''

"Did you tell him who we are?"

"Not exactly. I decided he might find my connection with the government a little suspicious, since the United States supports the present regime. I can't tell who the villagers support in this matter. I didn't think his knowing that you're a reporter would ease his mind, either."

"You never intended to tell him the truth, did you?" she accused, irritated with him.

He rubbed his jaw with his finger. "I told you I was prepared to lie if I got any hint that we might find ourselves being held here. Neither one of us wants that to happen."

She glanced around them, but there was no one in sight. The priest had gone back inside the church. The men had disappeared, apparently reassured by something the priest had told them. "He seemed so nice. I don't think he would have seen us as provocateurs, do you?"

"I didn't want to take the chance."

She sighed. "All right. So what kind of story did you tell him?"

He cleared his throat. "It was something I was thinking about during the night, when I was searching for a possible reason, other than the truth, for our being in the mountains."

"Okay. What?"

He wouldn't meet her gaze. "I told him that we'd come to Dalmatia several weeks ago with a team of university professors financed by an anthropological grant to study the area for papers we're preparing. That the outbreak in hostilities had caught us off guard. I pointed out that we just happened to be in the wrong place at the wrong time when the shooting began." He fidgeted before adding, "I explained that the two of us were together when our car was shot at, which is why we're now on foot."

"Did he accept your explanation?"

"Not at first."

"Smart man. Neither one of us looks to be the scholarly type, you know." She glanced down at her fatigues and shook her head with a smile. "So what did you say to convince him?"

"Well, I, uh, I explained that we were actually searching for a priest at the time the car was hit. That since that time, we'd been hiking through the mountains in search of a town and we were delighted when we saw the church spires."

"Nobody's going to believe that we were wandering around the countryside in search of a priest, Graham. No wonder he's having a problem understanding what we're doing here. What earthly reason would we have to search for a priest?"

"I told him that during our weeks of working together, we discovered a growing passion for each other that became too overwhelming to ignore."

She jumped up from the bench. "Are you out of your mind?" She looked at the church, wondering if she should hunt down the priest and explain her traveling companion's sudden dementia. She turned to Graham. "Why would you make up such an outlandish tale?"

"It was the only reason I could think of that would explain our sudden pressing need to be married immediately."

Chapter Five

She waited for a moment, waiting for him to smile and admit he was teasing her. Instead, he looked away from her, intently studying their surroundings.

Finally, she said, "This is some kind of joke, right? You're just kidding me, aren't you?"

When his gaze met hers, she could see no amusement lurking in his dark eyes. "I said what I felt it was necessary to say. When I implied that we had... anticipated our wedding vows and now wanted to rectify our mistake before possible repercussions, he immediately understood our urgency. He became open and friendly, pleased to see that we were willing to do the right thing."

"The right thing! You mean you led him to believe that you and I— That we— Now he thinks that I've—"

"That you've slept with me, yes. Which isn't really a lie. We fell asleep together yesterday, so technically I didn't lie."

"You know good and well that he thinks we did anything but sleep! How could you stand there before a priest and lie like that!"

"I told him that I loved you and that I wanted very much to marry you."

"Yes! That's what I'm talking about. How could you lie to a man of God, regardless of our circumstances?"

"I said whatever I could think of to convince him we had no interest in local politics. It was either that, or have him turn us over to those armed men who had it in mind to hold us for questioning for who knows how long."

"I'd prefer a third option," she said through clenched teeth.

"Sorry. That's the best I could do on short notice."

Katie closed her eyes and concentrated on regaining her composure. After all, she'd been in tight spots before. She'd faced angry mobs, sniper fire, Mother Nature at her worst. She could handle this. Of course she could.

"Don't fall asleep on me now, Kincaid," he muttered. "It would help a great deal if you could look properly lovesick and eager to tie the knot."

Her eyes flew open. "Lovesick!"

"Eager would do."

"You can't get married just like that, you know," she said, thinking furiously. "I'm sure there must be all kinds of red tape to go through, especially in a foreign country."

"Don't you think I know that? The priest wants us to come inside and speak with him. He'll probably explain that we'll have to wait until we get back to the States. We'll act sheepish and properly contrite, then ask if there's any transportation that could get us to the border and help us on our way."

She let out a sigh of relief. "Why didn't you say that in the first place? I thought you were talking about a real wedding here."

"Of course not. What I wanted to do was create a smoke screen that gave us another reason for being here rather than the truth."

"What did he say to that woman when he called her over?"

"I couldn't follow everything. I think he was seeing if she might be able to feed us, or let us stay at her place overnight."

"Hopefully, we'll be out of here before dark," she replied.

"Well, let's go hear what he has to say." Graham took her hand and Katie thought about how to look lovesick.

Once in the priest's office, everything seemed to become surreal to Katie. From what she could understand of the conversation, which was a mixture of the two languages, the priest was not informing them they could not be married in Dalmatia. Her worst suspicions materialized when Graham turned to her after a long and incomprehensible discussion with Father

Xabier and in a low voice said, "Do you have your passport?"

"Of course. Why?"

"We need to show it to him."

"Why?"

"So that he can fill out the license."

Her horrified gaze went to the priest who was making notations on a piece of paper. "What license? I thought you said he wouldn't agree to this?"

He shook his head slightly and in the same low voice, said, "So far, he's being very understanding. But even if we do go through some kind of ceremony, it certainly doesn't mean that we'd actually be married. I mean, I'm sure it wouldn't be recognized by the local government."

"Oh." She fumbled in her bag for her passport and gave it to Graham. He pulled his out of his pocket and handed them both to the priest.

Once again the priest asked questions that Katie had trouble understanding before he stood and motioned for them to follow him. Katie glanced at Graham and he gave a tiny shrug.

How could he be so blasted calm at a time like this? Legal or not, they were in a church telling a priest that they wanted to marry. Wasn't there something binding about intent? How could they pretend later that they hadn't meant any of it to be taken seriously?

The priest stood in the doorway and beckoned to them. They followed him to the doorway into the church sanctuary before Katie paused, looking down at herself in dismay.

A less likely looking bride and groom could not be imagined, she decided. "Excuse me," she said, causing Father Xabier to turn to her with a puzzled look.

Graham frowned. "What is it?"

"I was wondering if I could use the rest room."

Graham posed a question to the priest who nodded and rattled off what must be directions. Graham repeated them in English. "Down the hall, second door on the right."

When she stepped inside the small room and looked into the mirror, she didn't know whether to laugh or cry. Her gray eyes looked huge in her white face. The smattering of freckles across her nose stood out in bold relief. Her hair looked as though birds had been nesting there.

After using the facilities, she washed her face and hands and went to work on her hair. Eventually, the tangles disappeared and her hair hung limply around her face.

That certainly wouldn't do. Once again, she braided it and placed it in a coil at the nape of her neck. There. She looked a little better. With her new hairdo, she now appeared old enough to be her own grandmother, with no bridelike quality whatsoever.

The fatigues were hopelessly rumpled, their camouflage colors definitely not part of any real bride's color scheme. But then, she hadn't chosen them for their high-fashion appeal. She'd picked them because they were comfortable, utilitarian and tough.

Sighing at the sight in the mirror, she put on some lipstick that made her look like a clown. She wiped it off and walked out of the room.

And immediately ran into Graham.

"Are you all right?" he asked, a frown of concern on his rugged face.

"Just peachy," she muttered.

"You were gone so long, I was worried."

"If you must know, I was trying to make myself a little more presentable," she mumbled. "I don't think it helped."

He flashed her a brief grin. "You look fine." He rubbed his jaw. "Maybe I should take the time to shave. Anything to convince Father Xabier that I'm a blushing bridegroom."

"I believe it's the bride who traditionally blushes," she said.

"That's good to know. I wanted to make this ceremony as traditional as possible."

"Then there really *is* going to be a wedding?" she asked in a resigned voice.

"Yes. The priest mentioned that he's already contacted the village organist. His housekeeper is presently gathering a few flowers from her garden for your bouquet, and some of the villagers have wandered into the chapel to witness the festivities."

"Now I know how Alice must have felt when she stepped through the looking glass."

"The important thing is that we've convinced the village officials that we aren't here to take over their village and that the fighting in the capital has absolutely nothing to do with us. Nobody's after us."

"I hope you're right."

"So do I," he admitted.

Father Xabier was watching them from down the hallway. No doubt that was the reason Graham suddenly leaned down and kissed her.

"I'm sorry for getting you into this, Katie. It wasn't one of my better ideas."

"You can say that again."

"Do you have an alternative plan?"

"Not at the moment."

"Then we'll just have to go through with this charade."

"And hope that God will forgive us," she muttered, turning away and allowing him to enter the bathroom.

She was still having trouble believing all of this. It was happening too fast, Graham was too calm, and she was convinced she was going to wake up at any moment.

The priest beckoned for her to join him. When she did, she couldn't believe what she saw.

The woman who'd earlier posed for her had returned with several other villagers, all smiling and friendly, and were taking their places in the pews.

They had come to witness the wedding.

She turned to the priest. "You told them?"

He nodded. "Yes, stay with Greta this night."

"Oh, no, we couldn't impose. We'll find someone with transportation and—"

"Not possible. Not today. Maybe two days, maybe three. While you wait, you stay with Greta."

"Oh, but—"

She heard the sound of a door opening down the hall and Graham appeared with his bag, clean-shaven and enormously appealing.

Too bad she had such a strong urge to strangle him. In her sweetest tone, she said, "Ah, Graham, love, there you are."

He eyed her warily. "What's up?"

"It seems that Father Xabier has arranged for us to stay here in the village for the next day or so, possibly more. The lady he spoke to, whose name is Greta, I understand, has prepared us a place to stay with her while we're here."

He spoke to the priest in the native language. The priest nodded and smiled, obviously pleased with his arrangements. After a few minutes of conversation in the peculiar mix of language that she couldn't for the life of her understand, Graham turned, and moved her away from the priest. With surprising cheerfulness he said, "Sorry, but it can't be helped. He said that most of the vehicles here are too old to be depended upon for anything but local use. The only long-distance vehicle that is trustworthy belongs to a farmer who left a few days ago to sell the village produce at one of the markets. He's expected back in a few days."

"Swell," she muttered.

"It could be worse."

"How?"

"You could be holed up in that hotel, or being held as a political prisoner by now."

"I should have stayed and taken my chances."

"That isn't very bridelike of you, my dear. What must Father Xabier be thinking of you?"

She smiled brightly at the priest. He returned her smile and once again motioned for them to enter the sanctuary.

Ready or not, she was going to be married in a foreign country to a man she barely knew.

Katie kept reminding herself that this wasn't really a marriage. It was like a play. They were actors on a stage. Instead of playing the roles of threatening insurgents, which would have gotten them locked up, they had chosen the role of romantic lovers.

Her sisters would have loved it.

The church was filled with the scent of flowers and candles. She and Graham knelt before the altar. Their vows were witnessed by the small gathering of villagers and she and Graham received the priest's blessings on their impromptu union.

She repeated the priest's halting English words, vowing to respect the promises she was making to the man kneeling beside her. Late-afternoon sunlight beamed through one of the stained-glass windows, splashing color across the three of them in an artistic benediction.

After the last amen, they rose to their feet, thanked the priest, then left the small chapel, followed by the villagers. Greta came up and touched her arm, then pointed to her house.

"I think we're supposed to go with her," she said, glancing at Graham.

"I could stand something to eat. How about you?"

Food was the last thing she had on her mind, but she wasn't going to inform Graham of that. He was acting as though what they'd just gone through was an everyday occurrence to him.

She'd never spent such a strange day in her life. Now she was expected to celebrate her new status in life, a status that she'd never considered having, not even for a few days.

They entered Greta's home and were shown through the house to the garden in back, where a table had been placed. Several women were busily setting places and carrying food from their hostess's kitchen. Greta smiled, gestured to the women, the table and to the two of them.

"I think all of this is for us," Graham said.

Katie's eyes filled with tears. How could complete strangers be so welcoming and generous of their time, talents and food? The women were laughing and joking, gazing at the newlyweds and giggling. It was the giggling that caused Katie's cheeks to burn with embarrassment.

Graham took her hand and slowly raised it to his lips, placing a soft kiss on her knuckles. She stiffened and started to pull her hand away. He tightened his grasp and winked at her. "Don't be shy, Katie. These women are pleased to see us together. Don't you think we owe it to them to show some romance on our wedding day?"

"I think you're enjoying this!" she said through smiling lips.

"I'll admit that you make a very attractive blushing bride. Too bad you're the photographer. I would have liked to have had pictures of you."

"Of course you would. The bride wore boots—not to mention cammies. Who knows? I might start a new fad."

"C'mon, I'm starved." He pulled out one of the chairs for her, then seated himself across from her. The women took turns bringing them dishes from which to choose.

Katie had to admit that the offerings smelled wonderful and looked even better. Before long, she forgot her sense of being a fraud and savored each delicious bite.

By the time they were finished, the sun had set and Greta waved them back into the house. With an impish grin, she motioned for them to follow her up some steps to a small landing. She opened the only door there and stepped back, smiling.

There was a room beneath the eaves of her home, decorated with furniture that had been lovingly crafted. The bed was covered with a handmade quilt. Matching tables stood on either side with small lamps.

"This is beautiful," Katie said. She looked at Greta who'd been watching her. "Thank you so much," she said, touching her hand. She turned to Graham. "Will you tell her how much we appreciate her thoughtfulness?"

Graham's face had become an impassive mask. He carefully searched for words of thanks, haltingly spoken. Greta beamed, nodding. Then she went downstairs, leaving them standing in the doorway.

Katie moved toward the four-poster bed and stroked the gleaming wood. She heard the door close behind her.

"Katie?"

She turned at the peculiar note in his voice. "Yes?"

"You do realize that we're going to need to stay here together. Otherwise, this charade we've gone through will have served no purpose."

She looked around the room. Other than a small wooden chair, the small tables and a matching chest of drawers, there was no other furniture in the room. The bed took up most of the space.

"We'll have to share the bed. Is that what you're saying?"

"Yes."

She shrugged, struggling for nonchalance. "Well, it won't be the end of the world. We're both adults. We can—"

He made a chopping sign with his hand. "Don't sound like an innocent child. How do you expect me to share a bed with you and keep my hands off you?"

She looked up at him in surprise. "You make me sound like an irresistible siren, Graham. Just last night you made it clear that you weren't interested in some inexperienced female. I haven't gained any more experience in the past twenty-four hours."

"You were also sleeping in another area last night."

"So?"

"I'm not sure how to break the news to you, but I don't have an overabundant supply of willpower where you're concerned."

Pleased with his admission, she went up on tiptoe and kissed his jaw. "Thank you for that." She picked up her knapsack where it had been placed in a corner of the room. "I think the bed's big enough for two without crowding. Maybe by tomorrow, the farmer will be back and we'll be able to leave here.'' She dug into her bag. With her back turned to him, she added, ''Maybe I can get some clothes washed tomorrow. All I have to sleep in is the sweatshirt I used last night.''

''That's more than I have,'' he said in a low voice.

She turned and stared at him, remembering the night before. He'd been bare-chested, she recalled. The blanket had fallen when he'd sat up, when he'd pulled her into his lap and held her. When he'd— She swallowed. ''Oh.''

''Yeah. Oh.''

''Well,'' she said, frantically trying to come up with an answer, ''suppose I, uh, go downstairs and talk to Greta about my clothes. While I'm gone, why don't you, uh, get ready for bed. I mean, once you're in bed, there won't be a problem, will there?''

Graham listened to her naive suggestions and wondered once more what he was doing in this situation. It had gotten out of hand and he had no one to blame but himself. He'd honestly thought that the priest would not be able to marry them, but it hadn't worked out that way. In the eyes of the church, this woman was his wife. In the eyes of the state, he doubted very seriously that the ceremony would be recognized.

In his heart, though, he knew that he wanted to claim Katie Kincaid as his love and his wife in the fullest sense of the word. If he did, would she understand, finally, how he felt about her? Would she at least be willing to reconsider her attitude about commitments and marriage?

If he admitted his love to her, would she be willing to work out a relationship with him that would nurture both of them, or would she run as far and as fast as she could?

He needed more time with her, a chance to convince her that they could make a relationship work. The situation they were in now wasn't real.

So what were a few sleepless hours if he could use their time together to get her to trust him?

"I'll be fine, Katie," he said after a rather long silence. "We'll get through this just fine."

She nodded. "Of course we will." She sounded pleased that they were in agreement. "I'll knock before coming in, okay?"

Katie grabbed her knapsack and left the room. He took his time undressing, folding each item of apparel neatly and placing it on the waiting chair, until he stood in his briefs.

Gingerly, he lifted the covers and slid under them. After the hard floor the night before, he felt that he'd just stretched out on a cloud. With a sigh of profound pleasure, Graham allowed himself to sink into the comfortable bed. The long hike had taken its toll. So had the emotional crises since he'd rescued Katie from the hotel.

Within moments he was asleep.

Katie, meanwhile, went in search of Greta. Having found the woman, Katie pantomined washing the clothes. Greta nodded vigorously and led her to her laundry room, which was equipped with both a washer and dryer.

Katie stayed and waited through the cycles, spending part of the time trying to communicate with her hostess. She soon ran out of comprehensible sign language, and Greta reluctantly returned to the other room.

By the time Katie returned upstairs, she was feeling much calmer. She had a knapsack full of clean clothes. She would be able to sleep in her pajamas tonight, after all, and surely by now Graham would be asleep.

She peeked into the room and found that he'd left one of the lamps on for her. Tiptoeing in, she eased the door closed behind her, watching him to see if he'd heard her.

He lay on his side, facing her, his hair rumpled across his forehead. He looked younger, somehow, when he was asleep. The tension and lines in his face were gone.

Katie quickly changed into her pajamas, then slipped into bed beside him. She realized that she'd been holding her breath in an effort to be quiet, but if his relaxed state was any indication, she wasn't certain that a bomb going off nearby would wake him.

She tried to forget the events of the day, but they were too vivid and continued to flash across her mind like a videotape endlessly repeating herself. Legal or not, recognized or not, she had vowed to commit herself to the man beside her for the rest of her life.

She shivered, thinking about it. Hadn't she always said she would never marry, never give a man an opportunity to place her in a vulnerable position where she might have to depend on him?

The ceremony today had felt suspiciously like the real thing. Tonight was her wedding night, that time when traditionally a woman became a wife by giving herself to the man she loves.

Katie was more certain than ever that she would never be willing to commit herself to such a relationship. She was too used to having her freedom, going her own way, answering to no one. She drifted off to sleep still enumerating all the many reasons why marriage would never be a part of her life-style....

She woke up to discover that sometime during the night she and Graham had moved to the center of the bed. His arms were around her and he was nibbling on her ear, not at all an unpleasant experience.

He stroked her breast in a lazy movement.

Katie tried to come awake more fully, but the sensuous touch was also soothing and filled her with a sense of floating pleasure. There was nothing wrong in continuing to enjoy his touch for a while.

She shifted slightly, turning more fully toward him. He slid his hand beneath her pajama top so that his warm palm touched her heated skin. She shivered with the intimacy, holding her breath in anticipation of his next move.

Lazily he skimmed upward until he cupped her sensitive breast as he'd done earlier. But, oh! What a difference not to have the thin cotton material between them. She arched her back in encouragement and turned her head to find his mouth. When his lips covered hers, she sighed with contentment. He seemed to know just where to touch her to give her the most pleasure, how to caress her, when to become more urgent.

Such as now! The lazy stroking elicited a heated response from deep within her. Graham seemed to understand. He slid his thigh between hers, pulling her closer, rubbing his leg along hers until she felt as though she were going to burst into flame.

He raised himself and was shifting his body over her when he froze, unmoving, then pulled away as though he'd received an electric shock.

The combination of losing his body warmth and the covers at the same time brought Katie into full awareness of where she was and what she'd been doing. Meanwhile, Graham had stumbled out of bed and was muttering obscenities while he fumbled for his jeans and jerked them on.

Katie reached for the lamp beside the bed and turned it on. Blinking, she turned to the man standing as far away from the bed as he could.

"Graham?"

"I'm sorry, Katie. I never meant to— The thing is, I was dreaming that you and I were— Oh, hell. What difference does it make *what* I was dreaming. I shouldn't have—"

"Graham, it's all right." She was completely awake now, and shivering. Her body had been responding to his touch with enthusiasm. Regardless of their circumstances, she had discovered a side to herself that she hadn't known existed. She'd wanted him to continue touching and caressing her. She'd wanted to know what happened next, how she could find the fulfillment her quivering body was demanding.

"I didn't want to take advantage of the situation."

"You haven't. You certainly weren't forcing yourself upon me, you know."

He sighed in disgust, rumpling his hair even more than it was by running his hands through it. "That's beside the point. The thing is, I knew I'd have trouble keeping my hands off you. This just isn't going to work." He pulled on his shirt and stopped long enough to put on socks and shoes before he opened the bedroom door. "Go back to sleep, Katie. We'll talk about this later."

She watched the door close behind him and felt tears slide down her cheeks. She felt strange, flushed and shivering, aching for something she didn't understand. How dare he kiss and caress her, bring her to this quivery mass of sensation, then walk out the door!

Katie could feel her temper building, quelling her desire to some degree by focusing her tempestuous feelings on the man who had caused them.

Who did he think he was, making decisions for both of them? Couldn't he see what he'd done? He'd made her even more aware of him than she'd been before. No longer did she have to imagine what it felt like to have a man touch her so intimately. She would only need to remember these past two nights.

She jerked the covers up over her shoulders and curled into the pillow once again. Only then did she realize that she was on his pillow. It still carried the faintest scent of his after-shave on its smooth surface.

She buried her head in the pillow and sobbed.

Chapter Six

When Katie came downstairs the next morning, she found Graham sitting in the garden sipping coffee. Without saying anything, he poured her some and placed the cup on the table in front of the other chair.

"Thank you," she said, not looking at him. She took the cup in both hands, warming them, before sipping.

"It looks like it's going to be another nice day," he said after the silence between them had continued for some time.

"Yes," she agreed without inflection.

"I spoke with Father Xabier this morning. He's agreed to have one of his parishioners take us to the next village where we might be able to find transportation."

She looked up, suddenly remembering. "I didn't call the office yesterday!" she said in horror.

"You had other things on your mind."

"How could I have forgotten something so important?" She jumped up from the chair. "Does Greta have a phone?"

"No, but I'm sure that you can use the one at the church." He motioned to her cup. "Why don't you at least finish your coffee before you—"

"I can't. I have to—" She didn't bother finishing her sentence. Instead, she hurried into the house, rushed into the street, then trotted over to the church. When the priest opened the door, she explained her need and he showed her to his office before returning to another part of the building.

As soon as she got through to New York, she asked to speak to Lloyd Webster, her boss.

"Katie! God, it's good to hear your voice! Where are you? Are you hurt? Did you—"

"Whoa, Lloyd. I'm fine, really. I'm sorry I haven't called sooner, but—"

"Fine? Are you still in the capital?"

"Well, no, but—"

"Thank God you got out in time!"

"What do you mean?"

"The whole city is going up in flames. The news networks are transmitting horrific scenes there. When we didn't hear from you after the fighting began, I was afraid that—" His voice broke and there was silence on the line.

"A friend helped me leave right after the fighting began, Lloyd. Unfortunately, we had a little mishap with our transportation and we've spent a major part of our time hiking through the mountains.''

''Where are you now?''

''Etrusca.''

''You've got to get out of Dalmatia, Katie. All hell's about to break loose in that country.''

''But I wanted to cover what's happening. As soon as I can get some transportation—''

''I want you out of there. Now. We're getting all the coverage we need from the news networks. When things level off later, we can always send you there again, but for now, I want you to make tracks back here.''

''I'm sorry I wasn't able to let you know when the shooting started.''

''Listen, Katie. After almost three days, I was convinced you were dead. At the moment, I'd forgive you for anything. You're sure you're all right? You wouldn't lie to me, would you?''

''Of course not. I'm fine. We've been treated with courtesy and consideration.''

''We? Oh, you mean you and your friend. Who is it?''

''Nobody you'd know. Just a fellow American I've run into a few times over the years.''

''Are you going to be able to get out of there today?''

''I'll give it my best shot.''

''Then I'll see you once you're back in New York.''

She heard the slight click that disconnected them before she lowered the receiver into its cradle. Talking to Lloyd helped her regain her perspective. Lloyd was part of her real life. He was a symbol of the profession she'd chosen, the life-style she wanted.

Her unwanted feelings for Graham could be overcome. It might take some work, but she fully intended to dismiss him completely from her mind.

With that resolve, Katie left the church and returned to Greta's. Graham was still sitting in the garden. A basket of rolls were on the table. "Have one," he said, waving in the direction of the freshly baked rolls. Her stomach growled and Katie decided to take his advice. He poured her another cup of coffee. "Did you get through?"

"Yes. My boss wants me to come home."

"Smart man."

"He said I could return to Dalmatia later."

"Maybe not so smart."

"It's all part of my job."

He watched her over the rim of his cup. "I know."

Neither one spoke until she'd finished two of the rolls and her second cup of coffee.

"About last night," Graham began slowly as though carefully picking through a vast assortment of words.

"There's nothing to discuss," Katie said, meeting his gaze for the first time that morning. She was composed, no longer feeling uncertain. For a few hours, she'd ventured into a strange new place in life, pleasurable but much too risky for her peace of mind. "Circumstances forced us into a couple of situations where certain intimacies occurred. However, we're both adults. Nothing really happened. My virtue is still intact, if that's what's bothering you."

He emptied the rest of the coffee into his cup before answering her. "I'm glad," he said simply, concentrating on the liquid in his cup. "I'm not very proud of myself." He raised his eyes. "I had no ulterior motives in seeking you out at the hotel. I wanted to make certain you were safe."

She nodded. "For which I'm grateful. According to Lloyd, the capital is in chaos and the fighting is moving into the surrounding countryside. That's why he wants me out of here."

"Yes. I got my orders by phone this morning, as well." He looked rueful when he added, "As well as a royal chewing out."

"Because you've stayed too long?"

"Because I didn't tell them where I was when I called yesterday."

She frowned. "You mean they wanted you to stay in the capital?"

He shook his head. "They didn't know I'd left the Mideast."

"The Mideast. You weren't supposed to be in Dalmatia?"

"Nope."

"But you came, anyway?"

"Yep."

"Why?"

He seemed to search for the answer in the steaming liquid before him. When he looked at her, his eyes seemed filled with secrets. "I was worried about you."

She couldn't think of anything to say. What he was telling her didn't make any sense. If he was on assignment in the Middle East, then for him to come to

Dalmatia meant—meant what? "How did you know I was here?"

"I called the magazine asking for you. Your boss told me you'd come here to cover the aftermath of the assassination."

"He told you? That's not like Lloyd."

"I explained that I was a close friend and needed to reach you right away."

"So you came looking for me, you found me and—"

"Put you through a bogus wedding ceremony. Yeah, I know. Everything kind of blew up in my face—literally."

"I had no idea."

"I know. While I waited for the sun to come up this morning, I decided to tell you the truth. You've become very important to me, Katie. We're both fully occupied with our jobs and I know that. I understand. But I also want you to understand that you are very special and I..." His voice faded. "Anyway," he said, clearing his throat, "I managed to get myself into hot water because of the delays we've run into, which means I have to leave today, even if it means hiking to the border."

She was having trouble taking everything in. Was he saying that he...? Well, he had risked so much to come here and— "Graham?"

"Yes?"

"Thank you for risking your neck and your job for me."

"Will you promise not to take so many risks next time?"

She smiled. "I'll do my best."

"There are times when I wish I *were* a supernatural being, but since I can't claim that kind of power, I may not be around when you need help next time."

She reached for his hand that rested on the table. "I'm glad we had a chance to get to know each other a little better. Who knows where we'll be the next time we meet?"

He stood and turned slightly away from her, saying, "Let's go find Father Xabier. It's time to get back to our real lives."

Two months later, Katie sat taking notes at the weekly staff meeting.

"Are there any questions about this week's assignments?" Lloyd asked the people gathered around the conference table.

When someone responded with a long and involved question about possible perspectives for a particular assignment, Katie leaned back in her chair and let her mind drift.

She'd been doing that a lot since she'd returned from Dalmatia. She had to keep reminding herself that she was now back to her normal routine. This was her life. Sitting in meetings, catching planes to news spots around the world, researching stories, and rushing to meet deadlines were all aspects of the life she had chosen to live. She could hear the street sounds of New York coming through the windows. So why did her mind keep returning her to the mountains of Dalmatia? Why did Graham Douglas's face keep haunting her dreams?

She was acting like an adolescent with her first crush. Come to think of it, she hadn't had a crush at that age. Maybe that was it . . . she was going through delayed adolescence.

Well, whatever it was, she would love to get through it and get on with her life. Perhaps it was like a childhood disease. Once caught and experienced, she'd be immune for the rest of her life.

On returning home, she'd stayed busy. She hadn't wanted to dwell on that moment at the airport in Frankfurt when she and Graham were catching different planes. She'd had a sudden horrifying thought that she might not see him again. He was flying back into a very tense situation. A stray sniper bullet could find him.

The rush of fear had weakened her knees and caused her to shake. When had Graham become so important to her?

She felt as though something inside her had betrayed her when she wasn't aware of it happening. Some tiny part of her wanted to cling to him, beg him to be careful, promise him— Promise him what? That she would be waiting for him? That she— Her mind always went blank at this point, whenever she tried to place labels on what she was feeling. All right. So she'd developed a weakness for the man. She could live with it.

She would *have* to live with it, she'd discovered in the weeks since their parting, because it just wouldn't go away. Boy, wouldn't her sisters have a field day if they could see her now? They'd always said that one day she'd meet the man who would change all her attitudes toward love, marriage and commitment.

Well, that day would never come. She wasn't like her sisters. Graham had changed nothing. What he'd done was add new dimension to her life and her understanding of herself.

She'd discovered that she was a sensuous creature who enjoyed a man's kisses and caresses. It wasn't Graham she wanted. He'd just been the one who had awakened this sleeping part of her being. No doubt there were other men in the world who would have that effect on her, if she allowed them to get close enough. She just hadn't met one of them yet.

"Guess that's it," Lloyd said, reminding Katie where she was. She gathered up her notebook and pen and followed the rest of the staff out of the room.

Sally, one of the reporters and Katie's closest friend, fell into step beside her as they walked down the hallway toward their offices. "You okay?"

Katie looked at her in surprise. "Sure. Why?"

"You seem distracted."

Katie smiled. "Just the usual jet leg, that's all. I didn't get home until almost three this morning. If we hadn't had this meeting scheduled, I would have taken the day off and slept."

"You were in Mexico, right?"

"Uh-huh. Got a great interview with the president. It was definitely worth my losing a few hours of sleep and following him all over Mexico for a week in order to get an in-depth look at the country's economy."

"Better you than me. I like sleeping in the same bed every night...and waking up with the same man each morning," she added with a drawl.

"I'm sure your husband appreciates your sentiments. And for your information, I don't wake up with anyone—ever." Her thoughts immediately leaped to her stay in Dalmatia. She wasn't lying, she reminded herself. She had not found Graham in bed with her—except for that one night.... That one unforgettable, heart-stopping night when— *Stop it!* Couldn't she just forget about that entire trip?

Obviously not. She rubbed her temple and walked into her office. Sally followed her and helped herself to a cup of coffee. "You're shattering my illusions about your glamorous single life, Katie. I keep picturing you meeting all these fabulous guys who are eager to sweep you off your feet and into their beds." She sighed and rolled her eyes soulfully.

No. I will not think about him. I will not remember. I can train my mind to—

"There. You're doing it again," Sally said.

"Doing what?"

"I don't know what to call it. You just seem to drift off somewhere in the middle of a conversation. Maybe you should go home and get some rest."

Katie glanced at her watch. "I probably will go soon. First, I want to look at my mail, make an attempt at clearing off my desk and answer a few phone calls. By then, it'll be time for lunch. I've already told Lloyd I plan to take the afternoon off."

"Nothing like getting a head start on your weekend. Any big plans?"

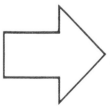

NO COST! NO OBLIGATION TO BUY!
NO PURCHASE NECESSARY!

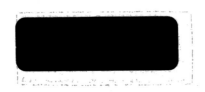

PLAY "LUCKY 7"
AND GET FIVE FREE GIFTS!

HOW TO PLAY:

1. With a coin, carefully scratch off the silver box at the right. Then check the claim chart to see what we have for you—FREE BOOKS and a gift—ALL YOURS! ALL FREE!

2. Send back this card and you'll receive brand-new Silhouette Romance™ novels. These books have a cover price of $3.25 each, but they are yours to keep absolutely free.

3. There's no catch. You're under no obligation to buy anything. We charge nothing—ZERO—for your first shipment. And you don't have to make any minimum number of purchases—not even one!

4. The fact is thousands of readers enjoy receiving books by mail from the Silhouette Reader Service™ months before they're available in stores. They like the convenience of home delivery and they love our discount prices!

5. We hope that after receiving your free books you'll want to remain a subscriber. But the choice is yours—to continue or cancel, anytime at all! So why not take us up on our invitation, with no risk of any kind. You'll be glad you did!

This lovely heart-shaped box is richly detailed with cut-glass decorations, perfect for holding a precious memento or keepsake—and it's yours absolutely free when you accept our no-risk offer.

PLAY "LUCKY 7"

**Just scratch off the silver box with a coin.
Then check below to see the gifts you get.**

YES! I have scratched off the silver box. Please send me all the gifts for which I qualify. I understand I am under no obligation to purchase any books, as explained on the back and on the opposite page.

315 CIS AQMH
(C-SIL-R-07/94)

NAME

ADDRESS   APT.

CITY   PROVINCE   POSTAL CODE

   WORTH FOUR FREE BOOKS PLUS A FREE HEART-SHAPED CURIO BOX

   WORTH THREE FREE BOOKS

   WORTH TWO FREE BOOKS

   WORTH ONE FREE BOOK

DETACH AND MAIL CARD TODAY

THE SILHOUETTE READER SERVICE™: HERE'S HOW IT WORKS

Accepting free books places you under no obligation to buy anything. You may keep the books and gift and return the shipping statement marked "cancel". If you do not cancel, about a month later we'll send you 6 additional novels, and bill you just $2.50 each plus 25¢ delivery and GST*. That's the complete price, and—compared to cover prices of $3.25 each—quite a bargain! You may cancel at any time, but if you choose to continue, every month we'll send you 6 more books, which you may either purchase at the discount price...or return at our expense and cancel your subscription.

*Terms and prices subject to change without notice.
Canadian residents will be charged applicable provincial taxes and GST.

0195619199-L2A5X3-BR01

SILHOUETTE READER SERVICE
PO BOX 609
FORT ERIE ONT
L2A 9Z9

MAIL POSTE
Canada Post Corporation / Société canadienne des postes
Postage paid   Port payé
if mailed in Canada   si posté au Canada
Business   Réponse
Reply   d'affaires
0195619199   01

Katie chuckled. "Other than catching up on the laundry, stocking the fridge and doing some reading, you mean?"

"Another shattered illusion. Why is it I expect single women to be out having dinner, seeing shows, taking moonlight strolls with some guy who's hanging on to their every word?"

"Larry ignoring you again?"

Sally shook her head. "Of course not. Not unless there's some sports event on television, you understand. Of course, the television is always set on the sports network, just in case."

Katie studied her friend for a long moment. "All that's part of marriage, isn't it?"

Sally shrugged. "I guess."

"I have a hunch you wouldn't give Larry up for anyone or anything, no matter how much you joke about him."

Sally made a face. "I know. I really love the guy and I know he loves me. It's just that, well, there's no excitement in our lives. We have a predictable routine that we've both come to take for granted. It's nice to have someone special in my life, but there isn't much spontaneity anymore."

"Then pretend you're single, that you've just met him, and begin to be a little unpredictable. Surprise him in some way. Think of new ways to have unexpected fun."

"Good point. What you're saying is that if I don't like it, I can change it."

"It's a thought, anyway."

Sally finished her coffee and tossed the paper cup into the wastebasket. "I really miss you when you're out of town, Katie. It helps to talk to you. You nudge me into seeing my life from a different perspective."

"I enjoy you, too, Sally. With my schedule, I don't have much time to cultivate relationships." She absently sorted through her mail. "Whether you believe it or not, your life is much more exciting than mine."

"Oh, sure. Suddenly getting caught in the middle of a war zone is much tamer than whipping up a tasty tuna casserole."

Once again, Graham's face hovered on the edge of her consciousness. "I suppose there could be exceptions," she admitted, looking up and smiling.

"Well, I'll let you get to work," Sally said, moving toward the door. "If you get bored over the weekend, give me a call. Maybe we can go see a movie or something. If the Mets are playing, Larry probably won't even notice I'm gone."

Katie laughed. "I may do that. We'll see."

After Sally left, Katie thought about their conversation. For the first time since she'd known her, Katie realized that she envied Sally. Like Sally, she'd been convinced that her life was exciting. The travel, the famous and not-so-famous people she met, the important events—all of these things were what she'd wanted to be doing.

Somehow, during the past few weeks, she'd discovered a new loneliness when she returned to her hotel room at the end of her day.

She'd fought the temptation to call Graham, to see if he was home, to see how things were going for him.

He'd given her his card, scribbling his unlisted number on the reverse side, and reminded her to call him whenever she felt the urge.

She was embarrassed to admit, even to herself, how often she got the urge. Thus far, she hadn't succumbed. She wasn't certain why. It had something to do with her not wanting him to see how vulnerable she was. She saw herself as happily independent. She wanted him to see her that way, as well.

She glanced at her watch. Another hour before lunch. Time enough to clear a few items off her desk before going home. She was just tired, that was all. She invariably fell into a state of introspection after a period of sleep deprivation. She'd just—

"Uh, Katie?"

Katie glanced up at the open doorway to her office. Sally stood there with a most peculiar look on her face.

"Yes?"

"There's, uh, there's someone here to see you."

No one ever came to the office to meet her. She always set up her interviews in the subject's home or office, where the atmosphere was more relaxed.

Puzzled, she checked her appointment book. She had nothing noted for today.

"Who is it? Did you ask for a name?"

She'd never seen Sally look quite so rattled. "He, uh, he said to tell you he's your husband."

Chapter Seven

Katie stared at Sally, her mind racing, searching for something to say, some way to explain. She hadn't told anyone what had happened in Dalmatia. There had been no reason to go into detail.

Then the true significance of Sally's announcement hit her. Graham was here in New York. In her office! Why in the world would he send such a ridiculous message? What was he trying to do, embarrass her in front of her colleagues? How could he be so—so—

"What should I tell him?" Sally asked hoarsely.

Katie struggled to maintain her self-control. Obviously, she'd need to exercise some damage control. She took a deep breath and stood, deliberately striving for a picture of calmness.

"Please show him the way to my office," she said pleasantly, feeling a nervous tic just beneath her right eye.

"Are you serious?" Sally asked in a hushed voice. "He's probably a mental patient that wandered off from whoever is supposed to be watching him." She paused, lifting her eyebrows slightly. "Although I must admit he is one good-looking dude. Too bad his mind had to go like that. I wonder—"

"Sally?"

"Hmm?"

"Please show him in, okay?"

"Oh! Sure thing, Katie. Maybe we can get a story out of this. Supposing this is some kind of modus operandi for this guy. If he goes around offices, visiting other professional women and claiming to be their husbands, think about the possible repercussions to a person's reputation. Maybe—"

"Sally!"

"I'm going, I'm going." Sally disappeared from the doorway and Katie rubbed her forehead, where a dull pain had begun to throb.

What was Graham doing here and why had he chosen such a bizarre way of announcing his presence? Did he think she'd refuse to see him, otherwise?

A slight noise in the hallway drew her attention and she lowered her hand from her face. Sally came into view.

Katie closed her eyes and sighed. "Wasn't he there?" she asked, starting around the desk just as Sally stepped into the room. Graham was immediately behind her.

For an instant, a strong surge of feeling washed over her at the sight of the man who'd been on her mind so much during the past two months. She convinced herself what she was feeling was anger, which she sternly controlled.

"Hello, Katie. Sorry to barge in on you like this." His deep voice, the voice that she would recognize anywhere, caused its usual reaction to her system.

Sally was watching him, wide-eyed, as though waiting for him to start babbling incoherently any moment.

Katie walked over to him and politely held out her hand. He took it, and her immediate response to his touch reminded her why she needed to keep a discreet distance from him. "Hello, Graham. Please come in and sit down." She hastily stepped back from him.

He was dressed more formally than she'd ever seen him. He wore a charcoal-colored sports jacket over a black shirt and trousers. His shoes glistened with a high gloss. Even his hair looked freshly trimmed.

Be honest, he looks smashing. How could she have forgotten how dynamic his dark good looks were?

Sally broke into her thoughts, sounding confused. "You mean you actually know him?"

With her best social smile, Katie introduced them, clasping her hands behind her. "Graham, I'd like you to meet one of my co-workers, Sally Haynes. Sally, this is Graham Douglas." She glanced at her watch, then at Sally. "Didn't you just mention that you were on a tight deadline?"

Ignoring Katie, Sally took Graham's proffered hand and smiled widely. "I'm so pleased to meet you, Mr. Douglas," she said brightly. Katie could see her friend visually measuring the breadth of his shoulders and the solid length of him. "I'm afraid that Katie has never mentioned you to me, which is an obvious oversight on her part. Otherwise, I would have known immediately to—''

"Goodbye, Sally," Katie said firmly. "We'll talk later.''

Sally reluctantly released Graham's hand and looked at Katie. "Oh, yes," she agreed with marked emphasis. "We certainly will.''

Once she was gone, Katie closed the door behind her and motioned to the chair in front of her desk.

"Have a seat.''

She returned to her chair behind the desk and sank into it, grateful for the support. "Was that really necessary?'' She'd lost her social smile.

He had the gall to look puzzled. "I beg your pardon?''

"There was no earthly reason for you to announce to the front desk that you were my husband, you know. Your idea of a little joke at my expense means I'll probably have to do a great deal of explaining.''

"Ah. Sorry. I didn't mean to create any speculation around your office.''

"Of course you didn't," she replied sweetly without looking away from his hooded gaze.

"I take it you didn't tell anyone about—''

The sweetness disappeared without a trace. "Of *course* I didn't tell anyone! There was nothing to tell. Thanks to your ridiculous story, we were—''

"Ridiculous? Hardly that, given the circumstances. Besides, it worked, didn't it? We got out of the country before all hell broke loose. If you'll recall, we were part of the last group of foreigners allowed out of Dalmatia, all of whom were innocent tourists—civilians who happened to be stranded there, just as we pretended to be. Do you honestly think we could have gotten out of there if we'd told them the truth?''

She waved her hand. "All right, we've already gone over all of this. But there was no reason for you to come to the office and blithely announce—"

"I guess I should have called first," he said, unbuttoning his jacket and looking very much at ease.

She glanced at the papers strewn across her desk while she made a determined effort not to leap across her desk and wrap her fingers around his arrogant neck.

"You were lucky to find me here," she said after a slight pause and several deep breaths while she counted to ten. "I just got back from Mexico late last night."

"I was already in town for a meeting at the UN Building and thought I'd take a chance on catching you at your office."

She folded her hands on the desk in front of her in an effort to appear calm. "Well," she said lightly, "you caught me."

His mouth twitched slightly. "In a manner of speaking."

"You've also left me with the ticklish task of explaining to people why you felt the irrepressible need to introduce yourself in such a way."

"You knew who I was, I trust."

She briefly closed her eyes and found herself counting once again. He actually appeared to be amused at her irritation. Well, she was tired of being the butt of his jokes. She just wanted him to state his reason for being there and to get out. She crossed her arms and waited for him to explain his presence.

After a lengthy silence, when he must have realized that she wasn't going to say anything more, he leaned forward in his chair. "I came by in hopes of getting you to go to lunch with me."

Ah. A social visit with a little mischief thrown in. It could be worse, she supposed. Katie unfolded her arms and leaned back in her chair, feeling a little more in control of the situation.

"It's kind of you to offer, Graham," she said, sounding ruefully sincere, "but as you can see from my desk, I'm really swamped. I need to spend time dealing with some of the more urgent matters before I can in good conscience leave."

When he didn't respond right away, she mentally reviewed her response and realized that she had sounded curt, almost rude. All right, so he'd decided to have a little fun with her earlier. Well, he'd had his little joke. It wasn't anything she couldn't handle.

Besides, hadn't she been wondering about him since they had parted? If she were honest with herself, she'd admit that she'd been delighted to see him when he stepped through her door a few minutes ago.

She'd still wanted to strangle him, of course. She wasn't sure how Graham always stirred up such a contradictory jumble of emotions in her. No one else in her life could affect her so violently. She seemed to bounce wildly between wanting to kiss him and wanting to kill him.

She glanced at her watch. "If you're going to be in town for a while," she added impulsively in the ensuing silence, "maybe we could meet later today." His expression didn't change. She smiled at him in an effort to show him there were no hard feelings on her part. "Once I'm through here, I intend to take the rest of the day off after a very busy week. How does that work out with your schedule?"

She waited for him to respond to her friendly overture. And waited. He sat there silently studying her for several uncomfortable minutes. When he did speak, she was certain she misunderstood him.

"Our marriage was legal, Katie."

She heard the words, but they made no sense to her, since her thoughts were on the present and the possibility that she would see him later today.

She shook her head slightly. "I'm sorry," she said, realizing she was more tired than she thought, unable to keep up with a simple conversation. "What did you say?"

In measured tones, he repeated his words. "I said that I just found out last week that our marriage is legal in Dalmatia and, according to the Justice Department lawyers who looked at the papers for me, it is recognized as legal in the States, as well." He waited a beat before adding, "I really am your husband."

She was already shaking her head. "No. That isn't possible. Didn't you explain to them that we couldn't possibly be m-m-m—" She stopped, unable to get the word out of her mouth.

"I'm afraid we are. There is nothing in Dalmatia's laws that prohibits foreigners from marrying there. Although unorthodox, the license was issued by the priest and later ratified by the village clerk."

"Oh my God," she whispered.

He inclined his head in a brief nod. "Exactly."

"How did you find out?"

"I was called into my supervisor's office and handed a package from Father Xabier that he'd mailed to me at the office."

She stared at him in dread. "A package?"

"Yes, containing copies of all the documents we signed. Since my supervisor was already aware that I'd been to Dalmatia at the beginning of the fighting there, he was quite curious to know what had been sent to me."

"You mean he opened the package?"

"No. But he wanted to know why I was receiving something from a Catholic priest in a country currently fighting a bitter civil war. I showed the papers to him and explained that I didn't believe them to be valid. He, in turn, sent them to be examined by lawyers at the Justice Department." Graham shifted in his chair and scratched his chin. "If it makes you feel any better, Kramer—my boss—was appalled that I had used a marriage ceremony as a way to get out of the country. Of course, he was already incensed over the fact I was there in the first place. He's convinced I'm way overdue for an extended vacation," he muttered, almost to himself. "Maybe he's right."

She was giving little attention to the problems their bogus wedding had caused him; her mind was too busy darting in all directions with the implications his announcement had on her and *her* life.

The headache that had been warming up earlier was now in full swing, pounding furiously behind her eyes. She leaned her head into her palm and massaged the ache while all kinds of thoughts raced through her mind.

"This is absurd. We can't be married," she muttered. Feeling cornered, she blurted out, "Why, we don't live in the same city...not even the same state!" Actually, she found the thought almost reassuring. It gave her a sense of welcome distance from both Graham and the whole situation.

She tried to concentrate. "Maybe there's been some kind of mistake. Maybe if we contact Father Xabier and explain to him why we pretended to—"

"I thought of that. Unfortunately, in the two months since the ceremony, the fighting has intensified to such an extent that most of the villagers, including the priest, have fled. According to the letter enclosed with the papers, Father Xabier wanted me to have copies of all the documents in the event the originals were destroyed."

She stared at him, her thoughts continuing to whirl chaotically through her head. "What are we going to do?" she finally whispered.

"I don't know. However, I thought we should get together and discuss some of the options." He paused, thinking. "I suppose we could meet later and—"

She jumped to her feet, wanting to escape the claustrophobic atmosphere that his announcement had generated. "You're right. We need to talk. Now. We'll go now." She glanced blindly down at her desk, seeing nothing but jumbled, incomprehensible pieces of paper. "I couldn't possibly concentrate on anything else at the moment."

Katie reached into her desk drawer and pulled out her purse, then froze, suddenly struck by a new realization. "That's why you announced yourself the way you did. You weren't trying to make a joke. You were being perfectly serious!" She wasn't certain whether she wanted to laugh or cry. She hadn't felt such turmoil since the last time she'd been around this man.

That should tell her something. She just wasn't certain what!

"To be honest, I didn't know how to break the news to you." He stood, watching her. "Would you like for me to explain to your co-workers what happened?" he asked quietly.

"Oh, no! Thank you, but no. I really feel that you've done quite enough, just by showing up here."

"I didn't know how else to reach you." He glanced at her, then away. "You see, I tried to call you the first part of the week. That's when they told me you'd be back today."

"So that's how you knew I'd be in the office."

"I was hoping you'd be here, since they wouldn't give me your home phone number or address."

"This is utterly ridiculous, do you realize that? You couldn't get in touch with your wife because you didn't know where she lived or her phone number!"

His mouth quirked into a lopsided smile. "You think that's bad? My supervisor asked me if I wanted to add you to my health care plan."

She had to get out of here before she came un-glued. Less than an hour ago, her biggest concern was getting home to catch up on her sleep. Now she was being considered for her husband's health care plan?

"C'mon, let's get out of here," she said, coming around the desk to his side. "Don't be surprised if half the staff falls through the door when I open it. Your announcement has no doubt created quite a stir around here."

He took her hand. "I can handle it if you can."

She made a face. "Actually, dodging bullets would be easier than dodging the gossip in this place... and both can be lethal to a life and to a person's reputa-tion. I guess I should be used to it by now."

As soon as they reached the street, Graham whis-tled for a taxi, which he obtained with amazing speed. Once they were inside the cab, he gave the name and address of the Hyatt Hotel in mid-Manhattan.

She raised her eyebrows and looked at him when he settled back beside her. "No ulterior motive, I prom-ise," he said, holding his hand up as though taking an oath. "I happen to enjoy eating there whenever I'm in town, that's all."

"You're not staying there?" she asked, still a little suspicious of his motives.

"Actually," he admitted, "I was. I checked out this morning but my bags are still there. I intend to catch one of the shuttle flights back to D.C. later on to-day."

Her mind had already returned to the purpose of this meeting. "It really shouldn't be difficult to get an annulment," she murmured, thinking out loud. "I just don't know how to go about it." She shook her head sharply. "What am I saying? How could I know details about something that has never entered my mind before now? I have a feeling it's going to be a little more complicated than our just going to a local court, since we live in separate states."

He didn't comment and they rode the rest of the way to the hotel in silence.

By mutual consent, while they ate, they avoided the subject that was on both their minds. Instead, Graham asked Katie about her recent trip to Mexico. He seemed sincerely interested in her opinion of the situation there, and before she fully realized what was happening, she was explaining to him what she had seen, who she had spoken with and some of her conclusions regarding the country's economic future.

With something close to surprise, she discovered that she was enjoying discussing her views with someone who could be trusted not to repeat them. He seemed genuinely interested, watching her with a slight smile on his face.

This was the man who'd risked his life, not to mention his job, to make certain that she was safe. It had been a heroic thing for him to do. Sitting across from him now, falling into their easy relationship once again, Katie reminded herself how much she'd missed him. Strange how those days together had forged such a strong bond between two people who had known each other only casually prior to the dangers they'd faced together.

She'd never pushed him to explain why he'd taken such risks for her. She couldn't recall anyone in her life ever doing something so quixotic for her.

"I've been doing all the talking since we got here," she said over coffee. "Now it's your turn. Tell me what happened when you returned to the States and faced your boss—Kramer, did you say? Was he very upset with you?"

"That's one way of putting it. There was talk about my finding another career, as I recall."

She stared at him, appalled. "Because you came to the assistance of a friend?"

"Because I was in Dalmatia in the first place. If I'd still been in the military, I would have been court-martialed. As it is, I still disobeyed instructions. The term 'insubordination' got kicked around for a while."

"Would they actually fire you?"

He leaned back in his chair and studied her with a cryptic smile on his face. It was times like this when Graham could be exasperatingly enigmatic. Perhaps it was part of his charm, she decided.

He finally responded. "Maybe," he replied absently. Then he continued. "Katie?" His smile disappeared.

A spurt of fear shot through her, and she wondered what had caused his sober expression. She wasn't at all certain she wanted to hear what he was going to say. "Yes?" she replied cautiously.

"May I make a suggestion?" he asked.

That didn't sound too bad. "Certainly," she said, relaxing slightly. She didn't have to take his advice if she didn't like it.

"You said you were taking the rest of the day off, didn't you?"

She eyed him with uncertainty. "Yes."

"I think we're going to need to spend some uninterrupted time together, in order to talk about this situation. We need to find a place where we'll be left alone, where nobody will be wondering why we're together and nobody will be making speculative remarks."

She thought about that for a moment. He'd definitely ruled out her office, that was certain.

"I don't actually have to be back in D.C. until Monday," he said. "Even before I knew you were in town, I've been toying with the idea of getting away for a few days—taking Kramer's suggestion and doing some thinking about what's going on in my life."

"It probably wouldn't hurt," she offered tentatively. "It sounds as though you've had a heavy schedule for some time."

"The thing is, I was thinking about renting a car and driving over to the coast for the weekend. Maybe if we both took off for a day or two, it would give us time to consider all our options." He leaned toward her slightly and asked, "Would you come with me?"

She wasn't shocked at his suggestion because it made a certain amount of sense. They *did* need to talk. The problem as she saw it was whether or not they could spend additional time together and not become more involved with each other.

Through a charade that she had participated in, she was legally tied to this man, a situation neither one of them wanted. The adult thing to do would be to calmly sit down with him and go over possible solutions.

Unfortunately, the thought of spending time alone with him did not make her feel like an adult. It triggered all of her personal insecurities.

Professionally, she felt capable of handling anything thrown at her. Personally, she was much more insecure and inexperienced. Take his offer, for example. There was nothing suggestive or provocative in his expression or voice to make her believe his request was anything but what he'd stated. But what about his unspoken expectations?

That was what bothered her. Were there unstated but understood strings attached to such an offer? He must be aware of how she responded to him whenever they were alone together. Was that what he hoped to encourage? Now that she was his wife, did he think that she might be willing to—

"I didn't mean to shock you with an improper suggestion, Katie," he said, obviously amused at her reaction. "You're looking at me as though I've just confessed to being an ax murderer." He shrugged his shoulders slightly. "So maybe it wasn't such a good idea. I just thought— Yeah, it really sounds stupid to suggest—''

''No! I mean, it isn't stupid at all.'' She gave a nervous chuckle, then attempted to disguise her nervousness with flippancy. ''It's just that I've never had a man suggest that I spend a weekend with him before.''

He studied her for a moment in silence before he shook his head. ''I see. A man wants a woman to go away for the weekend. It can mean only one thing to you, right?''

She could feel herself blushing and fumbling for words to explain. ''Why do I feel like such a fool?'' she finally mumbled. ''Of course we need to talk about our situation,'' she said. ''The consequences for both of us are serious and we have to deal with them.'' Katie took a deep breath before forcing herself to meet his intent gaze. ''I just think we should be clear about what you expect from me this weekend.''

He took her hand and squeezed it. ''I don't expect anything from you, Katie, except for you to be honest. Honest with yourself and with me, okay? I don't intend to put any pressure on you. We'll book separate rooms and you can set any kind of boundaries that will make you feel more comfortable.''

She felt reassured by his straightforward attitude. ''Did you have any particular spot in mind?''

''No. Any suggestions?''

''Well, there's several places along the coast that I've heard are very nice.''

"Then let's not plan ahead. We'll get a car, take off and drive until we feel like stopping."

She tried to think of all the reasons that she probably shouldn't do this. This man had a strong effect on her, one she wasn't certain she could control.

You also happen to be married to him.

You don't have to remind me.

You can't be afraid of him!

Of course not. Maybe it's *me* I'm afraid of.

A little self-honesty here? How quaint!

Is he going to expect me to go to bed with him?

Didn't he offer to get separate rooms . . . and have you set whatever boundaries you wanted?

All of that sounds great. The problem is, I've never considered doing anything like this before. The whole idea makes me nervous.

Gee, I would never have guessed.

"So? Who's winning?"

Startled, she looked at him. "I'm sorry, I don't know—"

He placed her hand between both of his. "You have a very expressive face, Katie. One moment you looked scared to death, the next very irritated. I was wondering if I could help in any way."

"Believe me, you've done more than enough. Here's a bit of honesty for you. I was doing just fine in my life before you came along and turned everything upside down. I don't know where I am any longer. Nothing is what I thought it was. As if that isn't enough, you suggest we go away together for the weekend!"

"But not for illicit purposes," he pointed out dryly.

She gave him a wry smile. "You're sure about that?"

"I'm very sure. My intentions are quite honorable, actually. When you think about it, all I'm asking is that we spend a little time together. Is that too much to ask of my wife?"

Chapter Eight

Several hours later, Katie sat beside Graham in a rented convertible, her hair tied in a scarf, feeling as if she'd just run away from home.

Actually, that was exactly what she *had* done. When she'd decided to accept Graham's offer, she had, in effect, dismissed the waiting pile of dirty clothes, the empty pantry and refrigerator and her plans to spend the next two days catching up on her sleep.

She glanced at Graham out of the corner of her eye. After lunch, he'd gotten his bag at the hotel and made arrangements to pick her up at her apartment once he obtained the car. The next time she saw him, he had changed into more casual clothes for their trip to the coast. However, he still wore black. He'd also added aviator glasses that reflected her image to her whenever she looked at him. Just what she'd needed to help her relax, of course. She was seated beside a mysterious-looking male who happened to be her husband.

Ever since he'd sprung that cheerful piece of news on her, the thought was never far from her mind. She'd mulled over the information during the cab ride to her apartment, while she was trying to decide what a liberated female packed for a weekend away with an attractive and intriguing male, and then later while she waited at her window, watching for him to drive up.

A husband was a foreign being to her way of thinking. Since she'd never aspired to having one, she'd never given them much thought in connection with her.

She recalled her earlier conversation with Sally about Larry and their relationship. She raised her head from the car seat and turned to Graham. "Do you like sports?" she asked, speaking for the first time in more than an hour.

He glanced at her. "I thought you were asleep."

"More like fading in and out," she admitted.

"In answer to your question about sports, I'm not particularly interested in them. Why do you ask?"

"I dunno. I guess I've always thought it would be un-American for a male to admit to anything other than absolute devotion to sports." She thought about that for a while before she asked, "What sort of things *are* you interested in?"

He didn't answer right away. When he did, he sounded a little surprised at his response. "Give me a rousing political debate anytime," he said, a smile lurking around the corners of his mouth. "Politics and government have always held a special fascination for me."

"Really?" She straightened in her seat. "Me, too. Isn't that strange? We've got more in common than I would have guessed."

He laughed, reached for her hand and squeezed it. "Hold that thought, would you?"

Why did his laugh, his touch and his provocative comment have such an impact on her?

At the moment, she was too tired for much soul-searching. She just wanted to enjoy the rest of the day in the presence of this particular man.

It was a beautiful afternoon, the breeze felt refreshing and she needed a break from her hectic schedule. What more could she possibly want?

With the weekend stretching ahead of her into pleasant fantasies of sun, sand and surf, Monday seemed in the far distant future.

She slid down in her seat and leaned her head back to catch the sun. Eventually, the steady drone of the tires on the road sang a somnolent song that lulled her into a deep sleep.

The next time she opened her eyes, it was dark, the car was stopped in the driveway of a resort hotel and Graham was nowhere in sight. She stretched and idly glanced at her watch.

Good grief, she'd been asleep for several hours! Why hadn't he awakened her? She opened the door and started to get out of the car when she heard Graham's voice.

"Sorry to take so long. There was quite a line looking for rooms. I guess the good weather convinced a lot of people to enjoy the seashore this weekend.'' He got into the car and waited for her to close her door before pulling around to the side of the hotel and parking. They both got out and he began to put the top up on the convertible without saying anything more.

Katie folded her arms and leaned against the car, watching him. "Don't tell me,'' she drawled. "Let me guess. They're all booked up—except for one room that we'll have to share, of course.''

He stopped and looked at her. The sunshades were no longer in evidence but she still couldn't see the expression in his eyes. "What a trusting soul you are,'' he replied, opening the trunk and taking out their two bags.

"Isn't that what you were going to say?''

"No,'' he said quietly, "it isn't. We have two rooms... two *separate* rooms. They are not connecting. However, they *are* on the same floor. If that bothers you, I can probably have one of the rooms changed to another floor.''

She felt a flutter of shame and embarrassment at her behavior. Why was she acting this way?

That's easy. You're so afraid of making a mistake with this guy that you're making a fool of yourself every time you open your mouth!

Oh, shut up!

"Did you say something?'' he asked, turning toward the main entrance to the hotel.

"Uh, no. I mean, yes. What I'm trying to say is...I'm sorry for behaving so ridiculously. Would you consider blaming it on jet lag and ignoring me until I become more used to our situation? You may have noted that I'm a little nervous about this weekend."

"So am I," he said without looking at her. He continued walking toward the hotel lobby.

She hurried to catch up with him. "You're kidding, right?"

He glanced at her. "Why do you think that?"

"Well . . . because. I would imagine a man as attractive as you has had plenty of experience at this sort of thing."

They went into the lobby, walked across the wide expanse of patterned carpeting and entered one of the elevators. Once the door closed, he glanced at her with a half smile. "You think I'm attractive?"

She fought to control her expression. "Of course," she replied, with dignity.

"Thank you."

"You're welcome." She studied the lights of the elevator with great intensity, wondering if he found the small space as warm as she did.

The doors slid open with a hiss and they stepped out. He pointed at one of the signs with room numbers and arrows. "This way."

Halfway down the hallway he paused and opened one of the doors, then stepped back. "I understand the rooms are alike. You can take this one if you want."

She walked in and looked around. "This is really nice." He brought her bag inside and placed it on the luggage rack before retracing his steps. He'd reached the entrance and started to close the door, when he seemed to remember something else. He stepped inside the room, gently closed the door behind him and walked over to where she stood watching him. He leaned down and kissed her, a warm, possessive kiss that set off all kinds of jangling alarms deep within her. Then he stepped back and smiled at her.

"Thanks," he said. "I needed that."

Just before he closed the door behind him, he said, "I think you're very attractive, too... I'll be back to take you to dinner in an hour."

She stared at the door long after he'd left, bemused that with one kiss he'd rekindled a flame that had been smoldering since their last night together in Dalmatia.

This was exactly the reaction she'd been afraid of. However, Katie knew she was no coward. She was determined to face the next few days with fierce courage. She would treat it like an assignment. She'd stay detached and wary. She was not going to allow her personal reactions to this man to influence any decisions she might be called upon to make.

Through a series of unusual circumstances, she was now legally bound with him. It was a temporary inconvenience, that was all. What she needed to do was to relax a little, enjoy his company and learn to cope with the strong attraction between them.

The weekend would be good practice for her, help her sharpen her social skills. She'd stay calm, cool and collected, regardless of her inner turmoil.

She repeated that thought over and over, like a mantra, while she showered and changed into her most feminine-looking outfit. Tonight would be a test she was determined to pass.

* * *

By the next afternoon, Katie wondered what she'd been in such a stew about. Graham had continued to treat her as he always had—courteously, though served up with a certain amount of teasing.

They were on the beach this afternoon, beneath the shade of a giant umbrella. She'd taken one look at Graham Douglas in a swimsuit and decided not to look anywhere but at his face. She didn't need any visual reminders of what a virile male he was.

Although to all appearances they were just another couple enjoying a few idle hours, their conversation was serious and to the point.

"I haven't done anything about our situation," he explained, stretched out on one of the hotel towels beside her, "because I wanted to discuss the matter with you first."

"Thank you. I appreciate that."

"I was the one who got us into this and I want you to know that I'll take responsibility for resolving it."

"Fine."

She kept her eyes closed, refusing to look at him. At the moment, she concentrated on the soothing sound of the waves breaking nearby.

"There is just one thing I wanted to point out...."

Slowly she opened her eyes. He'd taken off his sunshades. She was lying close enough to see the tiny wrinkles around his dark eyes that disappeared whenever he smiled. "What is it?" she prompted when he didn't say any more.

"Have you given any thought to the idea that we could stay married?"

She felt as though a fist had caught her in the midriff, knocking all the air out of her. "Stay married?" she echoed on a wisp of air.

He came up on his elbow and turned to her slightly, his knee brushing against her thigh. "I know it sounds a little strange at first, but I've been thinking about it. Do you remember when we were talking in Dalmatia about our life-styles and how sometimes we get lonely? What would be wrong with keeping our relationship the way it is? We could keep our same apartments if you like and visit whenever we were both in the States at the same time. We could..." His voice dwindled as he watched her face.

She sat up and faced him, folding her legs in front of her. "Are you suggesting that we stay married as a matter of *convenience?*"

He drew a circle on her kneecap with his finger. "Sounds a little odd, but it might work. Just think, if you ever have need of an escort to some news function, all you have to do is call me."

"Do you think I can't get a date? Is that what you're saying?"

"No. Of course not. I guess I was trying to tease you a little. You're always so serious about everything. I was trying to lighten things up."

"If taking things seriously means that I resent being considered a convenience to you or anyone else, then that's just what I am. I have no intention of being a wife to anybody, which happens to include you."

"What does that mean to you?"

"What does *what* mean to me again?"

"Being a wife."

"Are you teasing me?" she demanded.

"No. I'm being serious." His hand brushed the sand off her calf, then he ran his fingers lightly along her ankle and foot in a soothing, mesmerizing pattern.

She tried to ignore his touch and focused on his question. "A wife is expected to be domestic. I've never been very good at that sort of thing."

"Is there a rule that says a wife *has* to be domestic?"

"Wouldn't you want her to be?"

"What would you say if I told you that I wouldn't care what kind of wife I had as long as it was you?"

His voice had dropped to a low pitch and he was no longer looking at her.

"Graham?"

He slid his hand from her ankle to her knee, still without looking at her. "You've got some strange idea that I have a lot of women in my life . . . and that's not true. I've been too busy, too focused on my career, to devote any time to meeting people." If anything, his voice had gotten lower.

He was looking down and she couldn't see his face. Suddenly, it was of vital importance for her to see his expression.

She stretched out beside him once again, so that their heads were at the same level.

"Why do you think I risked my career to go looking for you in Dalmatia?" he suddenly asked. "I thought you would have guessed when I told you the truth about my being there." His eyes met hers. "I was worried about you. I was afraid you'd take too many chances and get yourself killed. I realized that if anything happened to you, I'd be devastated." He looked away. "That's when I knew that you were more important to me than my career."

She placed a very shaky hand on his shoulder. "I had no idea."

"I know. You see yourself as just one of the guys out there in the trenches, doing your job. I tried to keep the same perspective for a long time, until word reached me that the rebels were about to launch a major assault on Dalmatia's capital." His jaw clenched. "That's when I knew on some level that I was fooling myself where you were concerned."

"I don't know what to say." She hadn't wanted to examine how she felt about him or how he might feel about her. Now he was giving her no choice.

"I might as well tell you the rest."

She almost flinched. "There's more?" she asked faintly.

"I had a long talk with Father Xabier that first day. I told him I loved you and that I wanted to marry you, but that you weren't interested in getting married. I told him that if I could get you to go through the ceremony, it would give me some time to convince you that we could make a relationship work. I felt that you respond to me and that you might care for me more than you realized. I wanted to buy myself some time. We had so little time together. Months passed when I didn't hear anything from you or about you. I'd pour over your articles, reading and rereading them and trying to believe that you weren't risking your life to get them."

"You tricked me." She stared at him as though she'd never truly seen him before. "You lied to me. You told me our getting married was the only way. You said the ceremony wasn't legal. You even slept with me that night—"

"That's the operative word, Katie! I *slept*. I was exhausted and I knew I'd played a dirty trick on you. It wasn't my finest shining moment, believe me. I realized I was a coward by not admitting how I felt about you. I tried, earlier at the cottage, to turn the conversation in that direction, but you made it clear that you had no intention of getting married, ever."

"And you feel that gave you the right to force me to marry you, anyway?"

"No. Of course not. If you want to annul the marriage, I'll see to it."

She stood, picking up her towel. "Yes, Graham...I want to annul the marriage. What you've done is unforgivable. I trusted you. For me to trust any man is amazing, but I did. I really thought I could depend on you. I thought you had integrity...and honor...." Tears clogged her throat. "I feel like such a fool, believing that the ceremony was just a fake. I was so gullible. You must have had trouble keeping a straight face."

He, too, stood, facing her. "On the contrary. I will never forget how you looked, standing there at the altar, the light from the stained glass window surrounding you with a translucent robe of color. You were beautiful and very precious to me. I felt like a heel for not admitting the truth to you—I mean, the whole truth, because what I told you was also true. I don't think any of those men would have let us leave if I hadn't convinced them we wanted to get married.''

"So why didn't you seduce me that night? You could have, you know.'' She hated admitting that to him.

"Because I love you, dammit, can't you understand? This isn't about hopping into your bed. I thought I made that clear to you. I don't want to have an affair with you. I don't want an occasional romp to take the edge off before going back to work. I want to share my life with you. I wanted time to convince you we could make it work.'' His gaze veered toward the water. "I just want some time, okay?''

Katie had an insane desire to burst into tears. This man could jerk her around more than anyone she'd ever known. She hated him! She was certain of it! Stay married to him? Was he out of his mind?

Her eyes fell to his broad chest and she remembered how she'd felt in his arms.

Don't be ridiculous. That was lust, pure and simple. The only reason he had a definite edge was that she had never allowed any other man past her defenses enough to arouse her. But it wasn't enough. How could she possibly— How could anyone expect her to— He was just like her father. She couldn't trust a man to—

Like her father? Where had that come from? Graham was nothing like the man she'd heard about from her mother and sisters. Her father had decided he didn't want to be married, to have a family, to be responsible for others.

Graham, on the other hand, had gone to a great deal of trouble to prove the opposite was true for him.

She raised her gaze until she met his eyes once again. She was shocked by what she saw. The mask was gone. The mysterious male was no more. In his place stood a man strong enough to show his vulnerability.

He'd just shown her how deeply he felt about her. He'd been strong enough to confess the truth to her, a truth he'd known she wouldn't want to hear.

"How much time?" she asked, her voice trembling.

"As much as you'll allow."

"You want us to stay married so that you can prove we can make a marriage work, no matter how unconventional it might be?"

The bleak look in his eyes slowly changed to hope. "Yes. That's what I want."

"You actually think we can continue living the way we are now, with one major difference—that I'll be Mrs. Graham Douglas?"

"You don't have to change your name. Katie Kincaid has a definite lilt to it. You've made it famous." He took her hands and placed them on his chest, cupping his fingers over them. "I guess what I'm trying to say, Katie, is that I want a chance to show you that I don't want to take anything from you. I don't want to turn you into somebody you're not. I want to give to you. I want to have the right to call you. I want to be listed as your next of kin, as scary as that thought is. I want you to think of me sometimes, and know that I'm thinking of you." She had never seen his eyes more intense. "Eventually, and only if you agree, I want to wake up in the middle of the night and find you asleep beside me. I want to see your face the last thing at night and the first thing in the morning whenever our schedules permit.''

''Graham? Graham Douglas? Is that you?''

Graham's speech had left Katie speechless. She had no idea how to respond, but as it was, she didn't have to because a long-legged brunette in a bikini was trotting toward them, her white teeth flashing in her deeply tanned face.

Katie watched Graham glance around with a frown, then a startled look of pleasure swept across his face. ''Georgianna? I can't believe it! GeeGee. I haven't seen you since college.''

As soon as she was certain she recognized him, the brunette launched herself into his arms. If he hadn't braced himself at the last moment, Graham and GeeGee would have hit the sand in a tangle of arms and legs.

Katie hurriedly stepped back and watched the woman who was a good six inches taller than she was and still a couple of inches shorter than Graham, give him a long hug and an even longer kiss.

With her best reporter's objectivity, she noticed that he wasn't putting up a struggle. Her first reaction was to turn around and walk off. Whoever she was, this woman had the sensitivity of a water buffalo. Surely she could tell that they had been in the midst of a very important discussion. Where did she get off leaping into the middle of them like that, mauling him?

''GeeGee, I still can't believe it,'' he was saying. ''How many years has it been?''

She laughed, a deep smoky sound that even Katie recognized as sexy. GeeGee tossed her hair back from her face in what Katie considered a very affected manner and said, "More years than I'll ever admit to, believe me."

She turned to Katie and smiled brightly. "Hi. Sorry to come barging in like that—"

Was the woman a mind reader as well as drop-dead gorgeous?

"—but when I saw Graham, I couldn't believe my eyes!"

Katie smiled back just as brightly. "No problem. I was just leaving, anyway." She threw her towel over her shoulder.

Graham stopped her by grabbing her hand. "There's no hurry, is there?" he said in a friendly voice. "Katie, I want you to meet GeeGee." He turned to the other woman. "The last time I knew you, your last name was Sawyer, but I bet that's changed."

GeeGee nodded. "It's Conrad now, although I've been divorced for several years. How about you, Graham? Did you finally . . ." She glanced at Katie's ringless fingers and paused.

"The very topic under discussion, as I recall," Katie said, her smile still bright. "Other than a few minor technicalities, Graham is as free as the wind, right, Graham?"

He watched her through hooded eyes but made no comment. However, Katie's comment was all the encouragement GeeGee needed. "Well! This calls for a celebration, wouldn't you say? Why don't we—" she paused and looked at both Katie and Graham "—have dinner together tonight? I want to catch up on what's been happening in your life. You went into the army as soon as we graduated, as I recall.''

"And you planned to spend the next two years in France," he finished for her.

"Which I did."

"If you two will excuse me," Katie said with quiet dignity, "I think I've had enough of the . . . sun . . . for one day."

"We'll see you tonight, won't we?" GeeGee asked, her breast snug against Graham's arm. "I'd love to get to know you better. You know that old saying, 'Any friend of Graham's is bound to be a friend of mine.'"

Katie couldn't believe the riotous impulses running through her. She'd never seen this woman in her life, knew absolutely nothing about her, yet for some inexplicable reason, she wanted to snatch the woman bald.

"I wouldn't miss it for the world," she said brightly. "I'll meet the two of you in the lobby at eight."

Wrapping her towel around her like a toga, Katie marched up the beach to the hotel.

Chapter Nine

By the time she'd finished with her shower and drying her hair, Katie had worked herself into an old-fashioned snit. That was what her grandmother had always called them, anyway.

The most bewildering thing was that she didn't understand why she was so angry. Not that she didn't have a reason. Several, in fact.

One, Graham had lied to her.

Two, he had tricked her.

Three, he had used her.

Strike that. He hadn't used her. What he'd done was to risk his neck to make sure she was safe.

All right, then. Three, he had— Well, he was— Just who in blazes was this GeeGee character, and how well had they known each other? For that matter, what were they doing right now?

She had walked away from them, leaving the field open to Ms. Conrad to continue to rub her practically naked body all over him.

Did she care?

Now, that was the question of the day. If she didn't care, why was she so furious? If she did care, why hadn't she stayed on the beach, announced to the woman that she was Graham's wife and that—

But she wasn't his wife. Not really. Not in any but the most narrow technical sense. That was the reason they were here together for the weekend, to discuss that narrow technical connection.

Marriage wasn't something to be bandied about like a disease that could be contracted and then medicated. It was a state of being, it was a new perspective, it was a commitment, a lifelong commitment.

Commitment. She shuddered as a sudden and overwhelming awareness shook her to her very soul.

She'd been wrong. All these years, she'd been wrong.

It wasn't that she was afraid she would find a man like her father. No. That wasn't what she'd been afraid of. She had spent her entire life running from the thought that it was *she* who was like her father—afraid of responsibility, and commitment, and of not being able to stick around when things got sticky, or boring, or a hassle, or—

Katie sank onto the side of the bed and stared into the mirror of the dresser across from her. The face in the mirror stared back in shock.

All these years she had shied away from any possibility of a serious relationship, blaming her behavior on her father.

Was that why she'd chosen her career? She'd found all the excitement she'd wanted, sometimes more than she could handle. She'd gotten to fly around the world, visit some places she'd never known existed. She'd witnessed world-changing events...and she'd run from herself.

Then one day, Graham Douglas walked into her life, treating her like one of the guys, a buddy, tricking her into believing that all he wanted from her was friendship, a casual one at best.

She'd believed him, even when he'd done things that might have caused her to question that belief. Was friendship enough to cause him to jeopardize his job? Did he kiss his friends the way he'd kissed her that night in the cottage?

Suddenly, she leaped off the bed. He'd better not! she thought, remembering GeeGee. The idea of his kissing anyone the way he had kissed her, the thought of his being in bed making love to anyone but her—

Friendship?

She loved him! Why hadn't she seen that sooner? Of course she loved him, if loving someone meant he could make her laugh harder, cry louder, experience more intense happiness and more aching pain than anyone else she'd ever known. If that were true, then she loved him.

With that admission came a sense of peace and purpose the likes of which she'd never before experienced ... until she remembered GeeGee, the woman she'd left snuggled in Graham's arms.

No longer confused, she put her reporter's mind to work. After making several pages of notes, Katie got dressed and left her room. She went downstairs and out to the main entrance where she found a taxi waiting.

"Could you take me to a shopping area, please?"

"Certainly."

She hummed to herself as she watched the passing scenery. "Do you want to go to the mall or to the collection of boutiques along the water?" the driver asked a few minutes later.

"How far apart are they?"

"A couple of miles."

That was nothing in her line of work. "The mall." If necessary, she would walk to the boutiques later.

Fifteen minutes later, she hopped out of the cab, paid the driver and began her expedition.

"You love her very much," GeeGee said, sitting across a small table from Graham at the outside lounge of the hotel.

"I'm that obvious, am I?" he replied, making wet circles on the table's surface with his drink.

GeeGee smiled, the mischievous dimple in her cheek flashing. "Actually, you're anything but obvious. It's just that I've known you for a long time, and at one time I knew you very, very well."

He raised his eyebrows, appearing shocked by her statement.

"You know what I mean! If we'd ever gone to bed, it would have been the end of a beautiful friendship. As it was, we could share our deepest, darkest secrets with each other and feel safe. That's true intimacy, of course, but back then we were too young to understand that."

"So how did you know how I feel about Katie?"

"The mask you wear when you don't want anyone to know how vulnerable you're feeling... You've been open with me, or at least as open as your job permits, obviously, since you had no trouble telling me when you couldn't talk about what you do. But when I mentioned Katie, your face closed."

"Good thing you don't work for a foreign government. You'd get all kinds of secrets out of me."

"I don't want your secrets, honey. Not if you don't want me to have them. I care about you. I always have. I was really sorry when we lost touch with each other."

He lifted his glass, which was filled with a mixture of tropical fruit and a hint of something stronger. GeeGee had ordered two of them when they sat down, something she used to do years ago—order for both of them—always under the misguided notion that she knew what was best for him.

"I looked for you at the reunion and was really disappointed when nobody knew where you were," he said.

She sighed. "I know. I was out of the country when the invitations were sent out, plus I'd moved a couple of times. By the time the poor battered notice found me, it was too late."

"Sounds like you're enjoying your life, GeeGee. I'm glad."

"Oh, I am. I'm a little lonely at times. Guess that can't be helped. I tend to intimidate some of the men I meet."

"No!" he said, grinning. "Imagine that."

She laughed. "I don't care. I don't want a man I can intimidate. I keep looking for someone like you. I thought Neil would do, and he did fine for a long time. I was devastated when we split up."

"I'm sorry, GeeGee. You don't deserve to go through so much pain."

"None of us do, honey, but we keep finding it, anyway. Human nature never ceases to amaze me. Take you, for instance."

"What about me?" he asked, eyeing her warily over the tiny paper parasol in his drink.

"You've obviously come to this fancy resort with Katie. So what are you doing sitting here having a drink with me when you could be with her?"

He decided to remove the parasol, rearrange the fruit hanging on the side of the glass, then taste the liquid before responding to her question.

GeeGee had always been a walking, talking, human lie detector, at least where he was concerned. Besides, he didn't want to lie to her. What he wanted more than anything was to confess what he'd done. He hoped to find a sense of forgiveness in the act of confession.

He set the glass down very carefully, then looked into the brilliantly blue eyes across from him. "Katie and I are married, GeeGee," he said quietly.

He waited for her to comment, but outside of a slight widening of her eyes and a quick flare of her nostrils, she did nothing more as she waited for him to continue.

"That is, a couple of months ago, we went through a wedding ceremony that she thought was phony. We've never slept together." He twirled the little parasol between his fingers. "What I mean to say is—"

"You don't have to explain the intimate details, honey. I get the drift."

"Yeah, well. I finally told her the truth yesterday, as though I'd only recently found out myself and I convinced her to come down here for the weekend to talk about this so-called new development."

"With the idea of seducing her running around in the back of your mind, by chance?"

"What is it with you women! That's the first thing she thought of, too!"

"Well, you know how we women are, our minds always in the locker room."

"Very funny."

"All right. So you're down here together—"

"In separate rooms!"

"In separate rooms," she parroted obediently. "And then what happened?"

"What do you mean?"

She shrugged. "Why didn't you introduce her as your wife, or why didn't *she* say something, instead of shooting daggers at me out of those flashing and very expressive gray eyes of hers?'' She lifted her glass and took a dainty sip without taking her gaze from him.

"Daggers?"

"Uh-huh."

"Do you think she was jealous of you?" he asked, suddenly feeling lighter than he had in several days.

"A woman never misjudges another woman on something like that, honey. Believe me."

He grinned. Then he laughed out loud. "Jealous! No kidding. That's the best news I've had in a long time."

"You haven't answered my question."

"Well, just minutes before you came along, I told her the truth about the wedding, that I had always known it was legal, and that I had set it up on purpose."

"She wasn't very happy with your disclosure, I take it."

"Actually, it could have been worse. At first, she got up to leave, really angry, but then she stayed and listened to my explanation and..." He shrugged. "I really don't know where we stand right at the moment."

"Except that she walked off and left you with me."

He frowned. "There is that."

"Ah, me. I have such impeccable timing. My, my, my. Another few minutes and you might have been in each other's arms."

"Or she might have thrown sand in my face and walked off."

"It didn't look that way to me when I walked up."

"You don't think so?"

"I would say that, if you'd been a car salesman, the little lady was seriously considering taking a test drive!"

"GeeGee!"

"What?" She raised her eyebrows at him. "Just where is your mind these days, honey? And you accusing us poor women of having all these lascivious thoughts. Mmm. Mmm."

He scanned the umbrella tables. "Are you staying at the hotel?"

She shook her head. "Oh, no, but I come by every day on my walk. Each summer, I rent a little beach cottage a couple of miles from here. For two months I do nothing, absolutely nothing but vegetate." She gave him a big smile. "It keeps me young."

"Something certainly does. You're looking great, GeeGee."

"And you're looking restless. So why don't you go find Katie, make sure she's all right and I'll meet the two of you in the lobby at eight tonight."

"Has anyone ever told you that you're a mind reader?"

"A time or two, but so far nobody's been able to gather enough evidence to hang me, so I guess I'm safe enough." She stood and walked around the table. Leaning over, she kissed him very, very thoroughly before drawing back far enough to say, "There! I hope that wife of yours was watching." She grinned and straightened. "Ah, the things I do for love." She wiggled her fingertips at him, turned and gracefully wound her way through the jumble of tables to the beach. Graham noticed that he wasn't the only one watching her progress. Every male over thirteen, including one or two septuagenarians, eagerly eyed the tall brunette as she followed the steps down into the sand and turned her face toward the afternoon sun.

Graham found the waiter, signed a tab, then grabbed his towel and headed for his room. As soon as he got inside, he called Katie. Even though he let the phone ring several times, there was no answer.

Where could she be?

After GeeGee's spectacular exit, he'd tried to spot Katie. If she was anywhere around, she'd been well hidden. At the moment, he wasn't sure how he felt about having her witness that kiss. The experience had been pleasant enough, but he got more heated when Katie brushed her hand across his cheek.

Yeah. He had it bad.

He took a long shower, reviewing his conversation with GeeGee. It *had* helped to talk to her.

So Katie had been jealous, had she? He smiled to himself, then dialed her room once again. Where could she be?

A sudden thought hit him, making him feel as if he'd received a rabbit punch to the gut. He grabbed the phone again and dialed the front desk. A friendly voice answered.

"Hello. Could you tell me if Ms. Kincaid is still registered in room 432?" he asked in as calm a voice as he could muster, considering the fact that his hand was shaking violently.

"One moment, Mr. Douglas, and I'll see," came the cheerful reply. He caught himself holding his breath, afraid to hear the answer. Suddenly, he was sure she'd left. He should have known she would leave. Hadn't she told him? Hadn't she walked away from both of them earlier today?

"Mr. Douglas?"

"Yes?"

"Our records indicate that Ms. Kincaid will not be checking out until some time tomorrow morning."

"Yes, I know that. I just wondered if—"

"According to our records, she's still registered to that room."

"Thanks. Thanks a lot." He dropped the receiver into the cradle, noticing that the handpiece was wet where he'd gripped it so tightly.

She might still have left. She didn't need to formally check out. He'd arranged to pay for the rooms. There would be no reason for her to notify the front desk if she decided ...

That line of thinking would lead to madness, he decided, wishing he hadn't sipped on that nauseatingly sweet drink. Maybe he'd go downstairs and try to find her, maybe get a sandwich to wash the nasty taste out of his mouth.

He was at the seashore, after all. He should enjoy the weekend, even if he spent the time alone. Besides, hadn't she said she would meet him and GeeGee in the lobby at eight?

The thought calmed him. She wouldn't have said that if she intended to return to New York. Katie didn't make appointments, then break them.

He stepped out into the hallway, whistling, and locked his door. He paused on his way past her door and knocked, waited, then knocked again.

There was no answer.

Graham went off in search of her. They definitely had some things to discuss.

Hours later, Graham sat in the lobby, watching the elevators. It was now a quarter to eight. He'd spent the rest of the afternoon on the beach—swimming, walking, sunbathing and looking for Katie.

The exercise had done him good. He felt better tonight than he had in quite a while. He also had a sense of anticipation that he hadn't allowed himself to feel in months. He would see Katie tonight. They would have dinner with GeeGee, of course. But afterward, after GeeGee went home, he and Katie would talk. They'd come up with some ground rules. They would work out whatever made her comfortable, as long as she was willing to consider keeping their marriage intact.

He would—

He lost his train of thought. Although he'd been watching each time the elevators opened, he hadn't recognized Katie when she first stepped into the lobby. But then, her own mother wouldn't have recognized her.

Graham pushed himself out of the comfortably overstuffed chair, staring in shock at the woman who was casually glancing around the lobby.

She wore a very snug, midthigh-length black dress with spaghetti straps to keep the skimpy bodice from slipping the few necessary inches to her waist. Stiletto-heeled black sandals adorned her feet. But to

Graham, the most shocking part of the transformation was her hair.

She'd cut her hair.

Instead of her adorable braid—and he'd had some great fantasies about that braid!—her hair was now shoulder-length, layered and curled so that it framed her face with its warm color.

She finally spotted him, smiled and came toward him. Even the desk clerk reacted to the swaying walk that was the only way she could move in that body-hugging dress and those high heels. As she came closer—he'd been too stunned to move once he'd gotten to his feet—he saw that she'd done something to her face.

Her freckles were gone...and her eyes seemed wider or something, tilted slightly toward the outer corners. Her lips glistened with warm color and her cheeks glowed.

"You changed your hair," he said in a stark voice.

Her smile wavered for a moment. "Well, yes... among other things." She glanced down at her dress as though for reassurance.

"It's too short for a braid now."

She touched her shoulder where a curl rested rather provocatively in the shadowed curve. "I suppose."

"I loved your braid, Katie," he murmured.

Her face lit up and she gave him a brilliant smile. "Really? You never mentioned it."

"I guess there's a lot of things I neglected to mention."

She tucked her arm into his so that her half-exposed breast brushed against his forearm. "It will grow back, Graham."

He took a deep breath and concentrated on sending urgent messages to his body, or her hair wouldn't be the only thing growing. He was a grown man, for Pete's sake. He should be able to maintain some sense of decorum in a public place.

"Ah, there you are," GeeGee said, sailing toward them. "My, but don't you look gorgeous, Katie. Why, that dress looks like it was made especially for you. You have such a tiny waist! Just a pocket Venus, aren't you?"

Graham noticed that GeeGee didn't look too bad, herself. She wore a flame-colored dress that draped over one shoulder, Grecian style, and the skirt was slit to her knee. With that thick mane of black hair cascading over her shoulders, she was very eye-catching.

Katie smiled at GeeGee. "Thank you. You look rather smashing yourself."

GeeGee laughed. "We're just a regular mutual admiration society tonight, aren't we?" She tilted her head and looked at Graham inquiringly. "Something wrong, honey? You look like you've just been pole-axed."

Graham cleared his throat. "No, nothing's wrong. Everything's fine. I made reservations for dinner here at the hotel tonight. I hope that's all right with you?" He swung his gaze to each woman.

Katie said, "It doesn't really matter to me. I thought their food was excellent last night."

GeeGee said, "Oh, and they have the best band. Did you hear it last night? Maybe we can dance later."

Graham could feel his collar cutting off his air. Dancing after dinner? He'd wanted to talk after dinner. Alone. With Katie.

Katie turned and gave him a sultry look from beneath long lashes. "I don't believe we've ever danced together, have we, Graham?"

"Uh, no. Don't guess we have."

When would they have had the chance? They don't hold too many dances during tense and hostile situations. Come to think of it, he'd expected this evening to be tense and hostile. More to the point, he'd hoped it would be. He wanted to witness Katie being jealous. Instead, she seemed to be making a bosom buddy out of GeeGee. At the moment, they were busy trading shopping secrets.

"Are you ready?" he asked, interrupting a fascinating dissertation from GeeGee on the best place to have one's nails done. "I believe our reservations should be ready." He made a show of checking his watch.

He made the same gesture several times in the next few hours. Never had time moved so slowly. In fact, twice he checked to see if his watch was working.

The women seemed to have no problem keeping the conversation going, politely including him whenever possible. GeeGee insisted he tell some of their college stories to Katie, which he did. Admittedly, she seemed to enjoy them.

Or him. Or something. He wasn't certain at this point what was happening. She didn't act jealous. She didn't appear angry. On the contrary, he'd never seen Katie look so happy. She positively glowed. She encouraged GeeGee to tell some of her outrageous stories...outrageous because Graham happened to know they were all true.

And she laughed. Graham had trouble concentrating on anything other than Katie's melodic chuckle. Dear God, how he loved her. Admitting it had merely intensified his feelings.

"There! You see?" GeeGee said to Katie. "I told you the music was great, didn't I?" She glanced over at Graham. "Are you going to be a gentleman and lead each of us around the floor a couple of turns?"

"Sure," he said easily, thankful that GeeGee had given him the opening. He looked at Katie. "Shall we?"

She glanced at GeeGee before answering him. GeeGee gave her a wicked grin. "Do me a favor, honey, and get that man out of here. There's a very distinguished gentleman across the way who's been trying to get up enough courage to ask me to dance. With you two gone, it'll make his job so much easier."

Katie reached for Graham's hand. They both stood, then Graham had the composure-testing privilege of following a swaying Katie to the dance floor. As soon as he could in all decency do so, he put his arms around her and pulled her snugly against him. "I don't know how you can walk in those shoes," he muttered.

He discovered that his hand, which was resting on her back to guide her, was touching bare skin. He ran his fingers over her back. All bare, except for those minuscule straps. "Doesn't this thing have a back?"

She rested her head against his shoulder. "Not much."

He became distracted by the fact that she was resting against him, her body relaxed against his while her feet followed him without hesitation.

"You're a very good dancer," she murmured. "Very easy to follow."

Since he couldn't take a breath without her becoming aware of it, following his lead must seem quite simple to her.

"Katie, we need to talk."

She lifted her head and looked at him through thick lashes. "You got me out on the dance floor to talk?" she asked in a disbelieving tone.

"I don't mean this instant, but we need to finish our conversation . . . the one we started on the beach."

"But not tonight, okay?"

"Why not?"

"Because I just want to enjoy the moment without thinking about anything else. This has been so much fun. I went shopping this afternoon, did you notice?"

"And got your hair cut."

"That, too. You really don't like it?"

He stared into her oval face, while she gazed at him with interest. The hair curled in wisps around her face. She looked like an innocent little girl. The problem was, she didn't feel like an innocent little girl against his rapidly overheating body.

"You look great, Katie. You must know that. Every man in the place hasn't been able to take his eyes off you since we walked into the restaurant."

"Nonsense. They were all watching GeeGee . . . and for good reason. I really like your friend, Graham. She's funny and blunt and seems oblivious to her own beauty. Oh, look. Someone's asking her to dance, see? He's—"

She stopped talking and Graham glanced around to see what she was staring it. GeeGee was right about the gentleman. He looked very distinguished and was tall enough to dance with her with ease. "What's wrong?" he asked, seeing the blank expression on Katie's face.

"That man. He's the one she said was trying to get up enough nerve to ask her to dance."

"So? He obviously got up his nerve."

They danced by GeeGee and her partner. Graham smiled and nodded and continued dancing past them.

"I wasn't kidding when I said every man in this place has been watching her all evening," Katie whispered.

"That's not unusual, you know."

"How did she know he was going to be the one to ask her to dance?"

"Who knows? Who cares? At least she isn't sitting there by herself while we're out here." He was actually glad of the distraction for a few moments. Holding Katie out in public was a delicious torment. He knew she couldn't avoid noticing his reaction to her.

However, he meant what he'd said. This trip wasn't about getting her into his bed. He had no intention of seducing her, of trying to physically convince her that they should be together. He wanted her decision to be based on the dictates of her mind and heart.

Now, if he could only convince his body to cool it for however long it would take her to make that decision, he'd be a great deal more comfortable.

They returned to their table when the band announced a brief intermission. GeeGee joined them, thanking her escort before sitting down.

"Looks like you made a conquest," Katie said lightly.

GeeGee grinned. "Not really. He's got too many things on his mind to be distracted for long. He's worried that his teenage son may be taking drugs and that his college-age daughter may be careless about protected sex. Plus his ex-wife is complaining about the low alimony payment he's been making."

Katie stared at her in surprise. "You mean he told you all of that while you two were dancing?"

GeeGee flashed one of her mischievous looks. "I seem to hear the darnedest things from people I meet." She shrugged. "I must look like the confiding sort."

Katie yawned suddenly and laughingly covered her mouth. "You can tell I still need to catch up on my sleep. I had a busy week." She picked up her small beaded bag. "Don't let me keep you two from enjoying the music and dancing. I'm sure you have a great deal to discuss...news to catch up on."

Graham shot out of his chair, but before he could protest her sudden decision to leave, she touched his sleeve and said, "We'll talk tomorrow, okay? Enjoy the evening."

She smiled at GeeGee. "I hope you'll keep in touch. I've really enjoyed getting to know you."

"Oh, I'm sure you'll be seeing me from time to time."

"Good. I'll hold you to it. Good night, all."

Graham stood there and watched her sway across the restaurant and disappear into the hallway leading to the elevators before he slowly sank onto his chair, feeling dazed.

"That's quite a woman you have there, honey," GeeGee murmured. "You'd be wise to do everything in your power to keep her."

"I want to, believe me. I wish she *were* my woman, even if I sound like a Neanderthal for saying it."

GeeGee laughed. "Ah, yes. We mustn't have you males sounding too possessive these days, must we?"

"You know, I don't remember your being this obnoxious in college, GeeGee. Is this something new you've developed?" he growled.

She laughed harder. "C'mon on, handsome. It's time you danced with me, for old time's sake. Then it will be time for you to turn in, as well."

Graham just shook his head. Women. He would never understand them. He wondered why he ever bothered to try.

Chapter Ten

Katie paused in the hallway outside of the restaurant before walking into the lobby. She prayed she could make it upstairs before giving in to the uncontrollable urge to kick her ridiculous shoes off and throw them as far as she could.

She'd had no idea they would be so uncomfortable. They'd looked so attractive in the store window. All she could think of when she saw them was GeeGee's tall figure standing so comfortably beside Graham. So she had bought them.

Now the soles of her feet ached with every step. As much as she had enjoyed dancing with Graham, the pain in her feet had been a constant reminder of the lengths she had gone to in order to get a positive reaction from him.

All he'd noticed was her hair.

She brushed her fingers through the curls. Too bad he didn't really care for the new cut. She thought she might get attached to it once she learned how to style it. Maybe he would, too.

Concentrating on not hobbling across the lobby, Katie made her way carefully to the front desk.

"May I help you?" the clerk asked.

"I hope so. I feel so foolish. I was in such a rush to leave my room earlier that I left my room key inside. I was wondering if you could give me another one."

"Certainly. And your room number is—"

"Room 460."

The desk clerk reached beneath the cabinet separating them and pulled out a key with a large holder attached. "There you are."

She gave him her brightest smile. "Thank you so much." She turned away and carefully made her way to the elevator, punching the fourth-floor button. As soon as the doors closed, she immediately stepped out of her shoes, wincing as the blood rushed to the pained area.

When the elevator doors opened, she scooped up her shoes and padded down the hallway to her room. Once inside, she tossed her shoes into the corner, grabbed a package lying on her bed, then slipped out of the room and into the hallway once again.

She continued down the hall until she found the right room number, inserted the key the desk clerk had given her and let herself inside. Graham had been right. The rooms were identical. Each had a kingsize bed centered in the room. Each bed had been turned down with a small candy resting on the pillow. A lamp had been left burning.

She only had to shrug her shoulders for the straps to slide down and the skimpy top to droop to her waist. She found the zipper in the skirt, released it and stepped out of her new clothes.

Then she sat down on the side of the bed and pulled off her panty hose. "I'm not really nervous," she whispered to herself as her shaking hands opened the package she'd retrieved from her room. "I'm not nervous. Really I'm not." Her brave words didn't stop her hands from shaking, but she managed to slide the thin white gown over her head and tug it down around her body. She peered at herself in the mirror, closed her eyes, then peered once again. She could see through the gown as though she had nothing on.

She ran her hand down the soft material. The lacy bodice cupped her breasts, then fell away into a filmy circle to the floor. It was really a beautiful gown. Still, she wondered if Graham would notice.

In the bathroom, she scrubbed off her makeup, unable to fathom how anyone could wear the stuff all the time. It made her feel as if she were wearing a mask. Then she returned to the bedroom and crawled into bed.

The light was in her eyes. She would just as soon not have it on when Graham came in. On the other hand, she didn't want to fall asleep before he got here, either. She remembered their wedding night when he'd been so tired. Well, tonight was their real wedding night. Tonight would change a narrow technical legality into a full-fledged, bona fide marriage.

She smiled. If it was a marriage of convenience he was looking for, then this arrangement would be much more convenient in her mind. She wanted to know what she'd been missing all her life. Graham had given her a taste a couple of months ago, just enough to tease and tantalize her with fantasies. There was so much she wanted to learn and she wanted Graham to be her teacher.

What if he isn't alone when he gets here?

What kind of question is that?

It could happen.

You've got a truly evil mind, you know that, don't you?

GeeGee's a gorgeous woman. Do you think any man would turn down a chance to go to bed with her?

They're friends.

But neither one of them said just how close their friendship was.

Evil and sick. I'm disappointed in you.

It isn't too late, you know. You can always slip back to your own room. He'd never know that you were here.

Add cowardly to that list while you're at it.

Don't say I didn't try to warn you.

Oh, shut up!

Katie flounced over to her side and punched her pillow. Graham loved her. She knew he did. She loved him. That was what was important. They were married. She was willing to commit to their marriage. She would do whatever it took to make their relationship work.

If he was so worried about her safety, maybe she'd request a change in assignments. She could become one of the magazine's domestic reporters and let someone else take over the foreign reporting. She smiled to herself. Maybe she wasn't particularly domestic around a house, but becoming a domestic reporter might be considered a good compromise for her new role.

She heard a slight sound just outside the doorway and froze, glad she'd turned off the light. She wasn't sure she wanted to see his face when he discovered that she had come to his room.

She heard the key rattle and the door open. After a moment, the door closed, leaving the room in darkness. She heard him flip the light switch at the door, but nothing happened, since she'd turned off the lamp at its base.

Graham muttered something under his breath and felt his way into the room. He went into the bathroom and turned on the light. When he turned around, he saw her lying in his bed, watching him.

"Katie?" he said in a disbelieving whisper. "Is that you?" He took the few steps necessary to reach the bed. He sat down and reached over, touching her. "I thought I must be dreaming."

"I hope you don't mind that I'm here."

"Mind?" His voice cracked. "Why should I mind?"

"Well, we were going to talk about our situation."

"We can do that."

"Not tonight. I don't want to talk tonight."

He began to unbutton his shirt. "Neither do I," he said thickly. "Neither do I."

He pulled his shirt off and tossed it on the floor, reached down and took off his shoes and socks, then stood up long enough to unfasten his pants and slide them down his long legs.

Katie watched every move he made, the bathroom light giving off enough of a glow for her to see him. She no longer felt shy. She had danced with him long enough tonight to be aware of every nuance of that well-hewn body and she wanted him with every beat of her heart.

He pulled back the covers and got into bed. "Do you want me to turn off the light?"

"No. I want to see you."

"Good. I want to see you, too."

She smiled at him with pleasure.

He returned her smile and smoothed his fingers over her hair, arranging it very carefully across her pillow. His fingers were trembling.

Katie shifted, feeling a rush of restlessness overtake her. She yearned for so much from him, most of which was only vaguely defined in her mind. She reached up and touched his jaw. He flinched and she jerked her hand away.

His chuckle sounded shaky. "Did you burn yourself?"

She felt as though she didn't have enough air in her lungs. "I thought I hurt you, somehow."

"Oh, you couldn't do that. I'm just a little overheated, that's all."

A slight crease drew her eyebrows together. "Are you running a fever?"

"Something like that, but don't worry. I know the perfect cure."

With a moan he leaned closer and brushed her lips with his mouth. She sighed and placed her palms on his chest.

"I love the feel of your chest. It's so firm and yet it has a sleekness and a—" She forgot what she was saying. Graham was kissing her again, making her forget everything.

She shivered when he stroked her body and slipped his hand beneath the gown. Even in their most heated moments, he'd never touched her quite so intimately.

Slowly he lifted his head and looked down at her. She could see her image in the sparkling black of his eyes. "Am I rushing you?" he asked hoarsely.

She shook her head, unable to find her voice.

"I'm sorry, love," he managed to say. "I've wanted you for so long. I never expected to—"

She brushed her hands down his chest and along his bare hip. His skin quivered everywhere she touched. He'd caught his breath and seemed to have forgotten that he needed air.

There were no more words. Her soft, tentative movements freed him from restraint. Katie felt as though she were melting into a new and more glorious dimension as Graham showed her what lovemaking could be.

He placed kisses all over her body as though determined to memorize each and every part of her. Unable to lie still, Katie decided to follow his lead, mimicking his moves and learning about him, as well.

The gown was now somewhere on the floor, unmissed, and Graham was kneeling over her. The soft light gilded his glistening body, making the planes and hollows gleam.

"Ah, Katie. You are so—" Words failed him. He showed her, instead. When he eased through the delicate barrier and buried himself deeply inside her, they both sighed with pleasure and completion. "I didn't mean to hurt—"

"Shh, you didn't, love. Oh, you feel so good to me.... Hmm, so—uh—" He began to move, slowly at first. Startled by the indescribable feelings that swept over her, she could only hold on to him tightly, exhilarated by the rush of emotions and physical sensations that were crashing all around her in waves of energy and passion.

She felt him stiffen and heard him cry out at the same moment her body tightened convulsively around him. She clung to him as he shuddered and slumped in her arms.

They lay there in the tumbled covers, legs entwined, bodies pressed together in the physical symbol of their souls' union. Katie had never before felt so much peace.

When he started to move, she protested.

"I'm too heavy for you," he murmured and rolled to his side without releasing her.

They lay there for long minutes without speaking. Katie allowed her mind to drift into a series of daydreams about their future. Graham's breathing gradually relaxed into an even rhythm that she mistook for sleep until he spoke.

"Tell me I'm not dreaming, okay?"

She opened her eyes. His were still closed while he trailed his fingers lazily down her spine.

"This is no dream, fella, unless I'm dreaming, too."

"There is that possibility."

"I don't think so. My poor imagination could never have conjured up what we just did."

He opened his eyes and looked at her. "There's no going back, love. I want you to know that."

She nodded.

"I would have accepted any kind of rules that you chose to make while you were working out whether you wanted to remain married to me. But not now. I can't pretend that this didn't happen, Katie."

"It's a good thing. I'd be insulted if you did."

"I'm serious."

"Who was it who told me I needed to lighten up a little, and not to take everything so seriously?"

"This is different. I can't make a joke about what I feel for you. If there had been any doubt, tonight would have convinced me."

"I love you, Graham Douglas," she whispered, placing soft kisses on his cheek, nose, chin and mouth. "I'm grateful that you tricked me into marrying you. Otherwise, my stubbornness would never have allowed me this opportunity."

He continued to run his fingers down her spine. "So tell me," he said in an obvious effort to be less serious, even though he had to clear his throat. "What convinced you that we were meant for each other? My wit, my charm, my—"

"—body?" she finished for him, batting her eyes at him.

"Now there's a Neanderthal remark if I ever heard one," he muttered.

"Sorry. I couldn't resist. To answer your question, I think GeeGee showing up here woke me up big time."

"I'm afraid I don't follow you."

"Or more precisely, my reaction to her throwing herself into your arms. I was really angry with you. I felt betrayed, tricked and lied to and I was seriously considering returning to New York. And yet, I became more angry when this unknown woman came on to you."

"So it wasn't my fantastic way with words that persuaded you to give us a chance?"

"Well, if you must know, I—"

The phone rang, startling them both. Katie looked at him with sudden suspicion. "Were you expecting someone?"

He reached over her without answering, but the look he gave her spoke volumes. He pulled the phone closer before picking up the receiver. "H'lo?"

"Tell me, sir," GeeGee said in a businesslike voice. "Are you entertaining a woman in your room?"

He grinned. "I'm not sure. I'll have to ask her." He winked at Katie.

"Well, I'm shocked," GeeGee continued. "Utterly shocked. I can't imagine what your wife would say."

"Since it's my wife I'm attempting—in my own humble way—to entertain, I don't think we have a problem here."

GeeGee's infectious laugh echoed over the phone. "Great. I couldn't be more pleased. Take care, now, and keep in touch." She hung up before he could respond.

He glanced at Katie and said, "GeeGee," as though the word explained everything.

Maybe it did. "How did she know I was here?"

"Who knows how GeeGee knows anything?" He tugged her closer. "Now. Where were we?" he muttered. As though reading from a script, he said, "I believe my hand was here...and my other hand was here...I was nibbling—"

Katie gasped. "I thought we were going to talk?"

"Tomorrow, Katie. And all the tomorrows after that one. We're going to have a lifetime of tomorrows together."

Chapter Eleven

Three months later, Katie hovered before the television set, her hand pressed against her mouth to keep from crying out with pain.

Their tomorrows had just run out.

From the television a solemn newscaster was speaking as a map flashed on the screen near his head. The map was of a small, seldom heard of country that had at one time been part of the Soviet Union.

"State Department officials have been unable to deny or confirm reports that three State Department employees are missing as a result of this morning's bombing at the American Embassy in the capital of Krezda. We go now to our Washington correspondent who is standing by with the latest report."

Katie watched and listened and prayed harder than she ever had in her life, wanting some ray of hope that Graham was still alive.

When he'd left Washington last week, he hadn't been able to tell her why he was leaving or when he'd return, but he had told her where he was going.

To Krezda.

In the three months since he'd told her that their marriage had been valid, her life had changed dramatically, starting with her first Monday back to work when she'd been met at the door with avid questions about her marital status....

"Since when has my love life been fodder for the office gossip machine?" she demanded when she was hit with a barrage of personal questions as soon as she walked into the magazine's offices.

"Since you actually developed a love life, Kincaid," Sally replied, laughing. "Come on. We don't need all the juicy details. Just most of them. Exactly when and where did you acquire that gorgeous hunk who calls himself your husband?"

"I picked him out at one of the eastern bazaars as a souvenir on one of my trips overseas," she replied, straight-faced. She stepped around the group hovering between her and her office. "Now, if you'll excuse me, I have work to do."

"C'mon, Katie," somebody said. "Who is he? How did you meet him? Are you really married?"

"So I understand," she murmured, reaching her office door. "I'll be sure to get a bulletin out with all the pertinent data before I leave today. In the meantime," she gave each of them a smile, "I've got work to do."

She closed the door in her curious colleagues' faces and walked over to her desk. The door opened behind her, then closed. She turned to her credenza and the coffeepot, knowing that she wasn't going to be able to dodge Sally's questions. Quickly counting scoops of coffee into the machine, Katie folded her arms and waited while the machine worked its magic.

"Katie?"

"Yes, Sally?" She didn't turn around.

"I thought we were friends."

She heard the hurt in Sally's voice. When the coffeemaker stopped making its peculiar burping and belching sounds, she filled two paper cups with the steaming liquid, then turned and placed one in front of Sally before sinking into her chair.

"We are friends and you know it, so don't think I'm going to fall for that poor pitiful Pearl voice of yours."

Sally eyed her closely. "You look different."

"I had my hair cut."

"No. I mean, you glow. I've always thought that sounded ridiculous whenever I heard it, as though a human being could glow like a light bulb. But that's the way you look. Like somebody turned a light on inside of you."

Katie smiled. "That about sums it up, all right."

"So what happened Friday? I thought you were in your office with that hunk—"

"His name is Graham Douglas."

"—that hunk, Graham Douglas, but when I checked, you'd both disappeared."

"Actually, he's a genie. We both went up in a puff of smoke."

Sally picked up her cup, looking crushed.

After a swallow or two of coffee, Katie relented. "All right. Enough of this hangdog expression. What is it you want to know?"

Sally immediately perked up. "Is he really your husband?"

Katie smiled, remembering the past two days. "Oh, yes," she replied softly.

Sally's eyes widened. "But how could that be? I mean, only an hour before he showed up, we were discussing your single state. You never gave any hint to me that you were seeing anyone, much less that you were—"

"I guess I'm just getting forgetful, Sally. Too much going on. The ceremony completely left my mind."

"But where did you get married?"

"In Dalmatia."

"Two months ago? You came back, wrote up your reports and calmly went about your business?"

"Priorities, Sally. We've got to keep them firmly in place."

"Does your mother know?"

Katie could no longer tease about the situation. "No. Nobody knows about it. If it will make you feel any better, Sally, you were the very first person in New York to find out."

Sally brightened. "Really?"

"Actually, you found out before I did." Katie couldn't hide her smile.

Sally stared at her, dumbstruck.

"You see, that's why Graham stopped in to see me. He wanted to inform me that what I had thought was a fake ceremony that we'd gone through in order to get out of Dalmatia hadn't been fake at all. He thought I should know."

Sally's mouth dropped open. She hastily closed it and swallowed. "You're making this up, aren't you? All right, all right. If you really don't want to tell me what's going on—" She stood, picked up her cup and started for the door.

"It's the truth, so help me God," Katie intoned.

Sally turned back and stared at her for a long moment. "So what are you going to do?"

"We haven't worked out all the details."

"You *are* going to have it annulled, aren't you?"

Katie smiled. "No way."

"You're going to stay married?"

"Uh-huh."

"Does he live here in New York?"

"Uh-uh." That reminded her. She picked up the phone and dialed an intercom number. When the phone at the other end was answered, she said, "Lloyd? This is Katie. Do you have time to see me this morning? I need to speak to you about something."

Had three months gone by since that morning? Katie thought now as she continued to stare blindly at the television as a series of peppy, bubbly commercials filled the screen. Time had flown by since then.

She'd had three months with Graham. That wasn't long enough, she whispered. There was so much they were planning for the future. What if there were no future for them?

He'd promised to do whatever he could to get back home for the Christmas holidays. They were less than a month away. Katie had promised her mother and sisters that she and Graham would fly to east Texas and spend their first Christmas together with her family.

He'd told her to go without him if he wasn't back by then. He didn't want her staying in Washington alone.

She'd moved to Washington three weeks ago. Until then, they had spent their married life commuting between the two cities. She'd put in a request with Lloyd for a change in assignment. She wanted to stay in the States. If she had a choice, she wanted to work out of the Washington office, to be closer to Graham. She wanted to be there waiting for him whenever he came home.

As she stared at the television screen she had to face the fact that Graham might never come home again.

The worst part was that she couldn't share her fears and her pain with anyone because she wasn't allowed to mention where he was. His comings and goings were secret. She'd had to pass a rigid security clearance once their marriage had been discovered.

There were still whole blocks of his life that he couldn't talk about. She might know where he was but not why. She had purposely requested to work on local and national topics rather than international, which had been her beat in the past.

None of it seemed important to her any longer. Not without Graham.

She tried to focus her thoughts on the too few weeks they'd had together. A collage of memories flitted across her mind. She remembered the first time she'd flown into Washington, the weekend after their trip to the coast....

Graham met her at the airport. She found him leaning against the wall watching as the passengers filed out of the jetway.

"Hi, sailor," she said, walking up to him. "Looking for a good time?"

Slowly he straightened. "I might. Unfortunately, my wife might object."

"Ohhh, I don't think so. I have a hunch she's a very understanding person." She leaned against him, going up on tiptoe to give him a lingering, heart-stopping kiss.

"You think so?" he asked hoarsely when she pulled away.

"Within reason, of course." She linked her arm with his. "How about taking me to your place, big guy?"

They began to walk down the concourse toward the parking lot. "I hope you're not disappointed. I mean, it isn't a big place because I don't spend much time there. If you want, we can look for apartments this weekend."

She touched his jaw just for the pleasure of seeing the slight quiver that went through him. "I have a feeling we're going to be too busy. We have so much to—talk—about."

They barely made it to his apartment before they were removing clothing from each other, admiring and stroking all the uncovered delectable spots.

They never left the apartment the whole weekend.

Katie realized that tears were streaming down her face. She didn't know how long she'd been crying. She didn't remember much of anything since the moment she'd turned on the television early that morning and heard the news from Krezda.

Just because three people had been reported missing did not mean that Graham was involved, but she knew in her heart that if he'd been all right he would have called to reassure her before she could hear the news on television.

She hadn't spoken to him in three days.

"Oh, Graham, please be all right," she whispered. "I love you so much. I haven't told you enough . . . I haven't shown you enough. I want that lifetime you promised me, to prove that you made the right decision about us."

She wandered into the bedroom and over to the closet where all of his clothing hung, neatly arranged, in shades of black. She smiled through her tears. She couldn't imagine seeing him in any other color.

She pulled the sleeve of one of his jackets up so that she could rest her cheek against its suede surface. She rubbed it against her cheek, spotting it with her tears. The coat still carried his scent of after-shave and the essence that was Graham to her.

She rubbed at the spot she'd made, thinking that she'd have a tough time explaining why she'd been crying all over his suede jacket when he got back.

She jumped when the phone rang behind her. Whirling, she stared at it, hoping, yet afraid to hope. Wanting to know something and afraid to know. It rang twice more before she could pick it up.

"H'lo?" she said softly.

"Mrs. Douglas?"

It wasn't Graham. She squeezed her eyes shut and fought to swallow the sob that was threatening. "Yes?" she managed to say.

"My name is Tim Kramer, Mrs. Douglas—"

Graham's boss! She knew the name. It was the only one that Graham ever mentioned to her when he spoke about his job.

"Yes?"

"I'm afraid I have some bad news for you," he began slowly.

Katie bit down on her bottom lip, tasting the blood. "Graham?" she finally choked out.

"Yes, ma'am. He was in our embassy in Krezda. There was a bombing there last night."

"I heard about it on the news this morning." She had to strain to get the words out through her constricted throat. She sank onto the side of the bed and leaned over, resting her forehead against her knees.

"I'm afraid that Graham is one of the men who is unaccounted for in the blast. There was considerable damage to the building. They have a crew digging through the rubble right now. We just don't know what they're going to find. Graham made me promise before he left to keep you informed in case anything ever happened that might affect him. He said you were a professional and could deal with whatever news might occur."

She caught back another sob, not wanting this man to think that Graham had lied to him. "Thank you for calling," she managed to say. "I appreciate it."

"It isn't an official call, you understand. We still don't know many of the details. I will call you as soon as we hear more." He paused. "Is there—uh—anyone there with you?"

"No."

"Do you have any family or friends close by?"

"No. I've only been here a few weeks."

He paused before continuing. "Would you like me to send someone over to stay with you today?"

The thought of having some stranger there watching her appalled her. If she had to be brave for Graham's sake, she wanted to do it in the privacy of their home. "No. Thank you for offering, but...no."

"I'll be in touch," he said before hanging up.

She went into the bathroom and washed her face. She had known he was involved. Somehow, she had known. "Oh, Graham, hang on, love. Don't leave me. Please."

After working to compose herself, she picked up the phone and called her office.

"Hi, this is Katie. I don't think I'm going to make it in today. It looks like I may have a touch of the flu or something." Her voice sounded thick enough to verify her story. She listened for a moment then tears spurted from her eyes once more. "No. I don't think it's morning sickness, Fred. Give me a break, here. We haven't been married all that long." Another pause. "I'll keep in touch. I'm just going to take it easy today. I'll give you a call tomorrow."

Tomorrow. A word with promise. A hope for the future.

What would tomorrow bring?

The phone awakened her. She fumbled for the light and lifted the receiver. "H'lo?"

"Mrs. Douglas?" It was Kramer.

"Yes?" She looked at the bedside clock. It was almost two o'clock in the morning.

"He's alive." He paused as though unable to go on.

This time she couldn't control the sob. "Thank God."

"And His miracles. I don't know how he survived this long. They found him in the rubble a couple of hours ago."

The air caught in her throat. "How is he?"

"He's considered in stable condition although he hasn't fully regained consciousness. Bones were broken, I'm not sure exactly which ones. He was trapped beneath a beam, but the beam gave him some protection from the other falling debris."

"Where is he?"

"They intend to fly him back here in the morning. They want him in a high security hospital."

"I understand."

"I know this is going to be difficult for you, Mrs.—"

"Please call me Katie."

"Thank you. I'm not certain that you'll be able to see him right away. I'll do what I can to clear the red tape. We'll have to wait to see what happens."

"But he's alive. He's going to make it."

Guardedly, he replied, "I'm counting on it."

"So am I," she whispered. "So am I."

Epilogue

"Wouldn't you know?" Katie's sister Suzanne said, shaking her head. "Married to the family tomboy for little more than three months and you're already on crutches."

Katie's mother, two sisters and their husbands were in her mother's living room visiting with Katie and Graham. The children had been banished outdoors so the adults could talk.

"Hey," Katie protested. "I didn't do this to him."

They all looked at Graham who had been placed in the recliner, her mother's favorite chair. His left arm and leg were both in casts. His ribs were no longer taped and the effects of the concussion seemed to have healed without leaving any residue of pain or discomfort.

He looked perfectly at ease as though he'd known all these people for years.

Katie had trouble leaving his side. She kept wanting to touch him in order to assure herself that he was all right.

"It's true," Graham said with a grin. "I just wasn't paying enough attention to traffic. Otherwise I would have seen that guy wasn't going to stop for the red light."

He squeezed Katie's hand.

"You could have been killed," Katie's mother said indignantly.

"Yes." Katie tried to swallow the knot in her throat. "But he wasn't and we made it home in time for Christmas."

The conversation flowed around her while Katie's thoughts went back to the first day she was allowed to see Graham after the explosion that had almost robbed him of his life. . . .

Two days had gone by since she'd received word that Graham had been found—two days of sitting beside the phone, waiting to learn if he had been returned to the United States, if he was still alive. Those days of uncertainty and unrelieved fear that she might never see him again would forever haunt her.

Then the phone rang. She grabbed it on the first ring.

"Yes?"

"Katie? It's Kramer."

"Yes?"

"I managed to get you a pass into the hospital, partly because I'll vouch for you and accompany you and partly because Graham's been muttering your name whenever he rouses at all. The doctors have convinced the security people that your visit would be beneficial to Graham's recovery."

She bit her lip in an effort to gain some control over her emotions. "When?" was all she was able to say before her voice broke.

"Can you meet me in an hour?"

"Yes. Tell me where."

He gave her an address, told her to take a cab and hung up. Once she arrived at the government office building and gave her name at the front desk, she allowed others to escort her from building to automobile and eventually through gates to a hospital where Kramer guided her down a long hallway.

"You won't be able to stay long," he said quietly as they paused by one of the doors.

She could only nod without looking at him. She wanted to push open the door that separated her from Graham. She wanted to see for herself that he was alive.

Kramer opened the door and allowed her through.

Her gaze went immediately to the still figure lying on the bed. His arm and leg were in casts. As she drew closer she saw a bruise on his forehead, a scrape on his cheek.

She slid her fingers around his uninjured hand and brought it to her mouth. Tears trickled down her cheeks.

"Oh, Graham," she whispered, brushing her lips across his knuckles. "Please be okay. I love you so much."

His lashes fluttered, then lifted, revealing his dark, sleepy gaze. After a moment he seemed to focus on her figure beside his bed. A corner of his mouth lifted slightly.

"Katie," he murmured.

"Yes. I came as soon as I could."

"To rescue me?" he managed to mumble, his words slurred.

"Seems fair to me," she offered lightly, ignoring the tears that continued to slide down her face.

He closed his eyes and said no more.

When Kramer opened the door several minutes later and signaled that she needed to leave, Katie attempted to pull away. Graham's hand tightened around hers.

"I have to go," she whispered, kissing his forehead, then his cheek. "I'll be back whenever I can. I love you, Graham."

His hand relaxed and his breathing deepened.

Four days—four agonizingly long days—later she was able to see him again. This time he was awake and impatient. "There you are!" he said as soon as she slipped into his room. "I told them I was checking myself out of here if they weren't going to let you come to see me."

She leaned over to kiss him. When she did, he wrapped his uninjured arm around her shoulders and held her to him while his mouth hungrily possessed hers. Eventually, she drew away from him. "I can tell that you're feeling much better than the last time I saw you," she said, a little breathlessly. "I'm so glad."

"I keep telling them I'm all right. They won't listen."

"You hate being trapped in bed, I'm sure," she offered with understanding.

"Alone," he added.

She looked at his casts a little doubtfully and he grinned. "I'm sure I could work out a way," he offered.

Katie placed her hand on his brow. "Perhaps you're a little feverish."

He took her hand. "When I realized I was trapped in that building, all I could think about was getting back to you," he said, his voice rough with emotion. "I didn't go to all of that trouble to get us married in order to make you a widow after a few months."

Tears came to her eyes and she couldn't speak. Instead, she squeezed his hand.

"Kramer said he called you as soon as he knew something."

She nodded.

"He also said he twisted a great many arms in order to get you in here to see me."

"So I gathered."

He sighed and closed his eyes. Despite his efforts to appear all right, she could see how much effort it took. He was still weak, despite his protests to the contrary.

"I need to go so that you can rest."

Graham opened his eyes and frowned up at her. "I don't want you to go."

She smiled, deciding he sounded like a cranky little boy. "I'll be back."

"I told Kramer I was resigning," he said gruffly.

She froze, wondering if she'd heard him correctly. "Resigning?" she echoed.

"Yeah. I should have mentioned it to you first, I suppose."

"It doesn't matter. I just never thought of you as wanting to do anything else."

"All the time I lay there, fading in and out of consciousness, I promised myself that if I made it out of there alive, I was through with overseas work."

"Is there something you can do here in Washington?"

His grin was touched with humor. "Oh, yeah. In fact, I was approached not long after I returned from Dalmatia."

"You mean something with the government?"

"No. One of the television networks asked me to head up a weekly panel, to moderate discussions about our foreign policies. Of course they aren't aware of all that I do in the government, but they considered me expert enough to know who to ask on the panel and how to use my connections to ensure lively discussions."

It was her turn to grin. "You're a natural for television, Graham. I've always thought so."

His eyelids drooped once again. "You think I can do it?"

"You can do anything you set your mind to and you know it."

He smiled without opening his eyes. "At least I'd stay here in Washington," he murmured. "We could be together every day."

"I'd like that," she whispered. "Very much."

"So would I," he admitted before drifting into healing sleep.

Katie listened to the conversations going on around her, content to sit beside Graham and enjoy having him there to meet her family. He had an appointment the first week in January to speak to the network people about their offer once he was able to move around more easily on crutches.

In the meantime, she could enjoy each moment they had together.

During the course of the day the women of the family enjoyed pampering him, while the men sounded him out on his favorite football team, a little puzzled by his lack of interest in the sport. They finally figured he must be a basketball fan... or possibly baseball. No accounting for taste, after all. They forgave him, considering the fact he wasn't from Texas, so couldn't be expected to understand football's importance in the overall scheme of things.

By the time the day was over and Graham had been settled into bed, there was no doubt in Katie's mind that he had been thoroughly initiated into the Kincaid family. He'd passed with flying colors.

"I like your folks," he murmured, stroking her hair as she lay with her head on his shoulder.

"I'm glad. My mother considers you a saint for putting up with me and my sisters can't seem to keep their eyes off you."

"I don't think your brothers-in-law can quite figure me out, though. We don't have much in common."

She grinned. "Doesn't matter. You and I have enough in common, which is all that's important."

He kissed her forehead. "I'm glad I was able to come with you. Kramer and I convinced the others that my injuries could be explained innocently enough.

I didn't have to be locked away until I could walk out on my own.''

''I can't begin to tell you how good it feels to have you here. I'd already told Mom that we might not be able to make it. I wasn't going to leave Washington without you.''

''Did your mother give you any flak about our getting married with no warning to the family?''

''Not really. She said she thought it was very romantic, how you swept me off my feet that way.''

''Will you ever forgive me for not giving you a chance to have a proper wedding gown and a family ceremony?''

She pulled away from him for a moment, so that she could see his face. ''I'm not sure,'' she said, thoughtfully. After a moment she added, ''Of course I'm open for some of your brand of persuasion.''

With a muffled chuckle he set out to show her just how persuasive he could be. The casts didn't hinder him in the slightest. Katie had always known that Graham Douglas was a resourceful man . . . otherwise she would never have ended up as an impromptu bride.

*　*　*　*　*

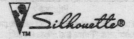

Take 4 bestselling love stories FREE

Plus get a FREE surprise gift!

**HE'S MORE THAN A MAN,
HE'S ONE OF OUR**

Fabulous Fathers

MAIL-ORDER BROOD
Arlene James

Leon Paradise was shocked when he discovered that his mail-order bride came with a ready-made family. No sooner had he said his vows when a half-dozen kids showed up on his doorstep. Now the handsome rancher had to decide if his home—and his heart—were big enough for Cassie Esterbridge *and* the brood she'd brought into his life.

Look for *Mail-Order Brood* by Arlene James.
Available in August.
Fall in love with our Fabulous Fathers!

Silhouette
R O M A N C E™

BABY BLESSED
Debbie Macomber

Molly Larabee didn't expect her reunion with
estranged husband Jordan to be quite so explosive.
Their tumultuous past was filled with memories of
tragedy—and love. Rekindling familiar passions left
Molly with an unexpected blessing...and suddenly a
future with Jordan was again worth fighting for!

Don't miss Debbie Macomber's fiftieth book,
BABY BLESSED, available in July!

She's friend, wife, mother—she's you! And beside
each **Special Woman** stands a wonderfully
special man. It's a celebration of our heroines—
and the men who become part of their lives.

TSW794

It's our 1000th Silhouette Romance™, and we're celebrating!

And to say "THANK YOU" to our wonderful readers, we would like to send you a

FREE AUSTRIAN CRYSTAL BRACELET

This special bracelet truly captures the spirit of CELEBRATION 1000! and is a stunning complement to any outfit! And it can be yours FREE just for enjoying SILHOUETTE ROMANCE™.

FREE GIFT OFFER

To receive your free gift, complete the certificate according to directions. Be certain to enclose the required number of proofs-of-purchase. Requests must be received no later than August 31, 1994. Please allow 6 to 8 weeks for receipt of order. Offer good while quantities of gifts last. Offer good in U.S. and Canada only.

And that's not all! Readers can also enter our...

CELEBRATION 1000! SWEEPSTAKES

In honor of our 1000th SILHOUETTE ROMANCE™, we'd like to award $1000 to a lucky reader!

As an added value every time you send in a completed offer certificate with the correct amount of proofs-of-purchase, your name will automatically be entered in our CELEBRATION 1000! Sweepstakes. The sweepstakes features a grand prize of $1000. PLUS, 1000 runner-up prizes of a FREE SILHOUETTE ROMANCE™, autographed by one of CELEBRATION 1000!'s special featured authors will be awarded. These volumes are sure to be cherished for years to come, a true commemorative keepsake.

DON'T MISS YOUR OPPORTUNITY TO WIN! ENTER NOW!

CELOFFER

CELEBRATION 1000! FREE GIFT OFFER

ORDER INFORMATION:

To receive your free AUSTRIAN CRYSTAL BRACELET, send three original proof-of-purchase coupons from any SILHOUETTE ROMANCE™ title published in April through July 1994 with the Free Gift Certificate completed, plus $1.75 for postage and handling (check or money order—please do not send cash) payable to Silhouette Books CELEBRATION 1000! Offer. Hurry! Quantities are limited.

FREE GIFT CERTIFICATE   096 KBM

Name:_____

Address:_____

City:_____State/Prov.:_____Zip/Postal:_____

Mail this certificate, three proofs-of-purchase and check or money order to CELEBRATION 1000! Offer, Silhouette Books, 3010 Walden Avenue, P.O. Box 9057, Buffalo, NY 14269-9057 or P.O. Box 622, Fort Erie, Ontario L2A 5X3. Please allow 4-6 weeks for delivery. Offer expires August 31, 1994.

PLUS

Every time you submit a completed certificate with the correct number of proofs-of-purchase, you are automatically entered in our CELEBRATION 1000! SWEEPSTAKES to win the GRAND PRIZE of $1000 CASH! PLUS, 1000 runner-up prizes of a FREE Silhouette Romance™, autographed by one of CELEBRATION 1000!'s special featured authors, will be awarded. No purchase or obligation necessary to enter. See below for alternate means of entry and how to obtain complete sweepstakes rules.

CELEBRATION 1000! SWEEPSTAKES
NO PURCHASE OR OBLIGATION NECESSARY TO ENTER

You may enter the sweepstakes without taking advantage of the CELEBRATION 1000! FREE GIFT OFFER by hand-printing on a 3" x 5" card (mechanical reproductions are not acceptable) your name and address and mailing it to: CELEBRATION 1000! Sweepstakes, P.O. Box 9057, Buffalo, NY 14269-9057 or P.O. Box 622, Fort Erie, Ontario L2A 5X3. Limit: one entry per envelope. Entries must be sent via First Class mail and be received no later than August 31, 1994. No liability is assumed for lost, late or misdirected mail.

Sweepstakes is open to residents of the U.S. (except Puerto Rico) and Canada, 18 years of age or older. All federal, state, provincial, municipal and local laws apply. Offer void wherever prohibited by law. Odds of winning dependent on the number of entries received. For complete rules, send a self-addressed, stamped envelope to: CELEBRATION 1000! Rules, P.O. Box 4200, Blair, NE 68009.

 ONE PROOF OF PURCHASE

096KBM

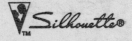